# TIDES OF LOVE

## GARRETT BROTHERS SERIES, BOOK 1

### TRACY SUMNER

## ALSO BY TRACY SUMNER

**Garrett Brothers Series**

Tides of Love

Tides of Passion

Tides of Desire: A Christmas Romance

**Southern Heat Series**

To Seduce a Rogue

To Desire a Scoundrel: A Christmas Seduction

**League of Lords Series**

The Lady is Trouble

The Rake is Taken

The Duke is Wicked (*coming 2021*)

**Multi-Author Series**

Tempting the Scoundrel

**Multi-Author Anthologies**

A Scandalous Christmas

(*coming November 24, 2020*)

Chasing the Duke: Seventh Day of Christmas

(*coming December 7, 2020*)

**Contemporary Romance Multi-Author Anthology**

Tangled Sheets (*coming July 13, 2021*)

# CHAPTER ONE

*"The first plan is the simplest and the one most usually adopted."*
~ C. Wyville Thomson
*The Depths of the Sea*
1898, Chicago

~

*N*oah marked four notches in the top of the ship's keel and pushed up his shirtsleeves, rechecking his measurements. He was adding the figures in his head faster than he could with paper and pencil when a knock sounded on the door.

"Coming," he muttered beneath his breath, but didn't rise. He disliked finishing a model section and leaving his materials spread over his desk.

"Garrett, I know you're in there." The door rattled on its tracks, yanked from the outside.

Noah groaned and stretched, crossed the room and let Bryant Bigelow, the ruddy-checked fisheries commissioner, charge inside.

"Dammit, Garrett. Freezing in that hallway." Bigelow blew into his hands and stamped his feet. His sodden pilot coat fluttered at his ankles, nearly brushing the floor. The former Navy captain, all bluster and brashness, stood just over five feet tall. "Christ Almighty. Freezing in here, too."

"Is it?" Noah grabbed a sweater from a rusty hook and tugged it past his head. He smoothed the scratchy wool, let his palm linger over his twitching stomach muscles. He pressed hard, sucking in a furtive breath. *Maintain a calm facade,* he ordered himself.

"Why in God's name do you live here? Never felt a colder place in my life." Bigelow advanced into the center of the enormous chamber, loosening a crimson scarf from his throat. "All this junk. Shells and"—he jabbed his boot against a rusted anchor—"ship models. And books. How many you have here, Garrett? A hundred? A thousand?" He angled his head, fixing his flinty gaze on Noah. His fleshy lips twisted in what he probably considered a smile. "You're the finest biologist I've ever worked with, but sometimes I think you're crazy."

The jarring squeal of the Union Loop Elevated kept Noah from having to reply. At first, he'd hated the metallic, ceaseless screeching on the tracks below. Now, he found sleep difficult without the train rattling the glass panes. Of course, he could live in Jackson Park with the other biologists or on Prairie Avenue with the educated elite. Admittedly, the space was impossible to heat during a typical Chicago winter. However, he could not, *would not,* explain his choice to distance himself from his colleagues.

Accounting for his idiosyncrasies made him decidedly uneasy.

"We have a problem, Garrett."

The blurred edges of Bigelow's face finally registered. Noah reached for his spectacles. "I would offer tea or coffee, as you look like a drowned rat but"—he slipped them on, blinked—"no facilities."

"You can't even boil a cup of water in this joint?"

"Afraid not." He shoved his hands deep in his trouser pockets, stiffening his shoulders, hoping the stance looked properly composed. He wasn't going to ask. Did not want to know.

Unfortunately, the rumors had made their way to his cramped office yesterday afternoon. He had been hiding in here ever since.

"I received another telegraph regarding the lab in North Carolina. Seems they prefer to work with a local. Soothe ruffled feathers of the fishermen or some such guff. You're from North Carolina, right?"

Circling toward the window, Noah squeezed his eyes shut. The sheer irony of life never ceased to amaze him.

Bigelow's leather soles cracked as he crossed the room, paused to fiddle with a row of horse conchs resting on a low shelf. "Anyway, we're ready to build. Need someone to supervise construction. You're the closest we have to a local, and you're the only man I have on staff who worked on the lab at Woods Hole. Our funding agreement contains conditions. Unfortunately, you've become one of them."

Noah watched a streetcar turn onto Dearborn Street, blue sparks spitting in its wake. "Last week, I received word a stipend has been approved for the trout acclimatization west of the Mississippi. I wanted to start working—"

"Give it to Thomas or someone on your crew. How many trout can one man save? Do you remember the disaster at Woods Hole? Didn't we learn our lesson?"

Noah heard a match strike, then Bigelow sucking on one of those foul cigars he loved. "You've been pushing for a second lab, Garrett. Well, here she is. A month or two living a stone's throw from some of the best barrier islands in the world doesn't sound terrible to me. Look at it this way, you can get research done, and you won't have to sleep or eat. Same as here, only warmer. Pilot Isle is perfect for you. No telephones. Hell, no electricity." He grunted, blew a noisy breath into the air. "I have to admit, this dawdling makes me question your commitment, son."

Noah shivered as ten years of grief and uncertainty, of raw, gut-wrenching fear, descended on his shoulders. *Commitment.* He would do anything to make the laboratory a success, was, in fact, the most devoted member of the fisheries department.

And Bryant Bigelow knew it.

"When do I leave?" he asked without turning, not wishing to record the victorious light in the commissioner's gaze or reveal the dread in his own.

"Soon as you're ready, Garrett. Soon, better be. Already leveling the foundation." He ground his heel to the floor, his smoking cigar stub no doubt beneath it.

Noah dipped his head, gripped the sill with both hands. A gust of wind off the lake rattled the windowpane in its frame, sent a frigid draft of air across his cheek.

After all the years of running, the past had finally caught him.

~

Noah had once believed nothing less than a decree from God would make him return to Pilot Isle.

Long ago, he'd convinced himself of his ability to live without his family, without Elle. Yet here he sat, bouncing across white-capped swells in a sturdy skiff clearly bearing the markings of his brother's design.

"You staying for the heated term, yup?"

Noah glanced over his shoulder. The old man sat at the stern of the boat, tiller in one hand, bottle of spirits in the other. He remembered the face, brown and withered, the pale scar splitting one cheek. He remembered the name, too—Stymie Hawkins. "You're pinching," he said without thinking, then frowned and turned toward the bow, wishing he had kept his damn mouth shut.

"Pinching?" The skiff rocked with Stymie's abrupt movement. A dry cough, then a slurp that sounded like a swig from the bottle. "I reckon I can get us to the Isle, young fella."

Noah squinted and swabbed at his eyes. The spray of salty water had made it necessary to pocket his spectacles, but he could see well enough. Too well, perhaps. They were three hundred yards from docking, sailing past a ship anchored close to the wharf.

"Ready about." Stymie swung the boat into the wind. "Little storm brewing, bit of rain. No nor'easter... nothing like that. Hope you have a place to stay. Lodgings, what little we got, all crammed tight with gosh darned whalers."

"I made the necessary arrangements," Noah said, watching a row of peaked cypress roofs burst into view, upper porches rising above wind-shaped oaks. He grasped the sides of the skiff, the reality of returning stabbing deep, the urge to flee hitting hard.

Stymie altered course, thudding the pockmarked pier as he angled in. "Only one fella ever told me how to sail."

Startled, Noah straightened to his full height, an action he avoided with much shorter men. The breeze took advantage and ripped his coat wide. "Excuse me?"

Stymie released a whistle-breath through the gaping space in his teeth. "Professor used to tell me how to manage my sail. Pert near right most times. I think I mighta been pinching at that."

"Nice story." Noah shoved a few coins into Stymie's hand and took off down the pier.

The first raindrop smacked his face as he crossed the wharf, shrieking seagulls and pounding waves a seductively familiar chorus. He shouldered past a throng of whalers, cast-iron try pots slung across their shoulders, their ribald laughter peppering the air. He skirted a fishmonger's wagon and stepped over a length of rope. An old man perched on an overturned water cask glanced at him, lifted a weathered hand in greeting. Noah returned the gesture reluctantly and turned behind a concealing wall of stacked oyster barrels.

Humid air arrived in gusts from the east, thick from the increasingly steady drizzle, the final nod to the question of whether to wear his spectacles. *Maybe it's better,* he reasoned, pausing in front of a house facing the bay, the double porch sagging above a foundation of ballast stone, the cypress shake roof dull gray. The enticing scent of the marsh on the far side of the island distressed him enough without clear vision bringing added misery, transporting him back to a time of security and love, family and friendship. While he stood there, trying to remember whose house this had been, the loneliness inside him awakened, overflowing his heart, forcing aside every other emotion. Eyes downcast and shoulders hunched, he traversed the shell-paved lane, the owner of the house forgotten.

Shaking rain from his face, he broke into a trot. He must remember the promise he had made as his train exited Dearborn

Station: he would not be drawn into wondering *what if;* drawn into reliving a period of his life he wished to forget; drawn into lowering his guard, allowing the people who had once meant the entire world to him to mean the world again. He had learned to survive on his own, after years of agonizing exertion.

No one to trust or lose trust in.

No one to risk his heart over.

By the time he arrived at Widow Wynne's boardinghouse, he had regained his equilibrium but lost most of his body heat. His wool underdrawers stuck to his skin, water dripped off his nose and slid past his collar. Cursing beneath his breath, he made a mad dash for the front porch and a reprieve from the storm.

The woman stepped into his path—or he stepped into hers. Her head bounced off his chest, his satchel landed in a puddle. His arms rose to steady her. "Excuse me, ma'am, terribly...." His voice tapered off.

Deep green eyes met his, glistening drops of water spiking the long lashes. A fierce ache started deep in his chest and moved to his gut.

Only one person had eyes as beautiful as these.

*Goddamn luck, he thought.*

Elle tipped her head, rain washing over her fading smile. She flicked a glance at the hands holding her. *"Juste Ciel,"* she said, her throat doing a slow draw as she swallowed. Her face paled, and she lifted a trembling hand to her forehead.

Noah braced his knees, fingers tightening around her slim fore-arms. For a moment, he feared she would pitch into the mud at their feet. But she simply mouthed his name as her gaze again fell to his hands.

Remembering she had always liked them, even impulsively called them beautiful once, he snatched them from her and searched blindly for his satchel, trying to escape the ringing in his ears, the darkness dimming his vision. Coming home had been a mistake. If it hurt this much to face Elle Beaumont, how would it feel to face his brothers?

"Wait. Noah, there's nowhere else to stay. Unless you want to go home."

He halted by the gate, threw his head back on his shoulders, and blinked the ashen sky into view. *Go home?* God, no. Water trickled in his mouth as he said, "Nowhere? There must be."

"I've already refused two fishermen. Widow Wynne returns from her niece's in a month. Then she'll accept boarders. Trust me, I would tell you if there were anywhere else."

*Trust her?* Oh, yes, *that* had turned out well before. Sighing, he cut his gaze her way, to find her standing in a shallow puddle, a sack of vegetables hanging forgotten from her fingers. A mannish blouse clung, somewhat indecently, to her bosom.

She had curves in places once flat and uninspiring.

So he stood there a moment, drenched and shivering, wondering how much better she would look if he had his spectacles on. "I could telephone—"

"No telephone. I petitioned the town committee for a public one, like they have in Morehead City. I proposed we place it at the mercantile." Swishing her toe through the puddle, she needlessly splashed her jersey gaiters with mud. "Mr. Scoggins planned to install it on the boardwalk post so his mother didn't have to see it. She threatened to move off the island if he did. Thinks spooks will creep along the line and into the store." She lifted her gaze, a mix of emotions crossing her face. Delight, caution, even a hint of anger, damn her. He read them all, like ink stamped on her forehead, the same as he could when they were children.

"We have a telegraph," she finally added.

"Impressive changes. There was a telegraph *before.*"

"Yes, well"—he observed in amazement as she pulled a watch from a narrow slit in her skirt and flicked open the tarnished copper cover —"impressive or no, the office closed forty-five minutes ago." She blinked rain from her eyes and pocketed the watch, faltering when she caught his look. "Oh. I have the seamstress specially sew the pockets." She stamped her foot, splashing more muddy water on herself. "Why should a man be the only—"

*For the love of God.* "A hotel?"

She shoved a sodden clump of hair behind her ear, the ends bright against her skin. "You think we've gone this long without telephones but suddenly have hotels?"

A fat raindrop hit his neck and slipped inside his collar, making him shiver. He wasn't about to stand around in a downpour and explore his limited options. "Tell me this isn't your home, Elle."

She lifted her chin, a flush sweeping her cheeks.

"Tell me you're married and have three children. Tell me you're only bringing the widow her groceries."

She shook her head, an angry circle of white rimming her mouth.

No way, not living in the same goddamn *house,* he vowed, and kicked the gate open. Elle emitted a squeak of panic and caught him by the wrist, throwing him off-balance and against the white pickets rising between them. Her breasts, firm and plump, bumped his chest, and he recoiled, but not much. She had a remarkably strong grip for a petite woman, and perhaps, if he were honest, he didn't want to move badly enough.

"Don't. Please don't. Not again."

Grief and remorse claimed him. "You don't have any idea what it has taken to get me here. But you have an idea what it took to make me leave, don't you?" He raised his hand in apology. "I've agonized for two months about this. I waited until I could... until I felt sure I could...." He tilted his head, icy drops of rain stinging his face.

"You're the marine biologist we've been expecting? The one I'm holding the coach house for?"

Nodding, he blew out a breath.

"I'll leave it to you to tell your brothers. I won't say a word. I promise. Caleb is gone for two more days, buying lumber in Durham. And Zach, well, Zach is here."

Noah closed his eyes, his skin prickling in anticipation and dread. Caleb and Zach. God, how he had missed them. "Too late for promises, Elle. Stymie Hawkins recognized me."

"Stymie Hawkins." She worried her bottom lip between her teeth. "It *will* be all over town by tomorrow then."

He tugged his hand through his hair. If he had a moment alone, he felt sure he could ease his discomfort. At least make a list of reasons for his return to Pilot Isle, something tangible to assess.

"Come in. Out of the rain," she said. "The coach house is very private. You have the second floor all to yourself."

A gust of wind pressed damp cotton against his chest, and he struggled to suppress a shudder.

"Some boxes arrived for you yesterday. Rory and I stacked them in the front room. Everything's clean, just a little dusty."

Who the hell is Rory, Noah wanted to ask? Her fiancé, most likely. *Good.* "Second floor?" he asked instead.

"It has a private entrance. Widow Wynne even had facilities installed last year."

"Facilities. Ye gods." Concentrating on the clank and rub of boats edging the dock and the bang of the unlatched gate against its post, he made an indecisive halt, a half turn. "I don't know, that is... I don't know if I can stay."

"I understand."

She probably did. Elle had always been able to sense his moods. As a young man, he'd had no choice *but* to keep his distance, when she read him like a blessed book. How he'd hated that. Every subtle expression, even the ones he worked to conceal, visible to her.

"Noah." Her teeth began to chatter, her breath chalking the air.

*Wonderful.* He shrugged from his coat and flung it over her shoulders, careful not to touch her.

He left her behind, rounding the corner of the house.

Elle huffed, struggling to match her stride to his, her hands fisted in his coat lapel. "The bottom floor is vacant, pretty much. Water damage. Needs repairs before it can be rented. Right now, I use the space for my school. Two classes a week. Tuesday and Thursday mornings. The typewriting machine *is* loud, but it shouldn't wake you."

He halted at the bottom of the staircase leading to the second-floor landing. So did she, her boots skidding across slick grass, her body, warm and soft, skidding into him. He set her back, trying to ignore

9

the teasing scent of gingerbread and soap. *"School?* What could you teach a child? How to break an arm rolling off a roof? Better yet, how to shatter the largest pane of glass in town with a misplaced kick?"

He watched her swallow her first reply, the only time he remembered seeing her halt a foolish word from tumbling past those lovely lips of hers. "For your information, it's a school for *women.* Anyway, climbing the trellis was Caleb's idea. How was I to know the roof was still wet? And I worked all summer to replace that glass." She shivered, possibly more from indignation than chill, and gripped his coat close. The sleeves hung well past her wrists, the hem hitting her just above the knee. She appeared fragile and defenseless, a facade surely, yet Noah experienced the familiar compulsion to protect.

He took the stairs two at a time.

"It'll be quite cold in there until you get the parlor stove lit."

*Parlor stove?* Chrissakes, he hadn't seen a parlor stove in ten years, wasn't sure he would remember how to light one.

"If it's too chilly, you can come inside."

He glared over the railing. "I live in Chicago, Elle. In a printer's warehouse. If it gets above fifty in there, in July, I'll eat my hat. So, thank you anyway, but no need to worry."

"Fine, Professor. Freeze your skinny rump off."

He leaned out. "What did you say?"

"Nothing." She forced a smile, her lips clenched.

He couldn't halt his study of her, the little not hidden beneath his pilot coat. Reddish strands of hair curled about her face. Slim fingers locked around his lapel, pallid against the black wool. He denied the urge to squint, to see if her lashes were as long and dark as they had appeared up close. The absence of his spectacles and the misting rain painted a fanciful portrait. She even looked—*God help him*—attractive, her cheeks flushed, her eyes wide and very, very green.

Noah wrenched open the unlocked door, ducked inside, and slammed it behind him. Elle Beaumont was trouble and would never be anything *but* trouble. *Forget about how much it hurts to look at her and remember the life I left behind.*

Years ago, he had protected her from everyone, including herself. He wasn't going to do that again.

The woman was on her own this time.

～

Fury propelled Elle across the street at a fast trot. *Wait until I get my hands on Zachariah Garrett.*

Noah lived in Chicago. Zach had mentioned sending telegraphs to the people building the laboratory. Telegraphs to *Chicago*. And as town constable, Zach approved all the construction permits. He had let her stumble upon, stumble *into*, the one person she wasn't sure she ever wanted to see again.

Much less *touch*.

A biologist. A marine biologist. How perfect. No one loved fish and seaweed, the stink of the marsh at low tide, more than Noah Garrett.

She banged her fist on the door of Zach's office. Oh, she hoped he was inside. If not, she would find him.

The hinges squealed. Zach popped his head around the frame, a delighted smile growing. "Ellie."

Brushing by him, she charged into the office, words tumbling free. "How could... *je suis*... I never...."

"Boys," Zach said to the group of men gathered round the wood-burning stove, "how about I meet you at Christabel's in fifteen for dinner. Rory'll be along any minute, and we'll come over."

With a chorus of agreement and a few wide-eyed looks thrown toward the woman they had all seen in a similar state before, the men shuffled out.

Zach turned to her when the door clanked shut. "What's wrong? Your father? Another attack? I'll get Doc Leland. After the engagement disaster, I don't blame you for not wanting to talk to him."

Elle slumped into the nearest chair, head dropping to her hands, the heat from the stove making her queasy.

"Do you have a fever?" Zach crouched before her, his knuckles grazing her brow. "This coat isn't helping. Blamed thing is more suited to the North Pole."

"Or Chicago," she said between splayed fingers.

"Yes, Chicago, I sup—" His heels popped the floor; he rocked back. "Noah's here." He grabbed her shoulders, slid her forward in the chair. "You've seen him? Where is he?"

She shoved his chest with both hands and jumped to her feet. *"You knew.* You knew he was coming."

He nodded, an eager glow in his eyes.

"Mercy above, you could have told me. Warned me, at the very least." She sniffed and wiped her nose on Noah's sleeve. A potent scent, as purely masculine as any she'd ever smelled, clung to the material.

Zach tipped her chin high. "Could I? Then what? You move to the mainland until he leaves? Hide in Widow Wynne's basement for a month? *No.* It's enough your father has driven you from your home, forced you into a desperate situation. A situation you've refused to let me help you with. Caleb and I are the only family you have right now. I did what I thought best."

"I wouldn't call my situation desperate," she said, angling her chin away. She couldn't look at Zach and fib at the same time. "Not truly desperate."

"You've taken up residence in a boardinghouse and act as an old woman's nursemaid to survive. All for refusing to accept a loveless marriage. In my book, that's pretty desperate."

Elle turned to the window, pressed her brow against the cool glass. She would not marry a man she didn't love. Being alone seemed a far better choice than living a lie for the rest of her life. She agreed with Zach, but she didn't feel comfortable discussing marriage with him. Not after he had lost his wife to consumption two years ago. Hannah had been the light in his life and only recently had the light begun to shine again.

"How did he look?" Zach sighed, his toe tapping the stone floor. "Did he seem glad to be back?"

Her heart sank. Steadfast, reliable Zach.

"Did he ask about me? About Caleb?" His voice weakened with each word.

Elle pasted on a smile and turned to face him. "Well, he's really tall." She held her hand high above her head. "Six inches, maybe more. He had to duck inside the coach house."

"His head almost brushed the frame? Imagine that."

"And his voice, you remember, kind of rough, like sandpaper? Sounds the same." His lashes were long enough to make any woman jealous. "Hair, his hair was a little darker, I think." A face so handsome she had experienced an absurd rush of anger. "Thin, he looked thin."

"Did he seem happy, Ellie?"

Combative, defensive, suspicious.

"I didn't have much of a chance to talk to him." She chewed her lip and glanced away.

The stove lid rattled as Zach settled wood inside. "I should go to him. Get this confrontation over with. He can't hide in a town this size for long."

"I don't think he wants to hide." Her lids drifted low as she pictured Noah's expression when he'd stormed through Widow Wynne's gate. Disbelief, certainly, and mistrust. A definite trace of fear. "He mentioned waiting two months before coming back. I think he wants to be the one to decide when you'll meet."

She opened her eyes to find Zach staring at her. "He tell you all that?"

"Of course not. He won't tell Saint Peter that much at the Pearly Gates."

Zach nodded and flipped the stove lid closed. "It's still there between you two."

"No, Zach, it's *not*."

"Lord knows I tried, but I never understood him like you did. Even when he was no higher than my knee, the questions he asked nearly knocked me from my feet. As if I had this special person to tend to, to watch over. I was a ship's pilot. What would I know about how shells are formed or how birds fly? And that nonsense, the fishermen treating him like a carnival fortune-teller. Professor. What a stupid nickname for a kid." He grabbed his coat from a hook by the door and shrugged into it. "Yet you, you always knew what he was thinking. Heck, I never did. Made me crazy to even try."

Elle trembled beneath wool still holding Noah's body heat. She wanted to deny the notion, call it a whim, a flight of fancy, but she *had* always known.

"He came along when I needed a protector, someone who didn't laugh at my accent and knock me into the dirt in the schoolyard. I guess I loved him for that. An immature infatuation, one I did not manage well." She sighed. "Clearly, I don't need a protector any longer. I'm not going to drink too much cider at the Spring Tide Festival and get sick on my shoes. Or tumble off a slick roof and break my arm. Noah doesn't have to save me anymore."

"You don't really believe—"

"Papa!"

A boy burst into the room, filthy coattail flapping past his waist, bootlaces tripping him up. Elle watched Rory fling his arms about his father's shoulders, snuggle his cheek in the folds of Zach's shirt. A swift jab of envy pierced her. If she shielded her sight for a moment, she could imagine he was *her* child, this lovely boy who shared an uncanny resemblance to his absent uncle. Only, she had loved his mother too much to do that. Hannah's smile, the dimple in her cheek, the shape of her nose, all lived in Rory's face. Her warm laughter rolled from his lips, her gentle touch from his fingers.

"Tomorrow, Miss Ellie," Rory mumbled around a mouthful of chocolate filched from his father's pocket.

"Tomorrow?"

"The beach. We're taking the skiff to the beach."

She fluffed his hair, traced Hannah's dimple. He smelled lovely, like sweets, dirt, and little boy. "I promised, didn't I?" Over Rory's tousled head, she captured Zach's gaze. "Caleb?"

Zach shifted from one foot to the other and popped two buttons loose at the neck of his shirt. Avoiding her question, he grabbed Rory's arm and hustled him through the doorway.

Elle just managed to pluck Zach's sleeve between her fingers as he moved past. "You have to tell him. Everyone in town will know by tomorrow. The next day at best. Caleb will be home by then."

"I know," Zach said, tugging his arm free.

"See ya, Miss Ellie," Rory called, racing down the jail's narrow walkway, trailing his father like a pup.

Elle sighed and sank onto a stiff wooden bench, the music of Pilot Isle wafting inside the open door. Pounding waves and squawking gulls, the crunch of wagon wheels over crushed shell, ships' flags snapping. She accepted the meager solace, willing to accept anything but the sight of Noah's eyes, guarded and full of torment. A deep, enduring sadness armored by a wall of restraint.

In his trenchant gaze, she witnessed every misstep, every foible, every foolish poem wrapped around a rock and tossed through his bedroom window. If he cared to differentiate, and of course, he did not, Noah would find an independent woman, not a bothersome child. A competent teacher, an active member of a thriving community, a woman no longer infatuated with a young man who did not return her feelings. She had become the sensible person he had encouraged her to be. The proper woman her father demanded. She had relinquished her hopes of true love and an education, prudent enough to realize they weren't in the cards.

A gust of putrid air filled the room, signaling a receding tide on the marsh. She wondered if Noah smelled the scent and remembered. Elle's slick palms slid along her skirt. She gripped her knees and bowed her head. The man she'd encountered this afternoon was a stranger, yet she'd recognized him in a purely elemental way. Detected his wounds, as visible to her as hers were to him.

She had nothing to fear; the silly girl in need of a young man's acceptance had departed years ago. The mature woman who'd taken her place had enough good sense to stay out of trouble.

Only, her *good sense* had come at the price of her dreams.

# CHAPTER TWO

"The tangles certainly make a sad mess of the specimens."
~ C. Wyville Thomson
*The Depths of the Sea*

~

*W* *alking along a narrow street, who, oh who, should I meet?* Noah pressed his cheek into the sand, humming the ditty he'd sung as a boy. The rush and swirl of the sea mingled with the lilting tune. A strange dream, he thought drowsily. He blinked. Darkness. And heat. Vapor fogging his spectacle lenses. The warehouse in Chicago never got this warm.

Pushing to his elbows, he knocked his hat from his face.

"No bite yet."

Noah turned to find a young boy sitting beside him, legs spread, trousers rolled to the knee, a fixed grip on *his* fishing pole.

The boy gestured to the hat. "Your face looked kinda burnt."

"Burnt?" Noah mumbled, his mind clouded by sleep.

"You come to Devil Island to fish?"

"Um, well, I came out here to"—*hide*—"yes, fish."

16

"Name's Rory."

*Rory?* The mover of boxes into his coach house Rory? Elle's fiancé? *Damn.* The kid looked about six years old, tops.

"You didn't sail here alone, did you?"

Rory laughed, the skinny end of the pole dipping toward the sand. "My pa'd skin me then." He jumped up and dashed to the water's edge. "My friend brung me," he yelled and reared, pulling hard on the line. "Can't swim near the dock in Pilot Isle, with the boats and all anchored about. Devil is the nearest beach."

Rory raced back and plopped to the sand at Noah's feet. "Got any more? I had a couple shrimp, but used 'em." He waved the empty hook, the bait long gone.

Noah passed Rory the bucket sitting behind him.

"Sand fleas?" Rory's expression soured. "No wonder nothing biting." He shrugged, secured the pole between his knees, and easily baited the hook.

"Did you bring a pole?" Noah plucked his hat from the sand and adjusted the wrinkled brim.

"Nah. I'll just use yours."

Noah coughed behind his hand, not wanting to hurt his feelings. And, he had not laughed in months.

It felt good.

Rory squatted beside him, throwing curious glances at Noah's rucksack. Noah pulled it close, removed a short length of wire and a pair of tweezers. His hook had taken a beating at the boy's eager hands. "Where is this friend of yours?" he asked, curling the metal. A worthless chaperon, that one.

"Oh, down the beach aways. She tried to do a somsault." He wiggled his tiny toes in the sand. "Pretty wet now."

Noah dipped his head, hiding a smile.

Rory tinkered with the pole, shifting from side to side on his scrawny buttocks. "Are... are you my uncle Noah? The one I look like?"

Noah dropped the tweezers. He jerked his gaze to the boy's face and cataloged features as meticulously as he cataloged species of fish. Square jaw. Tousled gold curls. Conceivably, the jaw could be... and the eyes. Gray, like all the Garrett men. He felt a sharp prick and looked to find the wire embedded in his palm. He winced, snatched it out, and thumbed the dribble of blood.

Rory poked his big toe in a ghost-crab hole. "I heard them talking once. Real loud. Mad. Uncle Caleb said it was the same as walking 'cross a ghost, seeing me." A shoulder jerk accompanied the confession. "Then I heared my pa talking last night, about you sailing in on Mr. Stymie's skiff."

Noah reached for the small chin, tipped it high. Rory stared, curious and hopeful. "Where did you hear this?"

"Warped door at Widow Wynne's. You can listen lots if you're quiet. My pa says everything at Widow Wynne's is warped or busted."

Noah let his hand drop, unable to do the same with his gaze.

"You a professor?"

Seagulls scurried past, searching for a piece of discarded bait. Waves surged, nearly brushing their feet. Rising tide. Noah recorded this in dazed silence as he watched the boy fidget and squirm, a trickle of love seeping past his hardened heart.

"You a professor?" Rory repeated, tapping the corked end of the pole against his hip.

Zach's son. Caleb's nephew. *His* nephew. He swallowed, throat clicking. "That's a, a nickname someone gave me a long time ago."

"Why?"

He shrugged. "I don't remember the exact reason. People used to come by the house. The house where I lived with your father and Caleb." Where Rory lived with Zach and Hannah? "They asked me questions."

"Where'd you find the answers?"

Noah grabbed the tweezers and made little roads in the sand between his feet. "Books, usually." What year was the cotton gin invented? Why don't the numbers in my ledger add up? Is this a King Mackerel or a Spanish Mackerel? The questions had been as preposterous as the nickname. "They weren't hard to figure out."

"There's my friend," Rory said, pointing with the tip of the pole.

He shaded his eyes in time to see Elle swagger over the packed

18

sand, her barefoot stride sure and even. In no hurry to reach them, she stopped once to skip a rock, again to stoop for a shell. The same girl, obviously. Head chock-full of mischief and frivolity. She waved at Rory and turned slightly, her stride faltering. Her hand dropped to her side. The other tensed around her basket handle.

*She hadn't known he was there.*

A moment's wicked pleasure flared in the face of her discomfiture. Hell, she had delivered enough in her day. He had left the coach house before dawn to avoid her.

Her uncertainty made up for his lack of sleep.

With a resigned shrug, she swiped her curls from her face, smoothed her hand over her shirtwaist, and started forward. He couldn't help noticing how her dress clung in moist patches—a result of her poor gymnastic ability and her immodesty. Clung to her hips, the curve of her breast.

*Look away, Noah.*

He gave his spectacles a recalcitrant shove. No need to retreat. He didn't care how refreshingly undone she appeared. Her hair lifted in the breeze, and she captured the strands between her fingers. Even in Chicago, few women wore theirs that length, just below the ear.

Noah preferred long hair.

When she got closer, he noted that her skirt was tangled in her hand, gathered above any point of decency. Trim ankles. Narrow, fine-boned feet. Too, the years had eased the dappled preponderance of freckles.

"Such a surprise," she said and plunked her basket to the sand.

He frowned and scooted as far as he could without actually moving to a different spot.

"Thank you, Rory, for leaving me wet and floundering."

Rory giggled. "I told you not to do the somsault."

"Som*er*sault. I agree. The first try was shoddy. Perfectly shoddy. Hence, I tried again, much to the delight of a group of fishermen sailing by."

Noah cut his eyes to her, his jaw dropping.

"Oh, Noah." She wrapped her arms about her stomach and

laughed. The only other word he understood was, he believed, "fussbucket."

*Fussbucket?* He moved to stand, sand squeaking beneath his heels.

She circled his wrist with a finger and a thumb, a gentle appeal. "Stay." She nodded to the basket, curls bouncing against her cheek, smile teasing her lips. "I've brought lunch. Enough for an army."

Yes, he smelled her lunch. He smelled *her*. Honeysuckle and a dash of something woodsy, like moist earth. "I couldn't—"

"Yes, you can. You're too thin. You must be hungry."

Famished, in fact. A turkey sandwich in the train's dining car had been his last meal. Still....

His gaze sliced to her feet, her pink toes digging in the sand. Skin as soft as it seemed, he would bet. Scooting over another inch, he stared hard at a flock of sanderlings bustling around a beached jelly-fish. "I don't—"

She shushed him, so he sat. Completely bewildered, while she chattered and shuffled, unpacking enough food for her army. Slices of ham, four chicken legs, a loaf of bread, a small round of cheese, three pickles, two apples, one orange, and a jar of lemonade. The necessities: tablecloth, napkins, forks, plates, cups. Once she'd placed the items in an admittedly handsome composition, she sat, skirt bunched beneath her.

She handed him a napkin. He folded the linen square neatly in his lap, yielding to the surge of relief to see her limbs adequately covered.

"I've brought dessert," she said and tucked Rory's napkin into his rumpled collar.

The males leaned forward, peering into the basket. A feast, a *child's* feast, lay inside. A chocolate bar, a bag of vinegar taffy, and at least ten different penny candies, everything getting mushy in the sun. Rory released a delighted whoop, which Noah silently echoed. He tilted his head her way as a small smile curved his lips, wondering if she remembered his sweet tooth.

A green-eyed glance, an impish smirk. He didn't know what to make of the teasing look. He had never known what to make of Marielle-Claire Beaumont. Mischief and shenanigans, pranks and rough horseplay, accidental touches and a fierce desire to protect. Helplessly, he glanced at her blotchy bodice, doing its best to dry under fixed sunlight and steady gusts of wind. Sinking his teeth into the chicken leg, he tore off a chunk and looked away.

Same old Professor, Elle noted with little surprise.

Deliberate chewing, measured swallows, a leisurely sip now and again. He ate like an aristocrat, long legs folded gracefully, hand propped on the blanket, not a smack or a slurp slipping past. When he finished, he plucked two apples from the basket and flipped one to Rory, who scrambled to catch it, hands cupped. Noah polished his on his creased trouser leg and took a neat bite. Rory mimicked, then attacked with enthusiasm. They shared a smile and a laugh, mouths full of apple bits.

Elle dabbed in the vinegar pooled beneath her pickle. It rattled her to see them together, looking like a matched set. Repeatedly, she turned to find Rory perched atop her kitchen table or squatting next to Widow Wynne's cat, and her vision would spot the hair, the eyes... suffering cats, the jaw. The square, handsome little face, the same stoic pout hardening the cheeks. She hated that look. Although she loved —had loved—both the faces.

In her youth, when one of Noah's dispassionate displays pushed her fury over the edge, she would make the mistake of gazing into his face long enough to witness a spark of loneliness, or merciful heavens, grief. Which only served to solidify her love like a clay pot in a kiln.

Slipping her finger between her lips, she sucked the tip clean of vinegar. The scent of wet wool drifted to her on a gentle breeze. Wool? Ah, Noah's sweater. She glanced at him, found him staring at her, a pale gray assessment. She popped her finger from her mouth as Rory hummed an off-key tune, a joyful, abstracted ditty. She wanted to know everything about him. Did he have a fiancée? *Juste Ciel,* a *wife?*

She searched, trying to read him. She could do it if he gave her enough time.

With a muttered oath, Noah bolted to his feet, scattering sand. "Rory, how about a walk?"

Rory jumped at the chance and raced toward the water; Noah followed with a stiff-shouldered stride.

Elle rose also. Her skin burned from humiliation, not heat. What did he think she was going to do, bite him? Of course, he *had* witnessed her letting the reins of protocol loosen a bit. And, she had been trying to trespass.

No matter, he was in for a blunt awakening. *Elle loves Noah* might be carved in every tree in the schoolyard, but that didn't make the message an eternal decree. He perplexed her, that's all, and if her knees shook, the shock of seeing him again made that happen. She stalked down the beach, determined to tell him what she thought of his haughty presumption. The nerve, the gall, oh—

She halted abruptly. Two sets of footprints cut into the sand. She shifted her gaze toward the water. Noah and Rory hunkered near the edge, heads nearly touching. Before she changed her mind, Elle settled her foot in the larger impression, heel over heel.

The smooth tickle under the arch of her foot sent a memory roaring through her mind. Running barefoot along the acorn-studded cemetery path, yelping as a sharp stem pierced her skin. Noah had stopped and offered his lanky back. She'd accepted without thinking twice and let him piggyback her the rest of the way. Accidentally, of course, and for just a moment at most, his fingers had brushed her ankle, circling and squeezing. He'd glanced over his shoulder, and something, something blustery as a summer thunderstorm, had passed between them. Something that made him avoid her for two weeks. Two weeks of tears and tantrums because the day after the incident, she found him kissing Christabel Connery in the darkened coatroom at school.

Elle blinked and lurched forward. She halted just behind where they crouched near the water's edge. Windswept and sun-kissed, they created an enchanting picture.

Her hands itched to touch.

A warning sounded, deep in her mind. Gripping her damp skirt in her fist, she leaned in, intent on telling Rory they had to leave. *Now.*

"There are two ways to determine its age," Noah said, flipping a bluefish in his hand. A ring-billed gull shrieked and danced nearby, begging for the pungent morsel.

"Deter?" Rory wiped a sandy fist beneath his nose.

"Oh. Tell. Two ways to *tell* its age."

"Is this one old? He's already dead."

"Well, growth rings on scales, or otoliths, would tell us." He tapped Rory's ear. "Otoliths are bones in a fish's ear."

"Fishes have ears?"

"Of course." Noah's lips parted in a smile as he leaned closer. "Have you ever chopped down a tree and counted the rings to tell the tree's age?"

Rory considered for a moment, nodded. "Yup, once with my uncle Caleb."

Noah stiffened, just the tiniest bit. "These... these are the same kind of rings." He drew a circle in the sand, then another around the first. "Two circles. The fish would be two years old."

"How old is this one?"

Noah shrugged. "I'd need a microscope to tell."

"Microscope? Do you have one?"

He nodded.

"Go get it." Rory flipped his hand toward Noah's gear.

Laughter, deep and clear, rumbled from Noah's throat; he bent from the force of it. "No, no. At the coach house. The rest of my equipment is being delivered tomorrow. Next time, maybe."

Rory shook his head fiercely. "We gotta check this fish. I'm afraid he might be young. A baby without a mother."

Elle held her breath. Noah arrested his movement to throw the bluefish into the sea. He brought his arm to his side, the stiff fishtail brushing his trousers. "No mother, huh?"

"Just like me."

Noah swallowed, working hard to recover from his shock. "I'm sure he's a rather old fish. A grandfather, at least, by the look of him. I can take him home and check. If it will make you feel better."

"It will," Rory assured him, leaning close to his uncle.

They could have been father and son, two casts from the same mold. Elle sighed and pinched the bridge of her nose. Merciful heavens, how had Zach not realized the reason behind her fascination with his son? Her body overheated, neutralizing the nip of cool water against her feet.

Maybe he did realize.

The boys rose, Noah's hand clasping his nephew's shoulder, Rory making no move to shrug away. When they turned to find her directly behind them, Noah took a deliberate step back, Rory an excited step forward.

"Miss Ellie, we got a grandfather! I'll tell you how old later." He waved the fish close enough for her to get a good whiff. She didn't know how old it was, but it had been dead a long time.

Pasting a smile on her face, she ruffled Rory's hair. "We'd better go. Your father will pitch a fit if we sail home in the dark."

"Do you want me to take him?"

"I'm quite capable of getting a child home, Professor." She grabbed Rory's hand and tugged him behind her. Halting at the food-scattered tablecloth, she began to repack the basket.

She heard him step behind her. "I only meant—"

"I know what you meant. I always know what you mean." She shoved to her feet. Rory stood to the side, jabbing a broken conch shell in the sand.

Noah sighed and blinked eyes so pale the edges dissolved into white. His left eyelid drooped, resisting a return to its previous position. "You'd better go. Before it gets dark."

A sick shot of remorse replaced her fury. Caleb's fist *had* done permanent damage. "Yes, I've—I've got to get back," she said, stepping forward. "Come on, Rory."

Rory waved, oblivious to the tension crowding the air. "The micrascrap, Uncle Noah. I'll see you tomorrow."

Noah's shoulders slumped as he recorded their brisk departure. He felt tangled in knots, an absolute snarl. He had a nephew, he thought, and experienced the first wave of love in ten years.

But, dear God, what had happened to Rory's mother?

He glanced down the endless stretch of ivory shore, bewildered and forlorn. Kneading the ache in his neck, he retraced his path. *Footprints somewhere along here.* He stopped. The larger held another impression. Noah traced the toes, dabs in the sand the size of a dime, and circled the firm imprint of a heel.

He had looked back while squatting near the water's edge and watched Elle place her foot *in* something. At first, he thought she had pricked her sole on a pin shell. Then, the look on her face as she stared at the ground, frightened or confused, maybe even excited, cranked an idea through his mind. A fantastical idea. Impractical and silly.

Perfectly, typically Elle Beaumont.

He outlined the mark of a feminine arch, drew his hand back when his fingers started to tingle.

Elle's fascination with him had never made sense. Summer heat and winter frost, they were disparate beings. He'd loathed her heedless nature, her inattentive squirming, her frivolous chatter. Laughing during church service, talking during school lessons. Tardy for everything. Most of the time, looking like a tomcat had spit her from its mouth.

How had she found anything to admire in someone as dissimilar?

Their differences, and his often blatant disregard, did not mean he had ignored her. Elle made it impossible *not* to notice. Sneaking into his bedroom, stolen apples crammed under her skirt; telling dirty jokes while perched atop a shell slab in the burying ground; gawking at him so often that Christabel Connery carved *Elle loves Noah* into every tree in the schoolyard.

At twelve, her antics had embarrassed him. By sixteen, however, he had come full circle. Disconcerted in an adolescent way, yet speculating, for the first time. Why her eyes flashed in that impassioned way whenever she looked at him, what he had done to warrant the attention, and, if he remembered correctly, what he could *do* with it. After all, how many times had he seen her crawling out or dropping off? Landing at his feet or in his arms. Skirt billowed around her knees, a bare ankle, or bony shoulder flashing.

A healthy young man could only take so much.

He tipped his head toward the sky, calculating. The sun sat low, a flaming ball coloring the water cherry. Still enough light to cross the pass, but he would check on Elle and Rory after he sailed in, just to make sure.

Old habits died hard.

He glanced at the footprint again and nudged his spectacles up. He would have expected this nonsense from the girl with apples stuffed under her skirt, the girl who had made sure Christabel's gibe lasted by spending an entire summer scratching the marks in deeper. What did this mean coming from the woman who flaunted surprisingly generous curves, ruby curls, and a plump bottom lip he could barely tear his gaze from? Noah dashed sand across the troublesome footprint and sank to his heels.

If Elle thought to tangle him in knots, he would show her he wasn't willing. He wasn't willing to let her read his mind either, even if he suspected her talent had faded long ago.

He entertained women out of necessity. Institute dinners, charity events, and alleviation of his sporadic pangs of desire. He didn't have the former to contend with and could live without the latter for a while yet. In fact, maybe he should tell Elle she didn't interest him. In the *slightest.*

Noah watched the sun slip low in the sky, his mood lifting. Life always progressed better with a plan in mind.

Elle rounded the corner of Widow Wynne's house, mumbling beneath her breath. A brisk breeze, close to cold, sliced through her coat but failed to cool her ire. What cheek! Questioning her ability to care for a six-year-old boy. Presumptuous, conceited... *man.* Noah Garrett could take his raised brows and his neat-as-a-pin clothing, his fish talk and his stiff backside, and—

"Marielle."

Elle pinched the bridge of her nose and halted. Mercy above, would this day ever end? "Magnus."

He sat on the porch's brick steps, long legs encased in striped trousers, ones tailored during his bimonthly excursions to Raleigh. An imported cigar dangled from his lips, the stink recalling their brief courtship. Favorable memories, most of them. Favorably dull. "You seemed to be in another world for a moment, Marielle. A little flushed around the cheeks. Is that ire on your lovely face?"

She raked him with a caustic glance she hoped would send him on his way. "What do you want, Magnus?"

He lifted a newspaper from his lap, offered it to her. "Just thought you might enjoy reading this. Tomorrow's edition of the *Weekly Messenger*. I stopped by the office to see if my advertisement had been placed. I'm announcing my new location, you may recall?"

She snatched the newspaper from his hand. Of course, she remembered. She had helped him select the plot of land.

"I think you'll find this of interest," he said, his voice wavering as it did when he tried to contain laughter.

*Her lips moved as she read, a habit she had never been able to break. Noah Garrett, brother of Zachariah and Caleb, sailed from Morehead City on the Adele—*

Elle crumpled the newspaper in her fist and raised her head. "Why are you bringing this to me? What can you possibly hope to gain? You humiliated me in front of the entire town, letting everyone know you decided to end our engagement. What more do you want? You have your pride *and* your medical practice."

Magnus's gaze began to smolder, no longer shining civilly for the sake of propriety. "You really are as unbalanced as some think if you believe the situation to be so simple. You made a fool of me, a circumstance I have trouble overlooking, my dear. Everyone knew you felt only relief when I failed to attend our engagement soiree."

She slapped the newspaper against her thigh. "A dinner party, Magnus. It was a simple dinner party."

Standing, he flung his cigar to the ground and descended the steps with a deliberate gait she realized contained a fair measure of anger. "A particularly fierce look was on your face when you rounded the corner of the house, Marielle. Who were you thinking of? I never witnessed any emotion except the unfocused, albeit attractive, expression of boredom. Pity even. What could paint such a rosy bloom on your cheeks? Or, should I say, who?" He moved forward, his elbow nudging hers, much too close for comfort.

In her haste, she stumbled over the bricks lining the walkway.

Taking advantage of her misstep, he grasped her chin, forcing her eyes to his. "You must be happier than you've ever been in your life. Noah Garrett back in town, and this time, you're old enough to cause real trouble. I applaud your efforts to keep yourself ready and available. I hear he's living in the widow's coach house. How convenient."

Her palm cracked his cheek with enough force to send him staggering. *"Get out."*

"Now, dear—"

"You heard her, Leland. Get out. Before I allow myself to get angry."

Magnus's hand paused halfway to his face. He swiveled around, his bark of laugher splitting the air. "My word, Garrett, how has our little Marielle survived without you?"

Noah had Magnus by the collar of his studded shirt before Elle drew her next breath. "I'm accosted often on the streets of Chicago, Leland. Trust me, you don't want to know what I've had to learn to protect myself."

Magnus craned his head, struggling to look his opponent in the eye.

"Have a care, Leland." Noah clenched his hand, his muscles flexing beneath his orderly cuff.

"You'd better take that advice as well, my friend." Magnus shoved Noah's arm aside, storming from the yard without another word.

Noah watched him go, then muttered an oath beneath his breath and stalked in the other direction.

She snatched his rucksack from the edge of the walkway and ran after him. She had never seen Noah use his hands for anything violent, unless you counted the lists he had made for Caleb detailing ways to solve problems *without* using violence. "I have no idea what bramble is stuck in Magus's paw," she said, struggling to hoist the rucksack over her shoulder.

He shot her a furious side glance, his gaze doing a slow burn. "No idea? Jesus, Elle, *you're* the bramble." He grabbed the rucksack and began to climb the coach house staircase. "You're everyone's bramble."

"Magnus and I broke off our"—she lifted her skirt above her ankles and scrambled after him—"our engagement months ago. Besides, why should he be mad? He made it very clear that the decision was his and his alone. Embarrassingly clear."

Noah stopped abruptly. Her head thumped him right between the shoulder blades, and the newspaper she had forgotten she held fluttered to the step.

He stooped and smoothed the newsprint over his knee, his head moving as he read. "Were you sorry?" he finally asked, his gaze lifting.

"Sorry about what?"

He adjusted his silver-rimmed spectacles. Behind glass, she saw that his eyes had cooled. "Sorry Leland ended the engagement."

Tell him yes. What better way to show Noah Garrett you haven't been pining after him for ten years? "I was terribly distraught. The entire situation nearly broke my heart. I looked so forward to being Mrs. Magnus Leland." Her voice cracked hard on the last word.

The muscles in his shoulders tensed; he shoved to his feet. "You're a terrible liar, Elle. Truly dreadful. Scares me to think you would waste a chance at marriage because of a silly"—he nudged the coach house door open with his elbow and ducked through the entrance —"*infatuation* when we were children."

She slapped the door wide when he would have shut it in her face. "Why you arrogant, boorish—" Her words caught in her throat.

Stacks of books covered every surface. The desk, the leather chair and ottoman, the faded settee that had once been dark magenta.

Cautiously, she strolled to the desk. She hadn't seen this many books since the long nights spent in the university library. She recalled rows and rows of chestnut shelves, covert laughter, and the smell of dust. The thrill of learning, of taking control of her life for the first time; sadly, the only time. Burying the burst of longing, she hefted a leather-bound volume as thick as her wrist. *"Depths of the Sea,"* she read and fingered the gold tassel marking the page. "This is magnificent, Noah." She turned the vellum slowly. "You know, I had an interest in biology once, but that, well, that was a long time ago." She shook her head, denying the impulse to tell him.

Why would Noah care about her dream of finishing university?

"They're books for the laboratory, mostly. The others are for research." Elle felt the heat of his body before she smelled him. A rush of warmth, then the tantalizing scent of sea and man. His arm circled her waist as he lifted the book from her hand. He brushed his finger across the mark Magnus's cheek had left on her palm.

Her fingers curled; her body swayed into the desk.

"This will bruise, more than likely," he said, his breath dusting her cheek.

She stared at his slim, supple fingers, the nails finely trimmed, the pads slightly callused. She had once pictured them exploring her body. Troubled, she tossed a careless smile over her shoulder, one she hoped would conceal her confusion.

Noah blinked, his gaze lowering. To her lips, she guessed, from the way they started tingling. She licked them nervously, deciding the insincere smile had been a bad idea.

Cursing softly, he stepped away.

When Elle recovered enough to face him, he had his back to her, hands braced on the frame of the only window in the room. The reddish glow of early evening spilled in, kicking glints of gold in the hair curling over his collar. "What Leland said, about you, about me. He was wrong, wasn't he?"

"Oh, that." Elle rolled her fingers into a fist to stop their trembling. "Of course he was. Magnus was always a tad jealous of... it's just, he remembered lots of things that happened... before. Nothing worth mentioning, things I'm sure you've forgotten by now. You're not the only one to light a fire beneath him. He hated Caleb, too. The proposal business rankled."

Noah slanted his head, a startled part to his lips. *"Caleb?"*

"He proposed at the Spring Tide Festival, five years after you left.

He'd been drinking, and when I refused his offer, he bent down on one knee, stumbled into the tent pole, and knocked the fiddler from his perch. Then, *he* fell into another tent pole. A crucial one, evidently. The entire length of canvas collapsed on top of us. Christabel took him home that night, something she's been doing ever since, I think."

"Why in the hell did he ask *you*, then?"

Her teeth clicked together. "Get the dazed look off your face, Professor. I've had a number of eligible suitors."

"Yes, I got a firsthand look at one of them today. In hindsight, maybe you should have accepted Caleb."

"Caleb felt an *obligation*. He struggled to be everything to everybody after you left. Instead of being my friend, he wanted to act as my protector. And a woman's protector, at least in his mind, is her husband. You may not want to hear this but your leaving and us hearing no word from you just about killed him. He was lost. Completely and utterly lost. When he found himself, he had changed. He grew into a man, a good man, but not the same man."

His hands dived into his pockets. "Caleb wasn't the only one who was lost."

She closed the distance between them. "I always wondered what leaving here, frightened and alone, would do to you. If the experience would change you into someone I wouldn't recognize."

"Didn't we establish in the damned attic that none of you knew me? Hell, I didn't even know myself." He laughed, but it sounded raw and reluctant. "So, am I still recognizable?"

Elle suspected he did not want to be. He believed change would shield him. But she could not lie. He had to face them, his fears and his family, sooner than he liked. "Yes, I recognize you, because I knew him. Deep down, I *feel* him. I see him. In gestures you make, he comes back to me. Bits and pieces I had forgotten. The curve of your hand when you adjust your spectacles, even the absurdly neat way you roll your sleeves." Against her better judgment, she added, "What you did today, sending Magnus away. My friend would have done the same."

He jerked his head, the light profiling his shuttered gaze. "I lived on the streets for months after leaving here. While struggling to

31

survive, I learned to smell a person's fear and recognize their anger before they turned it on me. I learned the hard way, each bruise a tough lesson I could not afford to ignore. When I rounded the corner of the house"—his shoulders stiffened beneath crisp cotton—"I reacted purely on instinct. Nothing solicitous or benevolent in the gesture, I can assure you. Don't take this for something it's not."

Her hand lifted, but he flinched before she'd even decided if she would touch him. "Would it be so terrible to find he's still in there? The boy who loved his brothers? The boy who trusted me?"

"He's dead and gone, Elle. These days, I'm the only one I trust."

She tilted her head, her neck aching from the unnatural angle. Behind glass, Noah blinked, eyes narrowing as he watched her watch him.

"Marielle-Claire!"

They leaned at the same moment, banging heads.

A hiss of breath slipped past Elle's lips, and she rubbed her brow. She looked out the window and saw her father standing in the yard below, his hand shading his face as he stared at the upper porch of Widow Wynne's house.

*"Juste Ciel!"* Elle dug in the pocket of her skirt. "Six-thirty," she said and glanced from her watch to her clothing. Dirt-streaked shirtwaist. Cuffs and collar missing. No belt. Hem dangling in two places. "He'll kill me. Alone in a man's apartment, late for our weekly dinner appointment, and dressed inappropriately. He will simply kill me."

Noah rolled his eyes as she smoothed the strawberry mess on her head. "It's no good. You still look like you sprinted down the street without passing a mirror."

She paused, expression frosting. "Thanks. Thanks a lot." Halting at the door, she squeezed the beveled knob until her knuckles paled and made another pathetic attempt to straighten her clothing.

And the damned urge to protect her hit him hard.

*"Wait." Ah, Garrett.*

Well, dammit, he had never liked her father.

She glanced over her shoulder with a weak smile.

"I'll help you this time. But this is it. I promise you, this is it."

Her eyes flashed. "Let's get this out in the open. I was infatuated, once, a long time ago. Time to move on, Professor. I've refused marriage. According to my father, the grand opportunity to improve my life. And I don't see any good prospects looming on the horizon. Not to break your heart or anything"—she angled her chin, training her stunningly green gaze right on him—"but that hasn't changed since you arrived."

He felt an odd tightness in his chest, although her pledge was exactly what he wanted to hear. "Good. We understand each other." He lifted his hand, staying her impatient jiggling of the door handle. "I'll do this, on one condition."

"Condition?" Her brow scrunched as her canvas boot tapped a tune on the planked floor.

"No more 'Professor' nonsense. Never again from those lovely lips of yours."

Elle raised her hand to her mouth, smoothed her finger over her top lip. "Of course."

Puzzled by what he'd just uttered, Noah dropped to his haunches and flipped through a pile of books. He motioned her behind the door as he approached, a burgundy volume in his hand. "Wait until I have your father's full attention, where you can see our backs are turned. Then run. Don't think, run." He stepped outside, then leaned back in. "Let me amend that. Think. *Please.* Don't trip crossing the yard or tumble down the staircase and break your leg. Only one doctor in town, I'll wager, and he's someone we want to avoid just now."

Elle glared and kicked the door shut, propelling him onto the small landing. "Fine show of gratitude," he muttered and yanked his cuffs.

Closing in on Henri Beaumont, Noah reminded himself that Pilot Isle differed greatly from Chicago. He had to get used to being part of a community, tipping his hat and making eye contact, engaging the fishermen he had come to soothe in discussions about the weather or the latest catch. Inane, completely harmless conversation.

Hell, he might as well practice his rusty skills on Henri Beaumont.

# CHAPTER THREE

*"We must console ourselves with the comparatively few things which come up entire."*
~ C. Wyville Thomson
*The Depths of the Sea*

~

*You cannot force me,* Elle thought to herself, her father's voice dissolving in her ears like mist in the sunlight. Her weekly dinners with her father were quickly becoming comparable to torture.

"Marielle-Claire, are you listening?"

Reaching for her wineglass, Elle drained it in one swallow. Her father kept a bottle of Bordeaux in the storeroom of Christabel's restaurant and insisted on drinking from his own crystal.

"Daughter, are you *listening?*"

"You cannot force me," she said, a kaleidoscope of color glittering across the tablecloth as she lowered the beveled glass.

"Force you? *Grands Dieux!* If I could force you, I would have. Long ago."

She drew a calming breath of air filled with the scent of smoke, fish, and Macassar oil. Strong enough to make her think every male head in the room was heavily slicked.

"You let Dr. Leland slip through your fingers, Marielle-Claire. Absurd, especially for a man, but I believe he wanted your love. Would not have *you* unless he had *it*, which, of course, he did not." Henri's lips parted on a sigh, a puff of smoke drifting forth. "Let there be only honesty between family. Your love is not available, now is it?"

She blinked and coughed, her eyes stinging. "Available? I've never loved a man enough to get married, if that's what you mean."

He flicked his hand, ashes from his cigar drifting to the floor. "Why do you insist upon believing in an antiquated ideal? Forget about a marriage based on love. I didn't love your mother. And she did not love me. We had a sensible relationship, a solid partnership. Love would have thrown a kink in a well-oiled piece of machinery," he said, candlelight revealing flaring nostrils and plump cheeks. Except for a hint of plumpness in her own cheeks, she and her father shared little. "If your mother had not been dead all these years, I would curse her for putting such nonsense in your head."

Elle dug her heels into the pine planks beneath her feet and prayed to God she could hold her tongue. She counted to ten, then whispered, "*Grandmere* Dupre filled my head with nonsense, if you must know."

"*Ah... cela n'a rien d'etonnant.*" Henri stabbed his cigar in the clump of creamed spinach on his plate, lips curling back from his teeth. "Not a surprise, to translate for you since your French is much like a child's. This news makes me regret, not for the first time, sending Marie our address after we moved to America. Is this what she wrote about in those cumbersome letters she sent every month? Cautioned you to marry for love? As she did, but, alas, as her beloved daughter did not? Imbecilic drivel from an old woman."

Elle swallowed her ire, wishing for another glass of wine to soften her father's cruel counsel. "Marie Dupre bore seven children with a man she cherished more than life. She believed in the power of love and urged me to hold on to love if I found it, no matter the cost." Of course, years ago, not long before Marie's death, Elle had made the mistake of writing to her about Noah. Every *cumbersome* letter from then on had mentioned his name, asking if he had returned to Pilot Isle. As if she somehow knew he would. As if it mattered.

"Don't look at me with blatant hostility on your face. You are my only child, a beautiful woman, and I love you. However, you tend to dream far too much, Marielle-Claire. Life is for those who grasp it in both hands." He made a fist. "Who *do,* not who dream. Sad but true, but you need a man to grasp life for you. You cannot do it alone. It's impossible. I made a mistake allowing you unlimited freedom. University, the disruptive group of women who encouraged you to attend those ridiculous rallies. The trouble you got into was easy enough to rectify. After I assured them you were going home, the officers released you without complaint. But the ideas, they remain a wall around you. *Grands Dieux!* Ideas of independence and feminine freedom, as if there were such a thing." He rolled the rim of his glass along his bottom lip, took a measuring sip. "Caleb would have put up with your nonsense. After all, he continues to."

"He's in love with Christabel. A tad late, I'm afraid." Elle smothered a yawn; she had heard these complaints many times.

"Well, well. Gossip travels."

Elle's shoulders lifted beneath her faded dress. She felt calm, overly calm. She wondered if her father's Bordeaux were to blame.

"Christabel Connery is nothing for you to worry about. I will talk to Caleb, if you wish. If you changed your mind, I could be persuaded to change his."

Elle gazed through flickering candlelight—across an incongruous setting of chipped porcelain and gleaming crystal—into a stranger's eyes. At times like these, her mother's comforting smile returned, and Elle experienced grief greater than any she could imagine. If only... *oh, damn and blast with if only.* "Papa, I don't care about Caleb and Christabel. I don't care about Magnus and Anna Plowman. If I married a man, shouldn't I care if he loves another woman?"

Henri reared, his thumbs snaking beneath the braided edge of his waistcoat. "I imagine you would care if the situation involved young Noah. He asked me to translate a science text this afternoon. Mentioned he's living in the widow's vacant dwelling. How opportune."

She slid her glass in a slow circle. Would she care if Noah loved another woman? Kissed another woman? The naive young girl would have cared plenty, and gone after them, claws sharpened. Elle rubbed her hand across her stomach, the sudden ache warning her the young girl still resided inside her.

*No.* A woman did not experience the unconditional love of a child. And, her love for Noah had been unconditional from the first moment. She could still see him shoving Daniel Connery from her path and turning to escort her inside the schoolhouse. Her mind had not understood every word spoken that day, but her heart had.

Her father's fist cracked down, upsetting a tin saltshaker and her wineglass. "Marielle-Claire, you must get him out of your mind. I would be happy to hand you over to him, believe me. But be reasonable. He does not want you. He never has."

Elle righted her glass and reached for the bottle. "Our relationship does not include sharing my mind, Papa. What's there is mine and mine alone." Commending herself for pouring with a steady hand, she took a long sip before she looked into eyes that scaled and stored.

Exposed, she buried her anguish deep.

Henri leaned forward, wadding stained cloth beneath each elbow. "Forget him, daughter. Right now, right this *minute*. You made a perfect ninny of yourself, but you were a child, and people will excuse a child's impropriety. They will not excuse a woman's."

Anger bloomed hot and fast in her cheeks.

"I can see by your intractable expression that I will have to unveil harsh truths to make you understand your position. A scented letter was waiting for young Noah at the post office this morning. From a Mrs. Bartram. Caroline, I believe. Return address Chicago. Unfortunately, Garrett retrieved the missive before I had a chance to intercept. Written proof would work wonders in convincing you."

"That's despicable."

His shoulders lifted in a careless shrug. "Dear girl, I no longer presume where you're concerned. I learned that lesson long ago."

"I no longer presume where you're concerned either, Papa. Those lessons blistered."

He vaulted to his feet, his chair skidding back. "You set yourself on a perilous course." He stuffed his crystal wineglasses in his coat pocket. "A dire one."

Knowing it would fuel his ire as mere words could not, Elle flicked her fingers in a dismissive gesture. It worked, she thought, watching him storm from the restaurant, cursing the tables crowding his path, cursing his daughter, cursing the small town he ran his shipping empire from.

"Whew, that was a good one."

Elle propped her chin in her palm, watched Christabel Connery sweep her maroon skirt to the side and plant her ample bottom in the chair her father had vacated.

"A quick-tempered male, I tell you."

"At least he didn't break any crystal this time," Elle said.

Christabel pulled a dented cup from her apron pocket and emptied the rest of the wine in it. "Oh, he's just getting sick of ordering those fancy glasses every month. Sees it's cheaper to flounce outta here spitting curses rather than throwing things. For the love of Pete, at least that's free." She swished wine from cheek to cheek and swallowed. "Have a fit if he saw me drinking this from a tin cup, wouldn't he?"

Elle laughed, or tried to, and dipped her head low. Her father's tantrum hadn't left the sick feeling in her stomach. Oh, no, Noah's love letter had done that.

"Oh, honey."

Startled, she glanced up, taking note of the compassion in her friend's dark brown eyes. Not able to stand anyone's sympathy just then, Elle dropped her gaze to the tangle of blond hair trailing past Christa's shoulder. Her father called Christabel a floozy; Elle called her a friend. "He's never going to sign my money over to me, Christa.

Never. He has no right to do this. My mother planned to give it to me for my education. She and Papa discussed the funds before she died. He promised her, promised me. And now, it's been so long. I'm too old to return to university."

"It seems he has every right, fair or no. Didn't your momma leave anything in writing? Anything at all? I don't know much about legal matters, but I do know you have to get it in writing."

Elle shook her head. Her mother's death had been sudden, three weeks after the headaches and dizziness started. There had not been time to sign papers and legalize things her mother had never dreamed would need to be legalized.

"Maybe you should marry—"

Elle's hand shot on, coming close to knocking the bottle to the floor. "Please, don't say it, Christa. Please, anyone but you."

"Honey, what are you going to do? Your school isn't a money-making business. Not enough, anyway. And what if Widow Wynne, bless her heart, passes on? You could open a shop, a millinery or something, like Carol Hudley. Except you can't sew worth a lick. And your cooking isn't good enough for even *me* to hire you." Christabel raised the cup to her lips, her words a hollow echo against tin. "You could still go back to Magnus."

Elle slammed her elbows to the table. "You must be joking."

Christabel lowered the cup, revealing flushed cheeks and a half grimace.

"Mercy above, you're embarrassed to even suggest it. How could you think...?" The words turned to a growl low in her throat.

"He still loves you, Ellie. Anna Plowman is a blind fool, I guess, not to see. Tell him you love him and didn't realize it before. He'd jump like you lit a firecracker under his tail end."

"I won't do it. Something deep inside tells me not to."

A dreamy smile rounded Christabel's lips as she took a lazy sip.

Elle leaned in and whispered, "Get that look off your face. It's not going to happen." She glanced over her shoulder, but no one appeared to be listening.

"Like your granny always said."

"Yes, yes, Noah's returned. Fat lot of good that will do me. My father just told me a woman is writing him from Chicago. Scented letters, of all things."

"Chicago's a long way, honey. Miles and miles. She's there, and you're here. Seems you have the advantage. Not so hard to make him fall in love with you if you put your mind to it."

A ragged laugh burst from her lips. "Noah Garrett, in love with me? Rich, Christa, really rich."

"Listen, from one woman who loves a Garrett to another who loves a Garrett but won't admit she does, it isn't that hard. You just got to make them see what's already there. Caleb never knew what hit him. Plain as the writing on a chalkboard most times. Men are just too stupid to read the message."

Elle shoved a spiral of hair behind her ear, wondering why her chignons never held for more than an hour. "Let me say this once, so I don't have to repeat it. I will never make a fool of myself over him again. I loved him, yes, I admit. *Loved.* A young girl's infatuation that is a faded memory now. As pathetically faded as this dress." She plucked at her bodice. "I avoided the post office this morning, because everyone is watching me, expecting me to swoop down, snatch Noah between my teeth, and fly off with him."

"Can you say you wouldn't enjoy flying off with *him* in your jaws? Can you *really?*"

Elle dropped her head to her hands and groaned. "Oh, Christa."

"I say you can't, because I saw him today, walking back from the docks. Honest, I nearly dropped my sack of potatoes. He grew up mighty fine." Christabel clinked the cup against her teeth. "Taller than any man on the street; a head full of hair the color of good scotch whiskey. Fancy fishing pole thrown over a broad shoulder. Picture spindly Noah Garrett having broad shoulders? Not as broad as Caleb's, mind you, but a surprise considering what a scrawny boy he was."

"He was never scrawny."

Christabel threw back her head and laughed.

"Stop it," Elle whispered. "Do you want the whole town to know what we're talking about? Heaven, that's all I need."

Christabel pressed her hand to her mouth, her head bobbing. "Sorry, sorry."

"I can handle this, I'm telling you. I can handle *him*. Don't go making a scene."

"Uh-huh. Did you see the clothes he wore? Slicked sharp as Sunday, neat as a pin. You always liked him spit-shined, didn't you?"

Elle pinched the bridge of her nose, a nagging headache creeping up on her. "Sure, I loved feeling fit for the rag box compared to him."

"Rag box? No, just a handful of trouble every now and then. Still are, I guess. But a man forgets all his arguments real quick when he looks into a face pretty as yours. Rag box? That's a new one." She gazed into her empty cup, her voice going soft. "Ellie, you and Noah were the sweetest things I ever saw."

"Sweet?"

"Oh, he acted like you rubbed him the wrong way, or acted like you didn't rub him at all. Once or twice, not long before he left, I know I caught him looking at you, a spark of interest showing." Christabel dabbed the frayed edge of her apron against her lips. "You see, honey, I recognize the spark of interest in the Garrett grays."

"Good for you. Good for Caleb. Just leave me, leave Noah, out of your spark-of-interest, Garrett-gray theory."

Christabel shook her head and sighed theatrically. "Sure a shame. Imagine the children you two would have. Smart as whips with a dash of spunk thrown in."

Elle's stomach twisted. Would they have had green eyes or gray? Hair the color of a burst of sunlight or dull, stringy red? Elle lifted her head to discover a shrewd smile crossing her friend's face. "Damn," she said and wrenched to her feet.

"Wait, honey, your daddy left this."

Elle grabbed Noah's textbook and skirted the crowded tables, ignoring the amused glances and the whispered comments.

All the way home, the book pressed to her bosom, Elle wondered how many people believed she still loved Noah Garrett.

Elle gave the dangling front doorknob a gentle twist, fearing it would fall off and roll into the tangle of shrubs surrounding the porch. Another chore to add to an unbearably long list. Tossing her shawl and gloves on the hall-tree shelf, she made her way along the darkened hallway.

Elle slid the pocket door aside and twisted the gasolier switch, flooding the parlor with murky light. Sinking to the edge of the tattered love seat, she turned her attention to the leather-bound volume in her hands. She read enough to see the red-and-gold slip marked an essay about coral erosion. Unfortunately, she could not read the text well. As her father had pointed out, her French equaled a child's.

Asking for a translation was a remarkably devious way of diverting her father's attention. Especially for a boy who had once dragged her into the mercantile and made her apologize for stealing apples.

Propping her feet on a tasseled ottoman, Elle hoisted the book against her ribs. She flicked her finger over the dog-eared pages, paused to read the notes scribbled in the margin.

An hour later, the case clock chimed; the book thumped to the floor. She reached for it, stopped, sighed. Noah's accomplishments were buried in the index at the rear: doctoral research, expeditions in the Pacific. He had even lived up to his childhood nickname. Heavens, she had eaten lunch with a true professor with her skirt hiked around her knees.

She kicked the book, then curled her toes in pain. She hated this feeling of... inferiority, of envy. If she had finished university, maybe she could converse about science or literature, history or mathematics. A semester of domestic economy wasn't likely to help her much.

Elle let her gaze stray to the pilot coat hanging over the arm of the love seat. She drew her hand back before her fingers brushed the sleeve. She and Noah did not have one interest in common except a thirst for knowledge, something he did not even recognize in her.

She wasn't sure who he was anymore. The person in the book; the biologist who had traveled the world and written research papers; the man who received perfumed letters from a married woman and stood so tall he had to duck through doorways.

She didn't know him.

She didn't think she would ever know him again.

Noah felt the stare burning into his back a full minute before he turned. Shading his face, he squinted into the sun, seeing only the darkened silhouette of a woman. A jolt of undesired anticipation tore through him, then trickled away when he caught the scent.

Fruity. Banana? Somehow, he knew Elle Beaumont would never smell like banana. An angry sea or a fistful of dirt, maybe, but never banana.

The silhouette hopped up a step, going from sunlight to shade. Flashing blue eyes tipped at the corner. Hollow cheeks, slim lips. Young and blond, very blond. Noah shrugged away his discomfort.

She took another step, her pleated skirt brushing his trouser leg. "Hello," she said in a laughing, breathless rush.

"Hello." He caught the nail that dropped from his lips. "Can I help you with something?" He perched his hip on the coach house railing, which wobbled precariously.

Another addition to his repair list.

"No." The young woman bounced on her toes, buckling her boots where the patent leather cap cut in. "My name's Meredith. I'm wait-ing"—she giggled and glanced over her shoulder—"for Miss Ellie to finish her other lesson. I come twice a week from three to four. She's teaching me to do my daddy's accounts. He owns the mercantile. I wasn't too good in school. Numbers and all, I mean. But Miss Ellie says I can do anything if I set my mind to it. Even add my daddy's accounts and not tangle them up worse than two tomcats in a feed sack. My daddy would rather have a son do them, if he had one. But he doesn't, so he's stuck. With me, and with Miss Ellie, who he thinks is tetched." She emphasized this by drawing a circle around her ear. "But it's only because she's smarter than he is."

Noah swung his gaze toward the coach house. The metallic ping of a typewriting machine had woken him from restless slumber, dreams idling just below the surface. Zach and Caleb... and Elle, circling a campfire on Devil Island, youthful faces glowing in the amber light.

"I remember you," Meredith cut in, before he had time to refocus on her face.

He glanced back slowly, raised a brow as he tugged his leather glove off with his teeth.

"You used to stop in my daddy's store when I was real little. Bought a lot of cotton handkerchiefs, for ship's sails you told me. Your brother Caleb even let me see the models one time, in his shed out behind your momma's house."

Noah loosened his fist, dabbed the fleck of blood where the nail had pieced his palm. Not much of a shed, more of an enlarged privy. He'd spent many hours in that dusty old shack, watching Caleb work his magic on piece after piece of wood, threading sail for Noah's favorite model, the American block sloop. The old shed stood less than a mile from here. He frowned and shoved the notion of returning from his mind. Caleb had likely smashed that shed to bits— along with his block sloop.

"Your name's Noah?"

"Yes, that's right," he said, and tugged the other glove free, a trace of unease mounting at her predatory look.

"The Spring Tide Festival is in two weeks." She flashed a crook-toothed smile, the first imperfection he had witnessed. "I didn't know if anyone told you about it. Or if you've decided who you might be squiring."

Squiring?

Meredith followed the statement with a bounce and a giggle. He almost reached out, fearing she would topple down the staircase. "The committee decorates a stretch of beach on Devil. A big tent, lots of pretty ribbons and white clematis, daisies and carnations if they bloom early. Old-time oil lanterns. Sailboat races during the day. Music and dancing at night. It's wonderful." She twisted her hands together and released a dreamy sigh.

Oh, yes, he remembered running after Caleb and Elle, struggling to divert some catastrophe. Pocketing the nail, he offered a tight smile. "I have a lot of work—"

"Work?"

"The fisheries laboratory. Out on the point."

"Oh." She slumped.

Across the way, the door to Elle's school opened, and a young woman stepped outside. No sign of Elle. Shrugging a bead of sweat down his neck, Noah barely harnessed a sigh of relief.

Meredith cupped her hand around her mouth and whispered, "I have to go. Miss Ellie is a stickler for punctuation."

Noah laughed; he couldn't help it. "I'm sure she is."

"Bye, Noah. Maybe I'll see you later." Lifting her skirt, she danced down the stairs, a wad of peach cloth clamped in each fist. "Maybe even at the festival."

He followed her progress through the overgrown grass, all the while marveling at the peculiarity, the sheer fickleness, of women. With the toe of his boot, he located the nail Elle had snagged her skirt on yesterday. Lifting the hammer, he pounded it in deep.

Elle settled her shoulder against the doorjamb below and took advantage of her luck. Dove gray clouds crowded the sky, dimming the flood of sunlight streaming over Noah. He shifted, knee flexing as he put his weight on it, and clamped a nail between his teeth. As he skimmed his fingers along the step above him, the muscles in his shoulders bunched beneath pressed blue cotton. She smiled; he looked dressed for church, not repairs. Swiping his wrist across his brow, he tilted his head enough for her to study his shaded profile, to determine the changes ten years had brought.

An air of masculinity, to be sure. Grooves chalked a mouth she would call virile and beautiful. Faint lines spreading from eyes the color of wood smoke. Gaze moving lower, she noted firm ridges of muscle in his arms and his thighs.

Looking away, she drew a breath of humid air and leaned in to see Meredith diligently working on her assignment. A pretty girl, a tad young, but not *too* young. Elle had seen Noah laughing with her. If he asked her to the Spring Tide Festival, Elle would have to watch him hold the girl against his chest and—

*You must get that boy out of your mind, Marielle-Claire.*

Her father's warning pounded through her, in time with Noah's hammer blows. She recognized the danger here. For her, Noah would always be a swift route to heartache. Corroborating the hazard, he shifted and the play of movement stretched his trousers over his firm buttocks.

"What are you doing?" she shouted, moving across the yard and climbing the coach house staircase with the grace and speed of a madwoman.

He shouldered a bead of sweat from his cheek and spit a nail into his gloved palm. "Hammering."

"Yes, I can see that. No need. And if there are repairs that need to be done, I can do them."

A gust of wind chose that moment to race in from the ocean and slap a loose shutter against the house. Noah lifted a tawny brow, the edges of his lips curling. "You're doing a fine job."

"The school takes most of my time. Besides, I'm not really very handy. Well, Widow Wynne can't afford workers and neither can—"

"A deal, Elle."

"Deal?" Clearing her throat, she forced the nip of suspicion aside. Deals created by men never seemed to get women anywhere in her experience.

He braced his elbows on his knees, dipped his head, and laughed. A stray lock of hair on the crown fluttered like a flag. Elle twisted her fingers in the folds of her skirt to keep her hands from wandering where they shouldn't. "What kind of deal?"

Noah's head lifted, his eyes warm and clear. "Don't look so dubious.

This isn't one of Caleb's deals. You don't have to worry about it biting you in...." He laughed again and rubbed his hand over his mouth. "You don't have to worry, that's all I'm saying. I worked as a laborer to put myself through university, so I'm qualified. I'll purchase the supplies and complete the repairs in exchange for help I'm going to need for the next month. Someone to transcribe my notes. A student of yours, possibly."

"There is one student." She worried her lip between her teeth. "Annie's trying to improve her penmanship, which is adequate, but her reading skills are good. Only, this sounds like a lousy deal for you. You pay for the materials *and* do the work?"

"Let me worry about that. You can't ignore the repairs any longer. This blessed place is collapsing around you." He nudged his spectacles higher on the slope of his nose. "And my notes aren't complicated, simple details concerning the lab's construction. I'm to wire Chicago once a week with a report. Took it by this morning, and the telegraph operator wasn't able to read my handwriting."

"It's not that bad."

He paused in mid-motion, the hammer dangling from his fingers. "How do you know?"

A gust of air swept her hair into her face. She brushed it aside, concentrating on the shadows pooling at her feet and the distant rumble of thunder. "I have your book, the one you gave my father. He left it in the restaurant, and I, I brought it home with me. I thumbed through a chapter or two last night. You made notes in the margins. Notes I could decipher. Easily." She shrugged.

"You read some of it?" He sounded incredulous.

She planted her hands on her hips. "I *can* read."

His thoughtful gaze skimmed her face. "I know that Elle. I just had no idea you would be interested."

"A long time ago, I had books similar to yours, but I"—no need to tell him she had been forced to sell her precious textbooks to raise money for the school—"don't have them anymore."

"Which essay did you read?" He propped the hammer against his hip and stretched out his legs. The eager expression on his face struck a deep cord, and she forgot his question. "Elle? Which essay did you read?"

"Um, something to do with average catches and the number of fish breeding. Nothing much."

Surprise widened his eyes; a faint smile curved his mouth. "By calculating average catches, we can demonstrate reduction in stock and generate an estimate of the number of fish breeding in a given area. It's what we call a skeleton study, time-consuming and exhausting, and basic. I'm going to conduct one here. God knows, I have the time. I went by the lab site this morning and Tyre Mcintosh, the master draftsman, told me to stay away for the rest of the week." He flicked a blade of grass from his shoe. "Said he didn't need some fish specialist hanging over his shoulder, telling him how to hammer."

"Sounds like Tyre. Interference doesn't sit well with him. Nor with the fishermen."

He grinned, the first truly genuine smile she had seen since his return three days earlier. "I'll use my considerable charm to persuade them."

Wondering if the time was right to discuss what he could no longer avoid, she said mildly, "Caleb has daily contact with the fishermen. He designs and builds their boats. You—"

He shot to his feet, sending the hammer tumbling. *"No."*

"Noah, he's your brother. You're going to have to face him." Sooner than he imagined. Caleb returned on the afternoon skiff.

"I'm not asking him to help me." His hands closed into fists, his voice dropped, clearly a man preparing for battle. "Never again."

The oak branches above their heads cracked together, nearly obliterating Elle's words. "You have it all wrong."

He flinched, his face losing color. "I found out just how much I could rely upon Caleb."

"He loved you, you must realize that. He still does."

She witnessed a wealth of emotion: remorse, uncertainty, and rage. "I don't know what to think. About myself or my family." Grasping her shoulders, he dragged her forward, the grief he fought to contain rising to the surface. "After ten years, I *still* don't know what to think."

A bolt of lightning struck, rattling a windowpane above them. They glanced up, then warily, at each other. Her skin burned where he gripped her. The air she drew into her lungs grew heavy, filled with the promise of rain and the threat of emotions she feared.

She wanted to ease his anguish but the words would not come when he stood so near she could see the curl of his lashes, the flecks of black in his eyes. See the fear sharpening every angle of his face.

She could only watch as his lightly whiskered jaw clenched, his hands leaving her so quickly that she staggered. "Keep out of my life, Elle. For once, just keep the hell out of it." He thundered down the stairs and shouldered past the shrubs separating Widow Wynne's yard from the next.

Elle gripped the railing, a splinter jabbing her hand. *Keep the hell out of my life.* Unfortunately, she couldn't. Not when he headed for the docks—and the skiff anchored there. How she knew, well, she just *knew.* The loose shutter whipped against the house, a reminder of the danger of sailing during a storm. She forced a brisk stride, but not reckless, which would draw attention she neither needed nor desired.

As she turned on Main Street, skidding on the oyster shells beneath her boots, a cold raindrop struck her cheek. She shivered and dabbed at her bodice, thinking she would be happy when summer began, be even happier when Noah returned to Chicago. Her heart gave a little jerk, exposing the lie. He had broken her once, sailing away without a backward glance. He had not contacted her in all those years, and, in a few short weeks, he would leave and never think of her again. She would help mend the rift between the Garrett brothers, because she had played a major role. That was only fair.

But nothing more.

Solving this mess wasn't impossible if she put her mind to it. The stubborn fool still loved Zach and Caleb, loved them with a depth of feeling she had often wondered if he even possessed. With Noah, you weren't sure how much he would *let* himself feel. She'd never seen a person hold a tighter rein than he did.

Running now, she didn't see the puddle but felt the grimy water seep inside her boot lacings. She saw the pitched roof of the jail and a glimmer of light glowing in the window. Noah would be angry with her for meddling, although he shouldn't expect anything different. Except, with a sudden mingling of pride and fear, she realized this *was* different. This time she would do what Noah had always managed to do for her.

She would save him from himself.

# CHAPTER FOUR

*"It is wonderful how soon things get into confusion..."*
~ C. Wyville Thomson
*The Depths of the Sea*

❧

The turbulent weather had driven everyone from the docks by the time Zach arrived. *Nearly* everyone, he noted, shoving his hands deep in his pockets. Icy raindrops streamed down his face, cooling his skin but doing nothing to relieve the furious pounding in his head. White-capped swells lashed the pier as he moved forward with a cautious step, the worn planks rocking beneath his feet. Through the dense fog rolling in from the sea, he saw the vague outline of a man standing in a flat-bottomed skiff moored next to the ferry bell. A tall man calmly working the sail's lines. For a brief moment, Zach wondered if Elle had been mistaken about Noah's distress.

Anxious to reach his brother, Zach stepped heavily, the thump rising above the storm's steady cadence. With a start, Noah glanced to the side and, before he recovered, his unguarded expression reflected such stark loneliness that Zach's throat closed. *Why,* he questioned, *why did this happen to* my *family?*

The wind ripped the slack line from Noah's hand, the sail billowing wide. He muttered an oath and rubbed his palm. "Damn her," Zach thought he heard him say.

"Don't." Zach shook his head. "Ellie did what she figured best."

Noah's shoulders stiffened, and he yanked the line taut.

Zach halted beside an overturned water cask and propped his elbows upon it. Ten years had passed since he had seen his little brother, and he wanted to ask everything, know everything.

*Hold on, Zach. Don't want to scare him off.*

"Weren't thinking of sailing in this, were you?" he asked, throwing a glance at clouds the color of wet ash.

"Of course not." Noah struggled to batten the sail.

Zach coughed and steadied his voice, though his words still came out rougher than he'd planned. "Good thought. I have enough people to rescue manning the lifesaving station without having to go after you. Had a shipwreck last month on the shoals, lost twelve sailors."

Noah turned his head and presented a glacial stare, as if, that night he chose to stay on Devil Island and observe nesting sea turtles instead of coming home, he had not been yanked across Zach's lap and spanked within an inch of his life. A wild gust billowed his sleeves, flicked his hair into his face, and the stare turned to a squint. Zach fought hard to contain the urge to tell him his spectacles sat in his front pocket.

After a long moment, Noah pressed his lips tight and averted his gaze.

Zach let a tense breath loose, not sure what to say or what to do. Except for the hostile expression and the hollowed cheeks, Noah looked much the same. His eyes were replicas of the ones Zach saw in the mirror each morning and the chin, ah, just like Caleb's. The shape of his face belonged to his father, most likely, and his height, it would seem. Noah had always been on the edge of pretty, to Zach's way of thinking, though he would have suffered before admitting it.

Zach had searched his memory for the face of the man who had loved their mother. Maybe he had passed him on the dock or spoken to him in the mercantile. Crazy as it seemed, he wished for this memory more than he wished for one of his *own* father. That he and Noah shared only one parent had never mattered to him, and he had recognized the truth since the day of Noah's birth.

Before Zach could move, Noah was halfway down the pier, skirting the boisterous group of whalers and disappearing into the fog. Zach strode forward until they walked side by side, pleased to note that Noah only had a couple of inches on him. He felt a smile break. Caleb hardly reached his shoulder.

Noah wrenched around, hair plastered to his brow, eyes dark and watery. "What the hell are you smiling about?"

Zach ignored the warning, disregarded the air of wariness, and threw his arms around Noah's shoulders before he stepped away. He inhaled a breath of salt air and ink. "I missed you," he said, because he had nothing else *to* say.

Noah hands rose to clasp Zach's shoulders for one brief moment, before he mumbled a denial and shoved hard.

"You didn't have to come." He turned toward the sea and tunneled his fingers through his hair. "Elle made a mistake running to you. I wouldn't sail in this mess. I just needed to think... not have everything crowding in. Sailing during a storm isn't sensible, and you know me." He glanced back, his smile flat. "Always the sensible one."

Zach's heart thumped, dulling the slap of waves against the jetty. Letting emotion seize him, he forgot his pledge to go easy. "Three years, Noah. For three years I watched the mail, the telegraph, reviewed every crew roster thinking you might have sailed in on a merchant ship and were hiding somewhere in town. Then I gave up, not knowing if you were dead or alive. Can you understand how that tore me apart?"

Noah tipped his head and blinked furiously, as always, considering before he spoke. "Did you think it was easy? Everything I loved was in this godforsaken town."

Too weary to stand, Zach dropped to the edge of the dock, resting his elbows on his knees and letting his legs dangle over the side. "Why, Noah? *Why?*"

Silence reigned for a long moment, then, surprisingly, Noah settled beside him. "I couldn't stay here. Things were... different. I didn't know who I was. I felt out of place, belonging to nothing and to no one."

"You're my brother, Noah, and nothing will ever change that. Not a thousand miles or ten years or sharing half the blood you thought we shared. Who cares if the bastard who sired me didn't sire you? I don't know why she chose to stray outside her marriage or even if she loved your father enough to make up for things. All I've ever known, clear to me as the sun rising every morning, is you and Caleb are my family. Nothing else matters."

"It mattered, Zach. It mattered more than I knew. You and Caleb were all I had, and I lost both of you that day." Noah dipped his finger into a gash in the plank, his gaze fixed on the sea. "The damage to my soul, my pride, my sense of family, was too much to overcome."

Zach splayed his fingers across his stomach, the unshakable conviction in Noah's voice scaring him. "Did you love us any less because we shared only one parent?" His expression steady, he waited.

Finally, Noah felt compelled to look him in the eye.

*Love?* Noah swallowed past the knot in his throat. He had forgotten the Garrett propensity—evident in both of his brothers—to blurt out what they were thinking without thinking first. Delaying the inevitable, he slipped his spectacles from his pocket and wiped them on the front of his shirt, pleased his hands shook only a little. He wanted to ask about Hannah, but if Zach fell apart right now, he was doomed to follow.

"Did you?" Zach's voice rumbled through air seasoned with the scent of his cologne. God, that smell had haunted his brother's pilot coat like a ghost, reminding Noah of the many times he had pressed his tear-streaked face against it.

"No." He jammed his spectacles into place, wishing he could lie.

Zach rocked forward, clasping his knees. "After Caleb had time to mull everything over in his rusty can and read Mama's diary from cover to cover, he wanted to die. He felt so protective, so responsible, and Lord, Noah, we had no idea where you'd gone, how you were surviving." His voice cracked, and he paused, hitching a noisy breath through his teeth. "When Caleb found out about your father, he let anger control him. And he ended up punishing the person he loved most in the world. It's his way. Act first, think later. You knew that. How could it have been a surprise?"

Head beginning to ache, Noah gazed across a turbulent, blue-black sea. A pelican swooped in to settle on a weather-beaten piling, its distinctive white coloring telling him it was no more than six months old. "The look in his eyes... this gaping void, some horrible absence of attachment. Like I was a stranger, or worse, his adversary." He flicked a hardened shrimp tail from the pier, where it plunked beneath the waves. "I felt weighed down with shame on top of devastation on top of despair. I ran because I didn't know what else *to* do. I couldn't go to Caleb, and I wasn't sure I could go to you. I know you knew, and you never told me. I felt tainted and dirty."

"I only have one question: are you still running?"

"What an asinine question. I'm here, aren't I?" He slammed his palms to the pier, shaken to the tips of his toes.

"In a way, yeah, you're here. For the laboratory. But I can't help thinking it's a weak link at best. Tenuous, Ellie called it, and I think that's what she meant." He picked a splinter from the plank and twirled it between his fingers. "I have to admit, she could always read you better than I could, so I'll take her word for it."

Noah snorted derisively. "Tenuous. Pretty big word for Elle."

"She's a very bright woman, Noah. If you weren't so gifted, maybe you would have noticed."

"It was hard for me to notice anything besides the broken arm and cracked teeth, the torn clothing and stolen fruit. Jesus, she and Caleb created chaos, day after day, and kept me busy repairing the damage. I never had time to stop and consider whether Elle Beaumont was an *intelligent* girl."

Zach sighed. "Not everyone pauses to consider every move in life before they make it, every word in life before they say it. Besides, all that happened a long time ago. Ellie is a woman now, not some silly kid."

"If you say so."

"Funny, I reckoned the tide was turning about the time you lit outta here," Zach said, not trying to hide the amusement in his voice. "Thought Ellie might finally get a chance to snag you. Lord knows, she worked hard enough."

"You're absolutely insane."

Zach raised his hands in defense. "Hey, just telling you how I remember it."

"Well, *big bro*, your memory is shot to hell."

Zach laughed, fueling Noah's discomfort and igniting a rare burst of recklessness.

"Listen, I admit to wondering." Noah's foot shot out, spraying water. "Dammit, she was always *touching* me. How could I not wonder?"

Zach drew his hand across his mouth, but Noah saw the wide smile anyway. "Maybe you should have given her a fast smooch under Mama's oak tree. Only, that would have been hasty, knowing you."

Noah jumped to his feet. "Don't try to push me toward her. It won't work."

"I'm not pushing anyone anywhere. Clearly, Ellie is over her juvenile crush. After all, she has her life, her school. Calm down. I think your virtue's safe."

"Virtue." Stalking along the slippery dock, he hoped he didn't slip and tumble into the ocean.

"Have time for dinner? Looking a bit on the wiry side."

He glanced back to find Zach dusting the seat of his trousers, shaking loose drops of rain from his collar. A gull flew past, squawking and diving into the wind. "Dinner?" he repeated, certain he would be hungry if he thought about it long enough.

Zach nodded, the raw yearning in his gaze and the answering pang in Noah's chest making the decision simple.

∽

Noah felt the Garrett net tightening around him, and he wasn't sure he minded.

Rory sat to his right, gravy smeared on his cheek, a dab of mashed potato clinging to the end of his nose. Zach sat to his left, waving a butter knife like a wand as he talked about the tribulations of being the town constable. They smiled and laughed often—something he certainly wasn't used to. Their behavior better suited a family kitchen, not a public restaurant. Some restaurant, Noah thought, and surveyed the crowded dining room. Dented tin chandeliers dripping wax to the floor, chipped porcelain atop tattered cloths, bowed chairs surrounding tables of all shapes and sizes. The stink of fried fish, whiskey, and hair tonic mingling quite favorably with the scent of the ocean flowing in the window.

A hoarse bellow from the adjoining saloon jarred him from his deliberation. He threw a quick glance at Rory, then lifted his gaze to Zach's. "What was—" The shatter of glass cut into his question.

"Uncle Caleb." With a vague motion, Rory sucked a lump of sweet potato pie from his spoon. "In the Nook and mad about something."

Noah didn't take time to think, the conviction in Rory's voice enough. Plus, in the deep recesses of his mind, the bellow had held a familiar ring. He shoved his chair back, pocketed his spectacles, and took the narrow hallway leading to the saloon at a near run. Pilot Isle's lone barroom was the place Caleb had given him his first lesson in drinking. Rum, he recalled.

The crack of wood and a grunt of pain had Noah shouldering past the crowd blocking the doorway, the fracas getting worse if the escalating uproar meant anything.

"Hey!"

"Wait a darned minute, fella."

Ducking inside, he knocked at the clutching hands, understanding these men wanted to sustain their entertainment. Fingers curled into fists he hoped he wouldn't have to use, Noah shoved into the central circle. Flickering light cast shadows across a multitude of besotted faces; their wrinkled clothing reeked of sweat and toilet water.

He squinted and took a step forward. Ten years had passed, but he recognized Caleb instantly. The hunched stance; the way he held his shoulders; blessit, even the coal black cowlick sticking up on the crown of his head.

Surprisingly, it wasn't bitterness filling his chest with warmth. No, the warmth felt quite like devotion.

Devotion bowed to fury when Caleb's head jerked from the impact of a blow. Loathing the part of his mind that sanctioned action above reason, instinct above logic, Noah nonetheless stepped into the fray.

Wouldn't be the first time he had taken a hard knock because of his brother's recklessness.

Clearly taking a beating, Caleb stumbled to his knees. Fist cocked and ready, his opponent advanced. Noah got a close look at the man's face—and time slipped away. As if it were yesterday, he watched his brother retrieve his spectacles from beneath Magnus Leland's boot, straighten them with clumsy fingers and rest them on his younger brother's nose.

"I'll be damned if you aren't begging for a drubbing, Leland," Noah said, his voice relatively calm considering the pulse pounding in his head. He held his arms by his side, figuring he could still reason this out. *Maybe.* If he avoided looking at Caleb, who lay in a dazed heap on the floor.

Magnus's arm dropped. He leaned into the light, ejecting a whiskey-scented breath and a bark of laughter. "Well, well. You actually *are* everyone's lofty savior, aren't you? Imagine, rescuing your brother after you neglected to mention your arrival. He was overwhelmed, to say the least, much to my enjoyment." He lifted his hand to his mouth, then frowned at the smear of crimson. "What happened, Garrett? Your dearly devoted little admirer couldn't keep you occupied? Admittedly, there's not much in the way of feminine solace in this town, but perhaps you might find something effortless compared to Mari—"

The first punch he threw split his knuckles; the second sent a shaft of pain up his arm.

Christ, it felt *good*.

Magnus tottered, launching a wild swing that caught Noah just under his ear. His teeth came down hard on his tongue; a flash of blue lit his vision. A warm trickle slid down his neck as his mouth filled with blood.

Without warning, hands gripped his shoulders, propelled him through the kitchen, out a back door, and into the night. The peppery scent told him exactly who led him. Shrugging free, he placed a steadying hand on the Nook's rough-hewn wall and dragged a breath of crisp air into his lungs. Blinking hard, he released it in a ragged chop.

"That was damned perfect! The two of you absolutely amaze me." Zach kicked a wooden bucket into the wall.

Noah shook his head and tapped the heel of his hand against his ear. "What?"

Zach leaned in and said through clenched teeth, "I'm the little bit of law in this town. I should throw both of you idiots in jail."

Noah rolled his head to the side, waiting for the wave of dizziness to pass. Zach stood before him, face white as chalk, brow beaded with sweat. Moonlight flooded the alley, throwing everything into silvery relief.

"Lord help me if one of you needs a doctor. He's out cold, draped over the only table left standing," Zach said.

"Good." Noah ducked his head and spit a mouthful of blood on the ground.

"Good? *Good?*" Zach paced to the edge of the building, hands propped on his hips, foot tapping a frantic rhythm.

"You've... learned a lot... little bro'."

Hair prickling the back of his neck, Noah stared at the blunt shape slumped against an overturned barrel. He dug in his pocket, slipped his spectacles on. "Yes, I learned a great deal, thanks to you."

His words appeared to knock the wind from Caleb, who dropped his head and flexed his hands, outwardly intent on his injuries. "I'm sorry," he finally said, his Adam's apple bobbing.

Noah sent his fist into the wall before he could think to stop himself. "Don't pull some damn remorse act on me, Cale. I can live without your recrimination. I have for years."

"Hold up, there." Zach grasped him by the shoulders and set him back with a gentle shove.

The kitchen door creaked, and the scent of baked apples spilled into the alley. "Zach? All clear? I have alcohol and bandages, if you need them."

"Yes, all clear."

After gathering her skirt in her hand, the woman stepped out. Noah had trouble piecing together names and faces but something about her seemed very familiar. She knelt before Caleb and placed her supplies beside her, whispering and turning his hands in hers, her touch decidedly intimate.

Ah, yes, Elle had mentioned Christabel Connery and Caleb. They had been together since Caleb's impulsive proposal.

Noah exhaled and stared at the puddle of water beneath his feet.

"Where's Rory?" Zach asked.

Christabel tilted her head, glanced at each doggedly set face before returning her attention to Caleb. *Stubborn fools.* "With my brother and Ellie. Daniel's ship docked earlier. You know how he's always asking her to dinner." She pressed a cloth against a gash on Caleb's knuckle, realizing she used a rough touch. "Cornered her this afternoon at the mercantile, didn't leave her much choice. They walked in as you went tearing out. She's in the kitchen, chipping ice. Should be here any minute."

"I have to go." Noah shoved from the wall.

Caleb staggered to his feet, blocking Noah's path. "Go on, get outta here. Like always."

Facing each other, they squared off, the air around them humming with emotion. Still, the wounds needed to be jabbed, allowing all the resentment and hurt to drain out. Christabel had believed that for years.

She discreetly shook her head when Zach started to move between them. Might be a fair fight, she guessed, squeezing the damp rag, scattering drops of water on her patent leather slippers. Noah stood six inches taller, but Caleb's arms were twice as thick.

After a moment, they eased back, cautious and unsure, muscles in their shoulders jumping. She watched Noah duck his head, his throat working, his lips parting, closing, and parting again. All the time, Caleb studied him, longing etched in each groove on his face. It was clear as daylight to her what they should do.

But, in the end, Noah turned and walked from the alley.

Zach raised his arm to hold Caleb in place. "Let him go."

Caleb spun to face them, his swollen lip curled. "I did that once, remember, and he never came back. I should have hauled him home by the scruff of his scrawny neck and made him understand."

"How was I to know he wouldn't come back? He was never anything *but* reasonable."

"He's thinking real reasonable, all right. So reasonable, he about knocked Leland's head off." Caleb's voice softened to a tone Christabel had only heard him use in bed. "And... he did it for me."

Zach tugged at his collar. "When he was a boy, I never knew what to make of him. Now, he's a man, and it's even worse."

Christabel handed Caleb a rag. He pressed it against his cheek and winced. "Well, you better figure it out. If you leave it to me, I'll go to that stiff-backed widow's right this minute and drag his—"

"No."

"What then, Constable? He can't stand to be in the same room with us for five minutes. How in the world are we ever going to resolve this mess if we can't even talk to him?"

"This isn't a room, Cale."

Caleb flung the rag to the ground. "Oh, hell, you know what I mean."

She covered her mouth, but a laugh burst forth anyway. Zach and Caleb twisted around, identical masks of confusion on their faces. She was beginning to enjoy this almost as much as she'd enjoyed seeing little Noah Garrett slug that high-nosed doctor in the jaw. "Noah didn't go tearing out of here because of you two."

"What are you talking about?" Zach asked, impatience narrowing his eyes.

All at once, the door banged against the outside wall, and Elle burst into the alley, washing bowl in one hand, strips of white cloth in the other. Her hair had come loose from its slapdash knot, bronze curls framing a face both ashen and flushed. Christabel smiled; she couldn't have timed the scene better if she'd planned it.

"Where is he?" Elle paused before she reached them, glancing into each darkened corner.

Zach's gaze locked with Christabel's; she nodded faintly. Figuring she needed to give Caleb an extra prod, she dug her elbow into his ribs.

He groaned and massaged his side. "Not there, darling."

"Where is he?" Elle repeated, panic accenting her speech.

"Gone, honey." Christabel grabbed the bowl and rags and turned Elle toward the kitchen. "Noah can take care of himself. A little blood and a thump in the head isn't going to kill anyone. Especially a Garrett."

"Blood?" Elle jerked to a halt. *"Juste Ciel!"* She whipped back, green eyes glowing, face devoid of color. "What did you do to him, Cale?"

Caleb raised his arm, then groaned and lowered it. "Not a thing. *Your* former betrothed was doing the damage. Some doctor, that one."

*"Magnus."* Elle stalked to the door and practically ripped it from its hinges.

"Good Lord, Cale, go get her. Honestly, I can't handle any more havoc tonight." Zach dropped his head to his hands.

Caleb jabbed Zach in the chest as he passed. "You and I are having a long talk later, Constable. I'm not so stupid I don't realize you knew Noah was coming."

"Yeah, yeah," Zach muttered as the door slammed.

Christabel perched her hip against the barrel, the bowl cradled in her arms. "What do you think about this, my friend?"

"Damned if I know what to think."

"Love would keep Noah here, sure as Moses parted that sea. Give him and Caleb plenty of time to mend fences, too."

Zach lifted his head, exhaustion shadowing his face. "True, there's *always* been something"—he made a vague motion with his hand —"between Ellie and Noah. Some kind of understanding, a keen insight into each other's feelings. But love? Love doesn't take this much figuring out."

"Honey, what you and Hannah had was a diamond sitting atop a pile of rocks. I watch idiots every day, drinking and searching for answers, and I can tell you, love isn't easy for most people. Bury deep what they don't want to see, go blind to what they're scared to feel. Using their heads, not their hearts." Christabel trailed her finger around the rim of the bowl, the sharp scent of alcohol stinging her nose. "Remember the first time we saw Hannah? Her daddy brought her to preaching just after they moved here from Atlanta. She wore one of those bonnets with all the ribbons trailing down, practically to her fanny. And some kind of yellow frock with lots of lace."

"Pink." He paused, stared into the distance. "The dress was pink."

"Pink." She coughed to regain her voice. Strange, how sorrow lingered.

"I'm terrified, Christa."

"Why?" she asked, shocked to the core. Zach wasn't the kind of man to fear much.

"In one split second, I lost my wife, my unborn child. And for a long while I lived just to make sure Rory got to bed on time and brushed his teeth. I wasn't much of a father for months after Hannah died and"—Zach drew a shuddering breath and paced to the end of the alley—"I almost failed him like I failed my brothers. Like I'm afraid I'm going to fail them again."

"You didn't fail anybody, Zachariah Garrett!"

"Somehow, I did, Christa. Yet, I can't for the life of me tell you what I would do differently if I had the chance to live each moment again." He settled his palms on the wall and leaned in, shoulders hunched, head hanging low. "My mother didn't leave me two boys needing protection and a switch against their behinds. She left me two young men needing I don't know what, changing and growing in ways that confounded the tar out of me. One with a temper I couldn't control, the other with a mind I didn't understand. I did my best by them." His voice dropped to a whisper. "Honest to God, I did."

Christabel stepped forward, a gust of wind trapping her skirt between her ankles. "This will all work for the best, Zach. You've just got to give the situation time."

"Time? Ten years hasn't helped. Did you see their faces? It about made me sick how much this still hurts them."

"Maybe Ellie could heal some of—"

"No." He knocked his boot against the wall, sending a flutter of caked mud to the ground. "I don't want her to make Noah run away again." He threw a sidelong glance at her, a tight smile locked in place, sorrow and self-hatred riding high on his face. "You see, I asked him about her today. Because I remember him looking interested a time or two. Watching her when she didn't know. He admitted it, said he did wonder, but mixed in his confession was this hunted look, like I was the hound, and he was the fox. After giving this some thought, I figure it might be better to keep that chest sealed."

"What are you saying?"

"I'm saying I think Noah's better off staying away from Ellie. And she's better off staying away from him. She says she doesn't care about him any—"

"And you believe her?" Christabel laughed.

"Of course, I believe her. Why would she lie?"

"Why, indeed." She slammed the bowl on the barrel and began folding the strips of cloth into needless squares. "Oh, maybe because the entire town teased her, always laughing and calling her the professor's assistant or no-beau-Beaumont. Or, could be due to Noah never showing a smidgen of interest, telling her as blunt as can be that he wasn't ever going to come around. That would be enough for me. Forget about the heartless drivel her father's been telling her for years."

Zach turned his head, his concerned gaze finding hers. "Are you saying she lied to me?"

"Good heavens, no." Christabel dropped the last pleated square in the bowl and sighed. Men were so feeble-witted. "Ellie's not lying to you." Supplies in hand, she paused before the door. "Honey, she's lying to herself."

~

He was lying to himself.

It *definitely* bothered him to watch Daniel Connery stand in the corner of Elle's porch for the third time this week, making last-minute adjustments to his lapel and dusting pollen from his creased trousers. Why would she want to go to dinner with a man who dressed so carelessly?

Tipping his head against the coach house wall, Noah observed the spill of indigo across a twilight sky, the cool breeze bringing Elle's laughter to his ears.

*Surely, the bastard's ship would sail soon.*

Powerless, he looked in time to see her step outside, Daniel holding the screen door, rumpled hat in his fist. A broad band of sunlight revealed the toe of a maroon boot, gloved fingers tying her satin bonnet ribbons, then a half turn as she secured the latch he'd repaired. She tended to use the back entrance after dark. Ever a circumspect man, Noah recorded this habit. In the past eight days, he had recorded far too many of Miss Beaumont's habits.

She liked to sit on the porch steps as the sun rose, fresh morning light sparking bursts of cherry in her hair. She preferred to leave the door open while she taught, her patient instruction and affectionate regard floating through the rotting boards, upsetting Noah's equilibrium and disrupting his schedule. In between lessons, she volunteered to assist repairing broken latches and rusted hinges, her enticing scent making him snarl and snap, then berate himself for his lack of control and his cruelty. He also berated himself for not being able to ignore the charming dimple marking her left cheek, the intelligent gleam in her eyes as she discussed politics or fashion or bicycles, one of a hundred topics she retained in her ravenous little mind. She craved information in any form—from collecting plankton using tow nets to tagging certain species of fish—and possessed a zest for life that amazed and confounded him.

He'd never had a student listen as attentively, grasp topics as quickly or as eagerly. Come to think of it, he had never talked as freely, and never, *ever*, about subjects he kept close to his heart.

"Hell," he said and snatched a conch shell from the railing. Placing it next to his ear, he held himself from straining for a better view.

Elle left the porch at a jog, striding down the path a full step ahead of her escort, striped cloth tapping her ankles. Noah worked his way up the threadbare dress that hugged each curve to perfection. Stopping at the side of the house, she took her coat from Daniel, her beautiful, plump breast outlined in shadow.

Noah felt his lips tilt in gloating, masculine satisfaction as Elle slipped her arms into his coat. The bulky cuffs hit her mid-thigh, the notched collar bunched beneath her chin. She should have returned it a week ago; he should have asked. Only... the thought of her scent overriding his made him hesitate, and he was damn sure he didn't want to examine *that* too closely.

As Noah debated calling out, telling the idiot sailor just whose coat she wore, Daniel offered his arm and Elle wavered, glancing to the side, her wide straw brim concealing most of her face. Noah stiffened and pressed against the wall, praying deepening shadows and blooming dogwoods concealed him.

She tipped her head, her face flooding into view. Her bottom lip slipped between her neat, white teeth. Noah groaned and closed his eyes, categorizing the marine specimens he had collected on Devil that morning.

In between razor clam and ribbed mussel, Elle's plump lip intruded.

Pink, soft, moist.

*Chrissakes, I'm going mad,* he reasoned and pitched the conch shell over the railing.

After counting to ten, he opened his eyes to find heightened darkness and an empty yard. His frustration only increased the throb in his temples, the ache in his back. Recompense for hunching over his desk in the coach house, reviewing sketches of the laboratory until daybreak. He completely neglected the narrow bed wedged in the corner of the bedroom.

His skin tingled from a week spent knee-deep in muck, specimen bag a heavy weight by the end of the day, the sun roasting him through his clothing. Rotating his shoulders, his gaze dropped to the plate by his side. Sometime last week, Elle began bringing him dinner. He had taken to eating on the coach-house landing, delighting in the lingering warmth, the animated fireflies and the boisterous crickets, the endless shush of waves rolling into shore. Vastly different from a spring night in Chicago. She had even eaten with him once. Over a dessert of apple cobbler, he had shown her how to trace her way from the Big Dipper to the North Star.

At the end of the lesson, she traced her way back.

Noah nudged the plate aside, wanting to do the same to Elle's hospitality. Only, coming home to find a warm meal waiting on the step felt—he searched his mind. Good, it made him feel *good*. After years of living in a city where he cared for no one and no one cared for him, he could pretend he had a real home here. Laughable, but the scent of fried chicken and black-eyed peas transformed Widow Wynne's coach house into a place he resided in moderate serenity.

Perhaps Elle brought the food to repay him for securing loose shutters, tightening wobbly doorknobs, and promising to replace the rotten floor in her schoolroom. Perhaps not. Scooting forward, he settled his arms on the uneven railing, let his legs dangle over the side of the stairs. He stared at nothing, yet saw Elle in her striped dress, a smile dimpling her cheek.

He dropped his chin to his arms and inhaled the scent of honey-suckle and cut grass. Underneath, if he really concentrated, he detected whatever Elle sprinkled all over her skin, her clothing. Moist earth and fresh rain, the slightest hint of something sweet sealing the package in gossamer wrapping. Nothing particularly feminine about it, yet the fragrance muddled his senses like no other. Clouded his mind. Made him think of tattered silk hiked past a shapely knee, a round bottom lifting off a leather bicycle seat, blazing green eyes and a dimpled cheek, plump lips parting on a sigh—

Noah's palm connected with the railing, the unwelcome rise in his trousers making him question, for the first time in his *life*, if a trollop would ease his troubled mind. Perhaps help him sleep better at night and think clearer during the day.

Did they even *have* trollops in Pilot Isle?

He didn't enjoy a woman altering his strict course by the way she smelled or the way her lips formed certain words. He had an established plan, a definite trajectory.

The plan allowed for the occasional tussle beneath scented sheets; a balanced, natural hunger that never bowed to control. Rather dispassionate, he supposed, but he carefully considered the circumstances before making love. After deciding years ago that he would avoid sexual encounters if they created the turmoil he found so repellent. Governing his impulses had never been a problem before—he gave his body what it needed and it quieted.

Perhaps a written list of reasons why he could not *afford* to react in this fashion to Marielle-Claire Beaumont would resolve the issue. Then his mind would send the signal to the rebellious part of his body. He could handle this trifling, sophomoric physical response. Easily manage it; of course, he could.

But, he'd already made a list.

Make that *two*.

A dull whack broke the silence. A shutter dangling from one of Widow Wynne's second-floor windows. He had missed that one. Actually, *missed* wasn't entirely accurate. He had climbed the ladder and glanced into a bedroom that looked like a tornado had blown through it. Dresses hanging from the bedposts, magazines and books stacked on a pine dresser, scattered cologne bottles, framed portraits, and undergarments. A lacy, frilly, stiff-looking contraption, yellow with slim black edging. Leaning in to get a better look, he cracked his brow on the glass and nearly tumbled to the ground.

"What a mess," he said and peeled a strip of paint from the railing post, imagining peeling one of those faded dresses from Elle's body. Finding a corset or chemise—the delectable undergarment he had spied—clinging to each lush curve. What would it feel like to sink into her as deeply as he could sink into a woman, suck her skin between his teeth, have her breasts swell beneath his fingers and her nipples pebble beneath his tongue?

*Spontaneous, uninhibited.*

He knew that's how it would be with Elle, recognized it as surely as he recognized his face in the mirror above his basin. The woman leaped headfirst into everything. Always had. Making love would be no different. Passionate, impulsive. That didn't sound similar to anything, or *anyone,* he had experienced. Passion always seemed rather tepid to him, a glass of tea left too long in the sun.

He didn't know why he wanted to control his life to the point of wringing it dry. He had analyzed this predilection many times. Since he left Pilot Isle, alone, frightened, and bewildered, he had not gotten close to anyone. A few friends, colleagues, people he could hold at a distance. Every time someone reached out to him, in friendship or affection, his thoughts, his feelings, crawled deep inside.

Caroline Bartram was the one person who knew about his childhood and what had happened to make him run. And, he only told her in a fevered delirium. She had found him, bloodied and shivering, lying between stacks of stripped pine outside a lumber mill. He'd left Pilot Isle little more than six months before, his anger too raw for his mind to subdue, and far too savage for his hands to defend. She had dressed his wounds and listened. Simply listened.

He remembered the relief telling someone brought.

Flicking another chip of paint loose, Noah sighed. Each day, he struggled to make room in his heart for his brothers. Although this scared the hell out of him. He recoiled every time Zach touched him, yet, deep in his gut, he suppressed the powerful urge to return the touch. *Crazy,* when he and Caleb had barely gotten past gruffly spoken greetings as they passed each other on the street.

This would have to change. Had already changed.

This morning, Noah did the unexpected: he asked Caleb for help. In an impulsive attempt to reduce the amount of time he and Elle spent together, he sent his brother a note requesting his aid in getting the fishermen to take him on their daily runs. With Caleb's assistance, the captains agreed, if Noah, in turn, agreed to salt fish and drain nets.

In plain truth, if he agreed to work like a mongrel. He welcomed the challenge, welcomed any excuse to leave the coach house before dawn and return after dusk, too exhausted to eat Elle's meals, much less eat them *with* her.

Unbelievable, given his vow to never depend on his family again.

He'd broken that easily enough. The other one he'd made since returning involved avoiding Elle. He cocked his head, listening for her lively step on the path.

Her buoyant laughter gave life to a hushed night.

He heard only the spiked chirp of a cricket and the crash of waves in the distance and denied the sharp stab of disappointment.

Noah angled his spectacles against his brow and pressed his knuckles beneath his eyes. The *Elle Vow,* as he liked to think of it, he must keep. Because he had no room for a woman in his life—in his heart.

He wasn't certain he'd left room there for anyone.

# CHAPTER FIVE

*"This may seem a trifling detail, but so great inconvenience constantly arises from carelessness in this matter."*
C. Wyville Thomson
*The Depths of the Sea*

~

*E*lle slipped on the stair's worn edge, banging her shin. Two more to the coach-house landing, then she completed a quick check of her dressing gown. Ties tied, buttons buttoned. Covered to the neck, albeit inappropriately. *Oh.* Shoes. She wiggled her toes and tried to shake off the grass and dirt. Sighing, she drew a salty breath of courage and pounded on Noah's door. No time to worry about him giving her the evil eye over such a minor detail as bare feet.

"Suffering cats, Professor, be home." A rumble of thunder sounded; she threw a frantic glance at the sky. *That's all I need,* she thought, and gave the doorknob a good tug. *Locked.* Merciful heavens, if Sean Duggan found them—Annie said he was staggering drunk—he would kill them both.

"Please, if you're there, let me in."

The door opened, the gas lamp in Noah's hand revealing tousled curls and a muscled chest sprinkled with hair. "Elle?" Noah fumbled for his spectacles. His eyes narrowed, his gaze lingering on her unbound breasts before lifting to her face. He mouthed one word —*inside*—and hauled her in by the wrist.

Elle jerked from his grasp before he could close the door. "I need your help," she said and dropped the wadded bundle of clothing she held to the floor. "Annie Duggan... oh, Noah."

He raised his head, stopped buttoning his shirt. "The student who's been transcribing my notes?"

"Sean, her husband"—she clutched his arm, dug her fingers into firm muscle—"he hurt her. I knew—I knew it was happening. Bruises on her arms, her wrists. I begged her to let me help her, but she protected him. *Why?* Now, it's gone too far, and I have to hide her. Somewhere. But not at Widow Wynne's. He'll look for her there. I pulled some clothes off the line. Hers are bloody and torn. I have to get her out of Pilot Isle on the dawn skiff. I have to."

"Take a breath and tell me where she is."

"Downstairs. In the school. When I got home, I noticed the door was open. I figured it might be Rory hiding from Zach. Might be you, fixing the floor or something. After Daniel left, I went inside. Under my desk, she was crouched under my desk, crying and moaning. I'm not even sure she recognized me. Sean will know to look at Widow Wynne's, but he won't think—"

"Calm down, Elle. I'll go get her."

"Thank you."

He studied her face, reading her like a book. "Stay put." As an afterthought, he pressed a soft kiss to her brow. Then he turned and strode through the doorway, his footfalls thumping on the staircase.

She wedged her shoulder against the wall, bringing her fingers to her brow. *Grands Dieux.* Had Noah just kissed her?

～

Annie's shrill scream jerked Elle from her contemplation, and she forgot Noah's command. Slowing as she entered the schoolroom, she glanced into each darkened corner, not knowing what she would find. Moonlight struggled past the pane of glass set high in the wall, coloring Noah in weak tones where he knelt before her battered desk.

"Come on, no one's going to hurt you here." His words were soft, his arm stretching toward Annie in a calm, gradual motion.

Annie whimpered and shifted, her cloth slippers and the border of her lavender dress disappearing beneath the desk.

"Trust me," Noah said, conviction in his expression, protection in the hand he offered. Elle did not have to see his face or grasp his fingers to know. When Annie remained hidden, he glanced over his shoulder, drawing Elle into silent consultation.

"Dear." Elle stepped in behind Noah, cursing the creaking planks. "I promise, we won't let anything else happen to you. I'll help you get home." This much, she *could* promise. She had just enough money hidden beneath her mattress to return Annie to her family in Atlanta.

"Home? Mother?" Annie scooted forward on her bottom, her gaze seeking, searching. A thin band of light slashed her face, highlighting the darkening circle around her eye and the streak of blood on her chin. A brawny fist had matted her hair close to her head. She rested a hand on her protruding belly, glanced at Noah, and whispered, "I had to run, Professor. My baby. He'll kill my baby."

Noah's fingers curled into a fist behind his back, but the hand he offered Annie did not so much as quiver. "Of course, you did. Come on, now. You're not doing the baby any good sitting here on a cold, damp floor." With careful movements, he lifted Annie's tattered shawl from her waist to her shoulders. "Elle brought clean clothes for you to change into. Come upstairs. I'll light the parlor stove, warm it up, nice and safe." Moving prudently, he leaned in, slipped his arms beneath her. "I won't hurt you," he whispered, lifting her high against his chest.

Elle stepped aside as he maneuvered his swaddled bundle through the doorway. She mounted the staircase, searching the overgrown shrubs for a wild-eyed man with whiskey on his breath. At the top, she rushed inside and slammed the door, flipping the metal latch.

Crossing the room, she watched Noah brush a pile of papers to the floor and settle Annie in a towering leather chair. The girl's bones seemed to melt, and she slithered to a half sit, head lolling, arms dangling.

Elle knelt before her, tucking a lock of hair behind Annie's ear. "Noah?"

He appeared by her side, light from the gas lamp in his hand shimming in his pupils. "I have few medical supplies here. Do you think I should get Dr. Leland?"

Unchecked, she flicked a glance at his right hand, the knuckles marred by gashes from Magnus's teeth. "No, um, I don't think Annie would want to involve him. I can handle this."

"Fine. What do you need?"

"Blankets, a towel, soap, water." With a gentle touch, she probed the swollen skin circling Annie's eye. "Liniment?" she asked, catching his gaze.

He paused, reviewing the list in his mind, then nodded. Placing the lamp on the desk at her side, he left the room.

Elle tugged Annie's ruined dress from her shoulders and hurled the rag to the floor. The one she had snatched from the clothesline would hang on her student's gaunt frame but at least it was dry. And absent of bloodstains. Elle swallowed her rage, lightening her touch as she slipped the peach cotton over Annie's head and smoothed the material past her thickening waist. She finished securing the bone buttons, then chafed her Annie's hands until her own stung, pleased to hear the girl's whimpers quiet to soft mews.

Noah reentered, a serving tray in his hands, a frayed towel looped over his arm, the scent of coffee clinging to him. He shoved the towel and tray at her. In a moment, he returned with a patchwork quilt, which he wasted no time in tucking around Annie. Forcing her to drink the coffee, Elle heard drawers being opened and turned to find Noah standing behind his desk, raising a corked bottle like a trophy.

"Got it." The flickering light reflected red-gold on the metal instruments and glass beakers cluttering his desk, blue-black on the tidal charts and detailed oceanographic maps tacked in neat alignment to the wall behind him. "Alcohol." He thrust the bottle toward her. "I couldn't find liniment."

Setting the mug aside, Elle jerked the cork loose and soaked the grayed edge of the towel, the sharp scent stinging her nose as she swabbed Annie's lacerated skin. Using the soap and water Noah had provided, she washed Annie's face, her neck, her arms and hands, slipped the ribbon from her own hair and secured the girl's in a damp lump. Abrasions doctored, she forced Annie to drink the rest of the coffee. The girl blinked sleepily, winced in pain, then slid into a restive slumber.

Rain began to plink against the window, a comforting distraction. Elle glanced at Noah, who sat quietly by her side. His calm facade didn't fool her in the least. His unlaced leather boot tapped in rhythm to the mantel clock, and his breathing sounded harsher than required when sitting still. Arms hooked around the back of the chair he straddled, a pad of paper in one hand, a gold-tipped fountain pen in the other, he frowned in concentration and scribbled, paused. Light bounced off his spectacle lenses as he tilted his head to stare at her through round wire rims. His gaze was thoughtful and shrewd... and held the slightest edge of anger.

He'd collected himself, she noted, taking a hasty sip of Annie's coffee. Hair finger-straightened and shoved off his brow, wrinkled shirt buttoned and tucked in. He wore no belt. Before she looked away, she noted that his trousers were faded at the knee, frayed at the waist, and probably threadbare in the seat.

Hands shaking, she tried twice before managing to jam the bottle cork in place. *Juste Ciel*, for a room sealed tighter than a water cask for two years, a room that should have smelled of dust and decay, it smelled fresh and alive, of pine needles, salt air, and *him*. The scent swam past her defenses and made her, for a brief moment, imagine racing into Noah's arms, pressing her cheek next to his heart, her lips to the hollow beneath his ear. She wanted to accept the protection he had offered another woman and hold it close.

Making room beside an aromatic horseshoe crab carcass and a textbook opened to the last page, Elle placed the bottle on the desk.

She had to remember her objective—to face Sean Duggan if he came looking for Annie. She had to handle him.

Somehow, she had to.

Giving her skirt a casual shake, Elle shoved the bloodied towel at Noah. Courage, she reminded herself, sometimes felt a great deal like fear.

"Don't even consider it." Noah yanked the towel from her and threw it to the floor.

"Consider what?"

"You're not going to wait for her husband alone." His voice lowered to a hoarse whisper as he glanced at Annie. "Look what that bastard did to his *wife*. Do you want him to get his hands on *you?* Have you completely lost what's left of your mind?"

*How had he known?* Frowning, she kicked the towel underneath the desk. She hated when he used undeniable logic and left her with nothing to say.

He slammed the raised legs of his chair to the floor. "Blessit, do you think I'm stupid? Do you think I would let you walk into a situation like that without, God help us both, my devoted protection?"

"Never in my life have I thought of you as stupid."

His face flushed.

Elle had to curl her fingers into a fist to keep from cupping his cheeks, the charming blush making him look all of sixteen. Her heart remembered what it felt for him then, because it started thumping eagerly, reminding her of a time when she would not have hesitated to touch him.

"So, her husband has beaten her before." He slapped the pen and paper to the floor as he straightened, lamplight playing over the muscles in his shoulders and his chest. With a gleeful flutter, Elle realized her mediocre cooking had chased some of the hard edges from his frame.

Lifting her thumb to her mouth, she nibbled the nail, directing her attention to the pad of paper sitting by his feet.

He nudged it beneath the desk with the toe of his boot. "Not the first time you've come between Annie and her husband, either, is it?"

She nibbled harder, wondering how to avoid this line of questioning. A sensible, rational explanation might do. She tilted her head. Maybe she could say—

"Quit trying to concoct a suitable reply."

Flustered, Elle promptly forgot her objective. "Twice. It's happened twice that I know of. Sean twisted her arm behind her back the first time, which left some nasty bruises on her wrist. The second"—she lowered her hand, felt a frown tug—"he split her lip, knocked a tooth out and loosened another. I begged her to go home, to her family. I offered to pay for the ticket to Atlanta. Or to let her stay with my friend Savannah, in New York, if she'd rather not go home. But Annie had just figured out she was pregnant... and he frightened her so." Sean Duggan had made threats she wasn't about to repeat to anyone— especially a man who had turned out to have a surprisingly ready temper.

When he continued to stare, she snapped, "To state this plainly, because I can see you're waiting for me to dig a ditch and crawl in, *everything* I've done for Annie has been against her husband's wishes. Including teaching her to read and write."

Noah bumped his spectacles up, drawing his knuckles across his eyes. Laughing, he said, "Just like you to make an enemy of every bully you encounter. Congratulations. That makes two this week."

"You think I'm still that silly little girl, don't you? Getting into one predicament after another. How incredibly insulting."

"You slip into trouble as easily as a warm bath, Elle. Be insulted if you like, but yes, that's what I think."

"For your information, Professor, not every problem has a solution. Sometimes people go by gut instinct, sheer, candid *emotion*. Fight fires when they catch a whiff of smoke, not wait until they trip over the burning building. Maybe my actions are a tad precipitate." She bent down, jerked the towel from the floor, and snapped the cloth into sloppy folds. "But at least I know how liberating it is to act without planning every move."

He lowered his hand, the spectacles resting on his brow stark against his sun-kissed skin. His left lid sagged slightly, giving him a reckless, rakish, thoroughly undeserved air. "How liberating"—his gaze traveled the length of her and back—"does it feel, sweet?"

"Don't call me that," she said and swallowed hard. *Trapped.* She felt trapped, her ankles chained to the floor. When he stared at her, grave and probing, she forgot her avowals of indifference.

*Damn and blast!* She didn't love him, this tall, well-formed man gripping the chair with bulging knuckles, his square jaw tense with frustration. If she loved anyone, it was the boy who had wiped tears from her face and blood from her knees.

She certainly didn't love this enigmatic, unreachable man.

Sometimes, she didn't even *like* him.

She lifted her chin, prepared to tell him, but her lips parted and no sound passed. His expression had gone hot. She couldn't think of another way to describe it. Eyes dark as a stormy sky, nostrils flaring as they caught a scent. Her scent? His hands uncurled, and he lifted his body enough to bring their faces in line.

Her fingertips tingled, her arms inching toward him.

Noah met her halfway, his breath hitting her cheek. She made a low sound in her throat, and he stilled. Cursing once, he shoved from the chair. It rocked from side to side and finally flipped with a crash. Before she could recover, he was standing by the door, holding a coat in his hand.

"Put this on," he growled.

"But—"

"You can't go running around in"—he tossed the coat over her shoulders—"your underwear."

"I'll be back—"

"I'm going with you."

"Annie—"

"She's safe here. Safer than you are at Widow Wynne's." He grabbed a rumpled fishing hat from the hall tree and stuffed it on her head. "This door will be cinched as tight as any on Pilot Isle. I should know, I installed the lock."

She tipped the hat, glaring at him from beneath the stained brim. He glared right back. Gritting her teeth, she said, "Now look here—"

"I have the only key, Elle. I'll be watching the coach house. That bastard won't get past me. And he won't get in here, I promise you."

"But—"

"If you say no again, I'll sit on your front step and wait for him. Do you want that?"

"No, of course n—"

"Keep the hat pulled over your face." He placed his hand in the middle of her back and gave a firm shove. "All I need is for someone to observe you leaving here in the dead of night."

She stumbled onto the landing, "All... all *you* need? Do you think it would do wonders for me, Professor?"

He swung her to face him. "Thought we had a promise," he said, his fingers cupping her jaw. "No more. I don't want you to call me that." She watched his lips settle against his teeth, and she opened her mouth to reply.

And inhaled his breath.

A teasing scent. Peppermint.

His half smile settled into a flat line. "You don't have to agree, sweet. Just move it." He jerked the coat lapels close to her chin, took her hand, dragged her down the stairs, and across the dew-slick grass.

She stammered, French tangling with English and gibberish coming out. Noah ignored the chatter, flinging her hand from his as soon as Widow Wynne's door closed behind them. Resigned to his interference, she fought a fierce surge of anger and prayed she would get through the night without killing him.

*Look what my damned illogical protectiveness has gotten me into this time,* Noah thought, flicking the maroon-velvet drapery aside and glancing into a sober night.

Restless, he prowled the length of Widow Wynne's gaslit drawing room, wishing his thoughts were as surefooted as his stride. What had happened in the coach house? Definitely wasn't a belated sense of duty that had made his body heat like a skillet over a flame. He'd simply been watching the wheels in Elle's mind spin, cataloging the emotions crossing her face because he could, and then something, a tender, warm expression had sent a jolt of raw need right to his heart. Making matters worse, he'd inhaled her scent, and *goddammit*, leaned in to kiss her.

The longing to touch her had all but brought him to his knees.

He fingered a frayed hole in the sleeve of his shirt, distancing his mind from his body. The wind shrieked outside, rattling the window-panes and shooting a draft of moist air across his face. He brushed his fingers past his cuffs, checking the buttons. These were work clothes, not ones he generally wore in the company of women. Then again, Elle had not even thought to throw a coat on over her *nightdress*. His coat—the one neither of them had the nerve to discuss—would have done well enough.

Now, blessit, she had both of his coats.

Suddenly, a vision of Annie spreading her hands over her swollen belly flashed in his mind. The smell of blood lingered in his nostrils. Returning to the window, he searched the dark street again, almost hoping for a sign of Sean Duggan. If that bastard *ever* got his hands on Elle, Noah would kill him. And Annie, dear God, what would happen to her if they didn't get her away from Pilot Isle? Somehow, they must. Noah had seen what years of abuse did to a woman, eroding her confidence and her dignity, leaving a vacant, pitiable shell. Caroline Bartram had denied her husband's mistreatment for years because she had felt indebted to him. Her previous occupation had not garnered many proposals, and the first one she received, she accepted. She had denied Noah's offer of assistance, until she finally understood that her husband would destroy her if she did not leave him.

Annie's situation seemed chillingly similar.

The door clicked shut, and he glanced back, releasing a relieved breath. Elle had changed into decent clothing, thank God, although the blouse looked fit for the rag box, too wash-worn to do more than cling to her lush bosom. The skirt was much the same, hanging in temptingly gentle folds from her hips. Why the hell couldn't she wear all those layers that normally kept a man from seeing a woman's true shape?

"Any sign of Sean?" she asked, her voice surprisingly controlled. He had to hand it to her—the woman was made of stern stuff.

"No." On his second pass around the parlor, he paused by the mantel, a dab of color catching his eye. "What is this?" He plucked a faded yellow ribbon from a brass hook.

"Oh, that." Elle cleared her throat and from the teasing scent invading his senses, took a step closer. "A suffrage bazaar ribbon. Widow Wynne let me put some of my things in this parlor when I moved from my father's house. He offered to keep them there but... I didn't trust him with, well, not with that."

"World's Congress of 1893, Department of Women's Progress. New York City." Noah turned the ribbon over and back. "Where did you get this?"

"At a rally."

"You've been to New York?"

Stepping forward, she took the ribbon from his hand. "I was a student delegate, not a full member."

He considered, trying to firm his slack jaw muscles. "Student?"

"Yes." Crisp as a fresh bill, no hint of inflection.

"You went to university, Elle?"

Bringing her mouth close to the mantel, she pursed her lips, and blew dust from a ceramic clown figurine. "For one year." Their arms brushed; the hem of her dress flapped against his ankles. She drew a breath, and he wasn't sure if he heard it or felt it. Or both. "There was trouble at the rally"—she gestured to the ribbon—"the university called my father and... that was that."

"Trouble?"

She slipped her watch from her pocket and checked the time. "I got arrested."

*"Arrested?"*

She snapped the cover and returned the watch to her pocket. "For two hours. The police herded us into the rear compartment of three wagons, not much more than grocer's carts. They only quarantined us to clear the streets they said, quite apologetically. The jail cells were clean. Not bad if you ignored the things etched on the walls." She frowned, remembering something unpleasant. "And the catcalls."

"A jail? With bars?"

"Yes, a *jail* cell. With bars. I wasn't scared. I knew from the astounded look on the lieutenant's face that he had no idea what to do. I feared my father's reaction much more than I feared a stranger's. Silver badge or no." She turned toward the window, thrusting the velvet curtain back as he had. Then she laughed, the sound both anguished and amused. "Actually, I found the experience rather exciting. A once-in-a-lifetime event."

"You call being arrested an *event?*"

She rubbed a scratch on the glass and shrugged. "I can't explain it, but I felt an incredible sense of freedom. Watching the crowd of women marching along Fifth Avenue, I realized life offered more if I only had the courage to grasp it. For the first time, Noah, I altered my destiny. My life finally took a turn I had chosen. A turn that did not require my father's sanction. Or society's." She rubbed harder at the scratch, weighing what she would reveal to him, he could tell. "Though the situation did not end well."

"Your father forced you to leave the university?"

"Oh, heavens, yes. He telegraphed the dean after the rally, threatened them with endangering my safety. They were glad to see me go, and I can understand. Many universities hesitate to start women's programs because of the additional responsibility." Elle cut her eyes his way, the pain in them making him wonder if she had talked about this with anyone else.

"He never wanted me to attend. He forbid me, in fact, vowing to withhold funds. I wrote to every eastern school accepting women and requested information. I had mail sent to a postal box in Morehead City. After a few months, he thought the matter, a whim, was forgotten. He didn't know I had money stashed in a spectacle case in my closet. Money *Grandmere* Dupre sent the year before she died. And what little I'd managed to save taking in darning and delivering groceries for the mercantile, anything I could do without my father's knowledge." She began a gradual circle of the parlor, her memories setting her in motion. "In June of 1892, I got a letter from Byrn Mawr that I had received a stipend for the fall term in exchange for working in the library four afternoons a week. I sent a reply of acceptance in July, took the train north in August. I stayed with Savannah, my roommate's family, until the term began in September. I returned to Pilot Isle a year later, without my degree."

*My degree.* Noah swiped his hair from his brow and felt a pinch of realization. Her voracious appetite for knowledge suddenly made sense. "Elle—"

"Oh, I know what you're thinking." She bounced up on her toes to adjust the gas fixture on the wall. The flame heightened behind etched glass, sparking an orange blaze in her curls. "I would have graduated if I had not gone to the rally, and you may be right. I've turned that over in my mind a thousand times, until I can't stand to think of it anymore. But, I would have missed my one, true moment of completeness, standing in a crowd of strangers, all of us experiencing our own sense of purpose. Also, I can't help but long for her, the girl who believed." She tilted her head to the side and a smile much older than her years graced her lips. "She was braver than people who fear the future because of uncertainty."

Using the edge of her sleeve, she swabbed the fixture's brass arm, injecting a cool tone into her voice. "I lost that naiveté, that self-assurance, when I came back. I still have no fear of the future, I simply loathe the certainty."

Noah propped his elbow on the mantel, a deck plank salvaged from one of Pilot Isle's many shipwrecks. As Elle paced the length of the Aubusson carpet, he realized: *I do not know this woman.* This engaging, puzzling, and entirely too attractive woman he denied desiring even as desire pulsed in steady jolts. He watched her frown and glide her worn slipper across the floor. The impulse to ask what made her brow crease was so powerful he gave in to it. "What are you thinking?"

She drew her head up, her foot stilling over a stubborn wrinkle in the carpet. "About the school. Why, if I didn't have the school, I would have nothing," she said, as casually as she recited a recipe.

Noah brought his hand to his neck and attempted to knead away the pressure. He did not want to know her this well, recognize her fears, understand her dreams, witness her vulnerability. Liabilities he might use to bring the balance to his side if he grew desperate.

And he might be getting there.

Elle Beaumont packed enough force to knock him from his pragmatically grounded feet.

Crossing his ankles in what he hoped passed for casual lassitude, he pretended interest in straightening his cuffs while covertly studying her. She twisted her hair into a careless knot and raised her arm to slide an ugly clip into place. The elbows-out posture thrust her breasts forward against the cotton blouse that, he decided again, belonged in the garbage bin. He would bet a gold eagle against her wearing an item of consequence beneath.

He would just bet.

As unsought images intruded, he suppressed a groan. This was not the time to let lust, a response he had learned to subdue years ago, gain the upper hand. All because a girl who had once been a thorn in his side had turned into a beautiful, intelligent, exciting woman.

He shook his head, denied the yearning, but the evidence chafed against his buttoned fly. He felt like acting, taking, *overpowering*. Without even pausing to consider the ramifications, perhaps make a detailed list of pros and cons to decide if he should act or not.

Which, of course, he shouldn't.

Without trying very hard, he marshaled five reasons for not touching her and would have recorded them if he had pen and paper. He tapped his finger on the mantel. One, he would return to Chicago in another month, six weeks at best. Two, children and marriage were not on his agenda before the turn of the century. And, if he pictured getting married, it wasn't to a woman who made the blood boil in his veins.

*No, thank you.*

Elle brushed past him, her enticing scent trailing behind. He let his arm drop, hiding his bulging trouser fly. A brief affair, maybe. Elle claimed to be a modern woman. She said she didn't want marriage, and he certainly didn't want marriage with *her*. He envisioned a marriage of respect and... restraint. He did not plan to invite this loss of control into his life for the remainder of it.

No, *no*. Affairs always resulted in lies and seduction. Things he had not had much experience with, which led quite logically to number three—

"Merciful heavens!"

Startled, Noah reached the window in two long strides and ripped the drapery aside. A drop of water hit his face. He wiped his cheek and let the velvet settle into place. "The roof leaks."

She smacked the heel of her hand against her brow. "I can see why everyone thinks you're a genius."

He shot her a hot look but didn't reply.

She snatched a wooden bucket from behind the threadbare settee and shoved it at him. "Make yourself useful and put this over the bleached spot. That's the worst leak."

He centered the bucket precisely and returned to Elle's side. "Why don't you have the roof fixed?"

"I hoped it wouldn't happen again," she said and crouched, mopping the floor with a rag.

His restraint slipped another notch. Of course, her dress was bunched beneath her knees, slim ankles peeking out, round bottom perched high.

"Hoped it wouldn't happen again?" He went to one knee beside her, slipped a handkerchief from his back pocket, and did what he could with it. Anything to keep his hands otherwise occupied. "How like a woman to think a roof leak would disappear." He swiveled to wring the cloth in a potted fern by his side.

"I'm not sure what you mean." She paused to rub her nose, splattering drops of water on her chest. "Widow Wynne hasn't any family in town to help her. I do what I can, in exchange for board and use of the coach house, but I can't repair the roof." She glanced at him from beneath long, thick lashes, a smile spreading. "You remember my luck with roofs, don't you?"

He laughed, and the tightness in his chest eased. He and Elle were *friends.* They could laugh and cross wits. Even eat dinner together occasionally. Friends did those things all the time. Relieved, he said, "I'm not suggesting you repair the roof. Hire someone." How about that lovesick idiot, Daniel Connery, he wanted to ask?

She twisted her rag over the fern's pot, then leaned back, taking her warmth and her seductive aroma with her. "Repairs take money, Noah. Widow Wynne doesn't have much, and I don't have much, either. In fact, sending Annie to Atlanta is going to take everything I have."

"I thought you had, I mean... I remember talk of a modest inheritance. From your mother, wasn't it? You used to tell me you were going to build a home for stray cats."

"My father controls that." The accent coloring her speech and her energetic scrubbing presented the only sign of agitation.

Before he comprehended his action, he'd captured her hand. "Why would he do that?"

She jerked her arm but not hard enough to pull from his grasp. "Mercy above, Noah. I'm an unmarried, twenty-five-year-old woman running a school which makes no money and is shunned by every man in this town. My father looks at me and sees a dismal failure, a frivolous spinster holding no prospects for the future, a dreamer lacking even an ounce of common sense." She swallowed, her voice dropping to a whisper. "He sees everything he hated about my mother."

Noah dropped his handkerchief to the floor, uncurled her knotted fist, and kneaded her palm until her hand sprawled open on his knee. Her skin was work-roughened in patches, marked by light blue veins and freckles, fingers long and slender. He traced the bones in her wrist, her pulse thumping beneath his fingertips. "Who cares what he thinks."

She hung her head. "It shouldn't matter, but it does."

"I understand." And he did. His brothers' respect had always meant more to him than anyone's. Colleagues, professors, students. Accordingly, their criticism cut the deepest and scarred the worst.

His grip around her wrist tightened, and she glanced up, slowly tugging her hand free.

A strained cognizance circled as rain pinked against the glass panes. She arched her back and swabbed the floor in a burst of intensity. The knot of hair at the base of her neck had begun to unravel. A lone curl brushed her collar; another lay beneath her ear. He lifted his hand and twisted the bright spiral about his finger. Her skin, moist and warm, lit the pad of his thumb afire.

A shudder rippled through her; her shoulders lifted. The delicate shush of air from her lips parted his on a strangled sigh. The heat radiated from her; a light sheen glistened on the nape of her neck. Taking a deliberate breath, he savored the fragrance that lingered in his dreams. Earthy and vital, the scent drew him. He wanted nothing more than to satisfy the reckless longing in his heart, ease the desperate hunger in his mind.

Giving in, Noah groaned low and curled his arm about her waist, pulling her against his chest. She gasped and dropped her head, exposing a patch of skin above her collar, an invitation he could no longer refuse. At the touch of his lips, the essence of her flowed into him, surging to the tips of his toes and back, leaving a mass of exposed nerve endings. He had never, never in his *life,* been crowded by as many images—sensual, intoxicating, enthralling.

Not a single lucid thought remained to suppress them.

"Sweet," he whispered and tangled his fingers in her blouse. He pressed light kisses along the edge of her lace-trimmed collar, following the curve of her ear to her jaw. His mouth parted over the hard ridge, desiring more, and moving toward it.

Elle murmured and sagged against him, giving him the opportunity he needed. Swiveling her around, he cradled her face in his palms, lifting her gaze to his. A fire burned in the green depths, one to match his.

A wave of virile self-satisfaction consumed him. *She wanted him.* Passion lived in each shallow breath she took, in the steady flush sweeping her cheeks. His hunger grew as he watched her lids flutter, her chin tilt, unwittingly bringing her lips closer. She had no idea the level of his desire, the crude images he entertained. And he knew somewhere deep inside that the touch of her lips would never be enough.

*How could it be enough when she has belonged to you since the first day you saw her?*

Noah reeled, the thought like a punch to his head. He opened his eyes to find hers fixed upon him, hooded and dreamy. Moonlight trickled in through a slit in the curtains, a golden glide across her slender shoulder, a fine-boned cheek. Her breath caught, body jerking beneath a blouse so revealing in its simplicity that he had imagined ripping it from her and taking her on the dirty *floor.*

Fear had him releasing her in a sudden wrenching movement; anger shoved him to his feet. Blindly, he made his way to the entrance hall, his hands trembling. His gaze stole back to find her kneeling in the pool of silver, her hair unbound and surrounding her, her eyes luminous and seeking. Blessit, didn't she know what it did to him when she looked at him like that? He forgot his plans for the future, his strict code of honor and his decency crisping in the blaze. He needed to remember she was an innocent woman, even if she stared like a courtesan.

He jerked a boot on, then fumbled for the other. He'd struggled to create a life from nothing. To let Elle into his heart would demand examination of a past he had already paid the price for. He grabbed his coat from the hall stand and jammed his arms in the sleeves. She roused everything he'd spent years burying beneath layers of self-sufficiency and detachment. Call him a coward, but he couldn't allow her to hold such power over him.

Her fingers grazed his arm and he flinched, turning to find her standing directly behind him. He felt a renewed burst of desire; he wanted to touch, kiss, *mate.*

The beveled doorknob slid from his grasp. Wiping his hand on his trousers, he tried again, ducking just before he hit his head on a low beam on the way out. The rain on his face was welcome. Hell, he would welcome anything that washed away the taste of her. Finally, when he was calm, he said, "Close the door, Elle. I'll be right here."

"Noah." His name on her lips sounded thick and tender, heavily accented, the way it had years ago. Starting to turn, he checked the motion before he had a chance to see her face. Tears might be enough to defeat him. He clenched his hands at his side and stared into the black sky.

*Let her cry. Let her despise me until the end of her days. Let her think I'm heartless. Cruel. A bastard. Just let her close the damned door and put something tangible between us.*

With a faint click, she did.

Noah released a tense breath he had not known he held and leaned against the porch railing, his heart aching. He relaxed his fists with some effort, fear still holding him in its grip. Sentiment born of emotions deeper than lust bullied him: *Go back. Finish what you started.*

How he had come to feel so much for Elle Beaumont in such a short time dumbfounded him.

Worse, how in the world could he conquer his feelings?

Elle slid to the floor in a boneless, breakable heap. Oblivious to the rattling pane of glass in the door or the steady drip soaking her shoulder, she dropped her head to her hands and prayed for the first time in months. Surely, God wouldn't let her... didn't plan for—

She slammed her fist against her bent knee, recognized she still held the damp rag, and flung it across the entrance hall. What did everyone in Pilot Isle expect her to do *but* fall in love all over again? Why should God be any different? Noah was handsome and brilliant and honorable, everything she had known he would be.

Why, he was close to perfect!

Knocking her head against the wall, she listened to his heavy footfalls. Six steps forward... a stagnant pause... six steps back. The cadence provided some level of malicious comfort. She could *hear* his confusion. He would never love her, but at least he coveted her. She understood enough from Magnus's inept groping and Christabel's candid clarification of men's motives. Elle had held Magnus off effort-lessly, never worrying about her ability to deny him.

She rubbed the tingling spot on her neck. He had sucked her earlobe between his lips, then swirled his tongue inside—something she would have guessed felt similar to a dog's sloppy kiss. Heaven, nothing was further from the truth.

Admittedly, the attraction they shared posed a problem. Was there a way to reduce it, like the flame on a gas lantern? She had no idea. She had loved Noah with a young girl's heart, never experiencing this, this... *physical* yearning that made her knees go weak and puckered her nipples beneath her shift. Nothing but a strong wintry gust or a swim in the ocean before June had ever caused this before.

Recalling the blatant terror on Noah's face brought a fresh burst of anger. It nipped a woman's vanity to close her eyes to receive her first real kiss, then open them to find the lover in question tugging his boots on like he had a fire to put out.

Only a fool would be pleased by *that* reaction.

And Marielle-Claire Beaumont was no longer a lovesick fool.

No, but she recognized her limits. Kissing Noah stretched those limits to the breaking point and threatened to plunge her into the throes of unrequited love. And this time, she would want more than friendship. She might go as far as demanding the things Christabel had explained in delicious detail.

A drop of water struck her flaming cheek. She blew out a breath as Noah continued to pace outside. Scooting across the floor, she captured the rag beneath her heel and dragged it into her waiting hand. She wasn't some pathetic schoolgirl, she reasoned, and viciously scrubbed at the water stain.

For once in her life, maybe the first time, she planned to follow Noah's advice.

And think with her head and not her heart.

# CHAPTER SIX

*"Every species appears to have an area for maximum development."*
    ~ C. Wyville Thomson
    *The Depths of the Sea*

❦

"*W*ell, daughter, you've definitely landed in trouble neck-deep this time."

Elle started, dropping the bundle of files she held on her father's desk.

How did he know about Noah?

Henri slammed the office door behind him and crossed the room in three angry strides. He stubbed his cigar in a crystal dish of rose petals Elle had placed in water that morning. A thin streak of smoke wafted past her face, the honeyed stench turning her stomach. "You had to help the little Duggan urchin, didn't you? Feminine freedom for all, correct? From whom has she gained independence, Marielle-Claire? May I ask you? Her husband? Who has every right to do whatever he pleases to her, which includes applying a firm hand? Did you know she is carrying his child? *Grands Dieux!*" He slammed his fist to the desk.

"Did it ever occur to you to remember Sean Duggan is the best pilot I have? My shipments are rarely delayed. He can navigate every inlet and shoal in the Banks with his eyes closed. Or should I say he is the best pilot I *had*. He tendered his resignation today, left to work for Elias Benton. When I requested a reason, he said he could not continue to associate with a family aiding in his wife's departure."

Before she had time to react, her father grasped her chin between his fingers. "Elias Benton is my competitor, Marielle-Claire. A ruthless competitor, who does not need the assistance of my only child to make a success of his business ventures."

She tried to open her mouth, but he tilted her head, forcing her lips together. "Do not speak unless it's to inform me you did *not* help Annie Duggan leave Pilot Isle, in which case you will apologize to Sean for his dilemma. He is worried, beyond measure. His wife has been missing for five days, and it appears she is not returning. The man has searched Morehead City thoroughly with no luck. Except to find a receipt of his wife's passage on the express train bound for Atlanta. He refuses to chase her as she has run home to her mother."

Elle jerked from his grasp and shoved to her feet, knocking the chair against the wall. "I did help her, and I would help her again. Tomorrow and the next day and the next," she said roughly, her throat dry from fury and frustration. "Think highly of that monster while you think poorly of your own daughter. But I will never, I can vow this on Mother's grave, apologize for helping Annie leave."

The slap rocked her head to the side. Without speaking, Elle walked around the desk, the pain in her cheek fading to a dull throb. However, the shock of her father's brutality had her heart pounding in her chest.

"Marielle-Claire, come back here," he called, but she was beyond hearing. Or caring.

The last, fragile vestige of family had been robbed from her, and she found herself racing down the staircase to escape.

The lively confusion of the harbor crowded round Noah as he maneuvered the gangplank leading from the *Nellie Dey's* deck. He rotated his aching shoulders, wondering how he would ever get in good enough condition to work the nets without his muscles screaming for relief. Stepping to the wharf, he tossed a scrap of fish to a shrieking gull and watched it seize the morsel in a swooping dive. Men dressed much as he was, in bib trousers and muddy brogans, bumped past, gill nets in hand, barrels hoisted upon their shoulders, crab pots clanking at their sides. All of them, him included, reeked of fish and hard labor, the stink worsened by the scorching afternoon sun.

"Aw, look at her, willya."

Noah shouldered his satchel of research materials and moved next to a group of fishermen circling a corked barrel of ale that would, no doubt, be recorded as damaged in transit.

"Wonder what the French bastard said to her this time?" Fat Jack asked in a singsong alto.

Noah looked over their heads, to the top of a staircase leading from Henri Beaumont's warehouse. His breath caught. Elle descended at a dangerously breakneck speed.

Her skirt flipped about her ankles; bright curls danced about her head. He squinted, imagined he saw a flush staining her cheeks. The sudden vision of his lips pressed against her smooth, moist skin pierced him like a hook beneath his.

"She looks to be in a fine fury, don't she?" This from a young New Englander who had sailed south aboard one of the whaling ships.

Jeb Crow, who claimed to be half Cherokee, but looked rather Nordic to Noah, laughed and ejected a stream of tobacco juice from his chapped lips. Noah grimaced and glanced at his feet. Whether he wore dirty brogans or polished oxfords, he preferred not to have his shoes spit upon.

"She gave old Beaumont the business end of a stick, I tell you. Trying to get her hitched, he is, and she ain't agreeing," Jeb said and spit again, this time closer to the New Englander.

"Can't blame Beaumont. Never married, never close even. If that was *my* daughter, I'd skin her alive," Walt Pepper stated, seeming to forget his daughter had run off with a Scottish sailor and nobody knew for sure if marriage had been part of the deal.

Jeb crammed another wad of tobacco in his cheek. "Miss Elle's nearly thirty years old. Way past time to marry and birth some babies. Make her forget that women's school nonsense."

Noah's gaze traversed the group. *Chrissakes, what a bunch of idiots.* He started to turn when, as often happens with men, the conversation degenerated.

"Look at her twitch. Put together nice, she is."

"Yessiree."

Noah glanced back in time to witness Elle hop to the boardwalk. He wouldn't call it twitching, but she did jiggle a little.

"You know what they say about orange-haired women."

"Maybe she hasn't found the right fella, yet. Maybe I should go calling." Crude sniggers and hard backslaps accompanied this suggestion, then the discussion halted. They turned in unison to stare at Noah. "Or maybe she *has* found him, but he just won't find *her.*"

Noah's hands closed into fists. What did these men know of Elle? Would they have been willing to defy an enraged, drunken bully who beat his wife? Had they fought for freedom they believed in and lost their dreams as a result? She had more courage in her pinkie finger than the whole lot of them put together. Noah forced his feet to move before he did something ridiculous, something completely out of character. Before he allowed a quintessentially masculine response to overpower intellect.

It seemed he fought this battle too often.

He sidestepped a rut in the shell-paved road, navigated a crush of lumber wagons and vegetable carts, and raised his hand in greeting three times to the call of "Professor" before increasing his stride.

The edge of Elle's skirt was mud-stained, the hem dangling. He struggled to ignore how the worn cloth clung to her hips and swayed with her brisk, rolling stride. She didn't walk like a lady, and she obviously didn't care who knew it.

Just when he caught her, she halted. He plowed into her and gripped her waist to steady himself.

"Noah, what are you doing?"

Doing? He had no idea. He woke each morning, his mind full of images he couldn't shake, desires he didn't want any part of. Physical labor served as his only savior. The captain of the *Nellie Dey* had even offered him a job for the season, telling him he had never seen a man work so hard for free.

"Hello, Noah?" She tapped his head with a slender finger. "Are you in there?"

"I'll be damned if I know."

"Don't you have some young woman waiting at the corner to walk you home? Why, in the name of heaven, are you hounding me?" Elle took a step, then stopped, and he almost ran into her again.

Noah rocked back on his heels, chastised. Perhaps *chagrined* better described the itch beneath his collar. Not for following her or watching her little show on the staircase, but because Meredith Scoggins likely *was* waiting for him on the corner. She had been there every day this week.

"That's right, shrug and wonder what possesses women to rant and rave. Hunch your shoulders like a boy who wants to crawl under his bed and hide. Go ahead. Congratulate yourself for your masculine restraint. Your superior intelligence."

"Elle." He patted her shoulder in an awkward gesture of peace, opposing emotions battling for advantage. To comfort, to flee. Only, her voice, though filled with anger, held a ragged edge that rallied right through the hardened walls of his heart.

"What happened?" he asked.

Her back rose and fell on a deep breath. "My father asked me to apologize to Sean Duggan for helping Annie leave town. He summoned me to his office this morning, and it was stupid of me, I know, but I thought he wanted to apologize for our argument. I showed up early, finished his records for the past week, and filed the invoices. He probably won't even notice. Every time I offer him a part of myself, he throws it away. I should know not to trust him. My father doesn't give his love freely. He never has."

"Elle."

"The discovery that nothing will ever change, that, in fact, things are worse than I imagined. Certainly none of your concern," she said and whirled right into the path of a dray loaded with crates.

Noah grabbed her shoulders and hauled her against him. "Hold on there," he whispered in her ear. Tremors shook her body, molding it tightly, *perfectly* to his.

"Watch out, Miss Elle," the driver shouted, and jerked the reins, bringing his nag to a stumbling halt, chicken feathers drifting to the ground.

*"You* watch out, Homer Crawford!" She slapped the side of the wagon and wrenched from Noah's grip.

"Women," Homer grumbled and plucked a feather from his lap.

Racing to catch Elle, Noah shoved her into the darkened alley running between the mercantile and Christabel's saloon. "Do you want to calm down and tell me what's going on?"

"Please, Noah"—she tapped the toe of her boot against a broken bottle, her voice wavering—"just leave me alone."

"What happened?"

She shook her head in denial.

"Tell me what happened. I'm a part of this, if you care to remember. I escorted Annie to Morehead City, not you." He pressed his elbows into his ribs, determined not to touch her.

She straightened her shoulders and lifted her gaze. It disturbed him to see grief riding a wall of ragged vigilance. But nothing disturbed him as much as seeing the bruise purpling her cheek.

Something shifted: in his stomach, in his chest. Something unrecognizable, something he was sure he had never experienced before. "Did he hit you?" His hand lifted, traced the mark. A dull wash of red clouded his vision. "Did your father hit you?"

She swallowed. "It doesn't matter."

"The hell it doesn't." He tipped her chin high. "Why, Elle, why did he do this?"

"Sean Duggan resigned today. The best seaman on Pilot Isle, according to my father. Because of me, he lost him to Elias Benton."

"He did this to you because of a business deal?"

"Yes."

Noah stepped back, folding his arms. Rage made him think terribly ugly thoughts. "Is he in his office?"

She grabbed his wrist, pulled him close. "You have to let me handle this. He's my *father*. Anyway, it didn't hurt, except in here." She pressed her palm over her heart. "And, sadly enough, that's mostly gone. You see, I *left* him, actually left him, when I moved from his home two years ago. Besides having dinner with him once a week, he gives me nothing, and I give him nothing. We share nothing. Heavens, sometimes it's hard to believe I'm his flesh and blood."

"You don't have to ask him for anything. Not after this. I can help you. I want to help you."

"I said no. Twice already."

"Elle, be reasonable. You used your savings sending Annie home, gave her the last penny you had. Take the money. I told you I made some very wise investments in Chicago. There's more in my accounts than I know how to spend. I'll give you enough to get you through the year."

She shook her head. "Knowing I can talk to you is enough. Maybe I was waiting for you to find me. Who knows? Old habits die hard, or so they say. I admit I felt the weight slip from my shoulders the minute you stepped behind me."

Her words raised the hair on his arms. "Behind you?"

"Oh, Noah." She laughed, a mix of impishness and frustration. "If you entered a room and the door was behind my back, I would know. I used to sit in school, waiting. The air changed temperature, closed in around me the second you walked in." She considered a moment, then shrugged. "It still does."

He took an unsteady step, grinding crushed shells beneath his boots. "Hush." Panic trapped his breath in his chest.

"If I can't tell you, who can I tell? I get tired of pretending. I don't understand why, but this connection has always been between us. At least for me it has."

"I don't know what you're talking about."

"How can you lie when we each need a friend so desperately?"

His hand shot out as his gaze snagged hers. "What if I lie? What the hell difference can it make to reawaken issues best left dead? How can admitting help either one of us?"

"Dead *issues?* Is that what you think of your past, your family, your childhood? As something dead?" She searched his face, observing too much. "You carry this grief around like baggage. It's foolish. Your brothers love you. You're blessed to have them, to have Rory, and yet, you have no perception of the miracle of family. Love is a gift. Not an obligation, not a burden."

Noah turned to pace the length of the alley. She had twisted him into a knot, as usual. Strong words and high-minded ideals. Brutal honesty. And what had he been trying to do? Comfort her. Protect her from harm because of the damned *connection* she spoke of. "I'm repairing the damage I've done to my family. In my own way, in my own time." *Without completely ripping my soul from my body,* he silently added. "What would you have me do? Cut a vein and let everything inside rush out?"

"Yes, if the rush brought you some level of serenity."

"Serenity?" He ripped his spectacles off and rubbed his eyes. "Don't I look serene to you?"

"You look haggard."

"A problem at the lab yesterday. The freight company lost a shipment of materials. And, I took beach patrol with Zach and Rory last night." He shook his head. "They're trying so hard to reach me and... I don't know what to do."

"None of this disappeared when you left."

"Stay out of this, Elle."

"Quit looking at me like a wild animal cornered by a predator. How can I make you believe I only want your friendship, which I would think you'd be willing to give? You can talk to me, even if you can't talk to anyone else. You always could."

She spoke of love and friendship, but what he wanted from her had nothing to do with those things and everything to do with her melting like butter over him. The cherished boy from her childhood wouldn't be contemplating throwing her to the ground in an alley, tangling his fingers in her hair as his body covered hers.

Noah fought the urge to run.

"Don't shut me out." She took a step closer.

"I *want* to shut you out. Better yet, shut you up."

A small wrinkle appeared between her eyebrows. "I don't know how to help with that."

He expelled a ragged hitch of laughter. "Yes, well, makes two of us." Pacing from her, emotion bombarded him. Did she honestly think what happened in Widow Wynne's parlor occurred between *friends?* Blessit, was she that naive? He'd wanted one brief taste, to see if she would equal his dreams.

Similar to an experiment.

Relief flooded his mind, and he smiled.

An experiment. So damned simple. Most of his torment the last week had been self-induced, pure conjecture. He had taken an instinctual sensual response of adolescence and transformed it into a man's carnal desire. The images crowding him were not drawn from past experience. In all probability, they were as spurious as a storm cloud that never brings rain.

Before he changed his mind, he dropped his satchel to the ground and turned to her. Elle flattened against the wall, chin angled high, frightened but defiant. She wouldn't run. Not this woman.

And for once, neither would he.

The humming in his ears the only sign of his discomfiture, he leaned in, pressing his palms to the rough brick on either side of her head. He had no choice, no longer able to live at the mercy of his emotions.

To expunge the temptation, he must yield to it.

"Noah," she said, half question, half plea. A warm breath skirted his cheek, one that smelled of apple. Her gaze skimmed his face, lingering on his mouth before lowering. She made a faint sound of protest.

"Friends, Elle." He lifted his hand and outlined her bottom lip. Closing his eyes, he concentrated on the way the moist skin clung to his. Continuing to the curve of her cheek, the crescent of hair above each eye. Expelling a strangled sound, she stiffened and left his hand dangling before her face.

"Friends," he whispered before he dipped his head. He paused, savoring the scent of her. With her next apple-breath, he guided his mouth to hers.

He felt her tremble. "Trust me, sweet." He dug his palms into the wall, thinking only of his goal, intent on ending his fascination. *Today,* right this *minute*, he would find out.

Find his dreams were simply dreams.

On a sigh of surrender, a shared release of passion, her mouth parted. Seizing the opportunity, he plucked her bottom lip between his teeth. He moistened and suckled, skimming back and forth. Grasping his forearms, she groaned into his mouth, and his mission dimmed. He deepened the kiss, sensation pricking every nerve. The scent of scorched rose petals; the rough edge of her front tooth; her tentative effort to get closer. She edged up the wall, her breasts chafing his chest, her eager hands tangling in his bib straps.

His heart slammed hard, out of control. "No," he said, and twisted away from her.

A rush of air shot between them, and Elle blinked, looking into his impossibly young, unguarded face. Eyes closed, his lips parted to allow a throaty breath free. She captured the image, realizing she would not see it again unless she caught him sleeping.

Merciful heavens, he looked like the boy she remembered. Her first day of school, a classroom smelling of chalk and vinegar. Herman Stanley apologizing for making fun of her accent. Noah giving her a smile of acceptance and unwittingly propelling love between two beats of her heart.

Just now, he had touched her with his beautiful hands before he touched her with his lips. Had stroked her face with the intent of enlightenment. Some of the gentle-hearted child had to be left inside him.

She curled her fingers around his bib straps and tugged.

*This is your chance, Elle. Take it.*

She ignored his grunt of protest and bounced to the balls of her feet, thanking her father for the ballet lessons. Slanting her head as Noah had done, she fit her mouth over his. She would use him for her own purpose, just as he used her for his. She threaded her fingers through the damp curls at the base of his neck, and, not sure how to ask for more, touched her tongue to the corner of his mouth.

Noah uttered a low groan of defeat and crowded her into the wall, his arms stealing around to cushion the impact. His heat scorched her skin; the taste of butterscotch filled her mouth. He had a sweet tooth, she remembered, dazed and dreamy.

Raising his hands, he held her head steady as his mouth, *finally,* truly captured hers. Her body slumped, a gradual melting. Caution, fear, logic, her father's cruelty, all liquefied, roaring like the ocean at high tide.

Lightly at first, then using greater pressure, he teased, raising the point of pleasure. He angled his head, drew his tongue across her lips, showing her what he wanted. She didn't care if the action was right or wrong, foolish or wise—she opened.

And he took.

The kiss was unlike any she had dreamt of. His mouth aggressive, his whiskered cheeks rough, his hands eager, gliding past her neck, her shoulders. Control slipped as he delved, bending, wrapping her in a gossamer web of need. *His need.* Of course, he would deny the lapse later. But right now, *this minute,* with his body joined with hers, she knew.

She had wondered the other night but now she knew.

He wanted her.

She did not mistake his need for love or consideration, kindness or respect. This blind ferocity, wild and undeniable, amounted to nothing more than overwhelming urgency.

A tortured sound rumbled deep in his throat. His lips trembled, his hands snagging in her hair. Her knees weakened, and he steadied her, fit her to his body.

*Desire.* Christabel had explained in vague terms what it meant to want a man so much you would do anything to have him.

"Closer," he whispered against her lips, his breath skimming her face.

*Juste Ciel,* she wanted to get closer. Already, his back bowed to accommodate for their disparity in height. The notion burned: they would not have this problem in a bed.

She stretched, trying. Almost... she almost—

He caught her under the arms and settled her astride his thigh. Her dress snagged between her legs as his knee wedged against the wall. His lips never left hers. Not once.

*My, how ingenious, she thought.*

She explored everything accessible. The muscles in his arm had grown from hauling nets and icing fish, his chest seemed broader, harder. Her mouth traversed the edge of his jaw, nipped at the skin below his ear.

How could a man who smelled of fish taste so wonderful?

She wiggled on his thigh, heat pooling between her legs. Whatever she searched for, she couldn't find.

"Let me show you," he breathed against her ear. Grasping her waist, he moved her forward, then back—a tantalizing abrasion. *Oh, yes.* She buried her face in his neck, a moan escaping before she could stop it.

A rusty creak penetrated the haze surrounding them; she lifted her head. Noah's mouth traveled to her cheek, to her lips. Elle fought the urge to close her eyes, drift on a cloud of moist, fervent kisses.

A gentle cough. Then another.

Elle pushed on his chest. "Noah." She forced the word between breaths, finally taking his face in her hands. "We're not... *alone*," she said, mouthing the last. Gradually, the music from the Nook filtered in. His eyelids flickered, opened, widened. Smoldering, charcoal gray. His nostrils flared on a rush of released air.

"Christ," he whispered, throat clicking on a hard swallow, chest rising and falling as he fought for control.

Bewildered, Elle could only stare, wondering if she looked as disheveled as he did. As appealingly undone. Gaze unfocused, lips swollen, hair plastered to his head in swirls of wet gold. Another burst of heat lit her. She wanted nothing more than to pull his mouth to—

"Stop looking at me like that. Do you want to end up beneath me?" He spoke harshly, but he was slow to release her, even slower to lift her from his thigh. The whole time, he shielded her from view, waiting for her to stand as she braced her palm against the wall.

Expelling a sigh, he slipped his spectacles on and turned.

Elle peeked around him to find Christabel standing in the Nook's doorway, hands fisted on her hips, her expression vacillating between amusement and curiosity. "Sorry to come across you in an indelicate state, but better me than some lonely fisherman." She glanced over her shoulder. "You take the back way, Noah. Honey, you come through the kitchen with me."

"What the hell do you have to do with it?"

"I'm the woman who's going to keep every gossip on the Isle from making your life hell, that's what I have to do with it."

Elle laid her hand on Noah's arm to diffuse his rigid stance. And, she couldn't stand so close and not touch him. Not when he had brought her body to life.

"Trust me, the men will be streaming in from the docks any minute, ready to drink now that the sun's set. Some are already in there raising the devil. End of the week and pockets full of money. No need to advertise you've been here. Poor man's bedroom, they call it."

Noah cursed beneath his breath and turned to Elle. His somber gaze captured hers as early evening shadows danced across his face. "I'm sorry, Elle. Sorry for this."

She stared at his lips as they moved, helpless to do anything but remember them covering hers. "I don't want you to be sorry. I'm not sorry."

"You will be." He stooped to grab his satchel. Frowning, he fiddled with the leather strap, his lips parting as if he would say more. His hand hovered near her bruised cheek. "I'm sorry," he said, his hand dropping.

The snap of shells beneath his brogans rang hollow and final in his wake. The mystical appeal of the alley departed with him, leaving only a slight chill, deepening shadows, and the stink of whiskey and fried fish.

"I waited as long as I could, but you don't need anybody seeing you tangled up like that," Christabel said.

Elle had no idea what being caught *tangled up* with a man was like. Although Christabel was right, of course. It wouldn't be good. Well, wouldn't be *wise.* Her father, Zach, Caleb. All of them would find out. She dropped her head to her hands. Her skin smelled of him, her mouth tasted of him.

How did a woman get past that?

"I didn't think he would stalk outta here. Boy, he has a nasty temper. Sure is a Garrett, that one. Do you reckon he remembers I carved *Elle loves Noah* into all those tree trunks?"

Elle laughed through her laced fingers. "Oh, Christa, however this ended, he wasn't going to handle the situation well. For a brief moment, the appalling happened, and he lost his beloved control. It's not your fault he's—" Scared. Stubborn. She wagged her head, frustrated to the core.

"Do you want to come inside? Have a cup of coffee? I make a mean pot."

"No." She glanced at Christabel. Blond and robust, she carried a lot of responsibility on her shoulders. Elle never underestimated her wisdom, no matter the packaging. "Thank you. I realize you did what you thought best. And you're right. I know that, too."

"Makes no difference if I'm right. Doesn't lessen the wanting. Anyway, no need to fret. I'll take care of him when he comes in tonight."

With a feeble half-turn, Elle swayed against the wall. *"What?"*

Christabel gave her a sympathetic look. Never had the contrast in their upbringings been more apparent. "He'll be back. Not a man alive who can walk away from what he walked away from and not seek a little relief." She winked. "And unless he comes knocking on your door, I provide the only relief in town."

Jealousy shot through Elle, vicious and unwelcome.

Christabel snorted and slapped her hands together. "Oh, honey, not *that* kind of relief. Whiskey is all I'm talking about. Sure, he could find the other if he wanted, but Noah's not that kind of man. Trust me, I can spot the scamps a mile off."

Elle chewed her lip, her suddenly tight clothing making her hot and itchy. "I didn't mean, that is to say, without doubt, I don't care what he does. This was simply a—a slip."

"A slip? What proper women call almost making love in an alley? Okay, honey, a slip." Christabel flapped her apron, her lips pressed to hold in a smile. "Now, get going. And, just in case Noah decides to *slip* with you again, dabble some toilet water between your breasts and put on a pretty dress. Maybe comb your hair."

Christabel's laughter, and her blasted advice, needled Elle the entire walk home.

# CHAPTER SEVEN

∼

*E*lle angled the paper into a shaft of moonlight and read the letter for the fourth time.

*April 2, 1898*

*My Dearest Friend:*

*I have enclosed an application for the scholarship program I mentioned in my previous letter. As you can see, each year the fund lends money to permit a promising young woman to attend college. Our last recipient chose Cornell. I know you considered returning to Bryn Mawr, but just look at the marvelous number of universities included in the program.*

*I admit to rallying behind you at the scholarship meeting last month, and dearest Elle, you are so deserving. Many on the committee feel your extremely high entrance scores are an added benefit as well as your proven dedication to furthering women's education. I am confident a completed application is all that is standing in the way of your dream.*

*Now, my friend, I can see you shaking your head and telling yourself the school cannot survive without you. Actually, Elle, I have felt a fair measure of discontent lately, an urge to accomplish more than I can in New York City. I hope you consider my offer to manage the school in your absence a serious one. I would be proud to work with your students.*

*I am speaking at a reform meeting tonight and hope to encourage the audience members to contribute generously.*

*To friendship,*
*Savannah*

The scholarship provided a grand opportunity to change her life, Elle thought, folding the letter and slipping it into her pocket. The application lay on her marble-top washstand, four pages of essay questions and personal queries. If she found additional means of income, even meager, she could survive.

In her entire life, she had only wanted *one* thing more than she wanted an education. She glanced at the darkened window of the coach house and realized no hope of that remained.

Reclining on the grass, she hooked her arms beneath her head and stared into a sky ripening from pitch-black to predawn blue. Birds had started to twitter, the only noise besides the distant roar of the ocean. No, not the only. She tilted her head, the thump of barrels being unloaded on the dock and a bell announcing a ship entering the harbor.

She rubbed her hand across her nose, the fragrance shooting a dart of chagrin through her. Sentimental absurdity to dab perfume between her breasts and behind her ears. A lone tear trailed down her cheek, and she scrubbed it away. How could she do this? Hadn't she learned her lesson years ago?

For her, Noah Garrett would always mean heartache.

He was not coming home, that was obvious. Elle could not picture Noah dousing his confusion in whiskey and cheap cigars. Nonetheless, Christa understood men better than she did.

Frankly, she was surprised he had not removed his possessions from the coach house. Fled to safer ground, as he would in preparation for a deadly hurricane. Losing control posed as grave a disaster in his mind. Perhaps he'd deemed it too much trouble to move the multitude of glass tubes, research books, and curious gadgets. In a sorrowful testament to her weakness, she knew they still littered every vacant surface. Darkness had provided the courage to climb the flight of stairs and peer inside. Unfortunately, a shift in wind startled her, causing her to knock a jar filled with murky water and a piece of gnarled driftwood from the landing. The driftwood she had put back in its place, the jar lay in pieces in the bottom of her garbage bin. She hoped she had not ruined an important experiment.

What had she been thinking? She twisted the damp edge of her dress in her fist. To let him kiss her as he whispered "friends" in her ear, to kiss him back, starved for his touch. Exposed, her mouth eager and open. This didn't make sense. She let him go the other night, stressing she would not fall in love with him, telling herself she was finished with men.

In fact, she told Daniel Connery the same thing not a day before. And she meant it.

Rejecting Noah had never occurred to her. She had raced into his arms. A reckless, gullible fool hoarding a vestige of absurd hope—imagining a twenty-seven-year-old man was innocent. Oh no, not after, not after the little—she groaned, but the memory loomed, terribly clear—*rubbing* incident. He had known exactly where to focus his energy, setting her atop his hard thigh, grasping her waist, and....

Where had he learned such a thing? And how many encounters had it taken to perfect his technique?

The image of Noah touching another woman made her queasy. He had obviously touched *many*. Mrs. Bartram of the scented letters, for one. He understood a woman's body too well. Living in a depraved city, who knew how many shared his bed? Elle closed her eyes, a sharp pain seizing her, riding hard from her toes to her head.

She rested her cheek on the prickly cushion of grass, images of Noah's hands upon her spinning round her mind like the phonograph in Christabel's parlor. The kiss represented a trifling part of what they could do. Even in her ignorance, she realized that. Too, she understood he had done much more at some point in his life. The presumption only made her sob and bury her face in her hands.

*Damn and blast,* she didn't need to wallow in the dirt when she owned only three decent dresses, and the one she wore represented the best of the lot.

Tears had never come easily or often, and they dried quickly. Crying answered no questions, abated no fears. Swabbing her face, she rolled to her back as the first delicate streaks of red and gold spread like a blush along the horizon.

*I wish Noah was here to share this with me.*

"I still love him," she whispered. "You fool, you still love him."

Sitting up, she pressed her hand to her chest, willing her heartbeat to return to normal. *Oh, blast. I still love him.*

A man armored against emotion.

She slipped her hand into her watch pocket and fingered Savannah's letter with a renewed sense of anticipation and dread.

The pounding ripped Zach from sleep. Shoving to his elbows on the bunk, he drew a hitching breath and let his head flop back. The muscles in his arms quivered; his heart raced. The dream returned in a series of flashes. Blood staining the sheets... Hannah's shrill, weak cries... his lungs burning as he went for the doctor... lifeless blue eyes and cold, stiff fingers.

A dream, Zach. A dream. The salty burn of tears stung, and he swallowed. *Am I going to dream about her dying for the rest of my life?*

Another round of knocking shook the door in its frame. "Coming," he shouted, praying a ship had not gotten beached on Diamond

Shoals. He would have to check his list to see whose turn it was to patrol. They had been lucky lately, but luck, Zach well knew, always ran out. His certainly had.

Flinging the thin woolen blanket to the floor, he found his coat hanging on the back of a chair and was just pulling his arms through the sleeves when he reached the door.

"Cap'n Garrett, open up."

The smell of smoke and whiskey drifted in the open door, attached to Bigby Dixon, Christabel's manservant, for lack of a better description. The hulking man stood beneath the jail's narrow lean-to, broad shoulder braced against a timber post, hooked grin riding his face. Zach's shoulders slumped. Bigby helped him organize the safety drills and scrubbed salt from the breech buoys on occasion, but he did not patrol the beach on a regular basis, and never alone.

"You might better come, Cap'n." Bigby dabbed his boot in the circle of light cast on the planks. "Miss Christabel sent me for you."

Captain. Zach had ceased being a captain before Hannah died, but Bigby would hardly know it. "Who is it?" he asked, digging in his pocket for his ring of keys, knowing exactly who it was.

Bigby's held tilted quizzically. "Ah, you know, Cap'n. Your brother."

"Of course." Zach crossed the street at a fast clip, Bigby trailing in his steps. They stopped twice. To look at a frog flattened by a wagon wheel and to count the masts rising above the peaked roofs of the warehouses. Zach reminded himself, gazing into Bigby's joyful face, that all the excitement and innocence of Rory's world filled this man's and always would.

When they arrived at the Nook, he sent Bigby to fetch coffee with a promise to let him sleep in the jail cell one night next week. Side-stepping tables scattered with cigar butts and half-filled glasses, he halted before Christabel's parlor doors. She settled Caleb on the striped horsehair sofa after he'd gotten particularly rambunctious, separated from the temptation angry words, cheap whiskey, and flirtatious women presented.

He knocked once, hard and furious.

"Zach?"

"Yes."

One of the doors slid into its pocket, a flood of light spilling across his boots. He strode past her, pulling his sleeve from her grasp.

"Zach, you might...." Her words faded to a whispered sigh.

The uncharacteristic hint of caution in her voice slowed his stride. Zach halted, his gaze drawn to the mammoth desk occupying one corner of the room. "Damn," he said and raised his hand to his face. "Damn."

"His spectacles." She tapped them against his wrist. "Didn't want him to break them."

Zach took the wire frames from her. "Lord knows, this isn't what I expected."

She tilted her head to the side and twitched her shoulders, a half-hearted shrug. "He's a man, Zach."

An inadequate explanation for finding his *sensible* brother slumped over her desk. Noah's arms sheltered his face, his hair bright against his rumpled black shirtsleeves.

"What happened?"

Christabel stepped beside him, the opposing scents of whiskey and flowers surrounding her. "Things were pretty quiet, most of the men summoned home by their wives long before Noah got here. He'd been sailing, I think. Had a wild glow in his eyes. Honest, I never thought he looked much like Caleb until then. I reckoned he would bust up one of my tables before the night ended." She stacked her fingers along the desk and leaned her weight on them. "Anyway, I brought him here right away. With a bottle. I knew, I just, well... oh, I probably shouldn't say, but good gracious, I want to tell someone." She knotted her hands together and recounted a story that left Zach feeling like he'd stumbled into a burning building.

"You found them *what?*"

She raised her hand to her heart and made a swift sign of the cross. "Kissing. And no sweet, decent kiss, either. Singed the air. I swear, plain as day, that's what I saw."

"Maybe, maybe—" His thoughtful gray gaze slid her way. "Are you sure?"

"Sure? Honey, they were practically clawing at each other."

Frowning, he watched Noah's chest rise and fall in a steady rhythm. "Do you think he loves her?"

She considered a moment, took in Noah's condition with a sweeping glance. "Whatever he feels, seems to me he don't want to."

"What should I do?"

Christabel cocked her head toward the heavy footfalls on the floor above, Bigby's childish laughter, and the sharp clink of silverware. "Take him home," she said.

Zach dragged his hand across his mouth. "What about Ellie?"

"What about her?"

"Doggone it, Christa, she's like a sister to me. I don't want Noah to hurt her again."

Christabel trailed her finger over the desk and laughed, a sound full of womanly wisdom. "Honey, how do you know she won't hurt *him?*"

⁓

"Christabel told you, I know she did," Noah said, an exaggerated drawl lengthening each word.

Zach tugged the spread as high as he could while keeping his brother's feet covered, although they dangled off the end of the bed. He nudged a wooden bucket across the pine floor, banging it against the frame. "If you feel sick, all you have to do is lean over." A trick he had learned from Rory.

Noah laughed, thin and worn. "I told you, I didn't... eat dinner. There's nothing." He patted his stomach. "Nothing."

Zach frowned. No dinner. He glanced at his brother's wrist, angled high on his flat belly. Sun-buffed skin covered muscle but bones protruded where muscle was scarce. "I put a pitcher of water on the table. A glass beside it," he said, tucking the blanket around Noah's shoulders, amazed, again, by how much Rory resembled him.

"She did, she told you. Don't try... to deny. Always a meddler, that one. I remember what she carved in those tree trunks."

"Yes, she did tell me." He unbuttoned Noah's collar and dropped it to the table. The cuffs followed, rasping against skin as Zach tugged them free. Thank goodness, Rory had gone fishing with Jason and his father. He didn't need to find his beloved uncle like this.

Noah's fingers fluttered, tangling in his black brace, the bones in his hand dancing. "I'm not sure why I kissed her. It's fuzzy... the reason."

"I'm sure everything is fuzzy right now." Zach grabbed the chair he had shoved from their path when they stumbled into the room. Straddling it, he leaned his arms on the back. Contradictory emotions tugged at him. He wanted Noah to sleep, knew he needed to sleep. Already, morning light colored the end of the bed; birds twittered and darted outside the window.

Another part, the part that had grieved—wondering if he would ever see his little brother again—rejoiced at the chance to talk to him without a wall standing between them. Zach had fought hard to destroy it. Two dinners at Christabel's. Unplanned visits in the guise of dropping off Rory at Widow Wynne's. Heck, he had even sailed on the *Nellie Dey*. The first shad run he'd been on since the year he turned twenty. Observing Noah—feet planted wide, body swaying with the roll and pitch of the ocean, recording figures in a book as thick as his arm, eyes faithfully scanning the horizon—had brought home how much his brother had matured. Drifted away. Become a stranger. A marine biologist who lived in *Chicago*. A man Zach often wondered if he would ever know again.

"Why do you suppose she does this to me?" The scar on his eyelid showed white against his tanned skin as he blinked. "Makes me all confused and wobbly. Never gotten wobbly before."

"The whiskey's making you wobbly." Zach tapped his palms against the slats of the chair and rocked forward on the front legs.

"Oh, no, she's more potent than liquor. Too beautiful. More than any woman I've ever seen. Intelligent. Fascinating."

Zach smiled. What the heck, he decided, Noah probably wouldn't remember the conversation anyway. "You're the scientist. What's your hypothesis?"

"Lust."

"Hmm, could be." He paused a beat. "Or, maybe you love her. Maybe you always have."

Noah's eyes opened, watery and bloodshot. He raised an inch off the mattress. "I don't love her. Impulsive, headstrong *woman*." He scowled and sank back.

"Be so bad if you did?"

His hand popped up on his stomach. "Disaster... a disaster. Like everything Elle involves herself in. Schools that don't make money and leaking roofs. Watch pockets and pocket watches. A nymph's body. Thanks, but I'll take a rational... judicious woman if I ever marry. No power over me. Disrupt my well-organized life. A proper wife."

"Rational and judicious? Proper? Sounds like a judge to me."

Noah waved this away. "You don't understand. I have a precise plan."

"For what?"

*"Everything."*

Zach banged the chair legs to the floor. "You have a plan for love?"

Noah nodded. "Since university."

"Then what are you doing kissing Ellie? Is she part of your plan?"

His smile dimmed, one eye slit open. "Course not. Unexpected bit of, rather... a circumstance I wasn't expecting. Except, she has lips made for kissing. So, I decided to conduct an experiment, a kissing experiment. Which failed horribly."

"A kissing experiment? You think you can control falling in love with a women like you can control one of your fish experiments?"

"When I have time to devote to marriage, I'll find the perfect woman."

"Perfect?"

"Someone sensible. Someone who doesn't expect me to lasso the moon. Who doesn't gaze at me with big green eyes full of emotion."

"What about not being able to take *your* eyes off her when she enters a room? What about cherishing the sound of her laughter, the way she whispers your name in her sleep? When you love someone, you'll want those things, you'll crave them as much as you crave the air you breathe."

"When I said I had a plan for love"—Noah jammed his thumb under his brace and jerked it clumsily past his elbow—"I guess I meant she would love *me*."

"Elle would love you, if you'd let her."

Noah's fingers clenched around the brace. "I don't want her kind of love."

"What other kind is there?"

"The kind I'm not tempted to return."

Zach gripped the chair, Noah's pain hurting him as badly as his own would. "That's not love at all, then. Noah, you have to let what happened fade into the past. You can't live your life watching over your shoulder, afraid to feel something in your heart. Afraid of what love will cost you."

Noah dropped his arm across his eyes; Zach wondered what he sought to hide. "I loved you, both of you, more than anyone could love his brothers." He swallowed, his throat doing a long draw. "I never wanted—I never wanted to hurt Cale. I couldn't think rationally when I left here. And I hated that. I made too many mistakes, following my heart instead of my mind. I lost both of you. I won't... can't risk that again. Ever again."

"You didn't lose anybody." Zach lowered the other brace from Noah's shoulder and slipped the top button loose on his shirt. As usual with *this* brother, he felt helpless. He didn't know what to say, what to do. Before the night they stumbled upon their mother's diary, the only emotion Caleb had ever shown Noah was love. Protective, fierce love. Zach imagined how Caleb's hostility—and it could be brutal—must have hurt him.

Zach waited until Noah's brow smoothed and his lashes lay motionless against his skin, then he rose from the chair, stretched.

"Home. I should be home," Noah murmured.

"You *are* home."

Zach turned at the sound of the softly spoken words. Caleb stood in the doorway, shoulder propped against the frame, legs crossed at the ankle. The wretched expression on his face belied his indifferent stance. He watched the bed for a sign of movement, twisting a worn hat in his hands.

Zach held a finger to his lips. "Not here."

Their boots thumped on the carpeted staircase, echoing off the sun-streaked kitchen walls as the door swung shut behind them. Zach poured coffee into two cups and sat with a fragile facade of composure.

Caleb slumped into a chair and dropped his hat on the floor. "Is he drunk?" he asked, gazing into his cup as he spooned in sugar.

Zach released a short beat of laughter. "You should recognize the signs of that well enough."

The spoon hit the table with a crack. Coffee splashed over the sides of Caleb's cup, staining the white tablecloth. "Holy Mother Mary, Zach, give me a chance."

"Give you a chance to what?" He pressed his tongue against the back of his teeth and counted to ten.

Caleb plunged his fingers into his hair, cradling his skull. His skin looked as filthy as the tangled strands. "You bastard. Do you think guilt doesn't eat at me every day? How can you do this?"

How *could* he do it? Caleb had mourned Noah's disappearance until Zach believed he'd lost both of them. "I'm sorry. I had no right."

Caleb stared into his coffee. "Don't apologize for speaking the truth."

"Let's cut the self-pity. Past time this family set things straight."

"Dammit, Zach! I've been to that old crone's back house, or whatever the hell you call it, three times. I talked to the fisherman and got him on the boats. What more do you want me to do? Kidnap him?"

"You don't have to kidnap him. I've done that for you."

Caleb's head lifted, his eyes shining like polished silver. "I guess you've got more courage than I do, brother." Pushing from the table, he dropped his cup in the sink and paced to the window. He shoved the curtain aside, his broad shoulders as unyielding as his pride.

Zach looked closely at the curtains for the first time in years. Yellow with little daisy things sewn around the edges. Funny, he remembered Hannah saying she liked them. Must be why they still hung there. "Where have you been?" he finally asked, skimming his cup in a gradual circle.

"The warehouse. A delayed shipment of sails. Fisherman coming down from New England for a boat next week." Caleb's gaze sliced toward Zach, a half smile twisting his lips. "Where'd you think?"

Zach shrugged, chagrined to admit he usually thought the worst.

"Obviously, Noah was keeping my space warm at the Nook." Caleb thumped his knuckle against the windowpane. "At least two of the Garrett men enjoy the entertainment Christa's has to offer. Remember those lovely creatures, Zachariah old boy? Called women?"

Zach ignored the familiar jibe. "I'm working this afternoon. Will you stay, talk to him after he wakes up? I'm not sure he's going to remember walking home."

Caleb stiffened. "How do you know he'll want to talk to me?"

"I don't."

"You'd love it if he blew outta here after telling me to go to hell, wouldn't you?"

"Oh, for pity's sake, Cale, don't be ridiculous." Zach's hand flexed around his cup. "For once in your life, just think before you charge in like a wild bull. That's all the advice I can offer."

"What went on last night? Something happen to upset him?"

"Start with that question. Should get the ball rolling."

"Not going to make it any easier on me, are you, Constable?"

"Nope."

"I saw him yesterday, on the boardwalk with Ellie. They were fussing, if I had to make a guess. I considered going on up to them, but the look on her face stopped me. She loved Noah so much. You remember. Heck, the whole town remembers, she made such a goose of herself." He tugged his hand through his hair, sending it into further disarray. "And you know tough-hide Professor. If he did feel anything for her, he never let it show. I always reckoned he just found it irritating, like a nagging rock in his shoe. We were only kids but"—he shrugged—"if the drinking spell has to do with *her*, I think I'm too much of a coward to ask."

"Just talk to him, Cale. Nothing more, nothing less."

Caleb braced his hands on either side of the window frame and propped his brow against the pane, a long sigh his only reply.

~

Noah reached for her.

He managed to grasp a lock of hair between his fingers, a cinnamon streak sliding across his skin. Elle laughed and kicked her feet, sailing higher. She smiled, and he felt a catch in his chest that could easily be called an ache.

In a slow backward arch, the wooden swing whizzed by him. He grabbed the rope and jerked it to his side, trailing his fingers along the empty seat.

Empty.

Noah blinked, squinted.

Where was he?

He reared from the mattress and groaned, a headache nearly splitting his head in two. His shoulders quivered as he struggled to sit, cradling his face in his hands. That didn't halt the crew building a modest structure in his brain.

He'd been dreaming of Elle, he realized, noting the effect the dream had had on his body. The blanket was puffed like a tent. Cursing, he flung the scratchy cover away and swung his feet to the floor. He touched his nose. No spectacles. Not on the table, either. Or in his shirt pocket. He squinted and glanced down. Maybe they had fallen.

Sliding to his knees, he searched the smooth pine. He jerked to a halt, fingering a six-inch gash running as deep as his knuckle.

*"Mama, what's that chip in the floor?" A sugary smell from the cookies she had made earlier in the day scented the fingers she brushed across his cheek.*

*"A Union soldier thought to chop wood in this room. My mother set him straight after one swing of his ax," she said and pressed her lips to his brow.*

Noah swiped at the gash, an ineffectual erasure of the past. Had he gotten so drunk he had come *here?* He searched, trying to remember.

Elle... the alley... sailing... the Nook... a woman's hand on his knee... Christabel pulling him into her parlor.

Zach, she must have called Zach.

Noah slumped against the bed frame, his head pounding with every beat of his heart. *Damn you, Elle, you wanted me to face them, and here I am, doing just that.*

Even at this moment, when he was likely dying, he could taste her, as if he had pressed a kiss to her mouth before rolling from the sheets. The tormenting image that had prompted him to guzzle an entire bottle of Christabel's rotgut whiskey returned, vivid and tangible. His hands propelling Elle's body across his thigh until the very core of her scorched him through his trousers. Blessit, he must have been out of his mind. Never, never in his *life*, had he handled a woman in a reckless, improper manner.

And they had been standing in an *alley*.

The images were so vivid that he questioned—feeling a faint twinge of desperation and a strong dose of fear—how he could erase them. He dropped his head to the mattress and groaned. Why had he bothered getting drunk for the first time in years if it left everything intact like a damned painting?

Glancing toward the window, he struggled to his feet. Late-afternoon sunlight flooded the room. Had he slept all day? With an oath, he straightened his braces and smoothed the wrinkles from his shirt. He had missed his morning meeting with Tyre Mcintosh, and he certainly couldn't go to the lab site stinking of whiskey. He brought his sleeve to his nose and sniffed, the action throwing him off-balance and into the bedside table.

God, he was a mess.

Feeling his way, he shuffled along the hallway and down the staircase. Familiarity eliminated the need for spectacles. He knew the house as well as he knew his face in a mirror. Luckily, his blurred vision kept the memories from burying him alive.

He entered the kitchen hesitantly. The smell of coffee and sausage greeted him, but no brothers. Swallowing hard, he rushed outside and inhaled a clear breath. *I'll never drink again,* he vowed.

It hadn't done any good, anyway. Elle still lingered.

What was he doing, stumbling around his family's house, waiting for a confrontation he didn't want? Or maybe he did want to face them... oh, hell, face *Caleb.*

Gathering his courage, he took a halting step. The shed, vague but tangible, sat in the back corner of the yard, sheltered from direct sunlight by a snarl of pine branches. Noah had always wondered if Caleb had chopped it to bits with the ax he'd used to destroy their models. The door creaked when he put his elbow to it, a harsh, forsaken sound.

A bird screeched and darted through a hole as he ducked inside. He mopped a cobweb from his face and turned in a slow circle. The smell of glue and raw wood had been replaced by the stale scent of abandonment. Smoothing his hand across the pine workbench Zach had made for them one Christmas, he found a tiny paintbrush tucked into a split and rolled it out with the pad of his finger.

A grinding sound fractured the silence. Noah turned more swiftly than his body could adjust to, and he bumped against the bench.

"Noah?"

He shaded his eyes. A muscular shape outlined by a thin halo of light, shoulders stretching the width of the doorway. Could be a hundred different men. But the voice called to him in his dreams.

"Caleb," he said, sounding as rusty as the shed's hinges.

"What the heck are you doing out here?"

He searched for an even tone. "Call me a sentimental fool, but I just had to see the place you redecorated with an ax. You've done a lot with it since then."

"Dammit, Noah." Caleb stalked into the weak stream of sunlight.

Noah rolled the paintbrush in his hands, his palms warming. He bent his head, shielding his expression from clumsy inspection. Beside his knee, a spider hunkered in a web spread between the bench legs. A hapless deerfly struggled in the lower corner. He watched the spider crawl toward its prey, experiencing a strange kinship with the luckless insect. "I was just looking for my spectacles. Have you seen them?"

"You and Zach are both heartless. Fine, if you want to be that way."

Caleb drove his fingers through his hair, leaving it sticking up in a half dozen places. The face in Noah's memory altered to the one before him. It was the first time he had been this close to his brother in ten years.

He inhaled deeply to return his breathing to normal. "I hate to tell you this, Cale, but there's a big black spider spinning a dazzling web right next to me. Probably babies scurrying across the floor. You know they hatch thousands at a time."

Caleb gingerly lifted one booted foot, then the other. He glanced into each corner of the shed. A shudder shook his shoulders and rippled down his arms. Uttering a growl and a curse, he curled his hands into fists and turned on his heel. The door slapped against the inside wall, flooding the enclosure with light.

Noah hung his head and laughed, gasping for breath, his head pounding until he feared he would be sick. The barrier he had erected in a blind panic years before crumbled beneath him.

"Get out here, you skinny bastard!"

Strangely, the jagged slivers scattered beneath his feet—fragments of models he and Caleb had constructed, their knees scraping the underside of the bench, glue coating their fingertips—flooded him with tender emotion. Devotion and security, hope and concern. He regretted the past, profoundly, but for the first time in years, he did not fear the future.

He stepped from the shed, a gust of wind pressing his shirt against his chest. He tipped his head, observing a blazing sunset of deep rose, blue and green.

Emerald green.

"Noah?"

Wagon wheels clattered over crushed shell, and a dog yipped in the distance, but he heard only Elle's accented, dulcet whisper. The paintbrush snapped in two in his fingers.

"You okay?" Caleb stripped a piece of bark from the tree he leaned against and sent Noah a worried frown. "How about coming inside and having dinner? I caught two flounder and four blue this morning. We can"—he coughed, shrugged—"talk."

"How big are the blue?"

"One's a good five pounds, at least. They were running like crazy in the edge."

"Bleed and ice them yet?" Noah lifted his finger to his nose, forgetting his absent spectacles.

"I'm not some blamed ocean scientist, but I think I can clean fish well enough to suit most folks."

Noah forced his feet to move until he stood by his brother's side, registering the jolt of surprise as he realized the top of Caleb's head barely met his chin. "We'll see. Cleaning them never was your strong suit. Or cooking them, for that matter."

"Heck, little bro', you can do the cooking." Caleb winked and strode along the worn path with the same reckless energy Noah remembered. Ejecting a labored sigh, he followed with the beleaguered step of one being coerced, but he could not deny the happiness in his heart.

Noah flipped the fish and leaned back, a bubble of oil bursting in the sizzling iron skillet. A drop struck his hand, and he cursed, sucking the singed skin between his lips. Behind him, the screen door squeaked and a small projectile slammed into his legs, throwing him into the counter.

"Oh, you're here," Rory said, the delight in his voice bringing a wide smile to Noah's face. "Uncle Caleb said you would never come here, ever again."

Noah pressed Rory's cheek against his hip. "What does your Uncle Caleb know anyway?" A prickle of awareness intruded; he lifted his head. Elle stood in the doorway, her hair tousled by the wind or impatient fingers, her eyes dulled by exhaustion. He snatched his hand from his mouth and willed his heart to slow.

Ignoring him, she smiled at Rory. "Go wash your hands. Wouldn't hurt your face to hit some soap, either."

Rory lifted shining eyes and fairly danced in place. "Are you staying for dinner? Are you, huh? Guess what? I caught a sheepshead fishing with Jason. I told him what you said, about how they use those pointy teeth to chew barnacles off rocks. He called me a liar, so I slugged him."

"*Rory.*" Elle stepped forward and lightly swatted Rory on the behind. "Upstairs. Now. And, I think you should apologize to Jason tomorrow or your father is going to find out what happened today."

Rory shuffled his feet. "Do I have to, Uncle Noah?"

Noah lifted his head, his gaze seizing Elle's and holding. His fingers itched to slip the loose tendril brushing her cheek back into her hairclip. He turned before his regard strayed to other parts of her body.

And that regard, in turn, affected certain parts of his.

"Miss Elle's right. You *will* apologize to Jason tomorrow." He grabbed a spatula and scooped the fish from the skillet. "Just because someone doesn't believe something you've said is no reason to slug them. Hitting never solves any problems. Trust me."

"Yeah, all right, I'll trust you," Rory said, clearly unconvinced. "But I still think Jason is a poop." Before Elle could get to him, he raced from the kitchen, his feet pounding on the stairs.

Elle's step was light and brisk, the swish of her skirt gentle music to his ears. Let her go, he ordered. *Let her go.*

"Elle, wait." He tossed the spatula to the counter and glanced over his shoulder to find her with one hand on the door, glancing over hers. "About yesterday." He snatched a dishrag from a hook and wiped his hands, his eyes everywhere but on her. "I don't know—"

"Save your awkward apologies, Professor. Merciful heavens, it's clear you *don't know.*"

He knotted the rag between his fingers. "What do you want from me? I let myself get out of control. I take full responsibility, and I'm sorry."

"I never asked you to take responsibility. Or be sorry. In fact, I told you *not* to be."

"Well, I am." A rush of apprehension threatened to buckle his knees. "Aren't you?"

She swallowed—a long, slow pull. "Of course."

*A pause.* A full second pause. He had seen it. "You're lying," he said. "What did you do, Elle? Oh, God, you didn't. Did you wait for me to come to you last night?"

In reply, a rosy streak grazed each cheek.

Her blush mirroring his desire, he spun around, afraid to look at her, yet obsessed with imagining how she looked. She had waited... wanting him and knowing what it would lead to. "So, that's the smell."

"Smell?"

"A different scent on your skin. Perfume. Real perfume." He slapped the rag to the counter. "Roses?"

"Honeysuckle. I usually put it in my shampoo."

He gripped the counter edge and prayed for restraint. His mind was trying to fool him into believing it had been years since he'd touched her instead of hours. "Elle," he said tightly, "you play a dangerous game."

"Yes, I've been told before."

He had her by the shoulders before either of them spoke or breathed. "What do you mean?" If Magnus Leland—

"My father. He... he told me that once."

Noah closed his eyes, shamed and infuriated by his reaction. He inhaled, then wished to hell he hadn't. Who knew a man could be thrown off his feet by honeysuckle? "Elle, I wish things were different." He halted. The squeaky floorboard just inside the kitchen. Turning his head, he watched Zach pile into Caleb, who stood stock-still in the doorway, jaw so slack it touched his chest.

Elle used both hands to brush past him. The door banged behind her. Noah glanced out in time to see her turning the corner, her hips swinging beneath another delightfully tattered dress. He pressed his brow to the rusted screen and sighed.

"What the heck—"

"—is going on between you two?"

"Nothing." Then he dared his brothers to dispute him.

# CHAPTER EIGHT

"*At the time, however, it was merely an expression of individual opinion.*"
~ C. Wyville Thomson
*The Depths of the Sea*

~

*a* sunset blaze of red and gold had seized the sky by the time Noah made it to the dance. He hitched his hip on the skiff and slipped on the canvas shoes he had purchased the day before. He surveyed the crowd of people gathered round the campfires, some dodging the sizzling flash of dripping meat, others using driftwood to bury potatoes deep in ash.

Lifting his head, he scanned the horizon, noting with a faint sense of unease the layer of mist drifting in from the east. As he glanced at the line of flower-bedecked skiffs, all waiting for steady hands to sail them home, his apprehension heightened.

As he walked along the packed sand, music, laughter, and conversation flowed from a tent constructed of hastily sewn blankets and yards of mosquito netting. Couples floated by, silhouetted by the glow of oil lanterns swinging in time to the whim of the wind. Was Elle inside, dancing with Daniel Connery or some other young man? Her skin scented with honeysuckle, perhaps, or bright sunshine and damp earth? Plucking a scallop shell from the sand, he traced the ribbed edges and wondered if the hot flare in his chest was jealousy.

In the three days since, there had been no mention of the passionate kiss or his brusque apology. In fact, there had been no conversation at all. An abrupt greeting in front of the post office and a lengthy stare across a packed mercantile shelf.

Did the empty ache mean he missed her?

Noah neared the tent, the hum of sound increasing. A group of drunken whalers dodged him, pouring from the V-shaped opening. Hesitating, he observed the joyful display of camaraderie with a sense of detachment. Here he was, a man of considerable means and education, yet he found himself seeking refuge in an emotional storm. Zach, Caleb, Elle. The three people in the world he had once been completely at ease with. Maybe *that* laid bare his childhood protection of Elle, not to save her but to save himself.

Bunched sprays of daisies and carnations brushed his shoulder as he ducked inside. He looked merely for the sake of curiosity, searching the outer circle. His height made the task easy. That, and the undeniable cognizance he experienced whenever she was near. A whisper of air leaked past his lips, and his body warmed. She stood just inside the tent's triangular back entrance, a crush of people whisking by her.

For days, he had been unable to erase this truth from his mind: *she had waited for him.* Put perfume on her skin and waited. Knowing he would take her virginity and... leave.

Then again, Elle had the courage to grasp what she desired.

She laughed and tossed her head, exposing the lithe arch of her neck. Smooth and sweet beneath his lips, he remembered. She tucked a stray wisp of hair behind her ear, and he marveled at his witlessness. Elle Beaumont was radiant, validated in the golden wash from the oil lamp by her side. It was not wholly physical, this radiance. It flowed from her lively green eyes, from the hands she moved so exuberantly in conversation, from the confident stride that carried her along the boardwalk.

Noah admired her vivacity, her sincerity, yet he *hated* the loss of control being near her brought.

Averting his gaze, he corrected his thought: he *feared* it.

Immaculate black canvas in a sea of dirty leather and sandy buck. Elle concentrated on those shoes as they moved through the crowd. She laughed during the appropriate pauses in conversation and nodded her head often, hearing absolutely nothing.

With covert glances, she peeked. Noah spoke to each man who stopped him with a slap on the back or a punch to the chest. He accepted the gestures of friendship, a calm facade hiding his bewilderment. She recognized his discomfiture as if it were her own.

"Elle, dear, what do you think?"

Startled, Elle glanced at the women surrounding her. She forced a smile. "That would be lovely, of course."

Heads bobbing, they agreed.

When the conversation lagged, Elle searched. Her fingers curled, nails digging into her skin. Meredith Scoggins stood next to Noah, her hand on his arm, her head lifted toward his. Blatant interest. A group of Meredith's friends circled, shifting Noah's cohorts to the outer circle.

A hulking, red-faced seaman tapped Meredith on the shoulder and she turned, giggling in delight. Noah's charcoal gaze immediately captured Elle's. He shoved his spectacles up, a scowl crossing his face.

*What?* Elle shrugged with a passiveness she didn't feel.

*Stop staring.*

*Me?* She patted her chest.

His gaze lowered then jerked to her face. *Yes. You.*

*I'm not staring.* Elle gestured to the oblivious, jabbering group of women.

He pursed his lips—an appealing pout, part-boy, part-man. A wave of desire swept from the tips of her fingers to her knees. Elle glanced around, frantic. The women chatted and fluttered, never noticing the color in her cheeks.

Daniel Connery, in the most fortuitous action of his life, chose that moment to ask her to dance.

She raced into his arms.

~

"See the way she stares at him, Doc. All dopey-eyed." Stymie shifted a wad of tobacco from one side of his jaw to the other, his watery gaze focused on the dance area. "Loony woman still loves the professor better than Peter loved the Lord."

"Shut up, you old fool," Magnus said and stalked off.

Stymie scratched his head and spit. "Wonder what put him in a stew."

Henri Beaumont linked his fingers over his bulging stomach, recording Leland's exit. Unfortunately Henri could not argue with the stinking fisherman's verdict.

For he had also recorded his daughter's impassioned display. *Mon Dieu.* She still looked at young Garrett like a lovesick pup. A blind pup. It made Henri realize he had been too lenient. By half. Waiting for his daughter to properly secure a promising future. Absurd to imagine a woman making a choice, *any* choice, and choosing well. Twice, he'd allowed her to go against his wishes. Against his better judgment. Evidently, a weakness of paternal love. University, for God's sake. What good had that done? His second mistake had involved allowing her to act as housemaid to a crotchety old woman.

What did Marielle-Claire think? That he would live forever? Provide for her *after* she came to her senses and moved back home? Didn't she realize she needed a man to guide her? Protect her? Didn't she realize *he*, Henri Beaumont, wanted grandsons?

Now this. *Merde.*

He had prayed the boy would never show his face on Pilot Isle again. Though he would have gladly kissed young Garrett's feet if he had shown an inkling of interest in marrying Marielle-Claire. Unquestionably the most handsome member of his family. Intelligent. Successful. Upon hearing of the boy's return, Henri had made it his business to discover which of the circulating rumors were true. Discreet inquiries.

Henri watched young Garrett shrug free of a clutching female hand. A marine biologist. True. He taught biology at a well-respected institution in Chicago. Furthermore, he had completed research aboard a government fishing vessel *and* written essays for a scientific manual.

Tapping his fingers on his belly, Henri struggled to recall the description the investigator used. Ah, yes: a rising star in his field. A rising star would have suited Marielle-Claire very well indeed. Exceptionally bright his daughter. And she had never lacked beauty.

Henri followed Noah's progress through a sea of simpering pouts, fluttering eyelashes, and teasing smiles. Yes, young Garrett would have forced the hand. Henri's grandsons would have been assured of possessing intelligence *and* good looks.

In this instance, his daughter had been an excellent judge of character. She'd recognized the boy's value long before the others. Yearned for him when he was no more than an ashen, bespectacled lad.

Henri exited the tent and headed for poor Leland, who stood with his back to the festivities. Henri wished he were home drinking a glass of Bordeaux instead of standing outside a homespun tent, sand lodged beneath his fingernails, sweat adhering his tailored shirt to his skin. *Mon Dieu,* how he hated the ocean. If not for his business interests, he would move inland as far as he could get.

Tonight's performance showed that young Garrett didn't want Marielle-Claire, would never want her. Oh, Henri didn't doubt the boy lusted after her; she probably threw herself at him. If Henri had devised a way to force the issue of marriage, involving the woman his investigator had located would have been unnecessary. Regrettably, the situation grew dire and required him to utilize the information he possessed.

Strange, but Henri found it hard to believe the boy had a married lover. He did not object; celibacy was reserved for feeble men and unmarried women.

His daughter, for example.

His fingers clenched over his paisley waistcoat. He would be damned before he let her make a mistake that would ruin her future.

～

As Daniel laughed and spun her through a wide turn, she returned his laughter. He liked her, she supposed. She also recognized....

Elle chewed on her lip, trying to remember the word Christa had mentioned to her. *Horny.* Daniel was horny.

But what did that matter? He was safe. He made her feel attractive without consequence. If he held her a little closer than she liked, it wasn't close enough to cause the church committee members to titter behind their hands. Moreover, he didn't make her heart miss even a beat. Hence, carelessly confident, she flirted.

Until she caught sight of Noah leading Meredith into the circle of dancers. The girl giggled and simpered, seeming to shimmy in her satin slippers.

Truly, she found it hard to record one man's movements while locked in another's arms, but she managed. Noah bestowed a slow, sweeping smile upon his dance partner, his fingers splayed across her back. Elle observed and pondered and felt sick inside.

"Daniel, can we stop for a moment? I need a breath of air."

"Sure, Ellie." Cupping her elbow, he escorted her outside the tent.

The night was pitch-black, the crescent moon's glow dulled by a layer of fog. The wind kicked at her skirt as she searched for a source of light. Saffron flames from one of the campfires, a ray of moonlight, anything. Worrying her lip between her teeth, she began to think she might have made a mistake asking a horny man to walk alone with her.

"Um, Daniel—"

"Excuse me, I'm afraid there's a problem with the flowers."

Elle turned, stumbling over a burrow in the sand. "Flowers?"

"Come along, flower girl." Noah grasped her wrist and yanked her behind him, contradicting his absurd pretext by dragging her away from the tent and any flowers to be found. When they neared the dunes, he halted and flung her hand away. "Elle, do you have any idea how long that man has been confined to a ship? With no women in sight."

"Six months, I believe he told me. I know, I know"—she dipped her toes into the sand—"he's very horny."

Noah's head whipped around. *"What?"*

Elle shook sand from her foot. "He's horny. Christabel told me it's the same as being lonely, except a special way a man is lonely. She said this feeling makes men confused."

"Dear God," Noah said beneath his breath.

"Well, does it?"

He dropped to the dune with a resigned sigh. "Yes."

Elle plopped beside him, crossed her arms behind her head, and rolled flat. Noah sighed again, but after a moment he followed.

For some time, they lay gazing into a sky absent of stars, listening to the warble of locusts and the wash of the ocean, the sand cool and solid beneath them. The moment seemed perfect, frozen in time. She feared a movement, a sound, a breath, would shatter it. The completeness flooding her heart was a delusion. Surely, it was a delusion.

"Shut your eyes," he whispered, close to her ear. "Listen. There's so much."

She did as he asked, opened her mind to the enchantment of a peaceful night, the allure of the sea. She wanted to witness the world through him. "I hear a bird."

"An oystercatcher. She's sounding an alarm because someone is nearing her nest."

Elle waited, more sounds coming together. "Scraping. The hull of a skiff against the sand as it shoves off. A crackle. Driftwood burning on one of the campfires."

"Good." She recognized the smile in his voice.

"I can hear... breaths slipping from your lips."

Sand shifted as he turned toward her, shifted again as he lay back. Finally, he said, "I can hear yours, too."

A wisp of wind carried his scent. She drew the fragrance in and

131

held it close, tucked it in the secret place where she tucked all her memories of Noah. Her love for him.

"Tell me about university, Elle."

Her arms stiffened beneath her head. "What's there to tell?"

"Did you ever consider going back?"

A hundred times. A thousand. "Once or twice."

He paused, seemed to deliberate. "Lack of funds stopped you?"

She laughed. "Oh, Noah, only a person with a surplus of funds would ask such a question."

"If the problem is purely financial, I could help."

"You offer from a sense of duty. The same sense of duty you curse for getting you into every pickle involving me." She blinked, startled by the haze of fog enclosing them and the clear notion she had of his thoughts. "I know leaving Pilot Isle would be easier if you believe my future is wrapped in a nice, tidy package. Check an obligation off your list and move to the next."

"Dammit, you twist everything until I'm not sure what I mean. Someone once offered me what I offer you. I didn't want to, but I took it."

She turned to her side, propping her chin on her hand. "Who?"

"It was a long time ago. Doesn't matter now. I paid the loan back. By any means possible." He rolled his head toward her, a fierce light in his eyes. "Elle, I wouldn't expect—"

She pressed her finger to his lips, ignoring the way their skin melded. "You're the first person to understand an education meant something to me besides the chance to leave Pilot Isle, and for that, I thank you. Sometimes, I think, people have to fight their own battles. *Need* to. I let you fight mine before, and it shot a gaping hole in my judgment." She considered a moment, then nodded. "I'd like to take the next step, whatever that may be."

His expression grew pensive; his gaze darkened. Beneath her finger, she felt his lips parting, his tongue—

Leaping to her feet, she followed the edge of the dune, her gait awkward in the ankle-deep sand. She lifted her fingers to her lips, her hand shaking so badly she couldn't hold it steady before her face.

"If you follow this path"—settling in beside her, Noah gestured to a break in the dune—"it runs through a forest of loblolly pine, to the southern edge of the island. I noticed some artificial light coming from the lumber wharf when I was collecting plankton samples last week. Loggerhead turtles will be attracted to the light come late July. Take Rory to see them deposit their eggs. You can't miss the flipper bites in the sand. Just look for a broad V-shaped impression."

She watched him jerk his shirttail from his trousers and swab his spectacle lenses. "You can show him, Noah."

"I'll be gone by then," he said without looking up.

"I don't understand. If you love this"—she gestured to their surroundings—"why choose to live in Chicago? If you love your family, how can you stand to be apart from them?"

He jammed his spectacles in place and climbed the dune, his attention centered on the sea. A layer of gray mist enclosed him, giving him a ghostly appearance. "I have responsibilities. A calling I'm dedicated to, one I treasure. My profession demands most of my time and my strength. I've gotten used to making sacrifices."

Lifting her skirt, she climbed after him. "Will leaving be a sacrifice?"

He waited so long, she thought he wasn't going to reply. "Maybe," he finally said.

"Stay, then," she whispered, shocked to hear the plea come from her mouth. *Stay, and I'll rip up Savannah's application, I'll run my school and....*

She shook her head, confusion robbing her of breath. For the first time, she did what Noah had been begging her to do her entire life. She listened to her *mind,* not her heart. One desire shone bright and clear. *I want to finish university.* She did not want to destroy the scholarship application. Not even for the sensitive, passionate, intelligent man standing next to her.

Not even for him.

Intent on telling him, she turned. Before she could, he had her chin between his fingers. Regret and torment darkened his eyes. "I can't stay, Elle. Please don't—promise me you won't ask again."

With a nod of finality, she promised.

"Thank you, flower girl." He trailed the back of his hand along her cheek. His smoldering gaze followed.

"Flower girl?" The words came out in a hoarse whisper.

His knuckle skimmed her jaw. "The other night. The scent of honeysuckle on your skin." His lips parted. "I haven't been able to erase the scent, or you, from my mind." He leaned in, his lids drooping low.

*A jolt of awareness shook her. Heart and soul, every inch of her readied for his touch. I love you. I won't ever kiss you again and not tell myself, tell you if you'll listen. You can fool yourself, Noah Garrett, into believing it's simply passion we share, but I know better.*

Just before his lips captured hers, a raw-throated scream broke them apart.

The situation at the edge of the surf came as close to complete and utter chaos as any Noah had ever seen. People shoved past him, stumbling toward, or over, the beached skiffs. Men grappled with lines and dug oars from the bilge, swaying from drink. Hoarse shouts of alarm and hands raised to the heavens became the pattern in a matter of a minute. He didn't have to ask what had happened. The distant, savage groan of a ship's hull being fractured against the shoals rang through the night.

A sound you only had to hear once to remember forever.

"Shipwreck," Elle breathed by his side.

Half-turning, he gripped her shoulders. "Don't even think of getting near the water. I mean it, Elle. Don't even *think* of it." He let her go—before he did something stupid like kiss the woman he had wanted to kiss all night—and plunged into the throng.

He scanned the beach for a sign of Zach. The fog made it impossible to see more than twenty yards. Blessit, what a night to put the test to the lifesaving crew's preparedness. Noah had not encountered one sober man yet.

He snagged Daniel Connery's arm. "Zach? Have you seen Zach?"

Daniel jerked the length of rope in his hands, tightening the square knot. "Hundred yards down. By the edge. Where the wreckage is washing up. Look for the flares."

Noah kicked off his shoes and sprinted, lungs near to bursting, eyes tearing behind his lenses. He caught sight of Zach, then Caleb, standing in a small group of men he recognized as members of Zach's patrol. When he reached them, his brothers were involved in a heated exchange.

"The ship's too far out to fire the breeches buoy, Cale."

"You can't go." Caleb shoved Zach in the chest. "I found you sleeping on the damned beach, and now, you want to be some hero? Nobody here is fit to sail. You aiming to lose one of your men, Constable?"

Wavering flares splayed a blazing ring of light across the sand, casting the men in brushstrokes of gold. With a shift in wind, Noah noted the potent stench of whiskey drifting from them. "I'll go." He shoved inside the circle. "Do we know the location? What kind of ship? How many men?"

"*Noah, no.*" Caleb flinched, equal measures of fear and fury etching his face.

Noah met Zach's startled gaze. "Instead of standing here arguing about what man in this group of six is fit to sail, you'd better worry about the group of fifty down the beach who aren't and are preparing to capture their moment of glory."

Zach yanked an unsteady hand through his hair. He looked from Noah to Caleb to the ocean and back.

"Go on, Zach. Take your men with you. Someone needs to control what's going on." Noah tipped his head in the direction of the tent.

Zach nodded and said to the man next to him, "Get Seaman Bennett." He gripped Noah's shoulder, squeezed once, then shouldered through the group.

"Dammit." Caleb slammed his fist into the open palm of his other hand.

A boy no older than sixteen appeared at the edge of the circle, a ragged blanket fisted at his neck, a mop of red hair standing at stiff angles about his head. Shivers shook his gaunt shoulders and rocked him where he stood. "Si-Sir?"

Noah stepped forward. "Tell me what you can, son. Anything you can. Quickly."

"I'm a seaman on the *Queen's Jewel*, sir. A wooden clipper, eleven on board. No passengers, praise be. Headed to Charleston with a cargo of woolpacks, printing paper, and ironmongery. We sailed past Hatteras without incident and the cap'n, he said making it past the watery graveyard should be cause for celebration. So he opened a crate of fine brandy, of which two hundred cases was stored below. The cap'n, he was the worse for drink lots of times." The boy glanced around and wiped his nose on the blanket. "But this time he was staggering before the breakers was even sighted. We weren't concerned, sir, reading the calm weather. Then the fog, she rolled in heavy as a mama's teat, and the cap'n, he mistook the Cape lighthouse for something it weren't." The boy shivered, his throat working.

"Go on," Noah said.

"At half past, the fog was swelling and the night getting darker and darker. Then, sudden like, the *Jewel*, she bounced hard on the shoal, sir. The man on lookout, he began signaling. We tried to wear around, almost got it when she swung, broadside on, with her head to the southward. The after port and starboard boats were cleared and lowered, both hitting water about the same time." The boy's lids fluttered and he quaked. "I was in the... lee boat, sir. Me and Deck O'Malley. The boat on the weather side, sh-she got caught by a swell. Dashed under the ship's counter like a finger... shoved her there. They screamed. And the sea? She just roared."

Noah swallowed past the rise of sickness. "Get him out of here. Someone get him out of here. Keep him warm and put some food in his belly."

Jeb Crow seized Seaman Bennett's arm and led him away. The boy turned and yelled, "O'Malley, he washed over the side. I tried to help him. Clinging to debris the... last time I saw him, sir. To a scrap of skiff, sir."

"A skiff." Noah closed his mind to the distant sounds of destruction. "Someone's skiff got tangled with the clipper."

Caleb wrenched him around by the shoulder. "I'm going with you."

"I've done this before, Cale. Remember?" He slipped his spectacles in his pocket and strode down the beach, the wind whipping his hair into his face. "I'd simply forgotten how ghastly looking for survivors is."

"Can you see without those things?" He nodded toward Noah's pocket.

"Well enough."

"Goddammit, I'm going. You can't stop me."

"Cale—"

"You need me on this one, little bro.'"

Noah halted by the boat and cocked his head, looking into stubborn gray eyes exactly like his own. "Maybe I do."

# CHAPTER NINE

*"They might have been caught on the way."*
~ C. Wyville Thomson
*The Depths of the Sea*

~

"**Y**ou let them go?" Elle hurried alongside Zach, trying to contain the quiver in her voice.

He stopped and waited for her to backtrack before he answered. "Do you think I wanted to send them out in this mess? Fog so thick I could carve a design in it." Swishing his foot through the bubbly froth at the water's edge, he said, "I can't allow anyone standing on this beach to go. I was lucky to find six capable volunteers. Lucky we're only searching for ten seamen. Plenty of space to bring them back if they're found. Maybe they'll even locate some of the cargo."

Elle seized a scrap of wood as it washed against her boot. A perfectly planed, smoothly varnished splinter. "Part of the hull." She let it fall to the beach.

Zach dropped to his haunches and covered his face with his hands.

The wind tossed strands of black hair against his fingers. "I'm resigning this post. Am I so responsible for these shipwrecks that I put my family at risk? How can I control what happens on those blasted shoals?"

Sinking beside him, she hugged her knees to her chest. Waves lapped at her feet. "I'm sorry I said that about letting Noah go."

"Oh, Elle." He shook his head. "Have you told him?"

She laid her cheek on her knee and stared into the fog. "What?"

"That you love him."

She tightened her arms about her legs.

"Tell him before he returns to Chicago. Tell him when his skiff lands on shore. Give him a chance to—"

"To cringe and back away as if I had the plague?"

"He's not that frightened of you."

"Close."

"What about Christa's—"

"She *told* you." Elle's hand shot out; a shower of water drenched his trouser leg.

"A little." He plucked at the damp cloth.

"Wonderful. Everyone in town knows I kissed Noah in the alley behind the Nook. Of course, they imagine I hauled him there. Poor beleaguered man."

"No, you're wrong. She only told me because...."

"Told you because of what?"

He stood and dusted the seat of his trousers. "I've got to get back. Make sure Jeb is keeping the boats anchored."

She yanked him off balance. "Tell me."

"All right! I had to get him at Christa's." He tugged his arm loose. "He was a mess. Almost as bad as Caleb at his worst."

"The parlor? Was he in the parlor?"

Displeasure hardened his jaw. "How do you know about *the parlor*, Elle?"

"Was he?"

Grunting once, he strode away.

Elle raced after him. "Zach, *please.*"

"I don't think he would appreciate me telling you this." He flicked a nervous glance at her. "I mean, he didn't say, not in so many words. Not to give you some idea he said anything. Blast, I just don't want to betray his confidence. He's always been, you know." He waved his hand in a circle at his side, rummaging.

"Private."

"Yes. Private."

She averted her eyes, refusing to beg. She'd done enough to last three lifetimes. A few feet up the beach, Seaman Bennett slouched against an ale barrel, the glow from a campfire revealing a face aged by tragedy. "I'll go to him." She headed the boy's way.

"Ellie?"

She glanced over her shoulder.

"Since the first day Noah brought you home, I've loved you like a sister. Caleb and I have never made a secret of it. But this"—his gaze shifted—"I'm torn in two about it. I don't know whether to push you two together, shove you apart, or stick my blasted head in the sand and mind my own business. I've never understood what Noah was thinking, and I guess this time, I don't have a good clue about you, either."

As his words battled past her bewilderment, a burst of love flooded her heart. "Zach?"

He abandoned his study of the sea, his eyes bright with fear.

"Noah's safe." She placed her hand on her chest. "I would know if he weren't."

"The other night, Ellie, I saw a flicker of something when he— when he talked about you. I think you should tell him how you feel, give him a chance to make good on it this time." He returned his regard to the sea. "I believe he wants to."

For the next hour, she comforted Seaman Bennett and watched the waves for a sign of Noah's skiff. The seed of hope Zach's words had planted in her foolish, forgiving heart flourished with each breath she drew.

∾

"Starboard, Caleb," Noah yelled, hand cupped around his mouth to elevate his words above the deafening roar of the clipper's hull splitting apart, seam by seam. He swabbed his spectacle lenses, practically useless from the spray kicking into his face.

He glanced at the two seamen huddled in the stern. They looked all of sixteen, tear-streaked faces and pink noses. He and Caleb had come upon them clinging to a section of the hull.

"Where?" Caleb threw his hands up.

Noah squinted, a dull ache beginning to pound behind his eyes. If only the moon shone brighter, and the blessed fog rolled out to sea. Still, something... a flash of color, fifty yards ahead. He pointed.

With a deft torque, Caleb circled the skiff and rowed like the devil, muscles bunching beneath the dark material plastered to his chest. He dabbed at the blood on his cheek, the result of a slap from the flat side of an oar. "Dammit, Noah." He maneuvered through the debris surrounding them.

"One more pass, Cale!"

Caleb slapped the oar to the water, his voice rising above the shrieking wind. "The fog... thicker... sucked under."

Noah stared at what remained of the clipper, knowing his brother spoke the truth. The ship lay port side to shore, a doomed position. Coupled with the fog and the hunks of debris keeping them from moving closer, the chances of finding anyone alive were slim. He and Caleb had already had a fierce argument in front of the wild-eyed young seamen. Afraid to terrify them further, Noah had relinquished the oars and agreed to leave. Only, some thread of recognition or... ah, he didn't *know*, but he had to try again. Holding up his finger, he mouthed, "Once more."

Caleb scowled and dug in, sending the boat in an angry skip.

Jagged fragments of wood cracked the hull as they cleaved the water in two. Pages from a book and a leather boot floated past. A pair of men's trousers. Noah gripped the sides and swallowed down a parched throat. Christ, why did he insist upon searching? Death surrounded them. He could sense it, imagined he could smell it, sour, like the scent of rotting meat. If only he was able to erase the image of Seaman Bennett watching Deck O'Malley float away on part of a skiff.

The boat slowed, and Noah looked back to find Caleb dragging the oars.

"No more. Too dangerous."

He shifted on the hard bench, the wind pressing his shirt against his chest. Searching the hazy distance, his urgency puzzled even him. That blessed speck of color would not leave him be. He tucked his spectacles inside the canvas shoe sitting by his bare feet. Catching Caleb's gaze, he dipped his hand down, then up—*I'm going in.*

Caleb wrenched the oar and cursed loudly enough for him to hear.

With a balanced movement, Noah slipped over the side. He lengthened his stroke, shoving debris from his path, the water a cool glide against his skin. Caleb had offered to swim out each time, but Noah excelled in the sport, an advantage that had given him hours of adolescent glee. Besides, he wasn't midway to intoxicated.

Just ahead, part of a skiff bobbed free. And atop it lay a body. Noah paddled forward, lungs near to bursting. *Too late, he'd arrived too late.* Closing in, he slapped his hand against the stern, brought his lips above the surface, and gasped for air.

"I thought your brother... had this skilled group of... sea rescuers. All I get is you."

Noah reared and swallowed water. He hauled himself atop the skiff, coughing.

"Please don't drown... on me, Garrett. I'm afraid I left my... medical bag at the office."

"Leland?"

"Who does it... sound like?" Ruining the show of bravado, the doctor's teeth began to chatter.

Noah dropped his cheek to the notched wood, gulping for breath. "I risked my life for *you?*"

"I'm sorry, Garrett. What does one do... when they helplessly watch men drown, screaming... as their ship is sucked into the sea? As it sucks them into the sea? You may think I'm a... bastard, and I suppose I can be," he said, his voice cracking. "Yet I am also a doctor. I prefer to save lives, not see them... being extinguished in front of me." He groaned, and Noah felt the skiff rock with the force of his shudder.

"Can you swim? Because I don't think I can carry you." Noah blinked, his eyes stinging as if he had shoved a fistful of lye soap in them.

"Of course... I can swim. I wasn't sitting here... waiting to c-catch my breath. Look around you. I didn't have... anywhere *to* swim. Because of the fog, I have no idea how... far we are from shore."

Noah hitched to his elbows. Magnus's bewildered gaze slid his way, and he felt the first real stab of fear. "Who else sailed with you?"

"We came upon the ship so suddenly, I couldn't... t-turn. A slow sail. Not much wind."

Not able to grasp Magnus's shoulders, he put the strength in his tone. "Who, Leland?"

"The clipper's mast, the main one, I think... crashed and caught"— he choked on a sob—"caught us right in the middle of the skiff. A-a clean break."

*"Leland!"*

The doctor's head lolled to the side as he stared into the distance. "She'll never love me now. Not when her father d-died in my skiff."

"Oh, Jesus." Noah pressed his stomach into the curve of the stern to keep from heaving. "Tell me Henri Beaumont isn't out here somewhere."

"On the other side of the skiff," Magnus whispered, his lips tinged blue. "I've been holding... his arm so he doesn't drift away. He's not heavy. Floating, he's floating."

"Holding his arm." Noah wrenched back, plunging into the water. "Cale!" he screamed at the top of his lungs.

Caleb returned a hoarse shout.

He screamed his brother's name again, his thread of control snapping.

A rumble and a shudder. The clipper going under. Noah felt the answering quiver along the surface of the water and the strong tug near his feet. "Hang on, Leland," he said, his teeth beginning to chatter. It sickened him to admit he meant, *hang on to Henri.* He watched the wave swell and braced against the edge of the stern. It roared over them, washing him into a large fragment of the clipper and washing Leland into him.

"We're going to die," Magnus cried and circled Noah's wrist.

Noah shoved Magnus toward the skiff. He nearly retched at the solid bump of another body. "Climb up, Leland. Do it. Caleb's coming." If Caleb's boat hadn't overturned. *Please, God, no.* Starting to shiver, he kicked his feet and grasped the underside of the skiff between numb fingers. "Leland, don't let go—don't let go of Henri."

"Still got him," Leland returned in a singsong voice.

*Hurry, Cale,* he prayed. The frigid water and the biting wind consorted to drive every bit of heat from his body. He never wanted to swim again, yet he dreaded having to step on shore and face Elle.

"I can see you. Just hang on."

He opened his eyes, unaware he had closed them. Kicking his feet, the surface of the water rippled, smooth and gentle this time. The knotted end of a rope thumped the skiff, emitting a startled cry from Magnus. "Leland take the rope."

"Leland?" Caleb leaned out. "What is he doing... Holy Mother Mary!"

Noah groaned. Water lapped against his chin and into his mouth. He coughed and spit it out.

"This is going to kill Ellie." Caleb's voice was rough.

"I'll be there," he said, wondering if that would be enough.

Along the shore, the occasional chip of quartz glittered in the dim moonlight. At the water's edge, a crowd of people gathered. Near the dunes, flickering bursts from a campfire danced across the sand. Long ago, Noah had stopped noticing the rancid smell and Leland's corresponding whimper at each crest and dive of the boat. Long ago, he had stopped feeling his teeth banging together or the searing pain in his side.

Now, Elle's pain consumed him.

When they reached the shore, the men greeted them, voices raised in jubilation and relief. Caleb released the oars as they dragged the boat to the sand. Someone slapped Noah between his shoulder blades and he pitched forward, scraping his palms on the bilge.

The joyful laughter ceased when the men got a look inside the skiff. No one proved quick enough to keep her from meeting them.

"Get her away." The crashing waves smothered Noah's hoarse plea.

He watched her drop to her knees in the edge of the surf, waves striking her beautiful body. He struggled to hold her back.

Her scream, Zach's curse, the boat shifting crazily as she threw herself against it. His lids lowered, obscuring the sight of her face, the horror and revulsion, the devotion. Brave and honest, Elle possessed a fullness of heart that gave her the faith to love when it would likely never be returned measure for measure.

He and Henri Beaumont shared this betrayal, Noah realized.

Swaying forward, he flailed, meaning to protect her. A barbed pain, violent and sudden, cut down the right side of his body.

With a gush of liquid heat, he felt nothing at all.

# CHAPTER TEN

*"The enormous pressure at these great depths seemed at first
sight alone sufficient to put any idea of life out of the
question."*
~ C. Wyville Thomson
*The Depths of the Sea*

~

" $\mathcal{C}$ ale, get off... my chest."

Noah's whisper had Caleb lurching against the bedside
table, nearly dropping the pitcher of water. He hadn't sat on Noah's
chest, threatening to let the long string of drool drop from his lips, in
fifteen years or more.

He hesitated, then took a step closer, gazing at his brother. Noah's
hair lay against his brow in a tangle of gold. His gaunt cheeks were
beaded with sweat, his usually clean-shaven jaw lined with stubble. He
had kicked the sheet off his feet, and the frayed edge of Caleb's work
trousers caught him mid-calf. He probably wouldn't be pleased
knowing he looked... sloppy. He'd never liked looking sloppy, Caleb
recalled.

Perching on the chair, he reviewed the list of things Leland had told them to do. *Change bandages daily.* His gaze flicked to the strip of white wrapped around Noah's chest. He tugged the sheet to Noah's neck and tucked it in for good measure. Thank goodness, Christa had promised to change the bandage when she returned.

*Apply cold compresses.* He snatched a rag from the basin at his side and wrung it with a twist. As carefully as if he placed flowers on a grave, he laid it on Noah's brow. His shoulders slumped in relief. Not a flicker of pain crossed his brother's face.

Chair wobbling beneath him, Caleb dug in his pocket. The least he could do was straighten Noah's hair. His hand shook as he began to comb. Not much experience with nursing. He and Zach were fit as fiddles, no need for doctors and sickbeds. Course, they'd never been slammed upside a splintered hull, either.

Leaning back in his chair, he studied the combing job, deciding it would do. This wasn't as frightening as he'd believed. Gave him a warm feeling actually. With a renewed burst of confidence, he plucked the damp rag from Noah's brow, dumped the cloth in the basin, and grabbed another. Turning, he slammed into a wide-eyed stare.

He yelped and dropped the rag on Noah's chest.

Noah blinked. "Cold," he said. His throat worked in a slow swallow.

"You're cold?" Caleb raced to the closet. Stretching, he tugged a blanket from the shelf above his head. It smacked his face, and he hurried back to the bed.

Noah grimaced and lifted the rag to his brow.

"Oh, you meant... I see." Caleb slumped into the chair, the blanket still wadded in his arms. "Yeah, we've got ice in there to keep them cold. Doc's orders."

"What time... how long have I been?" He coughed, trying to strengthen a voice frail from disuse.

"In and out for two days." Caleb hurled the blanket to the floor. "Have been too much to let me know you'd split your side open getting washed into something?"

Slowly, Noah lifted the sheet.

Caleb rested his hands on his knees and leaned in. "You got slammed into a jagged piece of wood, looks like. Cut into you like a knife."

Noah let the linen drop. "I just figured... the pain"—he flicked his fingers—"a bruise."

"A bruise?"

His eyes closed, and Caleb thought he had slipped into sleep.

"How is Elle?" Noah finally asked.

"Not so good."

"Funeral?"

"Today."

Noah's lids lifted. He struggled to rise to his elbows.

Caleb subdued him with one finger on his shoulder. "No, way, little bro'."

"Someone needs to... be with her, Cale."

"I realize you think that someone should be you, but Zach and Christa will have to do."

His throat clicked off a dry swallow. "Why aren't you there?"

Caleb poured a glass of water—then belatedly remembering another of Leland's orders—quickly stirred in a pain powder. He slid his arm beneath Noah's shoulders. "Because I never liked him. He treated Ellie as poor as a fistful of dirt, and she loved him too much to return the favor. Zach was scared I wouldn't be able to hide my *distaste for the man*. I think that's how he phrased it. A pretty way of saying I hated the bastard. So, here I am playing nursemaid to you."

With a pained grimace, Noah wrenched from Caleb's hold, sending the rag from his brow to the wall. Clumsy as a baby, he grabbed the glass and emptied the contents in three long gulps.

"Easy, partner." Caleb frowned and snatched the glass out of his hand. "If you vomit all over yourself, Zach will hang my butt in a sling."

"Typically vulgar," Noah said and slumped to the mattress, his skin pallid beneath a fevered flush. "Whatever you put... in the water tastes like—"

"Hush and lie there, grouchy little man." Caleb slapped a new rag in place.

Noah edged the cloth from in front of his eyes. "What kind of... nursemaid are you?"

"You scared us to death, Professor." He drew a breath that stunk of camphor and rubbing alcohol.

Noah waved away the concern, his lids drooping. The white scar on his eyelid held Caleb's attention, a beacon signaling their rocky past.

"Do you think this is a joke, what we feel for you? Watching you topple over in that boat, a river of blood gushing down your side?" Caleb's chair skidded back, and he stomped to the window. He flicked the curtain aside—ones they'd always detested but kept to spare Hannah's feelings—and glared into a blustery charcoal day that completely suited his mood. "Ellie was raving mad. You bleeding on one side of her, her father all mangled on the other. Stymie sailing in with three bloated bodies piled in the stern. It was a holy mess, the likes of which I never want to witness again."

Noah ached to the depths of his soul, but the pain was not merely physical. Elle had lost her father, and he couldn't protect her. Through a wealth of anguish and confusion, he searched for the part of her living inside him. It came to him gradually, then in a swelling tide.

Alone. She felt alone.

"I need a drink," Caleb said.

"Go find one," Noah challenged in a weak tone.

Caleb stalked to the side of the bed and stood, feet braced. "Let's get this done right now. No more secrets, no more tiptoeing around. I'm sorry for what I did to you, hitting you in the attic. Not understanding what my anger would do to you. I'm so damned sorry, I can't tell you how much. Every day since I've puzzled about it, worried over it. I was just"—he plunged his fingers through his hair—"stunned and... hurt. And mad. But not at you. At *him*, for leaving. Mama tried to make up for it. I know she did. But I wanted a father. I needed one. I hated him for leaving. Then I hated him more for making me crazy and making you leave."

"I chose to leave, and I'm sorry, too. I wish I could go back in time and handle the situation in another way."

"You don't have anything to be sorry for. That's what I'm trying to tell you. If you're still angry, if you can't forgive me, I want to know. Right now, I have to know."

A wave of dizziness swept over Noah. "Cale, I was very... lonely for a long time. Maybe angry. But I forgave you." He closed his eyes. "I did it to myself. Stupid to run away. A coward's way out."

He heard Caleb's boots strike the floor, then the soft creak of the door. "You're part of this family. That isn't *ever* going to change. Quit expecting it to."

"Cale?"

"Yeah?"

The church bell chimed, signaling the lowering of Henri Beaumont's casket into sacred earth. Noah sought to distance his mind from Elle, but she slipped inside, and he shivered from the impact.

"Noah? You okay?"

He tangled his hands in the sheet, ignoring the stab of pain beneath his ribs. "Has Elle been here?"

A minute ticked by. "This morning." Caleb coughed. "Only, she left. She had to leave in a hurry."

Noah slipped into a deep, drugged sleep before he could ask Caleb what he meant.

Caleb closed the door before Noah could ask more questions and backed straight into Christabel. The tray in her hands tottered, and he grabbed it to keep it from crashing to the floor. "Darn, Chris, what are you sneaking around for?"

Christabel smiled and tapped the edge of his jaw, as always, dismantling his wrath with her touch. "How's he doing?"

"Seems to be in some pain and really, really grouchy."

Christabel nodded. "Men make lousy patients. Why, do you reckon?"

Caleb shuffled from one foot to the other. "Chris, I, well you see, we had lots of things to talk about, me and Noah." His apprehensive expression was reflected in the silver tray.

She perched her hands on her hips. "You didn't tell him?"

He shook his head.

"Chicken."

He lifted his chin. "What do you want me to say? How you feeling, Noah? By the by, your married lady friend, the one none of us knew the first damned thing about, decided to pay a visit. Oh, and guess what else? Elle walked into the room to find her holding your hand and lit outta here like she'd seen a body hanging from the ceiling."

"Honey, if that's what you would have said, I'm glad you waited."

"Thanks." He stalked down the hallway, the tray clutched to his chest.

"You've got to tell him before that Bartram lady appears on the doorstep again, Cale. I met her on my way to the funeral. Plainly, she isn't leaving. Truly, this is a delicate situation."

Caleb cursed beneath his breath and wondered when exactly the tables had turned. For the first time in his life, he had to rescue his little brother from trouble.

Elle slumped against her father's mahogany desk and kicked at the papers scattered by her feet. The echo of the grandfather clock provided the only sound beyond her shaken, terse breaths. She hated this room. Despised the shelves of leather-bound books, untouched except for a yearly waxing; the emotionlessly amassed collection of art and antiques; the costly poplar-paneled walls; even the explosion of naked color on the ceiling.

She had perched on the horsehair sofa, caught between apprehension, rebellion, and love, during more dreadful paternal encounters than she cared to remember. From the time her father discovered her sneaking out her bedroom window, Noah and Caleb hidden in the shrubs below, to the time she quietly informed him she would not marry Magnus Leland, each episode had been a battle of wills, a contest of strength. Even now, his hostility held as heavy a presence as his cologne.

Elle grasped the official document, the crisp parchment stamped, signed and sealed. This scrap of paper had severed her affinity for her father more than all his cold-blooded threats. She rolled the paper into a cigar-shaped cylinder and blew a breath down the barrel. His betrayal, quite simply, left her numb.

Swaying to the side, she sloshed brandy in the crystal goblet and swabbed at a spill using the sleeve of Noah's coat. Her father would chastise her for using a goblet instead of a snifter, for sitting cross-legged on the floor, for being foolish enough to wear Noah's coat and, worse, for leaning in to sniff the sleeve with unerring consistency. She rubbed the wool beneath her nose, breathing in the warm embrace of Noah's smile, the heartfelt compassion in his eyes, the gentle caress of his fingers.

She needed him as much as she ever had, and yet, he could be in Morehead City or Chicago or, for that matter, on the moon.

Clinking the goblet against her teeth, she took a gulp of brandy, then choked and coughed. *Damn and blast,* why hadn't Noah's betrayal —in truth, no betrayal at all—left her numb? Why, why, *why* could she still feel everything? He'd made no secret of his correspondence with the woman in Chicago, sending off the letters pretty as you please, fodder for town gossip. Nevertheless, to see a woman sitting beside his bed, the bed he had tucked Elle into the night she'd broken her arm, the bed she dreamed he would one day return to sleep in—

With a curse, Elle flung the goblet against the wall. An amber trail trickled down the poplar paneling and to the Wilton rug.

Moonlight spilled through the window, a wash of silver across the rolled document in her fist. She flattened it on her thigh and skimmed the lines of text. Her father had left her penniless, or close to it. Enough for his burial and the employment of a solicitor to arrange for the sale of his business and his properties, the antiques, the art. In the bottom paragraph, he addressed the issue of his only child, Marielle-Claire. She would wed by May of 1899 or lose any entitlement to his estate. If she did not meet the terms, the estate would be transferred to a Banque National de Paris account in the name of Gerard Claude Beaumont, the deceased's cousin.

Elle tossed her father's last will and testament to the floor, where it glided beneath a tasseled footstool. She hoped Gerard Claude Beaumont, whoever he was, appreciated his good fortune.

Her father had misread her. She didn't care about his money. Of course, she would have liked to control the modest amount her mother left her, use it to complete her education and make the necessary repairs to the school. Perhaps repair Widow Wynne's roof. The rest, the estate of Henri Paul Beaumont, did not concern her in the least.

The savage cruelty of her father's last communication stung. She could imagine him dictating the marriage clause to his hawk-faced solicitor, a stranger who stank of Macassar oil and aided in sending paternal threats from the grave. A threat preserved in black ink for everyone to see. Elle felt humiliated, furious, and very disappointed.

Again.

These emotions gnawed at her, negating the grief that had bubbled forth when she got a good look at her father's lifeless body. Grief that swiftly turned to horror as Noah collapsed, a crimson streak slicing the side of the boat, following the path of his descent.

There could be no greater fear than thinking she'd lost the one man who would never be hers to lose. Much greater than the nagging uneasiness she'd felt long before Caleb rowed their boat toward shore.

She twisted her hands in the folds of Noah's coat, picturing the wash of blood down his side.

*He's not going to die.* No, but he would leave. And, sooner or later, he would touch another woman as he had touched her.

Elle wrapped her arms around her stomach, threw her head back, and laughed until her lungs burned. Caroline Bartram: another of her father's asinine errors in judgment. Unquestionably, he had not expected his daughter to be in his library at dawn, cleaning before a rush of consoling visitors stormed his house. The file lay open on the desk. Two large circles caught her eye. Printed in block letters inside them was a woman's name.

Smaller print below the vicious circles had given a great many particulars about Mrs. Caroline Beatrice Bartram. Age, family history, known associations, close friends, and presumed lovers. A detailed and rather fascinating report; it was news to Elle that you could buy a written account of someone's life. And Mrs. Bartram had led an interesting one, to say the least. This seemed a frightful intrusion, and she wondered, lacking any genuine interest, which drawer in her father's desk held Noah Garrett's life printed on cheap bond.

Noah and this woman knew each other well enough that an investigator had connected them. She dropped her head to her knees and swallowed past the choke of tears. Would she be listed in Noah's report?

Doubtful.

She sniffed and wiped her nose on Noah's sleeve, his scent sending a jolt of—*oh, God, she knew*—desire through her. Desire and the foolhardy love she wished to crush like a stick of chalk beneath her heel.

This morning, confused by her father's final thrust and eager to talk to Noah, Elle impulsively decided to take Zach's advice. She would tell Noah she loved him. She would never forget the sight of his blood on her hands. Never.

She loved him, and she wanted him to know.

She put on her nicest dress, which wasn't saying much, pinned her mother's brooch on her collar, arranged her hair in a shabby imitation of a French twist, and topped the ensemble off with a narrow little nothing of a hat she had purchased two years ago but never worn.

Following everyone's advice but her own, Elle dabbed the honeysuckle fragrance Noah liked behind each ear. Beneath the haze of grief and uncertainty, she felt joyously relieved. Joyously relieved, grieved, and uncertain, she opened the door to his childhood bedroom and her world tilted on its axis. A complete, soaring tilt. Backing out of the room, she then walked into town, and telegraphed Savannah.

*My father has died. Stop. No change in dire circumstances. Stop.*

If anyone found a visit to the telegraph office on the day of her father's funeral a strange occurrence, they didn't say anything. As for the odd looks, who cared? She'd been receiving those since the day she set foot in Pilot Isle.

She didn't think she could watch Noah walk away from her life again.

Therefore, she would walk away from his.

# CHAPTER ELEVEN

~

Caroline Bartram did not consider herself a person of exemplary moral fiber. She had grown up in a mill village in Solitude, West Virginia, in a squalid one-room shack. No running water, just a creek out back, newspapers stuffed into every hole and crevice, four children to a bed and three stretched beside it on the floor. Caroline had done things she was not proud of to escape.

She took a sip of tea, her pinkie angled away from the chipped handle. She remembered Ruby Garnet's lessons and used them well. She glanced from one man to the other, smoothed her hand across her bodice, and balanced her cup perfectly in its saucer. Her presence troubled them, Noah's brothers. The broad, rough one shuffled his feet and drank from the cup using both hands. The tall, thoughtful one, Zachariah, alternated between staring at her and staring out the window.

Troubled, indeed.

Patience waning, she asked, "Do you think a short visit would tire Noah too much?"

Zachariah pinned his brother with a hard glare. "Did you announce Mrs. Bartram, Caleb?"

Caleb's gaze flicked to her, to his brother, to the floor. He shook his head.

Zachariah sighed and swiveled toward her, his face set in lines of a serious nature. "Of course, Mrs. Bartram, since you've come all the way from Chicago. I just wanted"—he threw another heated glance at his brother—"to let Noah know you'd arrived so it wasn't a big surprise. I'm sure you understand."

"Is he all right?"

They both halted, studying her.

She placed the cup and saucer on the end table and tugged at the button on her glove. "I would love to see him now that he's awake." Vaguely, she questioned whether this constituted a breach of etiquette for a widow to visit a man in his bedroom. Ruby Garnet had never covered such a lesson that Caroline recalled.

Zachariah nodded and rose to his feet. "Right this way."

She brushed her gloved hands over her skirt and stood with a whisper of silk and crinoline. "Good day, Mr. Garrett."

"Mrs. Bartram," Caleb said, averting his eyes.

What they must think of her, she wondered, and climbed a narrow staircase in desperate need of a woman's touch. A spot of color would do nicely, a flower or two, a picture. She almost tapped on Zachariah's stiff shoulder and told him. Such rigid posture. She frowned. After all these years, people's derision still hurt. However, this time, she had lumped the scorn on her own shoulders. By accepting an offer to come to a place she didn't belong. Belated, perchance, but she hoped Noah would not be angry with her.

Zachariah halted before a door. Touching the dented knob, he said, "It's only been three days since the accident, and he might be sleeping, like he was during your visit yesterday. If he's not, he won't last long. The doctor gave him these pain powders and they snuff him out as quick as you can snuff out a candle."

"A short visit only, I promise. A quick hello, and I'll be on my way."

He pressed his lips together and peeked inside. "Awake, I think."

She thanked him and entered the bedroom, instantly recognizing the stench of illness. Caroline had doctored many people in her life, mostly women, and for ailments hospitals shied from.

He lay on his back, gazing through the window, his lids sleep-heavy. His hair was longer than she ever remembered seeing it, curling over his brow in streaks of color. She suppressed the maternal urge to sweep the strands from his face, instead, clutched her hands together, and slid into the chair by his bed.

His chest crested and dipped. "What are you doing here, Caro?"

"I came to see you, darling. What else?"

Gingerly, as if movement pained him, he turned his head. Skin shadowed and cheeks gaunt, but his gaze was clear and observant. "Are you in trouble?"

She laughed and yanked at a button on her glove. "I don't get into trouble anymore." Not terrible trouble, anyway.

The smile didn't reach his eyes. "Why, Caro?"

She shrugged and tapped her fingers together. "Maybe I wanted to see the place you've talked so little about. The family you've told me nothing about."

He laughed, then made a pained sound, and rubbed a spot below his ribs. "Now that you've seen it, seen them, do you think you'd like to tell me why you left Chicago?"

"Well"—she unbuttoned and buttoned her glove—"you remember my gentleman friend, Russell?"

"The lawyer."

"Apparently, Russell conducted some fraudulent business. Something to do with whiskey and illegal importation, if I understood the agreeable magistrate correctly."

"Good God, did you get arrested?"

"Oh, gracious, no. But they searched my house. Russell apparently used the back corner for a felonious reserve. Quite a stink on Prairie Avenue, I can tell you. None of the silk stockings want a former madam for a neighbor. Even if I keep my lawn neater than theirs and drive the grandest carriage on the block. Anyway, the magistrate suggested a short respite until they had Russell, bless his dear heart, locked away."

One of Noah's brows kicked high. "Do you have a place to stay?"

"My, yes. A kind whaler gentleman offered to bunk with his friend and give me the largest bedroom at the boardinghouse. Decorated in shades of pink and ivory. Reminds me of a child's room but lovely just the same."

"You ran to Pilot Isle to escape Russell the whiskey swindler?"

She frowned and clicked her back teeth together.

"I can hear the clicking, Caro." He yawned. "Dead giveaway you're withholding information."

"How about we have a nice, long chat tomorrow?"

"Hmmm, tomorrow the... mystery unfolds."

Caroline shook the wrinkles from her skirt and walked to the window. A shaggy-headed boy raced along the street, a mutt on his heels. A wagon crept past, loaded high with barrels and crates. A strong gust shook the branches of a tree and whipped the stalks of grass into a verdant frenzy. Long ago, Carrie McTavey might have known what kind of tree this was, what to call those red-and-white flowers surrounding the house. She might have understood how to let the simple joy of life overcome the everyday pain of living.

A kind, sweet girl, Carrie McTavey. Gentle and trusting. Completely happy to share a bed with three sisters and plug the holes in the walls with scraps of salvaged newsprint. Life had been as shiny as a new penny, even if the edges were dull. Then, her father's foreman put his hands on her on her twelfth birthday. After that, men touching her became commonplace. Expected. She shrugged and let the curtain slip from her fingers. She had harmed no one by earning money for the expected.

Noah mumbled in his sleep, and she glanced back. He looked so young. Worry lines smoothed by slumber. He was the only man, besides her da, who wanted to help her and didn't seem to want her body in return.

He had *never* touched her in a disrespectful way. At first, Noah's reticence hurt, because she'd come to understand men wanted her or else they didn't know she existed. Somehow, over time, Noah's view of her had become her own.

Caroline liked Pilot Isle, the picturesque avenues and earthy smells. Reminded her of Solitude, with friendlier people. They didn't scrunch up their noses when she smiled at them. Besides, Chicago had lost some of its charm, and more important, Justin would love the town. He hated the boarding school in Michigan. He wanted her and, gracious, she wanted him. In Pilot Isle, she could have him. What she wanted most in the world was to be a true mother to her illegitimate and much-loved son.

She glanced out the window as a young woman walked up the drive, a boy about Justin's age holding her hand. Her gaze lifted, and even from a distance, Caroline saw her eyes, green as the grass beneath her feet and spiked by long lashes. Not sure why, she moved out of sight. Through a slit in the curtain, she witnessed the play of emotion across the woman's face. Confusion, anger, and ultimately, love.

Evidently, this was Marielle-Claire Beaumont. The description matched well enough. A beautiful little thing. Exquisite face, lavish body. Caroline laughed softly. She could have made a fortune in the Pink House.

She looked back at Noah, his chest rising and falling beneath a bleached sheet. Frayed holes dotted the edge. She sighed. *Men.*

She remembered what little Noah had told her. Beaumont's daughter was a part of the discovery of his illegitimacy. Maybe he didn't want to have anything to do with the girl because of it.

She looked back to find the yard empty, the sun sinking low and throwing all kinds of vivid colors against the clouds. She saw more of the sky here than she could in Chicago.

She liked that.

Caroline knew from personal experience that small towns bred rumors faster than an alley cat bred kittens. A walk about town, a smile, a subtle question or two. She would ascertain enough to know if she'd made a mistake coming here.

~

Elle did not anticipate having Jewel Quattlebaum crash into her as the reporter tripped down Zach's front steps. "Merciful heavens, what's gotten into her?" Elle asked as Jewel strode down the path without issuing an apology.

"Noah, that's what."

Elle glanced back to find Zach leaning against the screen door, a yawn parting his lips.

"You look exhausted."

He stroked his bearded chin. "Frustration over tangling with a six-foot-two baby."

"That bad?"

"You won't believe what he told Jewel. She came here looking for details about the accident. Said Noah was a hero. Make a good story for the *Messenger* and all that. I assumed he would at least talk to her."

"And?"

Zach scowled, thoroughly disgusted. "He told her to climb on her gnawed-off pencil and ride it straight to hell."

Though she knew it would anger Zach, Elle laughed until her eyes smarted. My, she had not felt like laughing in days.

"It's not funny, Ellie, he's driving us crazy."

She nodded, struggling for breath, trying to agree.

"Go talk to him. *Please.*"

She straightened, the laughter dying in her throat. "No."

"What have you got in your hand?"

"The book you asked me to bring from the coach house. The one you said Noah needed."

"Talk to him. I beg you. Before I kill him or Caleb does. They've been going at it as fiercely as they did when they were children. I'm ready to run away from home."

"Zach, I—"

"I really believe you're part of this temper tantrum he's having. You haven't been by since the day of the funeral. Not that he's said anything, you know Noah. I told him you ask after him, and he just grunts."

"Me? Why would he care if—"

"What are you going to do? Avoid him until he leaves because of this woman? We don't know what to make of her, Ellie. Maybe they're good friends."

She hugged Noah's book to her chest, her father's file tucked inside. Good friends, indeed. "How is he?" she asked, unable to stop the question.

The door hinge squeaked as Zach stepped inside the house. "You've asked me a hundred times." He smiled at her through the torn screen. "This time you'll have to find the answer yourself. By the way, he's out back."

"Thanks a lot." A fine wind scattered her hair, tugged at her divided skirt. For a moment she considered leaving the book on the stoop and riding away on her bicycle. Except, she couldn't leave that despicable report for just anyone to stumble upon. For purely malicious reasons, she had decided to let Noah stumble upon it.

*I really believe you're part of this temper tantrum.*

Had her avoidance hurt him? Was that possible? Elle figured Mrs. Caroline Bartram would keep him entertained.

"Oh, the nerve of the man." She would give him his blasted book and then some.

Sunlight and dew sparkled on the blades of grass she crushed beneath her boot. A bout of rain the night before had cleared the air and hastened the transformation of spring. The scent of the ocean lingered, and through an open window she passed, the aroma of bacon and browning butter.

She rounded the corner of the house and halted, her fingers sticking to the book's leather cover. Noah sat in a rocking chair beneath the oak they had climbed as children, in a stretch of shade provided by a copse of branches. Wavering bursts of shadow and light swam across his profile, the pensive tilt of his lips, the taut line of his jaw. A table sat next to him, piled high with papers and books, and the box of metal instruments she had delivered two days earlier.

His hand swept the page of his notebook with rapidity she found hard to follow. He nudged his spectacles, then tapped the pencil against his straight, white teeth, staring into the distance. As she stood there, torn between love and dismay, Noah stiffened, the pencil sliding from his fingers. He cocked his head and looked directly at her, his reflective, unguarded mien hardening into the detached one she knew well. For a long moment, he stared, the expression on his face almost anticipatory.

Then he blinked and glanced down, a shrug of indifference his only reply.

Elle tipped her hat back and filled her lungs with a strong dose of courage. The wind shook the thicket of branches as she stepped beneath them and flattened a stray curl against his brow. She swallowed. He'd fastened nary a button on his shirt, leaving an open tangle of faded, blue cotton trailing past his waist. White gauze circled his ribs and a swatch of hair, darker than the hair on his head, peeked out above *and* below.

*Juste Ciel,* she thought, a pool of heat unfurling in her belly. Stunned, she dropped the book to the ground and plopped her rear end upon it.

Eyes still glued to his notebook, he asked, "Which one of my textbooks are you sitting on?"

She didn't answer, just watched the wind ruffle his hair and lift his floppy shirttails, exposing more of a man's body than she had ever seen except for an intermittent fisherman on the docks.

He snatched his pencil from the grass, then drew a hissing breath.

She rocked forward, the stance bringing her between his outspread legs. The scent of rubbing alcohol and soap filled her nose. "Noah?"

He lifted a finger, jaw flexing, face pale.

"Do you want me to—"

Before she could finish the question or rise to her feet, he had her by the wrist, his grip strong and convincing, his gaze centered on her. "No. Don't go." He glanced at his hand and abruptly released her.

She sat back, missing the book and bouncing to the ground. She tried again and said, "*Depths of the Sea,* I think it's called. Isn't that the one you asked for?"

"Yes. First textbook on oceanography published in English—1873."

"Mercy, I'm sitting on *that.*" She tugged the tome from beneath her bottom and thumped it on the table.

Noah dropped his head and laughed. "Oh, Elle." He dragged his fingers through his hair, his pale gaze traveling from her jersey gaiters to the feather sticking from her hat.

A leisurely stroke that set her skin aflame.

"What is this outfit you have on?" He propped his chin on his thumb and forefinger.

She glanced down. A calf-length divided skirt, a double-breasted jacket edged in black braid, a white blouse with detachable collar, a man's necktie. She would admit to affecting a masculine appearance, although the style was quite fashionable. Her father had berated her once too often, and she had hidden the clothes in the bottom of her wardrobe, forgotten, until she found them yesterday while packing. "I rode a bicycle here and traditional clothing doesn't work... because of the spokes." She shrugged, her cheeks heating. "I know they're a bit outlandish."

Noah stroked his finger across his lip, studying her. "I like them."

*"You do?"*

"Very practical, trousers. For a bicycle trip, certainly."

"Yes, yes, they are."

"The hat is nice, too."

Independent of her mind, her hand rose to touch. A burst of pleasure bloomed in her chest. "It's new."

"Ah," he said, and raised a brow.

Suddenly bashful, she pulled a weed from the ground, trying to think of something clever to say.

"Where have you been, Elle?"

She peeked at him through her lashes. He studied the pencil in his hand as earnestly as she studied the weed in hers. "Been?"

"I assumed you would stop by more often." He shrugged, then slid forward in the chair, rubbing his chest.

"Quit squirming." She rose to her knees.

He clamped the tattered end of his bandage between his teeth and struggled to untie the knot below his ribs.

"Here, let me help you." She leaned in, brushing his hands aside. She tapped his lips with her finger, and he parted them enough for the tattered end to fall into her palm. "Too tight, hmmm?" She loosened the knot as carefully as she could. "I bet Caleb tied this one." Her eyes met his as her hand settling over his heart. His intense gaze captured her, clear into her being. Her fingers curled in response, sinking into the hair on his chest.

She lowered her eyes and loosened the bandage. Hands shaking, she struggled to retie the knot. "I thought... you were sick and"—she swallowed—"I thought I'd wait for you to get stronger." *For* me *to get stronger.*

"Your cheeks pinken when you lie."

"I don't lie." She jerked the knot, avoiding his scrutiny.

"You just did. And I don't know why."

She drew a breath, the desire to touch him nearly overwhelming her meager supply of common sense. "Thank you for"—she glanced into solemn eyes difficult to delude—"for bringing in my father. I know... I know there was no way to save him. Magnus told me every-thing. He said you were helping them when you got hurt. He told me he apologized to you. I'm glad he did."

"Are you all right, Elle?"

She slid to the ground and let her hands dangle between her knees. Blades of grass pricked her through her skirt. She recorded the rush of waves to the shore and the mad dash of a squirrel along the branches above her. "My mother used to tuck me into bed and tell me how special I was. Her dear girl, *ma chere fille.* She told me she had prayed for me. And I believed her. Then she died and my entire world twisted inside out." With her pinkie, she recorded the plodding progress of a ladybug. "I tried to love him as much as I'd loved her. Heaven, I wanted to love him that much. But he never let me get close enough. I was a useless female, undeniably silly. Always, no matter how hard I strove to be responsible—" She halted, lacking a way to describe the person she had attempted to become.

Sighing, he reached for her. She pulled back in time to avoid the touch.

"Don't." She lifted her chin. "Truly, I don't need you confusing the issue by touching me and listening to my problems, making me think I can depend on you."

His eyes flared. "You *can* depend on me."

"Oh, yes, of course." She leaped to her feet and paced forward, pinching the bridge of her nose.

A baffled expression crossed his face, so little-boy-lost her knees threatened to give way. His lips parted, and he appeared to search for words. "You can depend on me."

"I can depend on you to *leave*. The lab is nearly finished. I've seen it."

"Be fair, Elle," he said hoarsely.

She *wasn't* being fair: accusing and belittling when she planned to leave as well. "You're right—" A whisper-soft tread rustled the grass behind them. Elle turned, her heart plummeting to her toes.

"I hope I'm not intruding. I'm Caroline Bartram, an old friend of Noah's."

Noah glanced between the two women and experienced a nip of unease. Caro could be quite mischievous if presented with a suitable opportunity.

"And you must be Marielle-Claire. I've heard a lot about you."

Elle jerked her watch from her pocket and spared it a nonexistent glance. "I've got to go. Teaching a reading lesson in ten minutes." She nodded to Caroline. "Mrs. Bartram, I left something of yours in Noah's book." Looking frightfully composed, she stalked across the yard, her stride, in his mind, comparable to a panther's.

Caroline followed Elle's progress as she made an angry pivot around the corner of the house. "Well, well. A little firebrand."

166

Noah knocked his head against the back of the chair. "What the hell was that about?"

Caroline presented an impish grin and settled by his feet. "For such an intelligent man, you can be terribly dull-witted."

"Dull-witted?"

"Severely preoccupied, blissfully ignorant." She tugged her gloves from her hands, finger by finger. "Please, choose what fits."

He rolled his head to look at her. She smiled in reply, a flash of white teeth and sympathy.

"Read what's in your little book, Noah. Unfortunately, I'm afraid I can guess what it is."

Hefting the volume to his lap, he flipped through the pages. Near the middle, a folded sheet caught his eye. He shook the paper open and read, line after glaring line. In the distance, the roaring tryst of land and sea called to him. How he wished he were there instead of here. An image of turbulent emerald eyes, agony and disbelief spilling from them, stained his vision.

Noah hurled the paper at her feet. "She thinks we were lovers."

Caroline smoothed the letter over the cushion of grass and bent her head to read it. "No, darling, she thinks we *are* lovers."

"Jesus," he said, and rubbed the spot on his chest that burned from the brush of her fingers. "Now I understand why she didn't come to see me. She's had this sordid report since the day her father died."

"Or, it could be because she walked in while I sat by your bedside, holding your hand."

He blinked, a stunned expression settling on his features.

"Why, darling, if I didn't know you better, I would think you actually cared about this girl."

"Of course, I care about her. She's been an unofficial part of my family since she was ten years old."

"Sounds like more than childhood affection to me."

"I'm not in love with her if that's what you're trying to intimate. Nothing even close."

"Intimate?" Her brow arched. "Is that the same as hinting at?"

He rolled his eyes heavenward. "Yes."

"Then I will admit to intimating you are in love with Miss Beaumont."

"I'm not." He dug his heel in the dirt. "Don't you think I'd know?"

Caroline licked her fingertip and smoothed a wispy curl on her head. "Unfortunately, no, I don't. In any event, would it be so bad if you were? She's a lovely woman. Absolutely lovely. Wild-eyed. Somewhat ferocious in a kittenish way. And, darling, if you could only see how she *looks* at you." Caroline's lashes fluttered. "I would give my soul to have a man look at me the way that little hellcat looks at you. Hot enough to turn wood to cinders." She laughed. "Stumbling upon the two of you, I admit to feeling the voyeur."

Noah's heart gave a violent twist. How *had* Elle looked at him?

In answer, an image surfaced. Elle, kneeling in the grass, her skirt spread around her, one delicate, stocking-covered ankle exposed. Her jacket molded to her breasts.

"Poor, darling, you have it bad."

A scowl tightened his lips. "I might, depending on your precise definition, but I'm not in love with her." Through gritted teeth, he said, "And quit grinning."

Her lips curled, her gaze straying to the front of his trousers.

A fever-hot flush swept his face; he shifted the book to his lap. "Blessit, Caro, surely *you,* of all people, understand the difference."

Caroline lifted a slim shoulder, an elegant shrug. "Fine. You don't love the little hellion. Perhaps, then, you should consider... other offers. The offer in her eyes. A woman like that could challenge a man's imagination. Tempt his mind. Rouse his soul."

"Stop reciting poetic verse, please. I don't want my imagination challenged." To his surprise, he lied, having pictured Elle in this fashion many times. No less than a hundred torturous times. Impulsive nature. Unrestrained enthusiasm. Instinctive sensuality. What would a woman like Elle do to a man? Brand him for life?

Noah couldn't afford to be branded for life.

"Afraid to take her up on it, darling?"

A gust of wind blew in from the sea, ripping at his stiff collar. "Completely terrified."

Caroline emitted an unladylike snort of laughter. "Oh, Noah, I *like* this girl. She's the first woman I've ever seen twist you in a knot. Gracious, the first I've even seen you look twice. Saints be praised!"

"I see we've moved to the Irish blarney."

"Stubborn fool, you wouldn't know a good woman if she kicked you in the head."

Noah slid low in the chair and crossed his hands over his stomach. "You suspected what was in the book."

Caroline pleated the hem of her skirt between her fingers, then stilled, realizing she clicked her back teeth. "You remember the other day, when I stopped by?"

"Vaguely. Those pain powders didn't do wonders for my memory."

"Well," she said, "Henri Beaumont telegraphed me and asked me to come to Pilot Isle. To keep you away from his daughter. I mean, at the time, I thought you weren't interested in staying. And, because of Russell and his sticky fingers—"

"How the hell did Henri Beaumont know about *you?* Where did the report come from?"

Caroline flashed a sad smile. "Darling, you really are naive. I've seen at least five similar communications about myself over the years. People can pay for a piece of your past. Simple as can be." She shook her head. "Don't you realize Henri Beaumont paid for your past, too? The little hellcat probably suspects. She's just afraid to go looking in her papa's desk."

"That bastard had someone investigate *me?*"

"How else do you think he got my name?"

Noah whistled through his teeth. "Chrissakes."

"A good account." Caroline turned the sheet of paper over and back. "Not entirely factual, but I've seen worse."

Noah inched forward, his fingers linked. "Did he offer you money, Caro?"

"Of course he offered money."

"Did you take it?"

She leaned in, her nose bumping his. "I'm not a prostitute anymore, Noah Garrett. Do you recall helping me leave the profession. So, wipe the affronted frown off your face. I could sell my house on Prairie Avenue and buy this whole town if I wanted to. To heck with Henri Beaumont's paltry offer."

"I'm sorry." He scooted back with a grimace of pain.

"You're the only man who has ever respected me. I don't want to think I've lost that."

"Oh, Caro." He sighed. "You haven't. I'm simply mired knee-deep right now."

"Make a list. What you usually do."

"I have a list. A growing pile of lists. One right there, beside you." He rubbed his fingers beneath his spectacles. "They're not helping."

She grabbed the pad of paper and tilted it into the light. "Well, well, a list of reasons to stay clear of darling Marielle-Claire. Not exactly the list I had in mind, but—"

He snatched the pad from her.

"I brought just the stuff to ease your troubles, darling." She tapped a leather-covered flask against his knee. "I keep it tucked in my garter. For strictly medicinal purposes."

He lifted the flask to his lips, the metal still warm from her skin. Before he drank, he threw a quick glance toward the house. The last thing he needed was Zach's censure.

"I heard about you and Marielle-Claire. Her idolizing you, you protecting her. A smelly old fisherman even took me to see the tree trunks in the schoolyard. It felt as if I was on a tour."

"Wonderful," he said around another gulp.

"I found the story a charmingly sweet testament to a girl's undying love."

"Elle didn't carve those in the trees, by the way." He grimaced. "But she went back later and dug the marks in deeper."

Caroline smiled. "And you think Marielle-Claire is the same willful, devoted child."

"Of course not. But she's still too impulsive." Too intelligent, interesting, vexing, beautiful. *Ma chere fille.* He shoved the cork into the flask, the taste of whiskey heavy on his tongue. Those few sips had softened the memory of Elle's torment, making it easier to catch a full breath. "She isn't the kind of woman to dally with, and when I decide to marry, *if* I decide to marry, I'll marry a woman who will not disrupt my well-organized life. Elle doesn't fit my plan, Caro. In fact, she'd blow my plan straight to Hades if I let her." He tossed the flask at her feet. "Regardless, I'm returning to Chicago once the laboratory is finished. I have a shellfish study to initiate and biology classes to teach. My life is not here anymore, and I'm not going to change that."

"Do you miss Chicago so much?"

He crossed his ankles and scowled. "Who said anything about missing Chicago?"

"Hmmm."

"Mind your own business, Caro. There's no future. Elle Beaumont and I are too different. We always have been."

She didn't answer, just hummed a soft tune.

Her silence annoyed the hell out of him.

"Uncle Noah, why can't you keep your hands off Miss Ellie?"

Noah dropped his fork to the plate. He glanced at Rory, who dabbed his spoon in the pool of gravy inside his mashed potatoes, and Caleb, who buttered his bread, a flush reddening his cheeks.

Rory wiped his nose and rocked the table as he swung his legs beneath it. Flaxen hair stuck to his brow in sweat-darkened clumps. "Huh, Uncle Noah? I love Miss Ellie, but she's still a *girl.* Have you kissed her? Johnny-Bob says you got to open your mouth for a real kiss. Yuck."

Noah lifted his napkin from his lap and wiped a dab of gravy from Rory's chin. "Who told you this?"

Caleb coughed. "Um, Rory, you're just playing with your supper. How about you go upstairs and wash up. I'll take you to Scoggins for ice cream."

"Yippee!" Rory raced from the kitchen, his chair swaying, his napkin fluttering to the floor, the subject of yucky kisses forgotten.

"Noah—"

"You know, you and Zach need to develop some other interests."

"Ah, come on." Caleb cracked a smile. "He must have heard us talking today."

Noah's chair skidded into the wall. "I think I'll spend the night at the coach house. There's a textbook I need to review before I make my next research trip to Devil Island."

"Heck, little bro', why are you angry if you *can* keep your hands off of her?"

Noah slammed the door in reply.

# CHAPTER TWELVE

*"They are conspicuous things, showing sufficiently bold specific characters, and thus they are less liable to confusion."*
~ C. Wyville Thomson
*The Depths of the Sea*

~

Noah left the laboratory site, head bent, gaze fixed on the wet planks beneath his brogans. The waves whipping the pilings almost erased the sound of Caleb's mockery. The promise of a storm scented the air and threw a solid punch into the wind coming off the sea. A fine mist struck his face and slicked his shirt to his chest. He crossed the deserted street and stopped to observe the flame wavering behind the globe of a streetlamp. Elle had mentioned petitioning the town committee for twenty and the insufficient approval for eight. Her cheeks had gone wild with color just talking about it.

He laughed, a sound that echoed off the warehouses looming on each side of him. No matter how much Elle troubled him, he was unable to deny her uniqueness, her inherent strength—or his fascination. Jocularity dwindling, he slipped his spectacles off, yanked his shirttail from his trousers, and swabbed the spotted lenses.

As a child, how had he missed those things about her?

He frowned and forced his spectacles into place. He'd squandered half his childhood running from her and the other half rescuing her from some farcical disaster. Who had time to wonder about—well, just to *wonder*? He had been doing ceaseless amounts of reflection since their passionate kiss behind the Nook. He touched his lips, imagining *her* fingers, her touch.

His heart picked up speed as his body betrayed him.

Cursing, he pulled the tattered scrap of paper from his shirt pocket and tipped it into the light, reviewing the list for the hundredth time. Five solid, irrefutable reasons to avoid Elle Beaumont, starting—

Lightning arced. A drop of rain pelted his cheek. Another smacked his chest, soaking to the skin. With a muttered oath and a shiver, he broke into a run. His brogans skimmed over a patch of shells, and he struggled to maintain his balance, his side beginning to throb in an impressive rhythm.

Relief poured through him when the next bolt of lightning illuminated Widow Wynne's pitched roof. Whipping off his spectacles, he slapped the gate back on its hinges. The heavy rainfall had unfurled a silver blanket, obliterating his view. Better that, he mused, taking the coach house stairs two at a time.

The key slipped from his hand twice before he jammed it into place.

Water streamed down his neck. He licked raindrops from his lips, the taste of salt invading his mouth. Shivering in the small entranceway, he ripped his shirt and undershirt over his head, and heeled his boots from his feet. He stepped to the landing and flipped the wet clothing across the length of twine he'd tacked between two posts.

A rumble splintered the air, and a chill claimed his body. He turned, tugging at the bandage circling his ribs.

A whisper of movement... a hiss of breath. Elle perched in the corner of the landing like a panther ready to pounce. A nightdress of cream muslin, drenched in all the right places, or hell, all the wrong ones, clung to her curves.

*She may as well be naked.*

The curtain of rainfall sheltered them from the world as they stared, immobile, seeing each other in a state neither had known existed.

Light illuminated her face: shock, curiosity, *greed.* She shoved her hair back, revealing brilliant eyes. Her lids fluttered, her gaze lowering to his chest. Her tongue peeked from between her lips, a promise intensely desirable in its innocence. In response, Noah exhaled, the sound muffling a distant thunderclap and the fierce thumping of his heart.

Passion scorched the air around them.

"What are you doing here?" he asked in a voice he hardly recognized.

When she continued to stare, he stepped forward, flustered and angry. His chest ached—longing, hunger, and pain. Repressed until he felt like a tin can ready to explode. *"What,* Elle?"

She hooked her arms beneath her breasts, unconsciously raising them above the drooping neck of her nightdress. "I wanted to make sure the roof wasn't leaking." Her chest rose and fell, adding fuel to the fire. "On your, your beautiful books."

He dragged his hand down his face, her goodness seeping into him. *I'm doomed,* he realized, and to prove it, effortlessly located her nipples beneath muslin. As he stared, they pebbled, tight and hard, as if he'd stroked his tongue across them. He swallowed, masking a groan, desire tensing every muscle in his body and melting in a leisurely slide to his groin.

Some of the lewd images spinning through his mind must have shown because broad spills of rose, much lighter than her nipples, stained Elle's cheeks. Her skin glowed, in a way he had never seen skin glow, how he imagined a newborn's would look.

Rejecting honorable intentions and prudent reluctance, he took a step closer, near enough to catch her fragrance. "Honeysuckle." He trailed his knuckle along her jaw, slipped his finger behind her earlobe. "Did you put it here?"

She swallowed and made a sound of fear or pleasure.

Noah discarded fear. Fear wasn't driving her to explore his naked chest, her look hot. "How about here?" He moved past her shoulder, circling her elbow, making a gradual sweep to her wrist. Her fist uncurled. Her pulse skittered beneath his fingertips. She gave a low gasp of surprise.

Rain coursed down her cheeks, a lock of cinnamon—hair he wanted spread under them while he plunged into her lithe body—lay tucked in the edge of her mouth. If he moved closer, he could use his teeth to peel it from her skin.

*Take her.*

"I want to make you mine, touch you everywhere, in every way," he said, surprising himself with the thread of need, the brutal honesty. His lips met her cheek, his tongue working the silken strand between his teeth, the taste of lemon filling his mouth. She arched and lengthened, dragging his lips over her jawbone to just below her ear. He brought his hand to her back, spread his fingers, and drew her near. "I want to explore your body in ways I've yet to explore, in ways I've yet to allow another to explore mine." The words rang true, yet he scarcely believed he voiced them. As it was with Elle, as it had always been, he could not hide behind a wall of indifference.

"Caroline," she said, and turned, presenting her back to him.

His arm circled her waist. "Never." His lips brushed her ear, skimming the nape of her neck. The faultless feel of her, the *completeness,* colored his desire in dark shades. A dizzying ribbon of anticipation wrapped itself around his mind and yanked, choking his fear. Defeated, he bent low and cradled her, her buttocks coming to rest against him.

"Never?" Her sigh captured him, tugged him deeper. Her cheek met his chest. She released a ragged inhalation that skated across his skin.

"Never." He tightened his hold and fit her to him. Like pieces of broken pottery, they slipped into place.

"I'm frightened."

"Don't be. Not of me," he murmured, fitting his fingers in the groove of her ribs, her heart pounding beneath his thumb as he swept it toward the rounded weight of her breast. He kissed from the sloped arch of her neck to her shoulder. A haunting chorus of sound, pelting rain and howling wind, mixed with their gasping breaths. A shiver shook her, her head lolling forward, inviting more. Unable to stop, he drew her skin between his teeth and sucked, hoping to mark her, a primal urge. She melted into him, her hand rising to cup his jaw. In turn, he breathed her in, her essence delicious and decadent on his lips.

"Sweet, oh, if you only knew how much I want you." She could have no idea how reckless, how savage and uncontrolled this was, to the exclusion of reason and rationale, the mainstays of his structured existence.

"How... much?" A shift of her bottom accompanied her question.

"Too much," he whispered, and returned the motion, rocking his hips into her. Leave it to this woman to find the precise movement to drive him mad. Pressing his face to her hair, the scent of citrus filled his nostrils, made him picture clear drops of pulp glistening on her lower lip, her dusky pink nipples.

He closed his eyes and pictured licking her clean.

What he could reach, he kissed, the edge of her mouth, her cheek, her jaw... starved, desperate, and impatient. He slanted his head, trying to seize her lips completely, thinking only to have more, much more.

Rising to her toes, she tangled her fingers in his hair and urged him closer.

A burst of liquid heat, passion in its most potent form, sparked and ignited. Bringing her with him, Noah swayed against the railing. He could hardly take it in. Could hardly believe his luck.

She hungered for him as desperately as he hungered for her.

*Trust me*, he thought. Or did he say it? With the roar in his head, who knew? Lifting his thumb, he rolled it over her nipple. Once, twice, until it puckered and protruded, ready to suckle. He groaned in a mixture of frustration and pleasure, the angle he held her insufficient.

He took her waist in both hands and propelled her forward. Kicking the coach house door closed, he turned her to face him, dipped his head, and seized her lips, his fingers tunneling through her hair. They were *alone*, utterly, temptingly alone. The gleeful knowledge seared the edges of his consciousness. Images of the woman of his dreams swirled, dulling reason and firing his senses. Pleasures he dared share, pleasures he had never wanted to share with another.

He traced the front of her teeth, a brazen invitation. "Like before," he said, beseeching her to remember their kiss in the alley.

She hesitated for only a moment before showing him she did, indeed, remember. She flowered; tongues tangled, a kiss of promise, earnest and absorbed. Mindless, Noah dragged his mouth to her cheek, bent low and wrapped his arm beneath her buttocks, the other across her back. He lifted her against his chest and recaptured her lips. Claiming every inch of her made it worth the dull ache in his side.

Ducking through the doorway, he halted by his bed, and let her slide down his body. Before her toes touched the floor, he laid her across the mattress in a gentle sprawl.

Her hair, bright and sleek, contrasted sharply against the linens, a seductive flame on a sea of ivory. Her unblinking regard revealed frantic desire. Raw and intimate, emotions a husband should see, but instead a lover would.

Lightning slashed outside the window, a burst of brightness. Through thin muslin, her generous curves stood in shadowed relief. He fought to stay focused on her face. Every tiny crease, every smattering of freckles. She shifted under his perusal, her legs falling open, Down a more dangerous path. Truly, he couldn't possibly govern *this* urge. Hadn't he wondered—even at the decidedly naive age of fifteen —if her hair was red all over? With a boy's uncontrollable provocation guiding him, he found her... dark and glistening. Heart hammering, his cock swelled, straining against his trouser buttons.

He exhaled raggedly and wedged his knees inside hers. "Do you know what I want from you?"

She licked her lips and nodded. Her gaze dipped low. A burst of air left her as she centered on his arousal.

His pulse pounded in his ears, hard and furious. He didn't recognize himself, a man who stood there thinking only of what he could do to this woman, not what it would cost him.

Or what it would cost *her*.

He vowed to go slowly and savor every damned inch of her. Tracing the delicate arch of her foot, he brushed his knuckle over each tiny, perfect toe. "If you're ever going to deny me"—he cupped her heel and raised her foot to his mouth, a delicious impulse—"deny me now." With a sigh, he trailed his lips over her ankle and up her calf.

She gasped, perhaps just realizing the man doing these wicked things to her was not her beloved protector. Wiggling from his grasp, she clawed at the mattress, digging her heels in. Her nightdress gathered in a sloppy roll at the bottom of her thighs. Unable, despite his warning, to restrain himself, Noah slid his hands behind her knees, lingered a moment to caress the rain-drenched skin, then stooped and jerked her forward. She glided across the sheets, legs dangling, muslin creeping higher, scarcely covering the triangle between her thighs.

He knew he should run as quickly as his quaking legs would take him. Instead, he tugged the last bit, the mattress edge cutting into her bottom. He angled his hips and burrowed. Warm velvet folds enveloped the strongest erection in memory.

"I know I asked you—" He swallowed, the words catching in his throat. Helplessly, he shifted to the right... to the left. So slight a movement, but he throbbed with each measure.

"Ask me again," she said, her hands sliding toward him. Her eyes snagged his, the eagerness in them stoking his hunger.

"Can I, sweet?" He skimmed his fingers along the outside of her thigh, hesitating over wadded muslin. He would never be able to sleep in this bed again, he surmised, curling his hand possessively around her hip. Not with the scent of lemon and honeysuckle and rich, brown earth driving peaceful slumber out, inviting carnal dreams in. "Can I touch you like I've dreamed of touching you?"

In answer, her lids skimmed low.

He inserted his thumb under the tattered hem and gave her thigh a languid stroke. "What would you do if I stripped this from your body?" He drew a deliberate circle. "I want to, if you're wondering. *Desperately.*" He raised the nightdress an inch—an inch closer to ruin for both of them. "What would you do? What do you think I would do?"

A rushed breath; a raspy, meaningless sound. She tried again, a teasing accent threading her words. "I... I don't know... for sure. But, I think I'd like it."

He snapped his head up and slammed into a sizzling, emerald wall. A powerful surge, privilege inspired by her reckless words, ripped every remaining shred of caution from his mind.

The mattress dipped as Noah washed over her. Knee, hip, stomach, chest. Points of startling, scalding, rain-drenched contact. His hands skimmed her arms, her back, fingers tangling in her hair. She made a noise he must have mistakenly interpreted, because he halted, shoulders quivering, his face hovering an inch above hers. His jaw tensed, flushed skin stretching over high cheekbones. With a willful shake of his head, he leaned in.

She prepared herself—*oh, heaven,* she really did.

Then, he claimed her—possessive and wild—and her preparedness vanished.

A hoarse groan rumbled from his throat, rattled beneath her fingertips. Pricks of sensation, a provoking, restless intensity. Heat pooled in her belly and between her legs, flooding her thighs and her buttocks. She pinched them together and burrowed into the mattress. Noah followed, pressing his hips against her. Her legs disengaged at pressure from his knees, embarrassingly weak pressure.

Then he fell into place.

Oh, merciful heavens, this was what she'd imagined in the alley. Height mattered little. And he knew it. Rocking, perfecting the fit, he knew it *all.*

"Sweet Jesu, you feel amazing," he said against her cheek.

In response, she explored with a vague, indefinite movement.

"This is what you're looking for." He tilted her hips and shifted between her thighs. A sense of fullness, one she didn't know how to describe, pervaded her, in a part of her body she knew next to nothing about. Saturated, a sponge filling with scalding water, while he, all angles, rigid and impenetrable.

Not understanding why she was compelled to, and never considering she'd shouldn't, Elle skimmed her hands down his back, grasped his buttocks, and arched against him.

In return, he attacked, ravishing everywhere at once.

"Open for me, sweet," he said, kissing his way along her cheek. "Only for me." He drew her earlobe into his mouth and sucked. His tongue swept inside, sending a bolt of heat to her toes.

A sigh slipped from her. He moved quickly, covering her lips and swallowing the sound. Color, sensation, exploded behind her sealed lids as he invited her to play. He tasted of mint and the faintest hint of whiskey.

Delicious.

The occasional boom of thunder and the soft tap of rain against pine shingles intruded little. Moist, openmouthed kisses, impatient bites, fierce sucking. Whispered sighs and ragged groans. His hands and lips worked, in faultless accord. A nail skimming her cheek, a finger dipping into her bodice. Muslin lowered; a rush of air crossed her breasts.

His breath warmed her. Then his tongue. An abrasive, skin-clinging stroke, a lazy rotation.

Her nipple fairly sizzled.

Why she craved *this* loomed far beyond her meager knowledge.

That she would beg if he stopped astounded her.

She attempted to speak but found she could utter nothing more than a dazed moan of entreaty.

He released a pleased groan and shifted to the other nipple, his fingers finding the spot his mouth had vacated. Arching, she presented her body to him, her tortured whimper breaking free, the sound echoing off the bedroom walls.

With a teasing flick to her nipple, he pulled back, the cessation she had feared. She blinked to find his gaze fixed on her; an engrossed expression. The same he wore when she caught him with his head buried in a textbook.

He slipped his spectacles from his face and swung them in a deliberate circle. Then he startled her by smiling, a mischievous quirk of his lips. Wicked, and very, very sensual. Licking her own, she fought to regulate her breathing by counting to ten in French and in English.

Shifting to the side, he stroked his toe up the inside of her calf. She could not suppress the weak sigh. His smile widened, and in a wonderfully inventive, astoundingly impulsive action, he circled her nipple using the rounded end of his spectacle frame.

A shudder racked her body. "Please."

He leaned in. So close, his breath grazed her mouth. "Please, what?"

She twisted her head from side to side, wadding linen behind each ear. "I don't know."

"This?" He brushed the cold lenses against the protruding nub.

"No," she panted.

"This?" His thumb fondled, circled once, fondled again.

"N-no." She placed her finger over his lips, then lowered her hand to her breast. Blinking past the haze surrounding her, she looked to see if he understood.

As she watched, his controlled blankness slipped away. As did his smile. His spectacles clattered to the floor. His hands cradled her face; his mouth captured hers. Parting her lips easily, his tongue swept inside.

She did not fight, did not care to try.

The kiss grew rough, rougher than any before. Tongues and teeth, a singular taste, one to dwell in her mind for eternity. Passion had never played a commanding role in her life, and she questioned, vaguely, if she would be able to live without it after this. Her fingers spread over his back, nails digging. Her hips matched his steady rhythm. A drag and pull like the tides. A rhythm the kiss followed, a rhythm that increased.

Moisture cleaved his naked chest to hers, the patch of hair stirring her nipples as successfully as his fingers and his tongue had. She moaned in delight and frustration, plunged her hands into the mussed locks on the crown of his head, and directed him lower.

He wrenched his mouth from hers and nibbled down the arch of her neck, a rich sound creeping from his throat. His chin brushed her ribs, the scrape of stubble making her shudder. Flicking a molten, heavy-lidded glance at her, he stared through golden curls untamed by pomade. Stared until her cheeks heated and pleasure thumped at the apex of her thighs.

Weak lid drooping, his gaze slithered low. Again, he displayed that wicked smile. "This, *ma chere fille,* is what you want. What we both want." He bent his head, she tilted hers, watching her erect nipple disappear between his lips.

*Sweet mercy.* Elle gasped and closed her eyes to the sight of him looming over her, helpless to ignore the heat, the frank intimacy, of his touch. Scarcely aware of the lumpy mattress beneath her, rather, she felt suspended in air.

Adrift on a sensual sea.

His mouth spread over her breast, his groan muted against her flesh. Animalistic, the things he did to her, the way he sucked her nipple between his teeth, rolled it beneath his tongue. Waves of ecstasy combined with sharp stabs of awareness. Ah... he was right, she concluded, pitching into a bottomless pit of carnality, her arms tumbling to the bed, her legs splaying wide. He'd given her *exactly* what she'd wanted: craved.

*Juste Ciel,* the man was remarkably skilled.

Sensation pressed in upon her. Noah's hips grinding into hers in a gradual figure eight. The crisp hair on his arms. The strain and release of muscle. His generous weight atop her. Damp cloth covering his arousal, a part of him she had never imagined, in all her dreams, would be so long, or so hard. His hands stroking the sides of her breasts, curling to cup them, kneading, drawing them into his waiting mouth. Callused palms gliding along her stomach, seizing her waist. Fingers plucking at her nightdress, tugging it higher. His tongue warming her, his lips welcoming her. His touch robbing her of thought or purpose, command or design.

Mental pictures provided taste and smell: fields of green, dark, red wine, sapphire clouds. A stormy blue-black sea stretching to the horizon. A slender boy nudging spectacles high atop his nose, his smile comforting and compassionate.

She invited the images into her mind, opened her legs to invite him into her body.

*Pounding.* Her heart slamming against her ribs. *Pounding.* Her pulse ringing in her ears.

Noah jerked atop her. Dazed, Elle watched him search for his spectacles, frown to find them missing. He straightened, his knees hugging her waist as he sat astride her. The hand he dragged through his hair trembled. His chest rose in rapid catches beneath the dangling strip of cloth covering his wound, the tattered end tickling her breast.

Bewildered, he looked completely bewildered.

The pounding inside her head started again. Then she realized someone pounded on the door.

# CHAPTER THIRTEEN

~

*E*xcept for the heavy footfalls on the staircase outside, the room was eerily quiet. Elle hiked to her elbows and glanced at Noah. Slowly, his look slid past her chest, to her hips, which were still wedded to his. He stared for a long moment, then muttered a ragged oath, and rolled to the floor in one smooth motion.

He strode to the window, his stride noticeably unsteady. He flipped the curtain aside, pressed his nose to the pane. "Caleb, I think," he said, his breath fogging the glass. "Looks like he's swaying on his feet." He swabbed the circle of vapor away using the ball of his hand. "Blessit, he lets everything upset him."

Elle waited for him to turn, perhaps finish what he'd started, but he showed no sign of doing either. Drawing the neck of her nightdress to a modest level, she lifted her bottom and yanked in an awkward attempt to cover her legs. A deafening rip filled the silence. With a sigh, she fingered the tattered piece of material. "Well, we can't all be as composed as you. Don't worry. He won't go to Widow Wynne's, see I'm missing and put two and two together. He's not that suspicious."

Noah turned, a sharp torque from the waist. "Right where he's headed," he said, sounding both shamed and flustered. "He's looking for me, and he knows I'm stalking you like some damned bloodhound." Again, he peered out the window when she understood good and well he couldn't see a thing.

She rubbed her eyes, breathing in the smell of rainfall and man. Feeling disappointed and unsatisfied, she considered Noah's ramrod posture, the tangled mat of hair on his head. It took considerable effort on her part to keep her hands where they should be and not where they wanted to be: tracing the muscled ridges of his back, the round curve of his buttocks. He had an extremely nice physique, sleek with just the right measure of muscle.

Scooting to the edge of the bed, Elle wriggled until her feet touched cool heart pine. Her knees wobbled when she put weight on them, but they held. Her toes curled from the chill. "Why do you suppose this is?"

His fingers knotted as he dropped his brow to the pane. A sweep of air fluttered the trailing end of his bandage. "Why, what?"

The soft pad of her feet reverberated through the room. She stooped to grasp his spectacles, moonlight sparkling off metal. Thankfully, he'd put no cracks in the lenses. "Why do you suppose we"—she pressed her lips together, figuring how to say this—"we react like this? I never felt this, hot and... and *itchy* about Magnus. About anyone."

A minute passed. Thunder rumbled in the distance. "How do I know? Happens to people every day."

She traced the wire frames with her fingertip, remembering what he had done with them. "Much like your married lady friend, isn't it? I'm not ignorant of life's basic truths. Most men have a lover and a wife. Extreme appetites, Christa told me."

He tapped the pane: three hard knocks. "You shouldn't be listening to Christabel. And, you're wrong about Caroline."

"Oh yes, I witnessed, *firsthand*, how wrong I am." Even now, she saw his hand folded in both of *Caroline's*, the woman stroking his fevered brow.

Another knock. "You're confusing what you witnessed."

"No matter. I kept her from your bed tonight. In fair recompense—"

All at once, he stood before her, his hands closing about her shoulders. "Don't say that." He shook her. "Don't even think it."

"How can I not?"

"I told you, before. I've never touched her." His gaze lingered on her breasts. "Like I just touched you. Never touched her at all. Whoever wrote your father's report wrote lies." His fingers tensed. "The desire I feel for you is more than I've experienced in my life. Nothing has ever come close. No one has come close."

For a long moment, they stared, caught in a world of their creation, a world Elle wanted to dive into, even as the rational part of her mind rebelled, begging her to remember they would not be in each other's lives much longer.

Wanting to test his resilience, she brushed the front of his trousers, curling her hand around his rock-hard flesh.

*"Stop."*

She dropped her hand.

"Stop looking at me like that. And touching me *there*." He shook his head. "Do you want me to go completely mad and—and tear your clothes off?" His gaze flicked down, then shot up. "What little you're wearing, of course."

Sinful images stormed her mind. Her lips curved against her best judgment.

He stumbled back. "Dammit, Elle."

"If it makes you feel any better, part of me thinks this is all a very bad idea. That part"—she shrugged—"I'm inclined to ignore. I usually do."

"For once in your life, listen to what the discarded fragment of your brain is telling you, because you and I are not going to happen." His eyes cut away. "Don't make this out to be something it isn't. You'll only end up hurting us both."

"What do you make this out to be?"

He wedged his shoulder against the bedpost and crossed his ankles, gazing past her, the wheels in his mind spinning as he reasoned in his systematic, professorial way. All right, two can play this game, she asserted, and struggled to allow her features to slide into lines of indifference. Hard to do when he stood before her half-clothed, hair mussed, charmingly undone. She chewed on her lip, fighting the urge to touch him.

As a clock counted off time, his eyes lightened, his fists unfurled, and his splendid arousal withered. Her hold over him, whatever that constituted, diminished with each annoying tick. "Elle"—he tapped the bridge of his nose, threw a quick glance at the spectacles dangling from her fingers—"I think we should stay far, far away from each other."

The edges of her temper crisped and curled. "That's what you came up with? Stay away from each other?"

A spark of fury lit his gaze. "What the hell do you want me to do? To say? I can't answer every question, find a solution for every problem. That blessed professor nonsense is a myth. I thought you understood better than anyone." He took a fast step forward. "Understand *this*. I want you. I sit awake, night after night, crammed in a stiff leather chair, lust eating me alive, picturing you twisting beneath me, or God help me, beneath another—"

With an angry oath, he swept his hand across the marble-topped bureau. The troublesome shelf clock struck the floor, a deafening shatter. Shards of glass glittered amidst the raindrops blowing in the window. "Forget him and let this... situation between us die."

*"Him?"* She pointed to the rumpled bed. "You believe this is still some sort of youthful obsession?"

Over his shoulder, his tormented gaze met hers, his chin lowering in what she had to assume was a positive reply.

"Maybe you're right. Maybe everything I feel *is* for that boy. The one who walked me to the doctor and held my hand while he set the splint. The one who helped me speak his language and protected me until I could do it well enough to avoid getting knocked around in the schoolyard. Maybe I'm yearning for *him*. Because I see his face when I look into yours. A figment of my foolish, sentimental imagination. Exactly what you expect from me, Professor? Fickle, flighty Elle Beaumont."

Noah flinched and jammed his hands in his pockets, as if the words he had practically begged her to utter disturbed him. "No, no, that's not what I expect from you at all. It's just, this attraction between us can't work. Some things don't make sense if you take a moment to examine them. *We* don't make sense. We're too different, you and I. And, the lure, the excitement, well, passion and—and love, love which comes from deep inside, are different beasts. Love is, love makes intimacy special. Inversely, lust roars around in your chest like a bear, clawing and slashing its way out. I guess I don't know... honestly, I don't know if one has much to do with the other."

Oh, how she wanted to tell Noah Garrett where he could stick his bungling rationale. Instead, she prolonged her departure by slipping his spectacles on her face. The room melted into ribbons of black and white. Seeing the world through his eyes deepened the ache in her chest. She swallowed hard and forced herself to say, "Then, what just happened between us was simply a spontaneous reaction to a—what would a scientist call it—some kind of primitive stimulus?"

He dropped to his haunches and began to place shards of glass in his cupped palm, his firm bottom resting two inches above the floor. "All I'm telling you, dammit, simply *asking* you, is to think. Use your clever little mind. Be sensible for once. You're too intelligent not to understand what I'm saying. We're oil and water, Elle, we don't mix."

Her heart shattered like the clock at his feet. "When have you ever known *me* to act sensibly, Professor?"

"Exactly what scares me," he said, the words hard-edged and determined.

Gravely determined.

Of course, she wasn't an impartial judge, but her feelings seemed indisputably genuine, shades darker than those she'd experienced as a child. Yet, as she studied him, she realized his oil-and-water theory might be true. He painstakingly selected a piece of glass, then paused to consider before selecting another.

She would have swept them up without regard for anything.

Despondent, she lifted his spectacles from her face and found him watching her, rotating a jagged shard between his fingers. A strange, almost fearful expression shaped his features. Then he averted his gaze, ending any argument she hoped to make.

Dazed and unsure, she dropped his spectacles on the washstand, navigated a pile of research books in the living area, and descended the staircase, head high, posture rigid. Pausing at the bottom, she looked over her shoulder.

Noah stood on the landing, hands gripping the railing, a wooden slat biting into his stomach. Water glistened on his clenched jaw.

*Tell me*, she pleaded, struggling to decipher the emotions sweeping his face. *Something, anything.*

In answer, he wagged his head slowly back and forth.

Noah let her walk away, her aggrieved sigh yanking his stomach to his knees. He wanted to go after her, drag her into that sorry excuse for a bed, and make astounding love to her. He threw back his head and expelled a choked breath. Hand trembling more than he liked, he dug into his pocket and lifted the scrap of muslin to his nose: the ever-present earthy scent, a touch of lemon, honeysuckle.

His sheets, hell, his entire bedroom, smelled of her. Couldn't go there.

The door slammed behind him. He tripped over a textbook, skidded across glossy pine, and sank into the chair he slept in most nights, where dreams of Elle slicked his skin to worn leather. Dreams that had him jerking awake and reaching for her.

They had ballooned to intense proportions, incredibly vivid, although he was able to rationalize them, or at the very least, his reasons for having them. He had recently read a commentary by an

Austrian psychiatrist who speculated that dreams revealed a person's deepest desire in its most blatant form. This made sense, because having Elle naked and writhing beneath him represented Noah's deepest desire at present. Nonsensical, but true.

He sloped forward, hands going to his knees. Dreams he could dispute. Scientifically, if this psychiatrist was correct. The agony crowding his chest, he had no argument for. Even worse, he feared his feelings as he'd never feared anything in his life. When he'd turned to see his spectacles perched on Elle's nose, her lovely eyes distorted by the lenses, it wasn't desire that galloped through him like a high-kicking mule.

Somewhere in the coach house, a branch slapped a windowpane. Tipping his head, he observed a spider spinning a web around the aged kerosene chandelier and realized he was in deep trouble.

*I'm falling in love with Elle Beaumont.*

Though precise classification would have been a blessing—he was not able confirm the assumption in definite terms. Besides love for his family, he did not completely fathom the emotion.

Or welcome it.

Just the same, there were far too many factual incidents for a scientist to ignore.

He yanked the scrap of muslin in two and flung the pieces to the floor. Zach spoke the truth. Emotions were *not* rational. Love didn't require precise classification. Hadn't the past month—being with his brothers again and unearthing the affection hidden deep in his heart —taught him that lesson?

It had, but familial love he *wanted.*

Somehow, Elle had worked her way under his skin.

Or, dear God, had she been there all along?

He slumped, dazed. She loved sunrises and chocolate ice cream. He liked sunsets and vanilla. She thrived on chaos. He loathed chaos. She dreamed impossible dreams. He renounced impossibilities of any kind. He was boring and predictable; she fairly glowed with dynamism and vigor.

A rational solution must exist.

He snapped his fingers and strode to his desk. Squinting, he shoved aside the latest Sierra Club *Bulletin* and an empty specimen bottle, grabbed his notebook, and flipped to the first blank sheet. He plundered through papers and located the fountain pen he had received for five years service with the fisheries commission.

Walking backward, his legs bumped the chair, and he dropped into it. He brought the notebook close to his face and drew a line down the sheet. Things he admired about Elle went on the right, things he despised on the left. He began writing, his hand sweeping the page. Dismayed when the right list grew considerably longer than the left, he ripped the sheet out and wadded the paper into a ball. It hit the floor with a crinkle.

He tapped his pen on the notebook and decided to approach the problem from a different angle. In the same fashion he would a research project where the conclusion was certain but procurable by various methods. *Outcome: mind free of Elle Beaumont.* The pen moved swiftly, until he had two pages of concise clarification and a systematic strategy for avoiding Elle—thereby reducing his engrossment, as he politely termed it.

Fine. Good. He had listened to the warning signs—like any decent researcher—and devised a plan. He would throw himself into his work and spend time with his family. No more kisses. Blessit, no more *anything* that involved touching her. No more daydreams— actual dreams he couldn't hope to control. No more considerate gestures. Eating dinner with her or repairing her shutters was forbidden. He had been planning to mow her grass; he would ask Caleb.

Also, he thought discussing the situation with Caroline might help. Perhaps, he could secure her assistance. Glancing at the plank-and-beam ceiling, he pictured the tangle of fragrant sheets covering his bed. His fingers tightened around the fountain pen. He lifted the notebook and scribbled one last notation.

Maybe it wasn't crucial, but he listed it anyway. Less urgency to tell Elle, which, remarkably, he found he really wanted to do. After all, what purpose would it serve to tell her that the astounding taste of her, the exquisite *feel* of her, had erased any sexual experiences in his past like chalk dust from a blackboard? He snapped his notebook shut.

No need to tell her. No need at all.

# CHAPTER FOURTEEN

*"I believe we have a simpler explanation."*
  ~ C. Wyville Thomson
  *The Depths of the Sea*

❦

*H*er mother's cameo caught a spark of sunlight as Elle pinned it to the collar of her percale blouse. Her father's solicitor, Mr. Hobbs, never realized this piece of jewelry served as the sole legacy from a devoted father to his wayward daughter.

Mr. Hobbs would be surprised, and her father angered, to know she had nullified the codicil two days before the reading. Reaching into her trouser pocket, Elle touched the scholarship-acceptance letter. She had telegraphed her agreement and had received a reply from Savannah this morning. The committee anticipated her arrival in New York City in no later than seven days. There were applications to submit, a lesson of study to organize, and an awards luncheon to attend. The largest responsibility would be preparing Savannah to manage the school during her absence.

This activity might keep her mind from straying to impossible dreams, even if her heart seemed captured for life.

She leaned against the staircase railing outside her father's office and tipped her face to the cloudless blue sky. A familiar voice filtered past the thud of ships edging the dock. A wave of heat—totally unrelated to the sun beating down on her back—lit her from the inside out. Closing her eyes, she strained to hear his words.

"...quantity *and* size. Blessit, Zach... need both. You volunteered... stupid questions."

Warm laughter traveled the distance. Lids lifting, she watched Zach pitch a fish at his brother's head. In turn, Noah pivoted, stuffing a thick book beneath his armpit, and snared the fish with one hand. "Nice try," she thought she heard him say.

She stared, wishing he stood a little closer, wishing fewer people crowded the street. Wishing the memory of his body pressing down upon hers would leave her mind for one blasted *minute.*

Noah poked inside the barrels circling the *Nellie Dey's* gangplank and turned to scribble in his book. A lock of hair fell into his face, and he flicked it back. Zach yelled a number, which he noted with a slight incline of his head and another furious scratch. An image of those long, sun-kissed fingers trailing over her shoulders, teasing her breasts and hauling her hips to his, forced her to wedge her knees against the wooden railing. To add to her humiliation, her nipples pebbled beneath her shift, an abrasive reminder of her weakness.

Forcing her legs to move, she shot down the stairs. Between swaying carts loaded with casks and piles of lumber, she caught glimpses of the man she had worked diligently to ignore.

Something seemed different. His trousers were wrinkled. Sloppily rolled sleeves capped his elbows and dirt soiled his knees. And his hair, curling about his head, lacked hat or pomade, and needed cutting. His appearance didn't keep Meredith Scoggins from yelling his name and crossing the street with an eager stride.

For eight days and fourteen hours, they had avoided each other. Except for one collision. Four days ago, leaving the post office as he entered. He had grabbed her arms and stared for a strained, impassioned moment into her face. Then, they jerked apart and departed in opposite directions.

At least *she* had gotten her mail.

Worming her way through a crowd of fishermen entering the Nook, she stumbled into a foul-smelling body. Her gaze traveled from mud-caked brogans to patched bib trousers. Sean Duggan, legs thrown wide, rage mottling his cheeks. His hands flexed into fists by his side. "I've been waiting to talk to you, *Miss Ellie,*" he said. Ale rode the breath buffeting her face, a repulsive comrade to the liquor seeping from his clothing.

He swayed on his feet, and a chill streaked down her spine. "What can I do for you, Mr. Duggan?"

He seized her wrist and squeezed hard, until she feared her bones would snap. "You scrawny little bitch."

She grimaced and breathed through her mouth, pain swimming up her arm. Her knees trembled, but she stared into his red-rimmed eyes, ignoring the discomfort and the stench, daring him to do more than this on a public street. He did not have the privacy of his home to lay an abusive hand on a woman half his size.

"You'd better step away, Mr. Duggan. I'm about to scream bloody murder. The noise is certain to alert Zachariah Garrett. His office is just across the street. Family friend, if you recall. He wouldn't take kindly to this brutality." She yanked her arm, but he held tight.

Sean's gaze flicked toward the constable's office. He released her, but did not back up, instead slapping his palm against the post above her shoulder. " I know where Annie went. And you helped her."

"Excuse me, but I think you'd better do as Miss Beaumont requested, or I may scream as well. I live in Chicago, among many desperate souls, so I guarantee I've had more experience. Besides, I *love* to draw an audience."

Elle edged around Sean.

"Never look a rabid dog in the eye, darling," Caroline said with a calm smile.

Elle linked her arm through Caroline's and whisked her down the boardwalk. Their heels clicked on the planks, the only sound for several minutes. Halting in front of Tilly's Nets, Elle jerked free. "Why?"

Caroline raised a brow, her gloved fingers closing around the package in her hand. "Why?"

Elle threw her hand out. "You've been trying to befriend me all week. Suffering cats, you've come to my house, stopped me on the street and... and today, you help me out of a disagreeable situation. Why?"

"Because I like you."

"Like me? You don't *know* me."

Caroline smoothed her hand over her frilled bodice. "I know Noah well enough, and he likes you. Quite a good recommendation in my book."

Elle felt the pounding in her head lower to her chest.

"And you love him, so you think you must hate me."

A group of sailors shuffled by, singing in slurred voices and stamping their feet; the first lazy days of spring were upon them. Elle watched the Nook's swinging doors swallow them up, then she turned toward home, neglecting to ask if Caroline wished to accompany her.

"What did I witness back there?"

Elle increased her pace. "Just another reason for me to leave this place."

"What was that?"

"Nothing."

"Darling, you must tell someone what happened. That man is a menace."

Elle halted, apprehension streaking through her. "You mustn't repeat anything about this, Mrs. Bartram. *Nothing*. Sean Duggan's problem is with me and no one else. I don't want—" Closing her mouth, she marched away.

Caroline's shoulder brushed Elle's as she stepped in beside her. "You don't want Noah getting involved."

Turning into Widow Wynne's front path, she kicked the gate open, and crossed the yard. Caroline stayed right with her. Frustrated and confused, Elle snatched her skirt and took the porch steps at a gallop.

She turned to find the annoying woman standing on the bottom step, grinning at her.

*"What?"*

"You've got dash, darling. And Noah needs someone with dash."

"Sorry to disappoint, Mrs. Bartram, but Noah isn't going to bother with anything without gills. You see, my father wasted his money."

Caroline's smile dimmed. "I never took any money from your father, Miss Beaumont, and I never intended to. I came for my own reasons, mostly."

"I'm sorry. Noah told me about the two of you being... friends." Glancing at her feet, Elle scrubbed mud off the toe of one boot with the heel of the other. "I've confused the issue enough. I don't need to speak without thinking and make the situation worse."

"Darling, how have you confused the issue?" Caroline shifted her skirt and perched on the step.

Elle settled beside her. "I keep mistaking the boy I knew with the man I don't. That's all I meant."

"Are the boy and the man so different?"

Elle plucked a withered blossom from the azalea and twirled it between her fingers. *Different?* Right now, the man was all she thought about, raw desire darkening his eyes, his lips parting before covering hers. "Sometimes I look at him, and I think my childhood friend is still there. Other times, the way he stares at me, the way he touches me, the bitterness on his face. I don't recognize him."

"I recognize him: a man who wants to love you and is fighting loving you like the very devil."

Elle crumbled the bloom between her thumb and forefinger, pollen dusting her skin. "Considering all the women he's been, well, you know." She cleared her throat. "Why does he get angry for thinking about that with me?"

Caroline covered her mouth, but not soon enough to keep the laugh from escaping. Noah Garrett had never looked *twice* at any woman. Of course, handsome and successful, women naturally flocked to him. He was considered an eligible bachelor in Chicago's elite circle. Beyond doubt, he had accepted an indiscreet offer or two, but nothing matching Miss Beaumont's presumption. Nothing at all. *Poor dear,* Caroline thought, and struggled to hide her smile.

"Laugh if you want." Elle ripped another bloom from the bush, her voice dropping to a whisper. "But he's very *experienced.* I don't know why it seems to disturb him to lust after *me.*"

Caroline gulped for air, propping her head on her knees.

"I'm glad to be a source of amusement for you." She waved, rebuffing Caroline's apology. "Don't worry, I'm used to the teasing. My feelings for Noah have always been nothing but a joke. They'll say I left because of him, too, I guarantee."

"Are you planning a trip, Miss Beaumont?"

Elle's hesitated before shaking her head.

"I'm sure you don't need my advice, or want it for that matter, but if you love him, you'd better stay and fight for him. You won't be the first woman who had to, I can assure you. No man on earth wants to admit falling in love, darling. No man I've yet to meet, anyway. They all need a kick in the seat of the trousers to set them in motion."

Elle murmured.

Caroline leaned in. "Again, please."

"Noah doesn't love me, I said."

"Are you sure?"

"Of course I'm sure!" She exploded off the steps and began pacing in front of Caroline, the hem of her cycling trousers bumping her ankles. "He thinks we don't mix. Like oil and water, he said. I'm too frivolous, too foolhardy. And believe me, I tried, at least I did years ago, to conceal my impetuosity. Think first, act later, that sort of thing. Aim to plan before do." She dropped to her knees beside a tilled square of soil, picked up a rusted spade, and stabbed it in deep.

"Try to put yourself in his shoes, Miss Beaumont. After all that happened here, Noah is overly cautious. What he reveals and what he hides are important decisions for him. To me, he's this little boy protecting a precious vase. He's so afraid the beauty of it won't last, he smashes the vase to bits just to ease his trepidation." She lifted the package of embroidered handkerchiefs to her lap and considered giving Elle one to wipe the smudge from her nose. "You mustn't take his word, all those silly reasons you two don't *mix*, gracious alive, as scripture. If you want him—"

"I don't need him." She snatched the spade from the ground, flinging dirt on herself. "Pointless, discussing this. He's turned me away at every corner. For my entire life, Mrs. Bartram. *Juste Ciel*, even *I* have some reasonable idea of when to abandon a sinking ship."

Caroline smoothed her finger over the corner of her package. "Are you leaving soon? On this adventure of yours?"

Elle's head swiveled in her direction. She looked like a rabbit trapped in a snare. "Will you tell him?"

"Will you?"

Her look grew unfocused as her fingers danced over the garden tool. Then her back stiffened, and she gave her head a firm, terse shake.

"You're a grown woman. What you tell Noah or don't tell him is your choice and no one else's. Despite this, I will tell you that I don't agree. I've witnessed the intimate glances the two of you share. Only a blind person would miss them. An attachment of such depth doesn't wither, or die." She curbed her counsel as suspicion filled the young woman's eyes. "I suppose you'll find out for yourself. Noah will, too."

The wind swept her hair into her face. "I can't endure watching him leave again, Mrs. Bartram. My decision is not an impulsive one, nor is the destination perilous. Regardless, leaving is better. He won't feel guilty about..."—she groped for words—"anything that's happened. And I can finish something, something I *want* to finish, and should have a long time ago." Looking away, she added, "Pipe dream or no."

Caroline sighed, wondering how she could help two of the most headstrong, gun-shy people she'd ever chanced to meet. Noah's love for the little hellcat was as obvious as those spectacles perched on the end of his nose, yet they didn't make him see everything. And Marielle-Claire, the way she looked when she talked about him almost made Caroline want to cry.

There must be something she could do *and* keep her promise. Caroline gave the package's ribbon a meditative tug. How to she gain the girl's trust?

"Miss Beaumont, could you do me a small favor?"

Elle started, pulled from a daydream that had left her eyes over-bright and her cheeks rosy. "If I can," she said.

*Trust.* "I want you to tell me about your school."

Noah couldn't help but wonder what she wore beneath those clinging cycle trousers. Since he'd peeked in her bedroom window and seen the lacy frippery hanging from her bedpost, he imagined it beneath everything.

The blade sliced into his skin. Dropping the knife, he brought his finger to his lips, the sour taste of blood filling his mouth. He swore, sick and tired of Elle's blessed undergarments monopolizing his thoughts.

"What is wrong with you?" Zach pitched a fishtail over the side of the dock. "You've been in a fog for the last hour."

Noah turned, unobtrusively wiping his hand on his trousers. What was wrong with him? *Hell.* He'd seen Elle across the street and had barely contained the impulse to go after her.

"Nothing's wrong." He slammed his notebook atop the oyster barrel. "Just thinking about materials for the lab, that's all."

"Wouldn't have to do with Ellie leaving her daddy's office and standing on the boardwalk watching us?"

He ripped a sheet from his notebook and wadded the paper into a ball. "For God's sake, Zach, drop it."

"Fine, I'll drop it." Zach shrugged his shoulders and tossed Noah's slide rule in a wooden bucket. "Consider it dropped."

"Easy there."

Zach glanced up, eyes full of mischief. "Boy, are you touchy."

Noah felt a scowl crack his cheeks. How could the scent of honey-suckle be stronger than the stench of fish? How could he have slept less the past week than he had the week before the Woods Hole laboratory opened, when he had been more nervous than ever in his life?

How could he want her so badly, a woman dissimilar to any he reasoned would make him happy?

"You coming for dinner tonight? Caleb caught a mess of cat. Promised to fry them up and make hot pepper corndodgers."

Noah looked toward the sunset spill sliding into the horizon. Waves thumped against the pilings; a fine mist dusted his lenses. He concentrated, searching for the contentment the sea brought.

"Dinner, Noah?"

He shook his head, gestured to the satchel by his feet. "Going to Devil for a day or so. I want to explore the mud flats on the south side of the island."

"You sure?"

He nodded, not sure of anything.

Zach patted his shoulder, then headed down the dock, the sectioned planks rocking beneath him. Shouldering his satchel, Noah stuffed his notebook inside the front pocket and sprinted to his skiff. Recklessness had him setting sail under more of a pinch than was necessary; the lines twitched in his hands.

Another hour in the coach house, knowing Elle slept less than a hundred yards away, was out of the question. A particularly vivid dream the night before had woken him, and he'd ended up at her back door, hand raised, preparing to knock.

*Excuse me, but I was hoping to make desperate love to you.*

He tugged the sheet and guy with a muttered oath. He had packed provisions for one day, maybe two. Long enough to figure out what to do about Elle. He had to do something. The avoidance part of his plan wasn't working. With each passing second, she became more difficult to resist.

He jerked a square knot in the line, and the gash on his finger split open and started to bleed.

Ah, yes, for the first time in his life, his span of attention equaled Rory's.

The wind whipped his shirt against his chest and the heart beating forcefully beneath it. Hanging his head, he sighed. His rigidly constructed world was falling apart. And *he* feared it would never be the same.

Feared he did not *want* it to be the same.

*Two days.* Two days to decide how to tell Elle he had fallen in love with her.

# CHAPTER FIFTEEN

*"Its sources are obvious."*
    ~ C. Wyville Thomson
    *The Depths of the Sea*

~

*A* jarring noise pulled Elle from the first genuine sleep she'd
had in days. She hitched to her elbow and blinked. She patted
her chest, realizing she had fallen asleep in her clothing. Must be the
jigger of whiskey Christabel and Caroline had forced on her at dinner.
Throwing her hand to the floor, she searched—

"Enough of that, sweet," Noah said and slid the glass out of reach
with the toe of his brogan. Her eyes grew accustomed to the darkness
as her gaze traveled his long, lean body. He dropped, grabbed her by
the waist, and pulled her into his arms.

"What... whe—"

He seized her words and her mouth, throwing her into a tempest
of emotion. Desperation and loneliness raged; passion consumed her.
She groaned and melted into him. Demanding and rough, the kiss
bruised her lips *and* her soul. She surrendered to her love and the

need she could no longer contain. She delved deeply, devouring as he devoured her.

He circled her wrists, his fingers tangling in her cuffs, and pressed her against the chaise longue. Chest heaving, he lifted his head, a look of complete bafflement crossing his face. "Not here... I didn't plan to... oh, hell."

With an oath, he pulled her to her feet and down the hallway, out into the moonlit night, grumbling beneath his breath along the way. Something about inquisitive brothers knocking on doors and how on this night, of all nights, she had to be inebriated.

"I'm not inebriated." Unfortunately, she followed the denial with a hiccup.

He sighed but didn't reply, nor did he look at her or slow his pace. Exhilarated for no good reason, she leaned in and sniffed his sleeve: woodsmoke and soap.

No hint of liquor.

Trying to track his lengthy stride, she stepped on the edge of a shell and gasped in pain.

Noah paused and swept her into his arms, looked both ways, then sprinted down the alley leading to the docks. His heartbeat thudded beneath her breast. He lifted her, a subtle shift that brushed her mouth against the underside of his jaw. Quite helplessly, she kissed him there, her lips lingering.

Noah moaned and halted in the shadowed recess of the seamstress's shop, braced his elbows on the wall, and lowered his mouth to hers, trapping her in his heated embrace. She hardly had time to loop her arms around his neck and thread her fingers through the hair curling over his collar, before he pulled away.

"I want to talk with you. Just talk," he said, a shudder working its way down his arms. "Not here. Not this." Peeking from their hiding place, he loped across the street, pressing a tender kiss to her brow. *"Not yet."*

She shivered at the intensity of his words and the alluring images they brought to mind, wondering how her clear sense of purpose had vanished so easily into the dark night.

The street was deserted. Other than the oyster factory, Noah's laboratory was the only structure on the eastern end of town. The lab stood tall and proud against a twilight sky, wooden shakes recently fitted to the roof. Aching deep inside at the look of completion about the place, she pressed her cheek to his chest, the warmth of his skin seeping past cotton and into her heart.

Stepping onto a narrow, little-used dock, he halted beside a skiff, secured and bobbing. He rolled her from his arms, his muscles tensing as he slid her down his body. Lids fluttering, he lowered his head. *Yes.* She tipped her chin, welcoming the rush of blood between her thighs, the tightening of her nipples. Oh... her body remembered, even if her mind sought to forget.

Mint and ripe apple riding his breath. Close... *closer.*

He jerked, an oath muffled by the hand he swiped across his mouth. "*Chrissakes,*" he whispered and steadied her with unsteady hands. Yanking his spectacles from his pocket, he hopped into the skiff.

Never thinking to ask where he took her, Elle watched him work the lines, the muscles in his arms bulging beneath blue cloth, each movement exposing his chest through the neck of his shirt. Knees beginning to tremble, her gaze dropped to his flat belly, the material there tucked haphazardly into form-fitting trousers. She blinked, curled her fingers, nails biting into her skin. A mismatched button on his trouser fly gaped.

*Juste Ciel,* she thought, and squirmed, a forbidden thrill racing to her nether region.

She lifted her head and encountered eyes the color of a stormy sea. The lines hung slack; his throat pulled in a long swallow. With a gradual movement, he extended his hand, palm up, fingers spread in invitation.

For a moment, she considered turning tail and running. From his rationalizations and the incredible power of his touch. She feared him in an elemental way, yet he remained a part of her, as essential as the blood coursing through her veins. Taking what he offered would not alter her love for him. Taking would only serve to heighten the pain of leaving him.

And, leaving him would be unbearable no matter what she did.

"I just want to talk with you, sweet. Please, come with me."

Decided by the faint tremor in his arm and the vulnerability on his face, she linked her fingers through his and closed them in possession. Stepping into the skiff, she ignored the warning her mind insisted on issuing: *the words he wants to say aren't likely to be ones you wish to hear.*

He settled her between his thighs, his arms circling her as he searched for the lines. The determined desperation in his movements sent a glimmer of feeling, *his,* through her.

Under a billow of white canvas, the flex of muscle at her back, Elle pressed her cheek against his collarbone and struggled to hold apprehension at bay. She had placed the power in his hands. If this was not how she pictured their relationship ending, her clothes damp and clinging, her hair curling about her face and neck, her hands clenched to keep from reaching... well, at least *she* had made the choice. Finally, even if the decision ended in grave error, she owned her life.

She owned her future.

Noah's chest expanded. He cleared his throat; his arms tensed. *Oh, heaven,* was he going to tell her he didn't want her in his life? Tell her he was leaving? That they had no future?

*We're like oil and water, Elle, we don't mix.*

Was he going to destroy her again?

She started, rocking the skiff. "Easy," he said, his lips against her ear. He drew back before he found himself tasting. She smelled different tonight, expensive and exotic. Almond and honey, a rich scent weakening his already weak resolve. "What's the new fragrance?"

"Caroline said you would like it."

Where had she dabbed perfume? Imagining *that* was sure to make him lose focus. Which he could not afford. He had planned precisely how he would tell her he loved her. Knew *exactly* what he would say. He had spent the last two days thinking about her every waking moment. Dreaming about her every sleeping one. He wasn't sure about the particulars, where they would live, and when they would get married, but he knew he didn't want to live without her.

Could not live without her.

The final determination had arrived last night. He had woken abruptly, his dream returning in fragments. Elle in the skiff with Leland and her father... a wave tipping them... her body tossed beneath the white-capped waves... a rapid descent into the depths of hell.

Expelling a terse breath, he fit her to his chest, his hands slipping on the lines, the awkward position making a laborious sail of a calm, easy one.

He didn't care; he wouldn't let her go again.

She shifted, and for a moment he feared he held her too tightly. Then, her lips grazed his neck, an arousing flutter, and he feared nothing at all. Her tongue, hot and rough, flicked his earlobe, her teeth digging in just enough to hurt. He leaned into the touch, his body kicking into gear, a frenzied rhythm it did not take long to find.

She kissed her way up his jaw, searching for his mouth. Her arms wound around his neck, giving him a plentiful view inside her gaping blouse. Of its own accord, his hand crawled higher, his knuckles, then the back of his thumb, brushing her taut nipple. She was exquisite, the wonder of her more extraordinary than all his dreams. Needing to prove she was real, he pressed his palm against her thumping heart as his fingers cupped her breast in blatant ownership.

She sought his lips, found them parted and ready.

*Stop her before she makes you forget what you're supposed to be doing.*

"Sweet." He grasped her wrists and pulled her arms by her side. "Please help me here." He struggled to speak. Blessit, he struggled to catch an even breath. With a quick glance off the starboard side, he saw they had almost reached the island. Another five minutes, and he could put his feet on firm ground, move a thinking distance from the warm, sweet-smelling bundle of seduction in his arms. "I can't think when you touch me."

*Damn,* why had he gone and admitted *that?*

She laughed—an empowered laugh that scared him a little—and

did something he had never imagined her doing, even in his rowdiest dreams. She reached between his legs and slid her finger into the mismatched buttonhole he had caught her staring at on the dock. Not a bold touch by any means, more of a grazing, playful stroke.

It was the most erotic caress he'd ever imagined.

Seizing her chin, he found her lips and plundered. She tasted of whiskey and citrus. She tasted glorious, and for a brief instant, he didn't care if he sailed them off course and out to sea.

Beneath her exploration, her innocent discovery, he swelled and throbbed. She unsnapped buttons, and he held his breath, his trouser fly spilling wide. He sailed them into shore as skillfully as he could with her hand closing about him, gently at first, then with a determined rhythm. His thin underdrawers presented little defense against her touch.

"Am I hurting you?" Her mouth skimmed his neck, a moist slide, her teeth catching, nipping.

He couldn't speak, but managed to shake his head as the skiff beached in the shallows. His collected plan, his grand design, disappeared in the sensual mist enveloping them.

Reclaiming her lips, he swept her into his arms, climbed from the boat and stumbled across the sand, never breaking contact. She worked the buttons of his shirt, one by one, palmed the exposed skin, then she paused to thumb his nipple. A woman had not touched him there and if one had, he definitely wouldn't have imagined it shooting a burst of heat to his loins. Of course, his vixen would find a way to arouse him to madness on her first try.

"What are you doing to me?" he asked in a rushed whisper as he approached the glowing fire. Shadows flickered and danced across the dune. The ocean rolled into shore, and somewhere in the distance, sand locusts croaked. Nothing penetrated but the sound of her blouse crinkling against his arm, the whistle of air past her lips.

She dipped her head and laved his nipple, tangling her fingers in his chest hair. She'd gone wild, and he loved it. "I want to know your body"—she sucked the hardened bud between her teeth—"as well as I know my own." She shoved his shirtsleeve past his wrist. "Better."

Before he lost the use of his brain and his vocal chords, he forced her eyes to his. He loved this woman. It all but knocked him from his feet to realize how much.

"Elle, I—"

She shook her head, covering his lips with her finger. Then she replaced her finger with her mouth. Aggressive and sure, doing all the things she knew he liked.

He could not deny her.

Not when he had, quite possibly, wanted her forever.

He walked the required distance, his makeshift pallet coming into sight. Cradling her against his chest, he dropped to his knees, the sand cushioning their fall. Her legs sprawled; he smiled. He liked the strange trousers she had worn of late. Liked them a helluva lot.

She tore at the cloth hanging from his shoulder, bucking her hips. He let her strip the damp cotton from his body. In reply, he slanted his head and deepened the kiss, taking her lower lip between his teeth and tugging, a sudden image of her lips tracing his arousal filling his mind.

"I want to press your body against mine. Explore every naked inch of you." He started at her collar, working the bone buttons free with systematic precision. He stopped himself from cupping her breasts. This time, he would wait until nothing stood between them.

She complied, guiding his hips up, tugging his trousers down, while her lips traversed his cheek, his nose, his brow. Tentative pillages, light nibbles and licks, sensation snaking into every exposed pore, setting fire to every nerve ending.

Although their fingers faltered often, it seemed easy to divest each other of clothing. Boots, he toed off. She wore none. Her divided trousers, he managed quicker than he could a complicated dress. She wore a simple shift, no corset in sight. He had dressed in a hurry to get to her and wore nothing but a pair of worn underclothing. She had no stockings; he had no socks.

The first touch of her skin against his sent was a shock to his senses. He lifted just enough to allow moonlight to cross her body.

Overwhelmed, he could do nothing but stare—and appreciate his good fortune.

She had grown into an incredibly beautiful woman.

"Noah." Embarrassed, she reached for his spectacles.

He shied away, emitting a husky laugh. "Oh, no, sweet. I waited too long for this, not to see clearly."

Her hair a wild, crimson riot flowing over the tattered blankets in such vivid contrast to the ivory sand. Her breasts plump and capped to perfection, nipples budding beneath his scrutiny. Her slightly rounded tummy, the bellybutton so feminine he wanted to smile. The need to smile vanished, the need to touch outweighing all else as his gaze dropped to her hips. Creamy skin and a round birthmark on her pelvic bone. Below, a swirling tuft of hair between her thighs.

Shapely thighs capping a pair of slender, surprisingly lithe legs.

"You're perfect," he said, and lowered his body to hers, the wind rustling the sea oats above them. "Simply perfect."

"No." A soft denial, followed by a breathless exclamation as he fully covered her.

He wrenched his spectacles off and flung them to the sand, kissing her cheek, her lips, her neck, wanting... wanting *everything*. His hand moved to her right breast, his mouth to her left. "Yes. Yes, you're perfect." Then he set out to prove it by catching her nipples between his lips and his fingers, lavishing them as he had dreamed of doing. *Oh, God, he was....*

*Dying*. She was dying.

The man she loved lay atop her, firm muscle to her sleek softness, half breaths rattling from his lungs with each slow grind of his hips, his fingers and teeth, his lips, all over her, everywhere at once. He groaned and in an instant of raw understanding, she realized his need matched hers.

Gliding her hands past his shoulders, she marveled. He found *her* perfect? *Juste Ciel. He* was perfect. If she could only get another look; a real, five-minute one. A vivid picture of his body bloomed in her mind, and she arched into the motion of his hips, capturing a whimper between clenched teeth. His hand had strayed, his fingers delving into the tight curls at her apex, a place forbidden except during bathing, and even then, under evidence of a heated blush.

He combed and stroked, diligently seeking, oh, merciful heavens... *seeking*. She stiffened and went on alert when he found what he sought.

"Trust me." His lips captured her earlobe, his breath sweeping inside. "I'm here, I'll always be here."

She shook her head and dug her heels into the sand, twisting the blankets and inching away from his hand. She didn't believe him... could not give him what he sought... not at all certain what he sought. It frightened her, the ease with which he molded her, as if she were a lump of clay in need of shaping.

Sensing her hesitation, he returned to her mouth and kissed her, seducing her, using whispered words and a velvet touch. She struggled through a cloud of half-formed pleasure. As his tongue began to match the rhythm of his fingers, heat rose from the tips of her toes, flowed up and out her fingertips.

She trembled, blood pounding in her head. "Please," she begged, unsure what she begged for.

A ravenous nip to the side of her breast... a rough tongue laving... hair chafing. Sliding his thigh between hers, he gradually forced her legs apart. Blinding sensation, each one of greater magnitude than the one before. She didn't know where this would end or how to end it; she could only hang on to him as a painter's splash stained her lids.

She clutched his shoulders, dug her nails into his skin as he dipped his finger into her moist folds. Desire clashed with fear, hunger with indecision. Tell him no, maybe, *yes*. She followed her body's will, arching, crowding into him, and sending his finger deep inside.

"Blessit, you're so warm," he whispered against her breast. He moved to her nipple, sucking, drawing her in. "So wet." His finger retreated, and she whimpered. "Let me pleasure you." Then he plunged. Again, and again.

A deafening roar, a mad pulsing. Mindless, breathless. A masculine scent on the hand she lifted to her face, moisture and sand on the arm she threw over her eyes. The hammering fury of the ocean, the hammering fury of the man she loved. She shuddered, then shuddered again, her toes curling into the sand. She moaned, perhaps she screamed. However loud, whatever sound, it pealed in her ears.

"I'll be here." He coaxed her, his voice thick, his touch direct and unrelenting.

Snagging her hands in his hair, she guided his mouth to hers.

He didn't follow, instead kissed his way *down*, swirling his tongue, lewdly, in her navel.

"Why?" She rocked against his finger as it went deep. His thumb found the erect nub nestled in her curls. He glided his tongue past her hipbone, stopped to suckle the inside of her thigh.

"I want to taste you, know every crease in your skin." The words blurred on a labored breath. "I would never hurt you. Trust me, sweet."

She did trust him, even as, unbelievably, his mouth replaced his finger.

One moment of suspended shock, then she broke apart, scattering in a thousand different directions. Need overwhelming reason. Delight overwhelming fear. She thrust her hips and demanded. Ecstasy, pure and undiluted, scorched a wide path, clearing her mind of everything but the reality of him caressing the most intimate part of her, his fingers working in delicate tandem with his mouth. She gasped, needle pricks of pleasure striking her, jettisoning her into a world of shrouded gratification known only to those who sought to grasp it.

Cool air brushed her skin, and she blinked to find found Noah poised over her, his weight held on his elbows, his gaze ravishing her, setting fire, inch by inch. She wiggled against the aroused flesh nudging the folds he had just vacated. He met her eyes, his as dark as she had ever seen them. The hunger in his gaze sent longing straight through her. Her knees swayed; her legs fell flat.

Had her heart ever felt this complete, her body this sated, her mind this calm?

A masculine smile of satisfaction crossed his face. Hands cupping her face, he leaned in, his mouth capturing hers in a long, deliberate kiss. She met each thrust of his tongue, desiring equal partnership. He groaned his approval, slanting his head and taking all she offered.

"Did you like it, Sweet?"

She closed her eyes, making a sound like a purr. Her arms flopping wide, she burrowed her fingers knuckle-deep into silken sand, uncaring that she lay before him, naked and complete.

His thumb smoothed her eyebrow, his hand trembling against her temple, passion building inside him, she knew. "I've never, well... I didn't know if you would like it. God, I wanted you to." His arm slid under her bottom, angling her hips as he settled against her. "This will be even better."

"Not possible."

She felt his slow smile. "Just watch." This said, he seized her lips, a kiss of savage possession, of mastery and crude compulsion. More blatantly sexual than any he had given her. Gone was the seductive, patient lover, the childhood friend. In his place, a man whose need had risen above his level of restraint.

Elle should have imagined how he would take her comment. Even as a boy, Noah appeared apathetic about swimming contests or boat races, the most unconcerned of the bunch.

Until dared.

She had never seen anyone work harder, by honest means, to win.

And now, he used his incredible tenacity, his talented lips and fingers, to drive her wild. She blinked into a midnight sky nestled with winking stars. As she stared, the world tilted on its axis.

"Where next?" His gruff query rang in her ear. "Here?"

He caught her nipple between his teeth and suckled. "Here?" His hand slipped through her moist curls, he sent his finger into her, once, twice, then a complete, teasing withdrawal.

Heaven, what had he done to her?

He pressed his sex against her. "Here?" he asked, each word he spoke more hoarse than the last.

She dragged her hands from the sand and clutched his shoulders. *"Yes."* A memory of her fingers circling him, followed by an image of them *joined,* shattered her coherence. Moaning, she urged him to sink into her.

He made a guttural sound and pressed her into the blankets. A creeping thrust; his hold on her tightened. Lifting her hips, she took him deeper. She hid her face in the crook of his neck and breathed in the mix of soap and sea clinging to his skin.

"So long, I've wanted you for so long." He captured her startled cry as he embedded himself inside her, hip to hip.

Her body bloomed in response to the unfamiliar fullness, each petal unfolding. The sharp pain quickly subsided, outweighed by pleasure. She smiled and gazed into his face. A muscle in his jaw jumped, a circle of white surrounded his mouth. He tilted his head and swallowed hard, obviously controlling his reaction.

Her hands skimmed his back, coming to rest above the rounded crest of his bottom. Tentatively, she moved her hips, a fresh torrent of desire claiming her.

His lids fluttered, his eyes meeting hers for the first time since he'd made her his. "Are you all right?" He pressed a feather-soft kiss to her cheek.

Amazed by the gratifying completeness, and so *all right* she could not believe it, she nodded. Grasping his waist, she made an impatient movement he could not help but understand. "But I think you need to... work harder... to win this bet, Professor."

He laughed and complied, the muscles in his buttocks bunching as he withdrew so far she feared he would pop out. "Yes, ma'am," he said, before claiming her lips and doing a gradual, glorious slide back.

Tender movements became fierce, amused expressions resolute. Restraint broken, he set a furious, steady pace, surging into her, each stroke seeming to touch deeper than the last. She rose to meet him, lost in a tide of tactile awareness. Whiskers scraping her cheek... teeth closing around her inflamed nipple... muscles, damp and hard, flexing beneath her fingertips... hips bumping, bruising and rough. Savage and untamed, fighting for subsistence, for the most basic gratification. And every place she hungered, he found: touching, licking, driving, tensing.

He raised her knee to his waist. She lifted her leg, locking her ankles behind his back, marveling at the wonderment of him thrusting, filling her completely.

*"Ma chere fille."* Low and ragged, the once-loved designation brought her closer, ever closer to the edge. For the second time.

"I'll be there, with you. Always," he whispered next to her ear.

A swift crest, a headlong dive. Harder, then harder again. The wind whipped the blanket against their hips, sand pricking their skin. She searched, thrashing and whimpering. He answered, his finger finding the nub of flesh he had teased before. Keeping his pounding rhythm, he touched her there, purposely.

And she exploded.

"Thank God, only so long I could think of fish," he said over the odd ringing in her ears. The ground shifted, and she arched into him, digging her heels into his calves, clasping him to her. Heartbeat to heartbeat, slick skin to slick skin. They fought for the same air, not enough for both of them it seemed.

As she drifted back, he called her name, his body shuddering. Driving deep once more, he buried his face in her hair and gathered her close, panting. For a long moment, they lay silent and dazed, limbs tangled in an intimate, damp jumble. Tremors shook him and passed to her.

He lifted his head, his gaze feral. A bead of sweat crossed his cheek; a rapid pulse beat at his temple. She smoothed her finger over the bulging vein, swept the drop of moisture away with her thumb. He leaned into her touch, his lids fluttering, the scarred one drooping. She smiled. She hadn't noticed before, but his nose was peeling, and his cheeks were freckled from the sun. The dark circles beneath his eyes attested to his lack of sleep.

Had she ever looked at him this closely? Would she ever again?

He released a weary sigh and rolled to his back, pulling her with him, pressing her into his side. He brushed her hair from her brow and laid a soft kiss on the crown of her head. "Better than candy," he murmured and yawned.

Fulfilled, she snuggled against him, the muscles beneath her cheek relaxing as he slipped into sleep. The arm around her went slack, the other lay across his belly, his slim, well-shaped fingers splayed wide. She searched for his hand, linking their fingers. Automatically, his tightened in possession.

Forever.

She would treasure what they'd shared forever, even if it *had* been the biggest mistake of her life.

Because, how long would it be before Noah began to regret?

# CHAPTER SIXTEEN

> "It is thus quite intelligible that a world of animals may live
> in the dark abyss."
> ~ C. Wyville Thomson
> *The Depths of the Sea*

~

*C*ontentment. Completion. The first of either Noah had truly
felt in twenty-seven years of living. Before this night, how
could he possibly have understood what holding the woman of his
dreams as he made love to her, her tremors of release shaking him to
the core of his being. He had never even slept in the same, well... never
spent the entire night with someone.

He liked it; he liked it a lot.

He smiled, amazed by his stupidity. By believing he could reason
his way out of loving her. He gazed at the sapphire blaze streaking the
sky and realized Elle was no longer chaste.

Then, neither was he.

Since he awoke to find her draped across his chest, her breath

218

teasing his skin, her hand clutching his, he'd struggled to remember a time before her.

A bit panicked, the answer struck hard.

Ten years ago, he left more than two loving brothers.

He stooped to grasp a conch shell, dusting off bits of sand. What if he had returned to find her married to Magnus Leland? A cinnamon-headed child bouncing on her hip, another man's child suckling at her breast. Another *man*. Noah flung the shell into the waves.

She was *his*; *he* would waste no more time on regrets and fear.

It wasn't entirely his fault, he reasoned. He'd always been rather possessive of her, fiercely protective and unable to shrug off the sense of responsibility. In some fashion, he had recognized the bond between them.

But Elle recognized the love.

Dammit, at seventeen, how could he know that he would never find another woman to match her, that she would be the one to fill the emptiness inside him? With all of Elle's foolishness and flippancy, chasing him down the street on a daily basis, he hadn't dared lower his guard long enough to find out.

Now, he would put the past behind him. Forge a solid relationship with his brothers, with Rory. Let the wounds of distrust heal. Take a chance on the future. Take a chance on love.

Love.

Water lapped at his ankles as he walked forward. The wave retreated and coquina shells pricked the pads of his feet. Why hadn't she told him she loved him earlier? How many years since he'd looked into her vivid green eyes and known for sure? Perhaps she had confused her fondness for a childhood friend. He had certainly accused her of that enough times.

He dropped to his haunches, his trousers getting soaked to the knee. He thought women always said those words after coupling. *During*, maybe even. Elle hadn't said anything remotely maudlin. Of course, he might have missed three little words, if she'd whispered them, or mumbled them against his neck or something.

He drew his hand across his whiskered jaw and sighed, his skin scented with almond and honey and woman. He sought to disprove the cold lump of suspicion collecting in his gut, the familiar fear of rejection, yet he could not.

Caleb's betrayal still stung. Of course, Noah was the fool; he should have stayed and let his brother beat him to a pulp, if necessary. They could have solved the problem a week later, not ten years.

"Noah?"

He wrenched around, landing flat on his bottom.

Elle stared, wide-eyed, for all of ten seconds, then she slipped her hand over her mouth and burst into laughter. She wore her shift and nothing more. Moonlight flowed through the thin material, silhouetting her body well enough to stir parts of his he had thought were satisfied.

He shoved to his feet, his trousers, minus underclothing, sticking to his legs like wet parchment. "You think scaring the life out a person is funny, huh?"

She shook her head, yet choked for breath, the laughter still bubbling.

He took a step forward. She took a step back. She broke into a run, and he was right behind her.

They stumbled up the beach, a faltering gait in the sand. He caught her about the waist, swung her off her feet, and against his chest. "Forfeit," he said, recalling a childhood game.

She giggled in delight, this woman who never giggled. "If you remember correctly, Professor, I never yield. You'll have to torture me first."

Her playful tone sent desire straight to his loins. He hardened against her bottom. "What kind of torture do you have in mind, sweet?" He seized her shift and tugged it to her hips in bunched fistfuls.

She gasped, not able to form a coherent response when his fingers teased, delving into the patch of curls at her apex, spreading, exploring, penetrating.

"Is this adequate punishment?" He found a bare spot on her shoulder and sucked.

Her head lolled forward, then back. She sighed in reply.

He settled her atop the blankets. Her shift fluttered to the ground; his shirt and trousers followed. Passion clawed at him, a ravenous beast demanding nourishment.

He fell to his knees; she spread her legs. Hip to hip, chest to chest, he entered her in a sure, swift stroke. Uninhibited, they mated like animals in the dawning light.

*Animals.*

Something Noah had never in his life thought to compare himself to.

Elle fished a threadbare sailor's cap from Noah's satchel and settled it over his face. He'd already blistered his skin, trudging around the island in improper attire.

She threw his shirt across his chest and watched it rise and fall on a long breath. He was exhausted, his cheeks dotted with stubble, dark circles beneath his eyes. His hair hung past his ears, far longer than usual. A memory of her nose embedded in the thick strands as he plunged into her curled her toes into the sand.

Nonplused, she concentrated on the break of waves on the shore; the call of seagulls in search of food; the rustle of sea oats on the sand dune behind her. Even after a hurried swim, she could smell the scent of their joining on her skin. Even after washing her mouth with salty water, she could taste him. Sliding Noah's satchel to the side, she slumped against the dune and groaned at the tender friction between her thighs.

They had made love *three* times. Once while waist-deep in the ocean. An hour ago, no more. How could she want him again so soon? How?

*Juste Ciel*, she had not expected this.

It's not as if she hadn't understood the mechanics of copulation. An indistinct, yet defined, sense of what happened between a man and a woman in a darkened bedroom. He positioned his sex accordingly;

she complied, stiff and sacrificing beneath him. This information circulated at every sewing bee and quilting circle, crossed every coverlet at every church picnic. Naturally, the married women stopped talking the minute she, unmarried and ignorant to the reality of wifely duty, entered their line of sight.

Until her engagement to Magnus Leland.

She had no mother, and they felt obliged to educate her.

Mrs. Scoggins explained in shadowy terms how thinking of household chores made the act go quicker. Widow Wynne listed excuses she once used to avoid *it* altogether. Jewel Quattlebaum detailed the necessary pain involved in a reporter's concise, unemotional manner. Lillian Quinn's description was the only one that sounded more pleasurable than tooth surgery.

Thankfully, lovemaking was nothing like those descriptions. Love made it truly wonderful. She reached out, needing to touch him. A muscular arm lay folded over his belly; the other stretched from his body, fingers nestled in the sand. Her breathing accelerated. She had touched much of him, with her hands, and later—at his urging—with her lips and her teeth. His sex's rigid shape was gone for the moment, but she could still see a firm outline beneath clinging cotton.

She had not imagined that circumspect Noah Garrett, the first to hesitate and weigh all the options, would take her with such confidence, such lewd boldness? As if he knew exactly what she needed and held no misgivings about giving it to her.

This excited her—in a secret place Noah had brought to life—to picture him, staid and fussy, buttoned up and pressed down, precise speech and polite bearing, panting and plunging into her, passion stealing air from his lungs, rational thought from his mind. She was amazed to find she could set him aflame, that she could shatter the composed facade he presented to the world.

She slid her hand closer, just one touch. Sighing, she forced her arm to her lap. He needed sleep. And she needed to conclude if this night had changed her plans for the future.

Leaning over him, she rolled his cuffs past his ankles, shading more of his skin.

She loved him, but he had not said he loved her.

Luckily, she hadn't admitted it, either.

Did he love her? She traced a faded scar on the sole of his foot. Indefinable lights, tender sparks of emotion flared in his eyes more than once last night. Especially the last time they made love. They left the water still joined, and he brought her on top of him in the sand as they attained bliss.

If there were the slightest chance he loved her, she would forgo the scholarship, and persuade Noah to take her with him. She remembered seeing a university in Chicago on the list of those offering women's programs.

Her hand stilled. What if he didn't want a wife who attended university? What if he didn't want a wife at all? Perhaps making love meant next to nothing to him.

She sat back on her heels. She could go with him anyway, make a life with him, somehow. She preferred this choice to the wretched one of never talking and laughing with him again, never being intimate with him again. Maybe a modern relationship was called for in this situation. Like Caleb and Christa had. Except, Caleb had asked Christa to marry him on more than one occasion.

She pulled her watch from her pocket and checked the time. Another half hour, and she would wake him. She glanced overhead: the sun was a bright, blinding ball in the sky. Looking at Noah, she noted that his cap shaded his nose and cheeks, but not his lips. Red and swollen, they looked well loved.

When they got home, she would make a baking-soda paste for his skin and spread salve on his chapped skin. She snapped her fingers. Maybe he carried medical supplies in his satchel.

She searched the shallow outside pocket. Two pencils, a metal measuring tool. In the larger section, she found a notebook and a leather-bound manual of some sort.

Normally not a meddlesome person, she took the notebook out, wanting only to read what he'd been studying the last two days. A garbled scrawl detailing migration habits for a fish she'd never heard of. On another, a rough sketch of the beach and back bay, marked off in specific sections, with complex names attached. She leafed through sheet after sheet of scientific terms, facts, and figures.

Wishing biology had been a part of her study plan at university, she turned a page and froze.

*Outcome: mind free of Elle Beaumont* was written in block letters and underlined.

Twice.

Her jaw dropped as she skimmed the lines of text. *Work longer hours. No more kissing. No more touching. No more daydreams. Eating dinner or repairing shutters is forbidden.* A circled notation reminded him to ask Caleb to mow her grass. She dug her toes into the sand, a furious quiver working its way down her legs. Obviously, he intended to share this list with her now that they had privacy to discuss the situation.

His lust, hell, *her* lust, had simply derailed his plan.

A sharp wedge of pain drive the breath from her body; she doubled over and sucked in air. A dull buzz sounding in her ears, she placed his satchel beside her and laid the notebook on top. Dazed, she covered him with the blanket, knowing he would swelter, but at least his skin wouldn't crisp.

She trudged toward the water, readied the skiff for sail, and found the strength to shove it through the bucking waves. She licked her finger and held it into the wind. She could make it to the dock in less than fifteen minutes, pack a bag, and have Stymie shuttle her to Morehead City in time for the four o'clock train. She would send a telegraph to Savannah and ask her to meet the train in New York City.

*I'll be here, with you. Always.*

Disbelieving, Elle tugged the lines taut and sailed from one dream and toward another.

～

For six months after leaving Pilot Isle, Noah slept in deserted rail cars and abandoned shelters, curled into a ball, fearful and tense. The dreadful experience had honed his instincts, razor-sharp, and when he woke, he realized instantly.

She was gone.

He blinked into muted light, flipped his sailor's cap from his face, and swore. Blessit, he was burning up. Shoving the thin blanket from his body, he rolled to his knees, praying Elle would be sitting beside him, a smile of happiness, of acceptance, on her lovely face.

A bead of sweat coursed down his cheek, another down his chest. He shook his head and calmed his breathing. *Think, Noah, think.*

That had always been easy before.

He stumbled to his feet, his stiff trousers crinkling. For a step or two, he followed the set of petite footprints, remembering his first day back on Devil and the picnic they had shared. He felt for his spectacles. No pockets. Hell, he didn't even have his shirt *on*.

He squinted, glanced anxiously around him, and turned a full circle. Where could she—

Two things struck.

His skiff, although he couldn't see clearly, no longer appeared to be on the shore. And his satchel lay in a spill, his notebook sprawled open beside it. He dropped to his haunches, and brought the paper close to his face. *Dear God,* he thought, the notebook sliding from his fingers. In the distance, the harsh grunt of a white ibis filtered through his bafflement.

Hadn't she known? Hadn't she trusted him? He had begged her to, told her he would be there for her. His list... it didn't mean anything. Nothing at all. Just an asinine way to try to expunge her from his system. Blessit, he *loved* her. Didn't she understand? Did she imagine he'd ever had a night like this one with another woman?

Impossible.

He tipped his head back and located the sun. Elle couldn't have left more than three hours ago. Four at most. He would straighten this mess out: tell her he loved her and explain the silly damned list. Plan in mind, he set about folding the blankets, spreading his campfire ashes, packing his satchel. Slipping his arms through his sleeves, he lifted his wrist to his nose, and inhaled deeply. He hoped he could persuade her to stay at the coach house tonight.

He was willing to grovel if necessary.

A shout sounded above the breaking waves. The wind ripped at his shirt as he turned toward the sea.

Caleb sailed into shore in a spritsail skiff of his design—one he had promised to construct for Noah. He glanced up the beach, his lips parting, words Noah couldn't catch over snapping canvas.

Was that Zach sitting in the stern? Noah fumbled for his spectacles. The troubled look hardening Zach's usually agreeable features triggered an alarm. He stood, rooted to a blistering spot of sand, trying not to let his imagination get the best of him. But... *both* of them? Why had *both* his brothers come? Like they performed some mission of mercy or something.

Zach reached him first; Caleb lingered by the skiff, clearly hesitant. Without saying a word, his brother dropped a wrapped bundle in his hands. Noah started to loosen the piece of cloth, then halted, staring.

He fondled the worn material, his anxiety building. "Where did you get this?"

"Where did you leave it?" Zach's tone held a faint thread of anger.

The material, once pale blue, was now the color of chalk. And stained in spots—with blood from a long-ago split eyelid. "The docks. Or Stymie's sloop, maybe. He ferried me to Morehead City that night. I changed into a shirt I grabbed from a clothesline." He swallowed, fighting the dread creeping higher. "Where did you get this, Zach?" But he knew, oh, he knew. Elle had kept his shirt for all these years. The shirt he'd been wearing the night he left Pilot Isle.

He wasn't sure *what* that made him feel.

Queasy, impatient, fearful.

"Noah, you know where I got it. She left you a coat, too."

"Left? Where is she?"

"Wherever she went, your friend Caroline went with her, so she's not alone, thank God." Zach retraced his steps, his stride chafing and furious. As he neared the skiff, he called over his shoulder, "I don't understand why Ellie wanted you to have that. You'll have to ask her, if you ever get to."

Noah flung the shirt to the ground and stared at the book in his hand. He had only seen it once, but he would never forget what his mother's diary looked like. Not when her secrets had cost him so much.

Why had Elle left this for him?

A moment passed and then he understood.

This was her way of saying good-bye.

"Are you going to go get him or do I have to?" Zach banged the skillet to the stove. A tarnished ladle followed.

Caleb slouched in his chair, hung his head over the back and groaned low, where Zach couldn't hear it. He drummed his fingertips on his thighs, wishing the aroma of dinner—fried ham and sweet potatoes—did something besides make his gut twist. He didn't want to face his little brother across the scant width of a kitchen table. Not right now. Ellie had been gone for three weeks and each day proved worst than the last.

"I don't like going there," he finally said. Shamed him, yes, because only children feared the burying ground. Shamed him, but truth was truth.

"I don't care what you like, Cale. Go get him. He's like Rory right now. Doesn't eat here, I don't know if he eats at all." Zach slammed a bowl of gravy to the table, rocking Caleb's glass of tea. "From the lost weight, I don't think he's eating anywhere *but* here, that's for sure. And what about the stunt he pulled with Sean Duggan, knocking him unconscious on the docks. Whatever Mrs. Bartram wrote in her letter, Lord, I believed Noah was going to kill the man. Someone has to talk some sense into him."

Caleb grabbed his wobbling glass in both hands. He'd been trying to get Noah's skiff ready, hoping that would lighten his brother's black mood. "I don't understand women. I've been asking Christa to marry me for nigh on five years, and she always says no. Holy Mother Mary! What do you want *me* to say?" He took a slow sip of tea. "Anyhow, thinking about him and Ellie, well, it kind of makes me uncomfortable."

Zach wedged a knife between the pan edge and a cake of corn bread, snapped his wrist, and popped the steaming loaf onto a plate. "Makes you uncomfortable to imagine your brother in love?"

Caleb wiped his chin and squirmed against the unforgiving seat. "Yeah, I guess. I mean, it is *Ellie*. Professor spent the night on Devil with her. God knows what they did."

Zach wedged a piece of corn bread into his mouth and chewed, a smile growing. "Doesn't take God to figure that one."

"Stop. I don't want to hear this. Practically my little sister you're talking about."

Propping his hip on the counter, Zach folded his arms, and settled his stoic gaze on his brother. *Damn,* Caleb hated that look. "I never understood Noah either, Cale, if that admission makes you feel better. Less than you, safe to say. Always a step ahead of me, a step ahead of any child I ever met. And then Momma died, leaving me to raise him. I tried my best. And when the two of you... well, I figured giving him some time to think was the way to repair things." He cupped his elbows in his hands and squeezed hard. "Let emotions settle. Only, he had the hurt fixed in his heart, so deeply fixed, there was no way to budge it. Every day that passed, he built these walls around himself, holding us out, betrayed and alone. And, he's doing the building again, only this time with Ellie."

"Maybe she'll—"

"She won't come back, not while he's here. You remember what he told us, the list she found? Hell, what's she to think?"

Defeated, Caleb scooted his chair back and rose, his shoulders hunched. He rubbed the nape of his neck, trying to remove the stiffness. "I'll go. I hate the danged burying ground, but I'll go."

"Just listen if he wants to talk. Simple." Zach turned to the stove. "Besides, I'm leaving to pick up Ellie's friend, the woman who's running the school. Savannah. I can't remember her last name." He jammed a dishrag in the waist of his trousers. "Anyway, I don't care how you do it. Drag him here by his toes. I'm not letting him withdraw from this family again. And you're going to help me, even if you have to spend the night in a graveyard."

Caleb put his shoulder into the screen door. "Not funny, Zach. Lots of spiders in that creepy place." The door smacked behind him as he stalked across the porch, Zach's laughter trailing him.

～

She could be pregnant.

Settling back, Noah rested his head against the gnarled wisteria vines circling the oak's trunk, wondering a little angrily if Elle had considered this fact. Three times posed significant risk. He hadn't minded taking the risk or asking her to. He assumed they would wed soon after. Dammit, every day spent imagining a child growing inside her pushed him closer to the edge.

*His child.*

He closed his eyes and let the unbidden images flow, accepting the agony as his due. To save his sanity, he allowed this painful process twice a day. When he woke, reaching for her, and again in the afternoon, after stocking the laboratory library. Nights were unbearable unless he labored to the point of exhaustion. Which should cover him tonight as he had just finished a twelve-hour shift on the *Nellie Dey*.

He searched for a comfortable spot, leaves crackling beneath him. Dappled sunlight danced over his unlaced brogans and seared his skin through his clothing. High above, branches stirred restlessly—restlessness he understood.

He located the marks in the tree trunk with ease. Like he did each day, he traced them: *Elle loves Noah.* Christabel had carved the words when he was fourteen, disfiguring two trees in the burying ground— which most people avoided unless lowering a loved one—and every tree in the schoolyard. It had taken her an entire summer to complete the project, she'd once told him. Naturally, he had been mortified.

Now... now he wished some of them read *Noah loves Elle*.

Because he did love her.

More deeply than he had believed was possible.

Would she have left if she'd known? Would it have made any difference? Hadn't he proven his love during their night on Devil? He assumed he had. Didn't such spirited lovemaking speak the same of her feelings?

Her betrayal, even if the fault lay at his doorstep, cut as deeply as Christa's marks. He questioned ever trusting Elle, ever trusting *himself*, again.

Behind him, the creak of the gate sounded, followed by a heavy tread on the path. Noah leaned out and a frown spread. He watched Caleb chart a hesitant course through the graveyard, dodging the shell slabs with devout consideration. He remembered his brother's fears: spiders and haunts.

Caleb halted, his fists diving into the pocket of his trousers. He stared at the vaulted brick Noah propped his left arm upon. "You shouldn't be leaning all over someone's final resting place, should you?"

Noah spared the worn tombstone a glance. "Navy captain, dead for fifty years. I don't think he minds the company."

Caleb fluttered leaves with a halfhearted kick. "Zach made dinner. Wants you to come home."

"I'm not hungry."

"Have you eaten today?"

Noah tilted his head, incensed for no good reason. "What is this? The damned Inquisition?"

"I don't know what that's supposed to mean, so I won't get mad. But, you'd better not think to push me too far."

Noah swore beneath his breath, a vulgarity he'd never said to his brother, never said to anyone.

Caleb jerked him up by the front of his shirt, brought them nose-to-nose. "Listen, you half-witted fool, I don't want to do this again. I lived through it once already. With Zach, after Hannah died. Crazy fits and black moods, not eating and not caring." Caleb released him, then grabbed Noah's wrist to steady him. "Ellie isn't dead. If you want her, find her. Quit rolling around in grief that isn't real. Real is the stone slab Zach puts flowers on every week. That's life lived without someone."

"You don't understand, Cale."

"I'm sure I don't."

He yanked a piece of moss from the bark and mashed it between his fingers. "I gave her all I had to give... and she left anyway."

"Yeah, you gave everything. Good aims are fine and dandy, but did you say the words?"

Noah didn't ask what his brother meant. Flinging the crumpled greenery to the ground, he shook his head.

"Aw, you *have* to say the words. Just whisper them a few times to yourself first. Then, they'll come spilling right out, even when you wish they wouldn't."

"I never got the chance to say them." He frowned and plucked at another bit of moss. "Not literally anyway."

"Literally? I guess that means you never actually said it." Caleb laughed and rocked back on his heels. "Funny how you can be so smart in some ways and dumb as a brick in others."

Noah cut his eyes toward Caleb. "What the hell do you mean?"

He threw his arm over Noah's shoulders, a stretch when he stood inches shorter. "I mean, little bro', you've joined the ranks of the unlucky souls who have to work for a woman's affection. About time, because you never had to work for Ellie's before. I guess I don't know much about women, confusing creatures, but I do know this much... they delight in the niceties."

"Niceties?"

"Little presents. A lace handkerchief or a colorful hair ribbon, maybe pretty flowers or a tin of powder. You could try those fancy words you think but never reckon you'll have to *say*. It won't get you far to keep quiet. You need to come right out and make a fool of yourself."

Noah snatched his satchel from the ground. "That's the most ridiculous advice I've ever heard."

"Maybe." He shrugged. "Only, who has a woman and who don't?"

"Woman?" Noah slapped dried leaves from the shoulder strap. "Hell, you can't even get yours to marry you."

"Mighty true, but at least I know where mine *is*."

Noah clenched his fists and took a furious step forward. "I could find Elle if I wanted to. I have some ideas, you know."

Caleb walked backward, shaking his hands, a silly smile on his face. "I'm sure you do, Professor. You always did have plenty of *ideas*."

"Elle left Pilot Isle with a woman who has been my friend for years. Caroline has a good idea where Elle is. Jesus, don't you think I would find her if I wanted to?" Actually, Noah had telegraphed Caroline three times. She had refused each request, once going so far as to advise him to stew in his own juices. "She left me, Cale, meaning she doesn't *want* to get married. What would you have me do? Drop to my knees and beg, give her the opportunity to rip my heart out completely?" He kicked the gate open and stalked down the sidewalk, Caleb right on his heels.

"Marry? Damn, you got to tell them you love them before you start asking. Though it hasn't worked yet for me." He clapped Noah on the back. "No wonder you messed this up. Like I said, smart in some ways, dumb in others. Makes me happy to realize I've got more brains than you about something."

"Realize? You don't realize anything." Noah shrugged from the grasp and crossed the street at a trot. He could see Zach's steep hip roof and the wooden shakes that needed replacing just ahead. Might as well go over there, he thought, all this talking had made him hungry.

Caleb jogged beside him. "Hate to disagree, but I do know one thing."

"Yeah, what's that?"

Caleb patted his chest, a smug grin plumping his cheeks. "Stopped by the post office on the way here, and I got a letter from your lady friend, Mrs. Bartram, right here in my pocket."

# CHAPTER SEVENTEEN

*"There is some rough rocky ground..."*
~ C. Wyville Thomson
*The Depths of the Sea*

❧

*E*lle passed a boisterous group of men wearing odd-looking shirts she had come to find they played football in. She acknowledged their subtle leers and soft whistles with a steady gaze, refusing to let them intimidate her. South Carolina College had eight female students in the fall of 1898, and horse-faced or winsome, they elicited a fair share of attention.

Attention she could live without for the rest of her days.

She slipped her watch from her pocket and gave it a quick glance. Lifting her skirt above her ankles, she took the steps to the college of science at a run. She couldn't afford to arrive late. She had petitioned the dean for entrance to this class, a first-year biology course, and he had agreed, albeit reluctantly.

Hushed voices echoed off the high ceiling as she entered the auditorium. With an swish, the door closed. She glanced around, found Piper Campbell, the only other woman in class, and slid in beside her.

Piper leaned in. "I thought I was going to have to search the halls for you."

Elle loosened the string binding her books and pulled the biology text from the stack. "I had a meeting with Dr. Collins. He doesn't think I can handle his European Chronicles class. After four years of accepting female students, I can't believe this university still expects us to take nothing but literature and domestic economy. Simple book-keeping is about the only class they'll approve without a fight."

"Collins?" Piper snapped her fingers. "Ah, yes, the one who wears a pince-nez and cracks his knuckles while he lectures." Her face tightened, a determined look Elle had come to know well. "Your duty is to go in there and score the highest mark, knock that dandified goat on his bottom."

Smothering a smile, Elle said, "No, no, Pip, I'll knock Professor Laurent on *his* bottom. When I signed up for his French course, I neglected to mention I spoke the language for the first ten years of my life."

At the front of the classroom, a loud clap silenced the hum of conversation. Professor Stanford, the youngest faculty member on campus, climbed three stairs to the platform and halted behind the lectern. Clearing his throat, he smoothed the thatch of dark hair on his head. "Students, I've made a slight adjustment to the syllabus, one I hope you will appreciate." He propped his elbows on the podium, where he would keep them the entire lecture. "I've asked a former colleague, a doctoral candidate teaching an advanced oceanography class at this university, to speak once a week on marine-science topics. I firmly believe an introductory class should present a wide variety of subjects to enable you to choose your next course with a clearer understanding of your interests and talents."

Professor Stanford announced his guest lecturer's name, and Elle's vision blurred. She gripped the edge of the desk, the kick of her heart all she heard.

Noah crossed the stage, his hand extended toward his colleague.

He had a notebook—the *same* blasted notebook—tucked under one arm, the familiar leather satchel looped over a broad shoulder. She drew him in like a long, cool drink of water.

And promptly spit him out.

Close-cropped hair parted slightly off center. Jaw square and clean-shaven. Cheekbones prominent in a lean face. Lips parting to reveal straight, white teeth. His formal attire—striped trousers, black sack coat, gray waistcoat, and four-in-hand knotted over a butterfly collar—befit a scholar.

"My, my, will you look at him," Piper whispered, her normally barbed tone thick as honey.

Elle vaulted to her feet, her textbook thumping to the floor.

Noah glanced up from the lectern, his spectacles catching a glint of light, concern crinkling the skin around his eyes. He heeded the lapse, his features smoothing. "Miss"—he glanced at his notes, then back with a half smile—"Campbell or Beaumont?"

She could have killed him, dashed down the aisle and pummeled him with her bare fists. If every female student didn't suffer at the emotional outburst of another in this world where they were watched so closely, she would have.

"Beaumont, Marielle-Claire. Sorry to disturb, *Professor* Garrett," she said through gritted teeth, then smacked her bottom to the bench, the hard spank exactly what she deserved.

A responding spark of anger lit his gaze; his smile flattened into a thin, harsh line.

She glared. He nodded.

Across twelve rows and two dozen students, they waged war.

"Welcome aboard, Garrett. Hope you're settling in. Unpacking the modest library I seem to remember you carrying with you years ago? I'm sure the jars of sand and rusted anchors are on the way." Martin Stanford leaned a shoulder against the doorjamb of his guest lecturer's office, his brilliant blue eyes lit with impish humor his students would have been shocked to witness. That he was a man once known as a flagrant profligate by the nickname of Marty would have also come as a surprise. "By the bye, you want to tell me what the little scene was in the lecture hall?"

Noah crushed his fountain pen in his fist, cursing his earlier slip. Thank God only two people in the room had noticed. "Excuse me?" He raised his brow in virtuous arrogance, hoping the ruse would throw Marty off course.

Marty dropped into a chair and hooked the heels of his oxfords on the desk. Noah had never seen an educator alter his personality so dramatically before his students. "Come on, Noah. I may not know you well, after all, you weren't the most gregarious fellow in my residence hall, but I know you well enough. Quite a show. I actually believed Miss Beaumont was going to leap on the stage and claw your face to ribbons." He whistled, lips pursed. "Scared me, my friend."

*Me, too,* Noah thought with pride and dismay, recalling the furious flush staining Elle's cheeks.

Marty rocked his leg in time to a personal tempo, patiently waiting. Finally, he said, "The silence is killing me. Fortunately, I don't have another class for two hours."

Noah sighed and dropped his pen to the desk, slipped his spectacles off, and buried the heels of his hands in his eyes. "She's a family friend." He rubbed hard, seeing stars. "Is that enough?"

"Not nearly."

"Sorry, but it will have to be."

Marty's feet hit the floor. "You contact me out of the clear blue, a terse telegraph asking me to bring you on for a semester *and* help you fund a research project on the coast. Admittedly, in light of your stellar reputation, your arrival provided somewhat of a coup for me, as I took all the credit for inviting you *and* for creating the research project." He waved his hand in dismissal. "No thanks are necessary. Glad to accommodate an old university chum. Without complaint, without question."

"Thank you. From the bottom of my heart." He replaced his spectacles, preparing to return to his work. He had to formulate a lesson plan for the oceanography course before four o'clock. And... until he figured out what to do about Elle, he wasn't clueing Martin Stanford in on anything.

Marty hummed a ditty and tapped his foot in time. "I'm Miss Beaumont's advisor. Worked with her a lot this semester."

Noah's head came up, greed overriding caution. He had missed her. In fact, he'd just about gone blind from missing her. Countless hours worrying and dreaming... and, a time or two, wishing he cursed her judgment as he cursed his. Damned helpless, he could not deny the impulse to ask, "Is she a good student? Is she happy?"

A wide, cat-got-the-cream smile crossed Marty's face. "Talkative, temperately disruptive on occasion. Slides in right under the bell, but notably intelligent and enthusiastic. In fact, she's impressed quite a few of the program's detractors, of which there are many at this insti-tution. At any institution accepting female students, I would imagine. Dane Cossin—you remember him don't you, came down in '94— anyway, he asked her to assist in his World Geography class. Grade papers, take notes, those types of duties. For that old cuss, a weighty honor."

"Cossin?" Noah's hand shook, sputtering ink on his paper. "Wasn't there a rumor about a liaison with one of his students in Chicago?"

"Yes, but the scandal involved his son, Daniel. Mathematics depart-ment. Dane is seventy if he's a day."

Noah slumped back, wishing Marty would get the hell out of his office.

"Is she a former student?"

"No."

"Had to ask." Marty shrugged, the first sign of chagrin. "I didn't think so. Excluding formal functions, I've never seen you in the company of a woman. But, I had to ask, you understand. Being a female student's advisor carries a peremptorily higher level of respon-sibility than I am used to."

"Give me her class schedule, Marty."

His gaze sliced back, round and startled. "I can't do that."

"Yes, you can. If you don't, I'll find a way to get it myself. Make it easy on me, an old university chum."

Marty unfolded from the chair. "What *is* this?"

"I'm going to ask her to marry me. I'm quite certain that's all you need to know." There, he'd said it. As Caleb had predicted, the words hadn't stung much. Only a slight twinge of discomfiture.

The next time he said them, probably wouldn't sting at all.

"You're in love?" Marty stumbled. "*You?*"

"What do you mean, '*you*'?"

"I had it all mapped out for you, Garrett." Marty fluttered his fingers, not even bothering to hide his incredulity. "Living in a decrepit house surrounded by shark's teeth and driftwood, bundles of archaic netting. But a wife? And marriage?" His arm stilled as he stared past Noah's shoulder. "Come to think of it, I *did* see a lot of interested women flocking around you in Chicago, but you never gave them a second look. Actually, I'd started to wonder."

"I never gave them a second look because of *her*." *I think I've loved her since I was twelve years old,* he added, too private a comment to make to anyone but Elle. Besides, it made him sound like a lovesick fool.

"Hell's bells, you must have a worse case of the sickness than I ever did."

"Have pity on me. I do." Noah slid a sheet of paper across the desk. "Either you give me her schedule or I follow her around campus, starting with your class on Wednesday morning." He tapped his pen. "Would the news you've invited a deranged marine biologist to teach in your department enhance your sterling reputation, Professor Stanford?"

Marty grabbed the pen and scribbled. "You're lucky I have a crack memory. Anyway, can't stand in the way of true love, now can I? I'm a romantic fellow, really. Always have been."

Noah linked his fingers over his twitching stomach muscles, hoping everything would be this easy.

∽

Elle opened the door and peeked inside. She held her breath and crept along the deserted hallway. The two hours the library remained open after dinner seemed the safest time to study; she was certain Noah would eat in the faculty hall and stay for the customary cigar and brandy. In the day since he'd shown up in her science class, she had not caught a glimpse of him.

But she had looked.

Around every corner, beneath every shrub. Releasing a hysterical giggle, she wondered if his appearance at the university symbolized nothing more than the mercilessly ironic will of God.

She turned into a back room that smelled of dust and leather. A comforting scent she would always associate with learning. Maturing. Heaviness settled in her chest, and she searched her mind for the source. Ah, yes. Now, she would also associate the aroma with *him*.

Settling at a table hidden behind shelves devoted to Roman history, she blinked the mist from her vision. Why did this have to happen? When she had finally decided leaving was for the best? She stared out a window overlooking the quadrangle, pine straw and horse dung littering the grassy expanse. The wind snatched at student's hats and pulled at the pages of their textbooks. Elle pressed her fingers to the pane, feeling detached and despondent, her heart and mind working against each other.

Merciful heavens, what could she do to forget him?

A dull screech signaled someone taking the other chair. She swiveled on the smooth seat, thinking to ask for privacy.

Noah. Elbows propped on the table, rolled cuffs hitting him high on his arms, wrinkled neckpiece twisted between his fingers. His hair mussed, his sun-kissed features angled in earnest regard. His lips softened into a half smile, faint and sorrowful, the corners tipped low. Hushed voices and heavy footfalls faded as his bewitching scent overwhelmed the stale one of aged parchment and learning—all crowding the air she breathed.

She almost lifted her hand to adjust his collar, dazed by the longing that set her heart beating like a drum. "What are you doing here?" she whispered.

He searched her face, considering. She saw a hint of sadness cross his, though his smile grew. "The best spot in the library. Quiet, an agreeable window."

She gripped the edge of the table and leaned in, close enough to see a tiny circle of stubble he had missed with his razor. "That's not at all what I meant, and—"

"What is this?" He dropped his neckpiece and used a slim finger to rotate her textbook. *"Basic Discussions in Biology.* I incorporated this text in a class once. Two years ago. What chapter does Marty have you reading?" When the silence lengthened, he said, "I could tutor you... if you need help."

A thousand memories crossed her mind. Carefree evenings spent at his mother's kitchen table, fireflies flitting outside the screen door, a scatter of pencils and paper, his hand guiding hers, gray eyes watchful and expectant. All the love she felt for him, absolute and powerful and unwelcome, flooded her being. Blind with panic, she grabbed the textbook and shoved her chair into the wall.

Reacting quickly, he grasped her wrist, her bones shifting beneath his fingers. "Don't run, sweet. Please, don't." The sight of her fear—raw, gut-wrenching fear—eroded his control. "I've only seen fear on your face once before, when I blacked out in Caleb's skiff. That emotion was *for* me." He let her hand slip away. "It really hurts to be the cause."

She drew a breath and perched on the edge of the chair. Her throat trembled beneath her lace collar. Noah wanted to press his lips to her pulse, love her with his heart and body. Share his soul.

He would tell her everything this time; he would show her she was not alone.

Forcing his hands by his side, he tried to disregard how beautiful she looked in what he thought was a new dress. "I'm sorry for shocking you in class. I'm also sorry for sneaking up on you today." He repressed visions of what she might be wearing beneath the butter yellow material.

"Caroline told you where to find me, I suppose." She linked her fingers and squeezed, presenting the crown of her head.

"After my fourth telegraph, plus two from Zach, yes, she finally did. You mustn't blame her. I left her no choice. Since then, I've been going crazy trying to get the lab on its feet and get to you."

Her eyes met his. "Get to me? Why would you want to get to *me?*"

"Elle, I"—he tunneled his hand through his hair—"I need to talk to you. Desperately. There are things I want to say. Words best spoken in"—he glanced over his shoulder and back—"private."

"I thought this might be why you'd made this journey." Her voice dropped. "I'm not pregnant, Noah. Thank God, for both of us. So you can go to Pilot Isle or Chicago or wherever it is the fish need you with a clear conscience."

He glanced down in dismay. He had *hoped* to find her pregnant. What would she think about that? "If you're trying to hurt me, you're doing a fine job."

"I'm, I'm not trying to hurt you."

"Doesn't matter. Nothing hurts as much as your leaving did. You didn't think it important to tell me you planned to return to university? I woke up on Devil *alone*, Elle."

"You don't need to remind me how much being left hurts, *Noah.*"

"Is that what this is? Revenge?" He leaned in, the scent of almonds and honey fueling his desire *and* his anger. "I wish I had never left. I wish I had given you your first kiss, been the one to hold your hand and dance with you, see you through university and the opening of the school. I wish... oh, hell." He banged his fist on the table.

"No use in wishing, Professor. We're like oil and water. You're the one who reminded me time after time, in your diplomatic way. Congratulations. Now I believe it."

His hand shot out. "You *don't.*"

She flinched, dodging the contact. "Yes, I *do.*"

He wrenched his spectacles off and gazed into her eyes. "Look into my face, Elle, and tell me what you see."

"I used to be able to see everything. Now... I, I see *us*, together, kissing and touching. Like the night on—" She flinched and her textbook hit the floor. "Why did you come, Noah? *Why?* You're not responsible for what happened. You were right when you begged me to forget the boy I loved. You should do the same and forget the girl you protected."

"I did say that, didn't I?" He laughed and scrubbed his hand over his jaw. "I once said far too many things." Before she could react, he was halfway across the table. His hands rose to cradle her face. "I hadn't planned to say this for the first time in my life in a damned library, of all places, although the irony isn't lost on me. However, another night cannot pass without you hearing me say it. The last two months I've said it in my dreams. Tonight I want to say it to you." He leaned in until their mouths brushed. "I love you, Marielle-Claire Beaumont. I'm deeply, hopelessly, helplessly in love with you."

Then he kissed her. And felt love flow from his heart.

Against his, her mouth formed one word—*no*—as anguish etched her face. With a cry that cut clear through him, she wrenched to her feet and rushed from the room.

He stared at the strand of hair wrapped around his finger, realizing he did not know where she lived, and that she had sprinted into a dark night. Shoving from his chair, he slipped on a smooth marble edge and cursed leather soles, inferior vision, and lack of foresight.

"Elle, stop!"

Chest hitching, he caught her as she turned into a dim passageway bordering the faculty residences. She shoved at his hands, tears streaming, dampening the hair hanging in her face. "Easy, sweet. There now. I'm here." He leaned against the rough bricks and wrapped his arms around her, drawing her close to ease her trembling.

"No." She slumped, the crown of her head slipping beneath his chin.

"Tell me why my loving you is a terrible circumstance." He turned his face into her hair. *Lemon,* he remembered, and inhaled deeply.

"What happened that night wasn't"—she burrowed her cheek against his chest, her sob tearing into his soul—"what you planned and... you don't know how to make it right. It's nagging at you... to make the situation right. Make me fit somewhere proper, somewhere decent. It's your way."

He cupped her chin, forcing her gaze to his. "You think my love for you is born of guilt? I don't feel *any* guilt over what happened between us. I'm incredibly awed by the beauty of what we shared. And I'm starved, actually somewhat desperate, to touch you again, but guilt?" He shook his head.

"Your list—"

Laughing softly, he fit his brow to hers. "Oh, sweet. Forget that ridiculous list. I've been making those since the day I defended a disheveled French immigrant in a crowded schoolyard. A thousand by now, at least."

"If you have, you hid them well."

A renewed burst of love swelled his heart as a renewed burst of desire swelled things elsewhere. He had not been lying when he'd said he was starved. For the sensation her body beneath his, arching to meet his thrusts, grasping his hips, and guiding his movements. Taking command in a manner unknown to him before her. His heart stuttered in remembrance. Sixty nights alone, dreaming and wishing for her companionship had proven to be a torturous experiment.

One he never wanted to repeat.

He lost sight of his purpose and lowered his head, thinking only of tasting.

*Oh, no, he's casting his spell.*

Proof of his hunger pressed into her hip, hard and long, as his mouth skimmed her cheek, his tongue flicking, stoking. Her thoughts scattered. Frantic and aroused beyond measure, she shoved against his chest. Then repeated the action more forcefully when he refused to move.

He backed off with a swear. "Elle, for God's sake, you're killing me. Tearing my heart from my body." He drew a shallow breath and let the air rush out. "I need you. Blessit, I love you. How can I prove it?"

She covered her ears, the pounding of her heart deafening. "You're confusing passion with love. You see, I went to the psychology section of the university library when I first arrived and spent an entire afternoon reading about... intimate relations. A classic example of misplaced affection, confounded by our childhood relationship. Also, I realize it's odd because, at one time, I would have sold my soul to hear you say the words you said to me tonight. I prayed to hear them, dreamed of hearing them. Only, I don't want to hear them now." She babbled and could not stop. "I can't depend on you. I have to depend upon myself. I've been trying to heal, trying to find my way. Trying to decide what I'm going to do with my life, now that my family is gone. You have your life planned, successful career, loving family. I'm alone now, and—"

He grabbed her shoulders, his fingers digging into her skin. Throat working, he glanced at his hands. Jerking them back, he turned to lean stiff-armed against the wall. His frenetic breaths echoed in the silence.

Had she imagined the glint of tears in his eyes? "Noah? I think, I think this would be better for both of—"

"Please," he said, an anguished, inaudible plea. "Don't say any more. I'll go crazy if you do." His fists clenched, his knuckles scraping the wall in what must have been a painful movement. "Not your fault. I expected too much after what I've said. The warnings." His head dipped low, and she watched him struggle, the muscles beneath his shirt bunching. "Just before you left, I figured this out, what it means, the rarity of the bond between us. I understand how poor the timing is. You've started university again. I intended to tell you that night on Devil, had every word planned, but you stopped me, kissed me. I never got my thread of thought back."

"You're a child with a new toy. You don't—"

He slapped the wall. "Don't presume to tell me what I feel, Marielle-Claire Beaumont. Don't you dare."

She swallowed, heartsick, and surprisingly, a tad angry. "It's too late." She added, *"You're* too late. Time will take care of this, for both of us."

"You little fool, time won't take care of a damned thing." His features settled into an intractable expression. "You'll marry me, Elle. Within the month. I'm not waiting any longer for you to come to your senses."

"Not waiting?" she asked, red coloring her vision. Stepping forward, she jabbed his shoulder. "Well, you'll wait a long time." Jab.

"I'm not marrying you." Jab. "This is my life, Professor, and you have no say. And thank you, but you can keep your romantic proposal."

He captured her hand before she uttered another word. "I love you, and I'll do whatever is necessary to make you believe it. Every day for the rest of my life. Swim the length of the Atlantic Ocean. Lasso the moon. You're the only person I've ever belonged to, and I'm not letting you give me up."

"No." He didn't hear her, as he was occupied with nibbling on her wrist.

"Yes," he said, and sucked her index finger into his mouth, rolled his tongue around her nail for good measure.

As if it were happening to someone else, she watched him make love to her hand. The same sweeping tilt she experienced when he kissed her, an earth-shattering shift, rocked her where she stood.

"This is what I want to do to your entire body, sweet. This is what I *will* do. I promise you."

A weak sound rose from her throat. A flush of need and embarrassment crossed her face. The juncture between her thighs caught fire; her nipples contracted beneath her corset.

Leaning against the wall, he hooked his feet at the ankles, a deceptive pose when she could see his chest lifting with ragged breaths. His gaze traveled from the tips of her new leather boots to the ends of her recently trimmed hair. "You desire me as much as I desire you. And you love me, even if you don't want to."

"Yes, I want you."

Raw hunger replaced confidence. His stance stiffened as he pushed off the wall. "Spend the night with me. Come to my house."

She walked back a step, stumbling over an uneven brick. He followed, his depraved expression exposed by a strip of moonlight.

Helplessly, she whimpered.

He squinted, his hands falling to his side. "You're terrified of me. Completely terrified."

"I am," she said, pride yielding to honesty.

Naked sorrow swept his face, making her feel the guilty party. "I'm sorry. I shouldn't have come here, forced myself upon you. I just figured with what happened on Devil." He closed his eyes and touched the bridge of his nose. "That you only needed to hear me say the words. I assumed my foolishness was keeping us apart." He turned and walked into a gaping recess of shadow. "I guess that's what my limited experience with women gets me."

Lacking reason, she raced forward and caught his sleeve between her finger and thumb. "What did you say?" Impatient and confused, and as always, impulsive, she said, "What did you just say?"

His gaze slid her way, and he blinked. As he remembered, a flush she observed even in the dim moonlight flooded his cheeks. "Nothing." He fingered the neat golden arch above his ear. "I didn't say anything."

"How you touched me, you were confident. Clever." She worried her bottom lip between her teeth, a movement he watched with blind attentiveness. "How many?"

His frown deepened, creasing his lips. "Elle, this isn't something we should discuss."

"Why? You've never kept secrets from me before."

"Secrets?" He groaned. "It isn't a secret."

"Then tell me." She swallowed, preparing for the worst. "How many? Too many to count?"

"Too many to *count?*" He leaned in, searching her face. "Is that what you think?"

She nodded.

"Sweet—"

"It's all right. Don't tell me. We're not children anymore, whispering under a spread of scrub pines, dangling our feet over the side of a dock."

Bricks shifted. A rock cracked the wall. "Two." His labored sigh echoed along the passageway. "In college, a professor's daughter. Engaged to a very wealthy man her father had selected for her. She was testing the waters, being rebellious, I suppose. She made her interest known, and I accepted her invitation. One time, at her father's summer cottage. Later, in Chicago, a woman I met at a university function. Widowed, attractive, not interested in an attachment. There were other, well, opportunities... but a nagging sense of discontent always held me back."

Elle opened her eyes to find him watching her, his gaze guarded and wary. "Once with her, the widow, too?"

He jammed his hands in his pockets and shook his head.

"Oh, now I understand what Caroline meant."

"What Caroline meant," he said and knocked the toe of his oxford against the ground. "Listen to me, the things we did, most of them were as new to me as they were to you. If it appeared I was overly confident or possessed a great degree of knowledge, hell, I don't." He lifted his head, a wicked smile growing. "Just beginner's luck."

"I'm scared," she said, startled to hear the confession.

His smile dimmed. "Why?"

"Everything's all mixed up." She pressed the heel of her hand to her throbbing temple. "My father attempted to determine my future, guide my hand. He told me so often that my choices were foolish, sentimental, and preposterous. I've come to wonder if he's right."

"Elle, he was not right. I told you the same thing, and I wasn't right, either. The young girl grasped our connection. She was wise and brave, and I loved her as much as I love you."

"You don't understand. I'm not a girl anymore, living on dreams of the future and believing in your love above all else. I can't pin all my hopes on you. Give you my heart like I could before. I just can't."

"Time? Do you need time?"

She bowed her head, the uncertainty on his face bringing to mind the boy she'd cherished. *Damn and blast,* it made her want to shout at the unfairness, the gross irony, of life.

"I'm going to the coast for a few days. Research at a commercial fishery in Georgetown. I had hoped to ask you to go with me, somehow schedule around your classes. I can see now, that won't happen."

"Will you come back?"

He tilted her chin, forcing her gaze to his. "You're slow to get the idea, sweet, but I'm not leaving South Carolina without you."

"But—"

He stopped her denial by capturing her lips beneath his, a kiss of gentle honesty, not persuasion. Entirely too compelling, this side of him. "I can't live without you," he said, then slanted his head, assaulting from another angle, his hands sliding into her hair to cradle her head. He tasted of citrus and mint, wonderful, appealing.

Time slowed as he leaned against the wall and spread his thighs, fitting her hips to his. She followed every movement, mirrored the thrust of his tongue, the rock and grind of his pelvis. Somewhere, the clang of a church bell and a horse's shrill whinny resounded. The world outside meant nothing. For her, there was only his thumb sliding beneath her collar, pressing against her pulse. His lips brushing her cheek and moving lower. Liquid heat, a shower of color —red, green, and gold. Her low mewl of assent. Her hands tugging at buttons, seeking what she knew he would give.

At the ingress of her finger through a loosened buttonhole, he set her from him. "Either we stop now"—he sucked air into his lungs—"or we make love on the ground."

"What?" She blinked, her vision blurred.

His jaw tensed. He fisted his hands by his side. "I'm sick to death of alleys and beaches. I want to lie with you on my bed, your bed, *any* bed. Wake next to you and listen to you breathe. Curl our feet together under the blankets. I want to be more than your lover. I want to be your husband, the father of your children. I want you, forever."

She could not stifle her bewilderment, just as he could not stifle his anger. "I'm leaving for Georgetown at dawn, sweet. When I come back, I'll find you. Don't think to run from me again."

"My life is here, why would I run?" Foolish to act confident with her knees knocking together.

He thumped his chest, for once, brute strength and mulishness. "Your life is with me. Don't ever forget that."

Dazed, she realized this was not the time to argue. She walked from the alley, not even sure which direction she took. He grasped her hand and led her to the library, where they retrieved his spectacles and her textbook. Not a word passed between them.

Noah dropped her off at the boardinghouse the female students shared, left her standing on the front porch with nothing more than an authoritarian glare of possession and a light, lingering kiss on her cheek. Elle watched him stride across the lawn, his tall form fading into the darkness.

Stark exhilaration raced through her, followed closely by sheer terror. Merciful heaven, against her wishes, or *because* of the thousands she'd once exacted, it appeared as if Noah Garrett meant to keep her.

# CHAPTER EIGHTEEN

~

The first gift arrived the next day. A square bundle wrapped in brown paper and sitting on the top step. He'd scrawled her name across the front in his now-familiar script; a yellow ribbon, one she had inadvertently left on Devil Island, held the package together.

She unwrapped the paper with trembling fingers, an autumn gust tugging at the loose knot of hair on her head. Her eyes stung from lack of sleep, from twisting and turning, from replaying everything Noah said to her and wondering if his words could be true.

Deep inside, praying they were true.

She opened the tin box, trying to deny the quiver of excitement. This was the first gift a man had ever given her, outside of a modest present or two for her birthday. Nudging the swath of velvet aside, her breath caught. Her mother's brooch lay amidst the plush maroon folds. Hands shaking, she pinned the piece to her collar, blinking past the tears. She sold it the day before she left Pilot Isle, to help pay expenses. Promising to keep the heirloom in her family, Mrs. O'Neil, the jeweler's wife, paid a fair amount.

How had Noah known?

Elle lifted the scrap of material to her nose, wishing his scent remained. She could visualize him arranging the velvet just so.

A slip of parchment fluttered from the box. Heart racing, she grabbed the sheet.

*Sweet,*
  *This belongs to you, as I do.*
  *I love you.*
  *Noah*

Elle replaced the velvet and closed the lid. With wooden movements, she followed the hallway to her set of rooms and collapsed on her bed.

She missed her morning classes.

～

Two days turned to four, four to six, six to eight. Her tension mounted with each package she found on the step, each hour that passed waiting for Noah to leap from behind a pine tree or pop his head from beneath her desk. As he had no doubt known would happen, her resistance melted, her love for him increasing each time she read one of his notes.

First the return of her mother's brooch. Then Noah's pilot coat wrapped around a set of leather-bound books she had admired, weeks ago, in the mercantile window. A parasol with pink-and-green ribbon loops came the next day. Or was it the shot silk dress, trimmed with black-velvet bands and guipure lace? The loveliest item of clothing she had ever seen, one she plainly had no place to wear. Sighing, she set the hat on her head. This morning's gift, trimmed with roses and a striped fabric, perfectly matched her parasol.

Noah had wonderful taste in women's apparel. With an angry kick, she scattered a pile of burnished leaves. Better to spend her time worrying about what she was going to tell him when he returned than imagining how he had come to have such good taste.

*I love you, and yes, I'll marry you.*

No, no, that sounded brazen, as though her earlier rejection had been a feminine ploy. But, she needed to have an answer. Soon. He had begun asking her questions in his daily missives. Blatant queries, often underlined for emphasis. *What church shall we say our vows in? Should we go back to Pilot Isle?* His methodical certitude made her smile and laugh aloud, her classmates looking on in stupefaction. Who but Noah would think to champion his cause, fact by listed fact, while never even showing his face?

And how had he known the tactic would work?

Curiosity killing her, she rose one morning at dawn and watched Professor Stanford creep into the yard and place a gift on the step. Although she should have resisted, she leaned from her window and yelled to him. He lifted his head, his face turning colors in the dawning light. Now, he avoided her gaze in class and had not called on her to answer a question once.

She expected to score a high mark in biology.

A sudden gust tugged at the lapel of Noah's pilot coat and sent a shiver down her spine. Elle shoved her hands in the pockets, drawing the wool close. She leaned her cheek against the material and sniffed. She punished herself by wearing the coat because it provided such an inescapable sense of closeness to him.

He had probably anticipated her reaction. She had to remember the man did nothing by chance.

Closing her fingers around the apple in her pocket, she brought the fruit to her mouth and took a healthy bite. Mrs. Holden really needed to hire someone to clean the yard—

Elle stumbled to a halt, the apple dropping from her hand. She spun in a small circle. Where was he? A black-and-white cat crossed the street at a dawdling pace, a grocery cart rolled past, the driver lifting his hand in greeting. Kicking the fruit from her path, she walked forward. Carved in the trunk of the only tree in the yard: *Noah loves Elle.* Not deep etching, like Christa's. This was a hasty attempt. She brushed the letters and raised her hand to her face. A raw scent clung to her skin; her fingertips glistened. Moist, the bark was still moist.

Calling his name, she completed another turn, even tipped her chin, and searched the copse of branches above her head. A sudden burst of emotion... longing, trepidation, inevitability. He was close; she could *feel* him. She sprinted across the yard, grass snagging in her bootlaces, leather soles skimming the scattered leaves. She watched a gust of wind suck the lace curtain inside her bedroom window.

She had closed the window before leaving for class.

The air was cooler in the hallway, a pale burst from an electric bulb lit her way. She tiptoed to her door. Something different.... She sniffed. A cloying odor, syrupy and floral. Hair on her arms rising, she twisted the beveled knob, and the door swung in without a murmur.

Candles covered every vacant surface, flames wavering in the open window's breeze. Rose petals, red and yellow, littered the heart-pine floor and the unmade bed. Elle closed the door and slumped against it. A faint sound, a whistling release of breath. She turned her head.

Noah sat in a chair in the far corner, arms folded over his stomach, feet propped on the rattletrap desk she and Mrs. Holden had moved from the attic. She stepped closer, saw he slept deeply. Candlelight lit every angle of his whiskered cheeks, silhouetted the gradual rise and fall of his chest. His frock coat lay in a tangle on the floor; his fingers gripped his neckpiece. The edges of his waistcoat curled, revealing a snowy white shirt open past the point of decency, and, *oh...* a wealth of chest hair showed.

Drawing the wrinkled cloth from his hand, she unbuttoned his collar, and dropped it to the desk. He murmured and sighed. She brushed his hair from his brow, slid his spectacles from his face, and placed them on a shelf above his head. Only after she had covered him with a thin woolen blanket, making sure his feet did not poke out, did she take a long, leisurely examination. She perched on her bed and she stared, marveling at her good fortune. Noah rarely let anyone view him like this—splendidly ruffled, utterly undone. She could look all she pleased, caress if she chose to. The notion of touching him sent a molten rush through her.

The candles dripped wax in melting plunks; the world retreated behind lace curtains and dying sunlight. The low flames bathed them in warm brilliance, creating an island of solitude and understanding. How had she ever imagined living without him? Pride, her damnable pride. Simply because he had not discerned his love as promptly as she would have liked. True, he had rejected her impassioned ardor at one time. But he had also been her closest confidant, her strongest ally. Wasn't that worth its weight in gold?

She placed her lovely hat on the floor and curled into a ball, sinking into the feather mattress, rose petals sticking to her skin. She blinked, yawned. In response, Noah mumbled her name, once, softly. Beautiful. Beautiful and brilliant, and he claimed to love her. She started to rise, to go to him, thinking to slide her hands inside the gaping neck of his shirt and press her lips to the tender area behind his ear, an act which never failed to drive him wild. She wanted to drag him to her bed and shock him with the strength of her desire.

She shook her head, determined to observe him until he woke.

They had time enough for everything.

For a long moment, Noah stood beside the bed, staring at the woman who meant more to him than life itself. The sun had set, leaving only a few sputtering candles to caress her skin, her hair, a glorious, rusty spill across the cream sheets. Funny, now that he had let her love into his heart, he could not bear to live another second without it.

When had Elle come to belong to him so completely? The first time he saw her, in the schoolyard? From that day forward, she had certainly thought *he* belonged to *her*.

Curled on her side, she stretched, innocently raising her skirt, baring a slender thigh he knew the shape of very well. Her cambric drawers did not hide much. No, not nearly enough. He remembered her legs wrapped around his waist, firm muscle tensing with each thrust. Groaning, he raked his hand over his face. He had to keep his mind free, clear. He needed to talk to her, wanted... *oh, God,* to explore the exceptional bond between them. He wanted to hear an accounting of every minute of her life.

He wanted to drink her into his soul.

As if she witnessed his struggle, and wished to destroy his good intentions, her mouth parted on a sigh, her tongue sneaking out to touch her bottom lip.

Ah, what was a man to do?

He pressed his knee into the mattress and it sank deep. Feathers, he realized, and smiled. He had never made love on a feather bed before. With a gentle sprawl, he lay behind her and pulled her against his chest. Elle was, if he remembered correctly, a very deep sleeper. Proving that, she shifted, crowding her buttocks into his groin, all the while humming low in her throat, her sensual kitten growl. The sound, and the press of her bottom, shattered the last of Noah's noble intent.

Nudging her hair aside, he placed feather-soft kisses along the nape of her neck, searching for, and finding the hidden nook behind her ear. He caressed her jaw, her temple, traced her arched brows with his lips. The scent of her drove him wild. The faintest hint of lemon and crisp autumn. And roses, he thought, smiling as he peeled a petal from her cheek. He unfastened the buttons on her practical blouse, wondering if she had worn the dress he had given her. He would have liked to give her lace-trimmed underdrawers, something secret and naughty for him alone. He had no word for the piece of clothing he pictured her wearing for him.

His breathing starting to escalate, he tugged her sleeve past her wrist, set his lips to her shoulder, his hand rising to cup her breast, heavy and warm in his palm as his thumb searched. She wore a corset, strangely enough. Stiff and unyielding, he pondered how to go about getting it off.

"Let me help you," she whispered, and turned her head, her mouth finding his, her tongue stroking, begging for entry. She tasted of apple, sweet and ripe. Knocking his hand away, she worked the ties on her corset, jerky movements that sent her elbow into his ribs.

He harbored no denial, only concerned with the quickest way to get inside her. There would be time for finesse and kind words later, time to remove every piece of clothing and pay homage to her body. Now, he *needed* her surrounding him, tight and moist and hot. Needed her badly. Her moans and sighs, delicious sounds of entreaty, convinced him rapidity would work for her as well.

He tore his mouth away and rolled her beneath him. Her thighs spread, and his hips slid into place, a consummate fit. "I'm sorry," he said, his lips pressed against the side of a freed breast and moving higher. "I want you too much to wait."

She laughed, which set her nipple quivering beneath his lips. "Wait? Merciful heaven, Professor, I don't want to wait. Hurry up and get your clothes off."

"Oh, sweet. A little clothing never hurt anyone." In impatient fistfuls, he drew her skirt to her waist, dismayed to find more than one layer. Her drawers were simpler, the matter of a knotted tassel or two. Promising to buy her new ones, he snapped the ties he could not easily undo.

Cooperative and eager, she went right to the heart of the problem, loosening the buttons on his trouser fly. Their lips met, their fingers trembling and slipping over buttonholes and ribbons. She removed fabric, grasping him, hand curled. Her teeth sank into his shoulder as she roamed the length of him... and back. Delirious with desire, he closed his eyes, his weight held on his elbows as he traced the curves of her body. Had he taught her to touch him in this fashion: a firm, assertive glide from tip to juncture? He must have, but he could not recall.

Right now, he could scarcely recall his own name.

Hand pressed to the small of her back, he angled her hips.

Lowering his lips to her ear, he instructed her to wrap her legs around him and hold on.

With a sweep of her thumb over the rounded tip of his arousal, a daring stroke that came close to ruining his fine purpose, she let him go. His hand drifted between her thighs, found her moist, swollen, and warm. He dipped deep, plunged, preparing her. He wanted, no, he *needed* to see her need match his. She tipped her head, throat muscles jumping as she swallowed. He glanced at the door, closed, but who knew how much sound would travel through it?

In a sudden movement, she raised her hips, bumping against the heel of his hand. The moan started deep, threw her eyes wide, rendering them dark, dark green. Acting quickly, he captured her groan of pleasure with his lips and entered her in one smooth stroke.

She gasped and together they found a fast, sure rhythm. Her legs tensed, then tensed again, her nails digging into his back.

"I love you," he said, his mind shutting down. Pulling her close, he thrust once more, hip to hip, thigh to thigh, and uttered a hoarse cry, flooding her with everything in his heart and his body. Every muscle strained and snapped like a taut band, leaving him limp. He kissed her, weak and clumsy, not certain if she responded. Still clasping her to his chest, he rolled to his back, moisture slicking their skin, their harsh breaths filling the room.

Elle slumped across him, her arm a dead weight beneath. He stretched, found his trousers circling his knees, snarled and damp. His shirt hung off one shoulder. Rose petals matted his cheek. And, oh yes, he thought and shifted with a groan. Elle had clawed his back to ribbons.

"*Juste Ciel.* I'm dying," she said, her voice cracking. She plucked at her skirt. "Good heavens, I still have my clothes on."

He smiled, pressing a kiss to her brow. "Actually, I ripped your drawers off. Ruined them, I'm afraid. I'll buy you a new pair, I promise."

"Drawers? Who cares about drawers? I can't even feel my arm."

Noah laughed and lifted enough for her to pull her limb free. Not wanting to let her go, he gripped her waist, and brought her atop him.

A dazed look ruled her face. Her lids slipped low as her head flopped forward. "Sleepy," she mumbled.

He tightened his hold, cherishing the secure weight of her. "It's all right. I'll be here."

"Love you," he thought he heard her whisper between a sigh and a yawn.

He checked the urge to kiss her. A stray tear he could *not* check streaked down his cheek. "I love you, too." Mere words did not even begin to describe what he felt. "Too much."

She hummed in response, a drowsy, sated vibration.

Footsteps echoed in the hallway; Elle tensed against him, lifted slightly. "Hush, sweet. I locked the door." He brushed his lips over her head, curls catching in his whiskers. "Besides, we're getting married. With this going on, I figure the sooner, the better."

She brought her hand to his chest, trailed her fingers through the hair she appeared to like so much. "When?"

He sank into the mattress, exhaled in relief. "How about this Saturday?"

*"Saturday?"*

"Preacher Ellis has been notified, the church in Pilot Isle reserved. Caroline's arriving on Friday afternoon. Christa's baking some kind of cake and throwing us a party or something. I bought our train tickets last week and—"

Elle reared, snatching a pillow from the bed and cuffing him in the face. "You planned all this, never even bothering to ask me first?"

He jerked his trousers to his waist and buttoned his fly. "Yes. I did. I told you I wasn't waiting any longer. Chrissakes, after this"—he gestured to the tangled sheets and scattered rose petals—"how can you argue? It's the only sensible option." *Uh-oh.* He realized after he said it that this would never be a good argument to present to Elle Beaumont.

"Why, you... oh!" She rolled to the floor and started pacing by the bed, hands fisted on her hips.

Noah rested against the rosewood headboard, beginning to enjoy this. The sight of her stomping around the room, bottom swinging beneath wrinkled satin, bosom bouncing beneath nothing at all, caused a miraculous erection to spring forth.

She glanced at him, glared actually, her gaze sliding down his body. She came to a sudden, shuddering halt. "Oh, no, Professor. Not again. Not as long as you're making all the decisions and not even asking me what I'd like to do. Stubborn, arrogant...."

He laughed and leaned over the side of the bed. Straining, he slipped his thumb inside the ribbon surrounding the box he'd hidden.

She raised her head from drawing her sleeves to her shoulders, her blouse still gaping, breasts rising on each furious breath. Her eyes widened when she saw what he had in his hands, her lashes fluttering. A flush of excitement crossed her cheeks as her fingers danced down her stomach to her waist. A rush of pleasure warmed him.

So, she'd liked his gifts.

Grinning like a lovesick fool, he nudged the tiny package toward the edge of the mattress. "This is the last one." He winked and crossed his ankles. "This week, anyway."

She took an eager step forward, a shy half step back. "You shouldn't have bought me all those gifts."

"I can return them, if you don't want them."

*"No."* Her cheeks reddened; her head lowered. "I mean, of course, I like them. I love them." She touched the flowing green ribbon circling the box. "It's just... I never... thank you."

"You're welcome." He shoved it beneath her hovering hand. "Go on, open it. Before I decide to pull you back into bed."

She looked at him then, dead in the eye. Her hunger caught him by surprise, and he reached for her.

Grabbing her gift, she skipped to the side. "Oh, no, you don't, Noah Garrett. Patience, you must have patience. Remember how you always used to preach the sacred value of patience?"

He flopped against the headboard, banging his shoulder on the rounded edge. "In the future, don't listen to me."

She smiled and climbed on the bed, settling Indian-style next to his feet. Her skirt hooked over her knees, gaping wide, giving him a wonderful view.

He knocked his head against the bedpost. "You're killing me."

She glanced down. A mischievous glint appeared as her gaze lifted. "Good," she said, and loosened the elegant bow. Sliding the ribbon free, she set it by her side with care. "This one is prettier than the others."

"Yes." He swallowed and struggled to breathe normally. "The store wrapped it."

She pushed the brown paper aside and stared at the silver jewelry box in silence. Wildflowers and roses embellished the casing. A touch of feminine nonsense, but he had guessed she would take pleasure from it. She outlined the ornate design, and he felt a moment's unease, a pang of uncertainty. Dammit, he wanted nothing more than to make her happy, to give her anything she desired.

She opened the box, a whisper of air slipping past her lips. "Oh, Noah."

He rocked forward, squinting to bring her expression into clear view. "Well?"

*"Juste Ciel."* She lifted the ring from its perch. The round emerald caught a ray of candlelight and threw a blazing spark to the coverlet. "Oh, my," she breathed, and slipped it on her finger, tilting her hand back and forth in the meager light.

"I looked and looked, searching for the perfect ring, one that *felt* right. But they were too fancy or too plain. Too big or too small. Too ugly." He shrugged, his cheeks heating. "Until I found this one. The stone is the exact color your eyes turned the first time we made love. After the night on Devil, it was burned into my mind. And... I knew, I thought, I mean, you would like it."

She launched herself at him with a cry of delight. "I love it. Oh, Noah. I love *you.*" She hooked her arms around his neck, feathering kisses along his jaw. "I always have, as you and everyone else in Pilot Isle knew."

"Thank God." He tightened his hold.

She laughed, sending a rush of warm air across his face. "Did you ever doubt it?"

"Once or twice."

Her delight faded. "Do you have to go to Chicago soon? How will we... what will we—"

"Chicago? Good God, woman, what kind of marriage do you think this is going to be? I'm staying *right here,* in South Carolina. We'll decide where to move after you graduate. You're not getting away from me for one day. I rented a house large enough for a family of ten, just around the corner on Senate Street. Marty is thrilled beyond words to have me teach the next four terms. Coupled with a research project on population dynamics of planktonic systems and making love to you as much as I can handle, I'm going to be incredibly busy."

"Marty? A house? Planktonic systems?" Her voice lowered. "Making love?"

"Never mind that, sweet." He flipped her to her back and settled in to kiss her soundly. "Right now, I think we have more important issues to worry about. Issues on, what shall we say... the rise."

She nodded. "History thesis due in two days. Biology exam next Thursday."

Determined to win this round, he slanted his lips over hers, nibbling and licking until she moaned low in her throat. "I'm not sure I can help with the history thesis, but I am a fair science tutor."

"Are you certain, Professor?"

*"Positive, ma chere fille."*

And, as any good biologist would do, Noah set out to provide concrete proof.

### The End

Read on for a preview of book 2 *Tides of Passion* featuring Garrett brother Zachariah.

Readers familiar with the Outer Banks may recognize Pilot Isle as Beaufort, North Carolina. Indeed, I loosely based my setting there, thanks in large part to information provided by the kind ladies at the Beaufort Historical Society.

I incorporated artistic license in these areas, mostly calendar changes, which I hope the reader will forgive. In 1902, the second Federal fisheries laboratory in the United States was completed in Beaufort—still there to this day. Woods Hole, the first, was established in 1871, actually placing its construction before Noah's birth. But I know he would have wanted to take part, so he did. The scholarship Elle received I based on the ones given by the American Association of University Women, founded in 1882. They bestowed their first loan, much as I described it, in 1901, three years after Elle received it.

The lifesaving program is a marvelous part of the Outer Banks history and well worth further research. Also, the University of South Carolina, in 1898 called South Carolina College, did admit female students. As an alumna, I wanted Elle to be one, too!

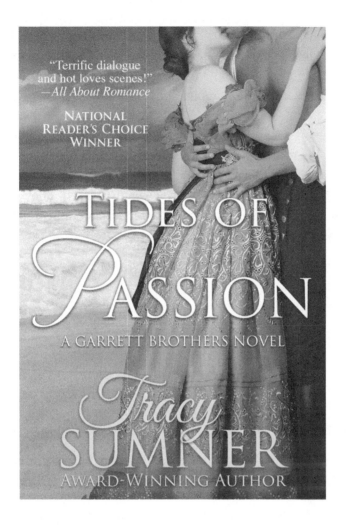

*She is his greatest temptation.*
*He is her forbidden desire.*
*A battle of wills leads to love.*

Spirited Savannah Connor is passionately committed to stamping out social injustice. Yet, when she arrives in Pilot Isle, North Carolina, ready to take up a new cause, she quickly finds herself on the outs with the town constable.

Zachariah Garrett is the most arrogant, infuriating, maddeningly attractive man she's had the misfortune to meet. And, suddenly, Savannah is fighting a whole new battle — this one against her own yearning for a man who is impossible to resist.

Ever since his wife's death two years ago, Zachariah Garrett has dedicated his life to keeping the peace. And, avoiding love. But Savannah Connor isn't an ordinary woman — and she proves hard to ignore. She's a beguiling beauty with the power to awaken emotions Zach thought he'd never feel again, and the tenderness to help him forget his fears. And risk his heart once more.

# CHAPTER 1

*Women can't have an honest exchange in front of men without having it called a cat fight.*
  ~Clare Boothe Luce

~

*North Carolina, 1898*

SAVANNAH KNEW SHE WAS IN TROUBLE A SPLIT SECOND BEFORE HE REACHED HER.

Perhaps she should have saved herself the embarrassment of a tussle with the town constable, a man determined to believe the worst of her.

However, running from a challenge wasn't her way.

She laughed, appalled to realize it wasn't fear that had her contemplating slipping off the rickety crate and into the budding crowd gathered outside the oyster factory.

No, her distress was due to nothing more than Constable Garrett's lack of proper *clothing*.

In a manner typical of the coastal community she had temporarily settled in, his shirt lay open nearly to his *waist*. She couldn't help but watch the ragged shirttail flick his lean stomach as he advanced on her. Tall, broad-shouldered and lean-hipped, his physique belied his composed expression. Yet Savannah detected a faint edge of anger pulsing beneath the calm façade, one she wanted to deny sent her heart racing.

*Wanted...* but could not.

Flinging her fist into the air, she stared him down as she shouted, "Fight for your rights, women of Pilot Isle!"

The roar of the crowd, men in discord, women in glorious agreement, eclipsed her next call to action. *There*, she thought, pleased to see Zachariah Garrett's long-lashed gray eyes narrow, his golden skin pulling tight in a frown. Again she shook her fist, and the crowd bellowed.

One man ripped the sign Savannah had hung from the warehouse wall to pieces and fed it to the flames shooting from a nearby barrel. Another began channeling the group of protesting women away from the entrance. Many looked at her with proud smiles on their faces or raised a hand as they passed. They felt the pulse thrumming through the air, the energy.

There was no power like the power of a crowd.

Standing on a wobbly crate on a dock alongside the ocean, Savannah let the madness rush over her, sure, completely sure to the depths of her soul, that *this* was worth her often forlorn existence. Change was good. Change was necessary. And while she was here, she would make sure Pilot Isle saw its fair share.

"That's it for the show, Miss Connor," Zachariah Garrett said, wrapping his arm around her waist and yanking her from the crate as people swarmed past. "You've done nothing but cause trouble since you got here, and personally, I've about had it."

"I'm sorry, Constable, but that's the purpose of my profession!"

He set her on her feet none too gently and whispered in her ear, "Not in my town it isn't."

As she prepared to argue—Savannah was *always* prepared to argue —a violent shove forced her to her knees. Sucking in a painful gasp, she scrambled between the constable's long legs and behind a water cask. Dropping to a sit, she brushed a bead of perspiration from her brow and wondered what the inside of Pilot Isle's jail was going to look like.

Fatigue returned, along with the first flicker of doubt she had experienced in many a month. Resting her cheek on her knee, she let the sound of waves slapping the wharf calm her, the fierce breeze rolling off the sea cool her skin. Her family had lived on the coast for a summer when she was a child. It was one of the last times she remembered being truly happy.

Or loved.

Blessed God, how long ago that seemed now.

That was how Zach found her. Crouched behind a stinking fish barrel, dark hair a sodden mess hanging down her back, her dress— one that cost a pretty penny, he would bet—ripped and stained. She looked young at that moment, younger than he knew her to be. And harmless.

Which was as far from the truth as it got.

He shoved aside the sympathetic twinge, determined not to let his role as a father cloud every damned judgment he made. Due to this woman's meddling, his town folk pulsed like an angry wound behind him, the ringing of the ferry bell not doing a blessed thing to quiet a soul. All he could do was stare at the instigator huddling on a section of grimy planks and question how one uppity woman could stir people up like she'd taken a stick to their rear ends.

No wonder she was a successful social reformer up north. She was as good at causing trouble as any person he'd ever seen.

"Get up," Zach said, nudging her ankle with his boot. A slim, delicate-looking ankle.

He didn't like her, this sassy, liberating *rabble-rouser*, but he was a man, and he had to admit she was put together nicely.

She lifted her head, blinking, seeming to pull herself from a distant place. A halo of shiny curls brushed her jaw, and as she tilted her head up, he got his first close look at her. A fine-boned face, the expression on it soft, almost dreamy.

Boy, the softness didn't last long.

Jamming her lips together, her cheeks plumped with a frown. Oh yeah, that was the look he'd been expecting.

"Good day, Constable," she said. Just like that, as if he should be offering a cordial greeting with a small war going on behind them.

"Miss Connor, this way if you please."

She rose with all the dignity of a queen, shook out her skirts, and brushed dirt from one sleeve. He counted to ten and back, unruffled, good at hiding his impatience. What being the lone parent of a rambunctious little boy would do for a man.

Just when he reached ten for the second time and opened his mouth to order her along, a misplaced swing caught him in the side and he stumbled forward, grasping Savannah's shoulders to keep from crashing into her. Motion ceased when she thumped the wall of the warehouse, her head coming up fast, her eyes wide and alarmed.

And very, very green.

He felt the heat of her skin through the thin material of her dress; her muscles jumped beneath his palms. Her gaze dropped to his chest, and a soft glow lit her cheeks. Blushing... something he wouldn't have expected from *this* woman.

Nevertheless, he stared, wondering why they both seemed frozen.

Zach was frozen because he'd forgotten what it felt like to touch a woman. How soft and round and warm they were. How they dabbed perfume in secret places and smiled teasing smiles and flicked those colorful little fans in your face, never *really* realizing what all that nonsense did to a man's equilibrium.

It was the first time he'd laid his hands on a woman since his wife died, except for a rescue last year and the captain's sister he'd pulled from the sea. *She* had thrown her arms around him, shivering and crying, and he'd felt for her, sure he had. Grateful and relieved and humble that God had once again shown him where the lost souls on the shoals were.

He hadn't felt anything more. Anything strong.

This wasn't strong either, nothing more than a minute spike of heat in his belly.

Nothing much at all. He didn't *need* like other men. Like his brothers or his friends in town. He had needed once, needed his *wife*. But she was dead. That life—loving and yearning and wanting—had died with her.

"Your mouth is bleeding," Savannah said and shifted, her arm rising.

*Don't touch me*, he thought, the words bubbling in his throat.

Cursing beneath his breath, the full extent of his childishness struck him. She would think he'd gone crazy. And maybe he had. Stepping back, he thrust his hands in his pockets and gestured for her to follow, intentionally leading her away from the ruckus on the wharf.

Buttoning his shirt, he listened to her steady footfalls, thinking she'd be safe in his office until everything died down.

"I'm sorry you've been injured."

Dabbing at the corner of his lip, he shrugged. He could still hear the rumble of the crowd. No matter. His brother Caleb would break it up. They'd argued about who got what job in this mess.

Zach had lost.

"What did you expect, Miss Connor?" he finally asked. "People get heated, and they do stupid things like fight with their neighbors and their friends. Hard not to get vexed with you standing up there, rising from the mist, preaching and persuading, stirring emotion like a witch with a cauldron."

She rushed to catch up to him, and he slowed his deliberately forceful stride. "Those women work twelve-hour days, Constable Garrett. Twelve hours on their feet, often without lunch breaks or access to sanitary drinking water. And for half the pay a man receives for the same day's work. Some are expecting a child and alone, young women who think they can disappear in this town without their families ever finding them. Their lives up to this point have been so dominated and environed by duties, so largely ordered for them, that many don't know how to balance a cash account of modest means or find work of any kind that doesn't involve sewing a straight stitch or shucking oysters."

She stomped around a puddle in their path, kicking at shells and muttering, nicking her polished boots in the process. "If you can reconcile that treatment to your sense of what is just, then we have nothing more to discuss."

Zach halted before the unpretentious building that housed Pilot Isle's lone jail cell, getting riled himself, an emotion he rarely tolerated. He didn't know whether he should apologize or shake the stuffing out of her. "I'll be glad to tell you what I reconcile on a given day: business disputes, marriages, deaths, shipwrecks, the resulting cargo and bodies that wash up on shore, and just about everything in between. What you're talking about over at the oyster factory has been going on forever. Long hours, dreadfully long.

The men may well get paid a higher wage—I couldn't say for certain—but they labor like mules, too. Do you think Hyman Carter is begging people to come work for him? Well, he isn't. It's a choice, free and clear." Reaching around her and flinging the door open, he stepped inside and, by God, expected her to follow. "What the hell can I do about that?"

Her abrupt silence had him turning. Savannah Connor stood in the doorway, bright sunlight flooding in around her, again looking like a vision of blamelessness, of sweet charity. She even smiled, closing the door gently behind her. Troubled, Zach reviewed his last words, racing through them in his mind.

"Oh no," he said, flinging his hand up in a motion his son knew meant no, flat out. "I'm not getting involved in this campaign of yours. Except to end it, I'm not getting involved."

"Why not get involved?" she asked, the edge back. "Give me one worthy reason why. You're the perfect person to request a review of the factory's processes."

Ignoring her, he slumped into the chair behind his desk, dug his cargo ledger out of the top drawer and a water-stained list out of his pocket, and began calculating entries. He was two shipwrecks behind. The town couldn't auction property—funds they desperately needed —until he, as keeper of Life-saving Division Six, completed the sad task of recording every damaged plank, every broken teacup, every sailor's shoe.

Work was good for the soul, he had always thought; it had saved *his* a couple of years ago.

Besides, maybe Miss Connor would quit talking if he didn't look at her.

Moments passed, the only sound the scratch of pen across paper and the occasional crunch of wagon wheels over the shell-paved street out front. When the cell's metal door squealed, Zach started, flicking ink across the page. He sighed. "I'm almost afraid to ask what you're doing."

Looking up from plumping the cot's pillow, she flashed a tight smile. "Getting ready for a long night, Constable Garrett. You're writing"—she pointed—"a summons for me in that little book, correct? What will it be? Disturbing the peace? Instigating a mutiny?" She shrugged, clearly unconcerned. "I've been charged with both of those before."

The fountain pen dropped from Zach's fingers. "*Arrested?* Ma'am, I've no intention of—"

"Thirteen times if you count the incident in Baltimore. That time, the police took us to a school instead of the local station. They didn't have a separate holding area for women and felt it would be inappropriate for my group to share quarters with common offenders."

*Thirteen.* Zach coughed to clear his throat. "I'm not arresting you. I only brought you here until things calm down on the wharf."

Savannah smiled, relief evident in the droop of her shoulders. "Then you'll help me. Thank goodness."

Gripping the desk, he shoved back his chair. "No way, no how. Are you deaf, ma'am?"

"Are *you*, sir? Did you hear those women out there today begging for equal rights? Women under your protection I might add."

His lids slipped low, the spasm of pain in his chest hitting him hard. *Protect.* Zach had spent his life trying to protect people. And so far he'd failed his wife, his brothers, and 81 passengers that he and his men had not gotten to in time. All events Reverend Tiernan said were in God's hands and God's hands only.

On good days, Zach agreed.

Opening his eyes, he forced his way back to his work, recording the wrong number in the wrong column. "Hyman Carter is a decent man. Pays his taxes, attends town meetings. He even donated enough money for the church to buy new pews last spring."

"He bought your loyalty in exchange for pews?"

His head snapped up. "No one buys my *anything*, Miss Connor."

She simply raised a perfectly shaped brow, sending his temper soaring two notches.

"Listen here, ma'am. That scene you caused today isn't the way to accomplish much in a town like this, though I'm sure it works fine in New York City. Personally, I don't cotton to taking orders from a mulish suffragette whose only aim in life is to secure the vote."

She took a fast step forward, her cheeks pinking. "Constable Garrett, you've grown too comfortable."

"That I have."

"No excuses?"

"Not a one."

"Well, you must know I won't rest until we come to a reasonable compromise."

"All right, then, you must know I can't change a man's way of running his business if it doesn't fall outside the law." He dipped his head in a mock show of respect. "Ma'am."

"Don't you realize that the situation at the oyster factory isn't *just*?"

A headache he hadn't felt coming roared to life. Pressing his fingers to his temple, Zach said, weary and unrepentant, "When did you get the idea life was just, Miss Connor?"

Savannah turned, pacing the length of the small cell, the sudden flicker of emotion in Zachariah Garrett's smoke-gray eyes more than she wanted to see, more than she could allow herself to. Feeling sympathy for an opponent violated a basic tenet of the abolitionist code. And whether she liked it or not, this man was the gatekeeper.

In more ways than one. She'd only been in town a week, but it was easy to see who people in Pilot Isle turned to in crisis. She had heard his name a thousand times already.

Just when she had devised a skillful argument to present for his inspection, a much better one strolled through the office door.

The woman was attractive and trim... and quite obviously smitten with Constable Garrett. Unbeknownst to him, she smoothed her hand the length of her bodice and straightened the straw hat atop her head before making her presence known.

"Gracious, Zach, *what* is going on in town today?"

Zach slowly lifted his head, shooting a frigid glare Savannah's way before pasting a smile on his face and swiveling around on his stubborn rump. "Miss Lydia, I hope you didn't get caught up in that mess. Caleb should have it under control by now though."

*Miss Lydia* drifted toward the desk, her clear blue gaze focused so intently on the man behind it that Savannah feared the woman would trip over her own feet if she wasn't careful. "Oh, I didn't get near it, you know that would never do. If Papa heard, he'd have a conniption. But I *was* at Mr. Scoggin's store and it was all anyone could talk about." She placed a cloth-covered basket on his desk. The scent of cinnamon filled the room. "Lands, imagine the excitement of a rally, right here in Pilot Isle."

Zach sighed. "Yes, imagine that."

"And"—Lydia glanced in her direction—"you've, um, detained *her*."

"I haven't—"

"Constable Garrett, if I may?" Savannah gestured to the cell door she'd shut while Miss Lydia stood in the threshold, hand-pressing her bodice. "I promise to be on my best behavior. It's just so hard to converse through metal bars."

"Oh, dear Lord." Zach yanked a drawer open and fished for a set of keys he clearly didn't use often. Stalking toward the cell with murder in his eyes, he asked in a low tone, "What game are you playing, Miss Connor?"

"Forewarned is forearmed, Constable."

With a snap of his wrist and a compelling shift of muscle beneath the sleeve of his shirt, he opened the door. "*Out.*"

"My, my, Constable, such hospitality for a humble inmate." She plucked her skirt between her fingers and circled him as he imagined a belle of the ball would.

Belle of the ball was called for with Miss Lydia, Savannah had realized from the first moment. The bored woman of consequence needing fulfillment.

And a cause.

Savannah would gladly give her one.

"If I may introduce myself." Savannah halted before Miss Lydia and flashed a hesitant smile. "Savannah Connor. Pleased to make your acquaintance."

Miss Lydia struggled for a moment but good breeding won out. In the South, it always seemed to. "Lydia Alice Templeton. Pleased, also, I'm sure." She gestured to the basket on the desk. "Would you like a muffin? You must be starved, poor thing. These are my special recipe. Cinnamon and brown sugar, and a secret ingredient I won't tell to save my life. Zach, oh." She tapped her bottom lip with a gloved finger. "Mr. Garrett, loves them."

"I'm sure he does," Savannah said, not having to turn to see his displeasure. It radiated, like a hot brand pressed to her back. "And I would love one. I'm practically faint with hunger."

Miss Lydia sprang into action, unfastening and cutting, spreading butter, and clucking like a mother hen. Savannah admired women who could nurture like that; Miss Lydia was a born mother when children scared Savannah half to death.

"Here, dear," Miss Lydia murmured, full of warmth and compassion. "Mr. Garrett, haven't you a pitcher of water?"

No reply, but within a minute a chipped jug and a glass appeared on the desk with a brusque clatter.

"Do you mind if I perch right here on the corner of your desk, Constable?" Savannah asked and bit into the most delicious muffin she had ever tasted. "Truly, these *are* good. Ummm."

"I win the blue ribbon every year at the Harvest Celebration." Lydia shrugged as if this were a certain thing in her life. "My father owns a commercial fishing company, and my mother passed some time ago, so I take care of him now. I bake all day some days." She turned her hand in a dreamy circle. "To fill the time."

Savannah halted, a mouthful of muffin resting on her tongue. She couldn't stop herself—really, the urge was too powerful—from looking up. Constable Garrett stood in the cell's entryway, shoulder jammed against a metal bar, feet crossed at the ankle, those startling gray eyes trained on her. Trained without apology.

"*No*," he mouthed. An honest appeal from an honest man.

She hadn't dealt with many honest men in her life, including her father and her brother. Also, she was confident she hadn't ever had as attractive an opponent. It was wicked to feel a tiny zing when she imagined besting him, wasn't it? Was that letting personal issues and professional ones collide?

Swallowing, she returned her attention to her prey. "You could find other ways to fill your time. I'm happy to tell you that this is precisely what I did."

"But—"

"My mother also passed away when I was a young girl. After that my life consisted of living in our home in New York City, while making a life for my father and my older brother. They were helpless when it came to running a household, so I took over. My childhood ended at that time, but later on, I made sure I would have something to show for it."

"Ohhh," Lydia said, clasping her hand to her heart.

Savannah ignored the audible grunt from the back of the room and continued, "One day I simply found the endless duties and tasks, many of which I was uninterested in, to be so monotonous as to make my life seem worthless. I forced myself to search for meaning— a cause, if you will. I attended my first women's rights meeting the next afternoon." She failed to mention she had been all of sixteen and had nearly broken her ankle jumping from the window of her bedroom to the closest tree limb outside. After dragging her home from the meeting, her father had locked her in her bedroom for two days.

Without food or water.

He didn't let her out until that lovely old tree outside her window no longer stood tall and proud.

"Miss Connor, I couldn't possibly attend a meeting like that here."

Savannah dabbed a muffin crumb from the desk and licked her finger. "Why ever not?"

"It's not... I'm not...." Lydia's voice trailed off.

"You're not resilient enough? Oh, you are. I could tell right away. Can you honestly say that you are satisfied with your life? What, pray tell, are you doing completely for yourself?"

"Redecorating my father's stu—"

"That's for him. Try again."

"Cooking."

Savannah smiled and shook her head.

Lydia snapped her fingers. "Oh, I have one! I host an information-gathering tea in the historical society office one morning a week. Although Papa feels it's shameful for me to work, even when the position is entirely without compensation."

Savannah relaxed her shoulders, dabbed at another crumb, as if the news weren't simply wonderful. The glow of heat at her back seemed to increase. "And how do you feel about working?"

"I love it. I'm very good at keeping records and tallying donations. I raised more money for the society last year than any other volunteer, even though Sallie Rutherford's total arrived at five dollars more than mine." She leaned in, cupping her hand around her mouth. "Hyman Carter is her uncle, and he gave it to her at the last minute to lift her total past mine."

*The wonder*, Savannah thought, dizzy with promise. "Miss Templeton, this is a propitious conversation. I need a co-leader for my efforts and until this moment, I wasn't sure I would be able to locate the right woman in a town the size of Pilot Isle." She smiled, placing her hand over Lydia's gloved fingers. "Now, I think I have."

"Me?" Lydia breathed, hand climbing to her chest. "A co-leader?"

Savannah nodded. "I have to govern Elle Beaumont's school in her absence. Teach classes and mentor her female students until her return. You may have heard that she's returned to university in South

Carolina. Yet, I couldn't possibly stay here and watch women live in a state of disability and not try to improve their situation. Women working exhausting hours for half the pay a man receives, for instance. Did you know about that?"

"The oyster factory? Well, I have to say, that is, yes." Her gaze skipped to the constable and back. "Although, I haven't ever been employed. Not in a true position of payment. And the factory," she said, voice dropping to a whisper, "isn't where any ladies of, what did you call it, *consequence* are likely to pay a visit."

"As co-leader of the Pilot Isle movement, you should make it your first stop. Let's plan to meet there tomorrow morning. Nine o'clock sharp. Bring Miss Rutherford, who even if she is a bit of a charlatan, might prove a worthy supporter. Too, she can gain access for the group without the burden of another impassioned assembly."

Savannah smiled and added, "Surely her uncle doesn't want that."

"Now wait a blessed minute."

Savannah glanced up as Zach's shadow flooded over them. Bits of dust drifted through the wide beam of sunlight he stood in, softening the intensity of his displeasure. No matter his inflexibility, the man was attractive, she thought.

"A problem, Constable?"

"You're damn right there's a problem."

A soft gasp had him bowing slightly and frowning harder. "Beg pardon, Miss Lydia. I apologize for the language, but this doesn't concern you." He swung Savannah around on the desk, her knees banging his as he crouched before her, bringing their eyes level. "It concerns *you*, and I remember telling *you* I wasn't putting up with this foolishness." He stabbed his finger against his chest. "Not in my town."

She drew a covert breath. Traces of manual labor and the faintest scent of cinnamon circled him. Savannah valued hard work above all else and never minded a man who confirmed he valued it as well, even if he smelled less than soap-fresh and his palms were a bit rough. Forcing her mind to the issue at hand, she asked, "Are we prohibited from visiting the factory, Constable?"

"After today, you better believe you are."

She arched a brow, a trick she had practiced before the mirror for months until it alone exemplified frosty indifference. "My colleagues, Miss Templeton and Miss Rutherford, will attend in my absence, then."

"No."

She scooted forward until the stubble dotting his rigid jaw filled her vision. "You can't stop them and you know it. In fact, I'm fairly certain you cannot stop *me* without filing paperwork barring me from Mr. Carter's property. That takes time and signatures, rounding up witnesses to the dispute. However, I'm willing to forgo this meeting. During the initial phase at any rate. For everyone's comfort."

Sliding back the inch she needed to pull their knees apart, she decided that for all Zachariah Garrett's irritability—a trait she abhorred in a man—he smelled far, far too tempting to risk touching during negotiations. "Don't challenge my generosity, Mr. Garrett. You won't get more."

"Are you daring me to do something, Miss Connor? Because I will, I tell you."

"Consider it a gracious request."

"You can take your gracious request and stick it...." Jamming his hands atop his knees, he rose to his feet. "Miss Lydia, will you excuse us a moment?"

Lydia cleared her throat and backed up two steps. Before she left, she looked at Savannah and smiled, her eyes bright with excitement. Savannah returned the smile, knowing she had won that series if nothing else.

"You must be crazy," Zach said the moment the door closed. "Look at the blood on your dress, the scrapes on your hands. Do you want Miss Lydia to suffer the same? The things you want her to experience are things her father has purposely kept her from experiencing and for a damn good reason."

She gazed at the torn skin on her hands and the traces of blood on her skirt as she heard him begin to pace the narrow confines of the office. "It's a mockery to talk of sheltering women from life's fierce storms, Constable. Do you believe the ones who work twelve-hour days in that factory are too weak to weather the emotional stress of a political campaign? Do you believe Lydia cannot support a belief that runs counter to her father's? A child is not a replica of the parent. The sexes, excuse my frankness, do not have the same challenges in life."

Watching him, his hands buried in his pockets—to keep from circling her neck she supposed—she couldn't help but marvel at the curious mix of Southern courtesy and male arrogance, the natural assumption he shouldered of being lawfully in control. "Engaging in a moral battle isn't always hazardous to one's health, you know."

"Doesn't look like it's doing wonders for yours."

"Saints be praised, it can actually be *rewarding*."

Looking over his shoulder, he halted in the middle of the room. "Irish."

"I beg your pardon?"

"You. Irish. The green eyes, the tiny bit of red in your hair. Is Connor your real name?"

"Yes, why," she said, stammering. *Oh, hell.* "Of course."

"Liar."

She felt the slow, hot roll of color cross her cheeks. "What could that possibly have to do with anything?"

"I don't know, but I have a feeling it means something. It's the first thing I've heard come out of that sassy mouth of yours that didn't sound like some damned speech." He tapped his head, starting to pace again. "What I wonder is, where are *you* in there?"

"I'm right here. Reasonable and... and judicious. Driven perhaps but not sassy, never sassy."

"You're full of piss and vinegar, all right. And some powerful determination to cause me problems when I have more than I can handle." He halted in the middle of the room. "And here I thought Ellie was difficult. Opening that woman's school and teaching God knows what in that shed behind Widow Wynne's, putting husbands and fathers in an uproar. Now you're here, and it's ten times worse than it ever was before."

"Do women have to roll over like a dog begging for a scratch for men to value them?"

"That and a pretty face work well enough for me."

She hopped to her feet, her skirt slapping the desk. "You insufferable toad."

"Better that than a reckless nuisance."

"There's nothing wrong with feeling passionate about freedom, Constable Garrett. And I plan to let every woman in this town know it."

"If it means causing the kind of scene you caused today, you'll have to go through me first."

Savannah laughed, wishing it hadn't come out sounding so much like a cackle. "I've heard that several hundred times in the past. With no result, I might add."

"Guess you have." Halting before a tall cabinet scarred in more places than not, he went up on the toes of his boots and came back with a bottle. Another reach earned a glass. "With thirteen detentions, I can't say I'm surprised." She watched him pour a precise measure, tilt his head, and throw it back. "Did any of them happen to figure out you were working Irish underneath the prissy clothes and snooty manners?"

She lowered her chin, quickly, before he could spotlight her distress. *Working Irish.* A term she hadn't heard in years. Every horrible trait she possessed—willfulness, callousness, condescension —her father said came from the dirty Irish blood flowing through her veins. Her mother had been the immigrant who had trapped him in an unhappy marriage.

A marriage beneath his station, thank you very much.

And he had never let his family forget it.

"Would you like a medal for your perspicacious deduction, Constable?" she asked when she'd regained her composure.

He laughed and saluted her with his glass. "Heck, I don't even know what that means."

"*Astute*, Constable. Which you are. Surprisingly so." She closed the distance between them and took the glass from his clenched fist, ignoring the warmth of his skin when their fingers touched.

"May I?" she asked and drained the rest, liquid fire burning its way

282

down. Looking at him from beneath her lashes, she smiled. "The Irish like the taste of whiskey on their tongues, did you know that? O'Connor was my mother's maiden name. Her grandfather changed it to Connor when he came through Ellis Island. When my father asked me to vacate his home the first time, I claimed the name because he said if I must disgrace the family, I could disgrace her side of it. So I did."

She handed the glass back. "Now that you know one of my secrets, I should know one of yours."

He went very still, the arm that held the bottle dropping to his side. Before he pivoted on his heel, his face revealed such wretched grief that she felt the pain like a dart through her own heart. It wasn't enough to offer an apology for the offense.

How could she when she wasn't sure what ground she had trespassed on?

"After she got released from jail, we had coffee she bought specially in New York City. About the best coffee I've ever tasted, too. And these hard, bready cookies that Savannah"—Lydia cupped her hand around her mouth—"I call her that now you know, said she has to go to a place called Little Italy in New York City to buy. Can you imagine? And I'm to be her co-leader. My goodness, I never would have thought anything this exciting would happen in Pilot Isle. Not in my lifetime."

"Your father?" Sallie Rutherford asked in a hushed whisper, pleating her skirt with shaky fingers.

"Oh, he'll shoot me dead when he finds out." Lydia fanned her warm cheeks, trying hard not to envision her father's certain fit of temper. "But I'm strong enough to handle him. Resilient, yes."

"And you're still planning to go tomorrow morning?"

She nodded. "With you."

"Oh dear me, no. Dwight looks like he's sucking a lemon most days as it is. Do you want him to move back to his mother's for *good*?"

Dwight Rutherford had married Sallie Smithe on the eve of his fortieth birthday and any disturbance on the calm sea of life sent him running back to his boyhood home and the welcoming arms of his mother.

"Savannah said there's nothing wrong with helping your fellow woman, Sallie. Why should we expect the men in this town to be happy about it, can you tell me that? It's a man's world; laws are men's laws; the government a man's government. We're merely set on changing that."

Lydia felt sure Savannah would have been pleased to hear her parroting with such accuracy.

"Well, what about Dwight? And your father?"

"Oh, posh." Lydia chewed the last of her iced fruitcake with renewed enthusiasm. "They can take a big old leap off Pearson's dock for all I care."

"But the quilting meeting is—"

"Hang Nora and her weekly quilting meeting! I need you to get past the men your uncle will undoubtedly have guarding the gate. Plus, he won't curse too much with you in the room." Lydia dipped her linen napkin in a finger bowl on the table and patted the cool cloth against her lips. She ignored the beads of perspiration rolling down her back. Insufferable summers. "After the historical society calamity last year, you *owe* me. How can you even consider refusing?"

"Why, I never," Sallie sputtered with all the indignation of an affronted peacock.

Lydia drew a deep breath, testing the air to see if the roast she was cooking for dinner needed checking. "Savannah's going to unpack the rest of her belongings today. Books, pamphlets, materials to make signs. Paint and paper, all the way from New York. She also has badges for us to wear. Red with the words Freedom Fighter in gold emblazed across it."

"Gold?"

"If you help us with this, you'll be a bona fide member of the Pilot Isle Ladies Freedom Fighters."

"My...." Sallie sank back against the plump cushions, a wistful look entering her eyes.

Lydia released a pent-up sigh, less frightened than good sense should allow she knew. Savannah and the rally and the chance to live life for herself just this once was too rare an opportunity to let slip away. Besides, Zach Garrett wouldn't let them dilly-dally for more than a day or two.

She needed to have her amusement now.

"I'll do it," Sallie surprised her by saying, quite clearly and without additional arm-twisting.

Lydia clapped her hands and giggled, giddy to the tips of her patent leather boots. "That is fine news. I'm thrilled and relieved. Gracious, now that that's settled, I must tell you what else happened at the jail. I shouldn't, but I simply must."

Sallie vaulted to a rigid position, eager for gossip.

"I really shouldn't say—"

"Oh no, please do! It's been so dull around here since Noah Garrett ran off with that crazy Elle Beaumont."

*Too true*, Lydia thought. The entire town had hungrily monitored the antics of Zach's youngest brother and Elle Beaumont, who, eccentric as she seemed to be, had snared the man she'd wanted since long before anyone could remember differently. It made her think of... well, today, at the jail, the way Zach had looked at Savannah, just for a hint of a moment when he thought no one was looking.

Not with interest, no, no, *no*. More as though he had been wound up like one of those new-fangled toys she'd seen in the window of Dillon's Goods in Raleigh.

*Agitated* was a good word for it. Which was all well and fine because women often roused men to a fever pitch.

Everyone knew that. It was just the way life operated.

Except it never seemed to operate like that for Zachariah Garrett. Even when his beloved wife was alive, he'd been calm and capable and strong. Why, if Lydia felt half a heart in love with him it was *because* she'd never witnessed anything but calm, capable, strong Constable Garrett.

She had never seen him agitated. *Never.*

Lydia wouldn't have guessed he had it in him.

Maybe there was something to this independence craze if it made a man sit up and take notice.

"Of course, this cannot go any further than this parlor," she finally said, tucking a wisp of damp hair beneath her bonnet. "And again, I shouldn't say, but I have to tell you that I've never seen such fire in Constable Garrett's eyes as I did today."

"*Fire?* Zach Garrett?" Sallie swallowed a bite of iced fruitcake too quickly and choked. "Are... are you sure? Why, he's so *collected.*"

"Without a doubt. Fire," Lydia assured her friend. "And Savannah Connor lit the match."

# ABOUT TRACY

Tracy's story telling career began when she picked up a copy of LaVyrle Spencer's Vows on a college beach trip. A journalism degree and a thousand romance novels later, she decided to try her hand at writing a southern version of the perfect love story. With a great deal of luck and more than a bit of perseverance, she sold her first novel to Kensington Publishing.

When not writing sensual stories featuring complex characters and lush settings, Tracy can be found reading romance, snowboarding, watching college football and figuring out how she can get to 100 countries before she kicks. She lives in the south, but after spending a few years in NYC, considers herself a New Yorker at heart.

Tracy has been awarded the National Reader's Choice, the Write Touch and the Beacon—with finalist nominations in the HOLT Medallion, Heart of Romance, Rising Stars and Reader's Choice. Her books have been translated into German, Dutch, Portuguese and Spanish. She loves hearing from readers about why she tends to pit her hero and heroine against each other from the very first page or that great romance she simply must order in five seconds on her Kindle.

Connect with Tracy:

facebook.com/Tracysumnerauthor
twitter.com/sumnertrac
instagram.com/tracysumnerromance
bookbub.com/profile/tracy-sumner